WESTERN

Small towns. Rugged ranchers. Big hearts.

Forgiving The Cowboy
Tabitha Bouldin

A Protector For Her Baby
April Arrington

MILLS & BOON

FORGIVING THE COWBOY
© 2025 by Tabitha Bouldin
Philippine Copyright 2025
Australian Copyright 2025
New Zealand Copyright 2025

First Published 2025
First Australian Paperback Edition 2025
ISBN 978 1 038 94063 6

A PROTECTOR FOR HER BABY
© 2025 by April Standard
Philippine Copyright 2025
Australian Copyright 2025
New Zealand Copyright 2025

First Published 2025
First Australian Paperback Edition 2025
ISBN 978 1 038 94063 6

This is a work of fiction. Names, characters, places, and incidents are either the
product of the author's imagination or are used fictitiously, and any resemblance to
actual persons, living or dead, business establishments, events, or locales is entirely
coincidental.

MIX
Paper | Supporting
responsible forestry
FSC® C001695

Published by
Harlequin Mills & Boon
An imprint of Harlequin Enterprises (Australia) Pty Limited
(ABN 47 001 180 918), a subsidiary of HarperCollins
Publishers Australia Pty Limited
(ABN 36 009 913 517)
Level 19, 201 Elizabeth Street
SYDNEY NSW 2000 AUSTRALIA

Cover art used by arrangement with Harlequin Books S.A.. All rights reserved.

Printed and bound in Australia by McPherson's Printing Group

Forgiving The Cowboy
Tabitha Bouldin

MILLS & BOON

Tabitha Bouldin has a bachelor's degree in creative writing/English from Southern New Hampshire University. She is a member of American Christian Fiction Writers (ACFW) and an avid reader when her three cats will allow her to pick up a book. Living in Tennessee her entire life, Tabitha grew up riding horses and adopting every stray animal she could find.

Books by Tabitha Bouldin

The Cowgirl's Last Rodeo
Forgiving the Cowboy

Visit the Author Profile page at millsandboon.com.au.

Trust in the Lord with all thine heart; and lean not unto thine own understanding. In all thy ways acknowledge him, and he shall direct thy paths.
—*Proverbs* 3:5–6

For my sister. It takes a strong woman to stand up every day and fight for her happily-ever-after. You are that woman, and your daily fight is an inspiration that encourages me to keep going, especially when life is hard.

CHAPTER ONE

TENLEY JACOBS HAD a major problem on her hands. She sighed and threaded the chewed-up scraps of leather through her palms. "You're in big trouble." She waved what used to be bridle reins at the rambunctious puppy bounding up and down the barn aisle. Unconcerned, the white German shepherd pounced on a patch of hay and yipped, tail wagging, little bottom wriggling left and right in a wild arc, as he looked back at Tenley. "Don't give me that look. I'm mad at you."

"Aw. Aunt Tenley, he didn't mean it." Six-year-old Jade Matthews added a whine to the new "aunt" title and dropped into a crouch beside the puppy. Her bright green eyes lit up with the first bit of joy Tenley had seen in weeks.

"Sure, he didn't." She tossed the mangled reins onto a hay bale and rubbed her hands over her face. They smelled of oil and leather. The familiar scent soaked into her bones, attempting to right the whirlwind the day had become.

Freckles, a leopard-spotted Appaloosa and Jade's equine therapy partner, whinnied from the stall at the far end of the barn, drawing Tenley's gaze toward the sunlight streaming in through the open double doors. "Come on. We need to start your lesson." She held out a hand in a stop motion. "But first, put your dog in the empty stall."

Jade opened her mouth, an argument brewing, with a look so much like her mother that it staggered Tenley and forced her to hug her elbows over her stomach to keep from throwing her arms around Jade and squeezing tight. Jade had been withdrawn since her parents' deaths, and Tenley didn't dare risk ostracizing her by offering unwanted comfort. Jade had made her feelings clear the first time Tenley gave an unexpected embrace.

Tenley hiked an eyebrow and put a hand on her hip. "That was the deal. You get the dog, but he stays out of the way. Especially when we're acclimating new horses. Or when someone is riding. Like you're supposed to be doing." Freckles nickered again, his trumpeting sound echoing through the barn. The Appaloosa gelding was Tenley's newest acquisition for her equine therapy program, and he'd quickly become Jade's favorite horse to ride. His only problem seemed to be an aversion to being alone—hence the constant nickering. A problem Tenley remedied by placing him in a stall beside Socks, a large black-and-white gelding who was as unflustered as they came. Currently, Socks didn't seem too thrilled with his new neighbor and was busy ignoring Freckles' need for attention.

"Will you let me ride Freckles on a trail ride?" Jade scooped the puppy into her arms and huffed when he wriggled. At eight months old, the pup was half Jade's length, and when he started flailing all four paws, he became almost impossible to hold. Jade shuffled toward the open stall door and dropped the puppy to the thick bed of straw. Before she could jump back and close the door, the pup shot between her feet and darted into the hallway. He lowered his front half and stuck his tail up in the air. It waved side to side, and he barked at Jade, his head bouncing when he jumped and took off running outside.

And that's why Tenley had resisted getting the dog in the first place. She worked with therapy horses. Her brother, Brody, was the horse trainer, but neither of them knew anything about training dogs. Her family's sole experience with canines came from owning a few random work dogs through the years to help keep coyotes away.

Tenley plodded after the runaway canine and stepped into the bright sunshine that coated the Triple Bar Ranch in a golden glow. The Blue Ridge Mountains poked their heads up in the distance, drawing Tenley's gaze. She loved her North Carolina home with a depth that filled her to bursting. Wild horses couldn't drag her away from the ranch she'd always called home. Especially not now that she'd finally gotten her equine therapy license and opened her own clinic alongside Brody's horse training barn.

Laughter drifted on the breeze from the round pen, and Tenley caught a flash of movement between the tall panels. Her brother Brody and his wife, Callie, worked a new horse together, their joy permeating the air and drawing a smile to Tenley's face.

Jade raced after the wayward dog, her steps light and quick. "Get back here you rascal."

"Maybe that's what we should call him." Tenley swiped a hand over her forehead, drawing away a line of sweat before it trickled into her eyes. Less than two weeks into May and the summer heat had already turned vicious. Winter could not come soon enough. She loved living in the shadow of the Blue Ridge Mountains, but she was tired of the heat and humidity that came with it. Give her snow any day.

Jade caught up with the pup and dove on top of him. They rolled in the dirt, laughter and doggie yips colliding.

Tenley grabbed the discarded bridle reins and hurried over, using them as a makeshift leash that she quickly tied to the pup's collar. "Take him to the stall, Jade."

Jade's lower lip stuck out in a pout, but she followed Tenley's directions.

Tenley tagged along behind her, doing her best to stay out of the way and let the girl find a measure of independence.

Even at almost seven years old, Jade had her mother's stubborn streak.

Jade led the pup to the stall, removed the temporary leash and closed the door before he could escape. She handed the leather strip to Tenley and hurried down the aisle to Freckles' stall with a big smile on her face. "Don't worry. We can ride now." She flung open the door and reached for the halter.

The gentle gelding followed Jade to the crossties and stood statue still while Jade brushed him down. She dragged the tall stool they kept for the younger, shorter riders over and began saddling and bridling him. Freckles settled under Jade's attention.

Emotion clogged Tenley's throat at the sight of Freckles leaning his head down to bump Jade's shoulder. She patted his jaw, then flung her arms around his neck and squeezed. Now, a horse, she would hug. This was why Tenley pushed for the equine therapy program. Not just for Jade, but for all the hurting people who could benefit from the horses.

She'd been one of those hurting people. A closet alcoholic who'd hit rock bottom and found herself sitting overnight in a jail cell in Bridgeport instead of getting ready to walk down the aisle. Thankfully, she hadn't hurt anyone, but the drunk-and-disorderly had kept her behind bars for her wedding day, and once she was released, she'd been too ashamed to tell Mac Mitchell, her fiancé, the truth about why she'd jilted him at the altar. She wasn't even coherent enough to make a phone call from jail… The memory stung intensely.

In the immediate aftermath, he up and left for Chicago without a goodbye or a backward glance.

He was clearly too hurt and too proud to fight for her. She couldn't really blame him though, not when her pride kept her in a prison of her own making. And she hadn't been ready to fight for him either. Not until it was too late.

Over six years of silence followed, and every year that passed made it that much harder to make amends. Even though she had six years, eleven months, and seven days sober under her belt and God's forgiveness in her heart, she doubted Mac would be able to see his way clear of her indiscretion. She didn't deserve his forgiveness. Or her dad's. She was the reason he'd been out driving the day of the hit-and-run and had been paralyzed. It was all her fault.

Her pulse hammered in her throat as she watched Jade. Amber, Jade's mother, was Mac's sister and Tenley's best friend. She'd named Tenley and Mac as Jade's guardians in her will when she found out she was pregnant. She'd given birth shortly before Tenley and Mac's wedding. Once things fell apart, Tenley had assumed that Amber changed the will.

According to Leonard, the lawyer who'd sought Tenley out after Amber's fatal car accident, she hadn't. Tenley and Mac shared guardianship of Amber's daughter—married or not.

Mac hadn't shown up for the funeral, a fact that needled Tenley to no end. She couldn't wait to hear his excuse when he finally did arrive. And she knew he would. Eventually. Her past forever lingered in the background of her thoughts. Mac's imminent return kept things churned up. The apology she'd never given, the reason she'd never explained. He deserved to know the truth, even if he never forgave her for running away. For once in her life, she'd protected him instead of letting him fight her battles for her. This was one battle she'd had to face herself. No one else could achieve sobriety for her.

She bit her lip until she tasted blood. Did he know they shared guardianship? Did he care? Leonard had tried to call Mac, but the last he'd mentioned to Tenley, Mac was unavailable for some reason he wouldn't disclose. When she pressed for further information, Leonard had given her a look that bordered on pity and said he'd keep in touch.

Jade finished tacking up her horse, snapped her helmet on, and peered over her shoulder, a smile blooming and showing the gap where she'd lost her front tooth last week.

"I'm ready." Jade patted Freckles' leg and waited.

Tenley nodded. "Okay. Take him out to the small arena. You can mount up at the gate, and I'll close it behind you."

Tenley allowed Jade to have slightly more control over the lesson than a lot of her other students, except when Jade joined them in a group ride. Unlike the others, Jade had grown up riding at the ranch, with Tenley as her teacher. These lessons on Freckles were more for Jade's psychological well-being than anything else.

Which brought Tenley back to Jade's earlier question about riding Freckles on a trail ride. Tenley hesitated to say no. Freckles was trained to take anything in stride, but trail rides were different. Anything could happen out on the trail.

Jade led Freckles from the barn, paused at the mounting block and climbed into the saddle. Once on Freckles' back, she shot another winning smile at Tenley and moved into the arena.

They spent the next twenty minutes going through Tenley's preplanned lesson. Jade walked, trotted and loped Freckles around the arena, her concentration showing in the way she frowned and sucked her bottom lip between her teeth. Just like her mother.

Tenley walked alongside her as she led Freckles from the arena and back to the crossties, where they removed the gelding's tack, rubbed him down and put him back in his stall.

"Alright, let's head to the house." Tenley opened the stall door where the puppy waited, tail furiously sweeping the ground.

Jade whooped and raced outside.

Tenley kept her pace slower, enjoying the slight breeze rustling the oak leaves on the trees lining the trails to her left. Her parents' house sat at the end of the long drive. Tenley's house was situated the farthest away from the main house and the barn. Her brother and Callie lived in the house behind the barn, and her sister Molly had chosen to build hers on the southern side of the yard, directly across from it. Molly lived there with her young son, Luke, who had turned out to be a great playmate for Jade. It had been hard on them losing Luke's dad overseas, but things were getting better. Grief was a long road.

"Uncle Mac!" Jade screamed and bolted for the main house.

"Jade, wait." Mac was here? Tenley's heart pounded in her chest, and fear shot through her like a runaway horse. Tenley ran after her, her boots slamming the packed dirt and sending jarring jolts up her legs. She shielded her eyes from the sunlight bouncing off her parents' tin roof and saw a tall man standing on their front porch.

A rangy canine stood at his side, ears up and alert, posture stiff.

"Jade," Tenley called again when the little girl continued her race down the rutted drive. Tenley stepped in a hole and stumbled several steps before she regained her balance.

The man on the porch never moved. He might as well be carved from stone.

Not Tenley. Everything in her seemed to go to war. Her heart raced, but she blamed that on the unexpected exercise. He'd finally come. She'd known he would but had hoped and prayed that she'd be given some kind of warning first. She didn't want to see him like this, out of the blue, totally unprepared. Her hands curled into fists.

Jade skidded to a stop at the bottom of the steps. "You brought Zeus." She flung her arms around the dog's neck and squeezed.

Zeus let out a pained whine.

Mac shifted his weight, and Tenley caught the flash of a grimace in his brown eyes. "Careful. He's not feeling well." He studiously ignored Tenley and kept his attention on Jade. Some unnamable emotion caught in his expression.

"What's wrong with him?" Jade ran her hands over Zeus's black-and-tan fur. Her brows wrinkled together in a perfect imitation of Mac. "Was he hurt?"

Tenley managed to stop before she hurtled into the porch railing. Gravel spewed under her boots, and her hat slid down over her forehead. She adjusted the black Stetson with one hand and shoved the other into her pocket while attempting to calm her breathing. She'd neglected her running lately, and it showed.

"Yes." Mac left it at that and finally, *finally* lifted his gaze to Tenley. His shoulders snapped back, and his lips tightened into a flat line. "Tenley."

She dipped her head into a nod. "Good to see you, Mac."

"Is it?" He asked sarcastically. His black hair looked the same with its close-cut sides that resembled a high and tight but longer. He wore jeans and a rumpled T-shirt that bore a Chicago PD logo. The sight snagged her breath and forced her chin up.

She didn't have the heart to argue with him. Not about this, though questions flickered in his expression before his eyes shuttered.

Maybe someday he'd ask. And maybe someday she'd tell him why she left him at the altar. But not today.

The puppy bounded up the steps and plopped onto its back, paws up in the air. It batted at Zeus's nose and tried to nibble the older dog's leg.

Zeus let out an almost human sigh, then lifted his head toward Mac as though asking permission. Mac made a hand movement, and Zeus lowered to his belly on the worn-out porch. Seconds ticked past, the roar in Tenley's ears filling her head as questions bombarded her from the inside.

Mom stepped out onto the porch. "Oh, Tenley, there you are. I was about to call the barn."

Dad rolled out behind Mom, his wheelchair bumping over the wooden planks. "Well, Mac, how are things in Chicago?"

"Hectic." Mac seemed determined to keep his responses short and clipped.

Tenley locked her jaw to keep from saying anything she'd regret. Mom and Dad didn't need her interference. She sat on the bottom step and drew her knees up to her chest, then stretched them out, loosening the tight muscles before they cramped. She really should start running again. Especially if she wanted to have a prayer of keeping up with Jade. Speaking of prayer, Tenley sent up a rapid-fire entreaty for guidance and peace.

"Leonard told me Jade was here with Tenley." Again, Mac's tone said more than the words themselves. He drew himself up to his full height, an impressive six foot two to her five foot seven.

Tenley resisted the urge to curl her shoulders up around her ears. The need to defend herself roared up and threatened to choke her. Not now. Not like this.

"Jade, why don't you come inside and have a glass of milk. I made cookies. They should be cool by now." Mom shepherded Jade into the house while giving Tenley a look that Tenley interpreted to mean she'd better get on the ball with smoothing the raging river of turmoil between her and Mac.

Easier said than done, but she'd try.

Relief skirted the edges of her anger, and she mouthed *thank you* over Jade's head. They disappeared inside, with Dad lingering the longest, his gaze darting back and forth between Tenley and Mac. Then he left them to it. The screen door smacked closed with the squeal of hinges in desperate need of oil.

She shifted sideways and put her booted feet on the step. "Jade is always here with me, except when she's at school." She filled her voice with accusation, the tone hot enough to blister. "It's what Amber wanted." So much for staying calm.

A dry laugh left Mac. "No. What my sister wanted was for me to take care of Jade." He waved a sheaf of papers in her direction.

Tenley snatched them from his hand and scanned the documents. Did he have a different will from the one Leonard showed her? Her breath locked in her throat. This could not be happening. Her mouth dropped open, and she snapped it closed just as quickly as relief overwhelmed her. It was the same will. "Take another look. I think you missed something." She handed them back. "Both our names are there."

MAC FORCED HIS gaze away from Tenley and back to the document. The papers crinkled in his hands as his grip tightened.

Tenley cleared her throat and rocked her boots back and forth. Heel to toe. Heel to toe. She wrapped her arms around her knees and pulled them under her chin. A breath whooshed out when she lowered her cheek to her knee and stared out over the yard. She wore a pair of tattered jeans with a rip in the knee and a T-shirt with their old school mascot on the back. Same old Tenley. She never threw away anything that might be useful later.

When they planned their wedding, she'd refurbished the majority of the decorations from yard sales and thrift stores, remaking them into beautiful pieces. Given what she'd done with ratty flowers and old ribbon, he'd been curious to see what her wedding dress would look like. He'd never found out.

He bit down on the wrenching feeling tearing open the wound she'd made the day she left him standing at the altar. Alone. No reason. No apology. She'd disappeared from the church and his life without a word. He couldn't let her distract him from his mission. From Jade. The last person he had in the world who mattered to him.

Straightening his shoulders despite the pain stiffening his arm, he brought the papers up to eye level. Tenley's name leaped from the page. Right beside his. The internal wound ripped apart, leaving him breathless. How many years had he dreamed of seeing her name beside his? Only in his dreams, it was a marriage certificate that held the honor of placing them side by side.

Not this. He shook his head. "Amber never changed the will." He should've known. Leonard tried to give him a warning. Mac had brushed off the older man's attempt with a stiff wave and bolted from the tiny office that stifled him.

It had taken all his inner strength—and the fact he was a police officer—to keep him from breaking the speed limit when Leonard told him where to find Jade.

This could not stand.

Tenley didn't deserve the right to raise Jade. She was irresponsible. She wasn't mature enough. A slew of other belittlements bombarded Mac. He locked them behind his teeth and massaged the pain shooting down his arm.

Zeus looked up at Mac and whined. The puppy continued to gnaw at Zeus's ear, but the older dog didn't seem to mind. Mac reached down to ruffle the dog's ears, reassuring his partner that he was fine.

Zeus lowered his head again, then wagged his bushy tail.

Shock coursed through Mac. It was the first time Zeus had shown any emotion other than concern since they'd both gotten injured. It made him want to call his boss and report the good news. Zeus didn't need to be retired. He wasn't too old for the job. He hadn't burned out. Neither had Mac.

Sitting with her legs drawn up, Tenley rubbed her cheek back and forth over her knee several times before lifting her head "We're both her guardians. It's right there in black-and-white."

What? Oh, right. The papers. Jade. Guardianship. He'd almost forgotten in the sudden flurry of emotion that erupted in him over bringing Zeus back to work on the force.

"No." Mac sliced a hand through the air. A hiss of pain accompanied the movement, and Tenley's eyes narrowed.

She rolled to her feet and stared up at him from the bottom of the steps. "What's wrong?"

Their different heights, along with the fact he stood on the top step and she on the bottom, put her at a disadvantage. Or it would have if she were anyone other than Tenley. She gave him a look, scouring him from head to toe before her dark brown eyes found his.

"My sister allowed you to be part of her will. That's what's wrong." He refused to let her see his pain. Pain she'd caused and pain from the bullet wound that had left a hole in his shoulder and put him off the police force for the next few months. Or so the official statement from his boss read. The unofficial one bit deeper. Those things were no longer her business. He rolled the stiffness from his neck. "I'm taking Jade back to Chicago with me."

"Nope." Tenley stomped up the steps and slammed her hands onto her hips. Her eyes met his and fire sparked in the depths. "You can't take her from everything she knows and drop her into a place like Chicago. I won't allow it. She has two weeks of school left. You can't consider yanking her out now and forcing her to start in a new school."

"You won't—" Disbelief forced out a raw laugh. He shook the papers. "This means nothing. You have no right to be her guardian. I'm her uncle. You're *not* family." Tenley's face turned redder than a Rhode Island Red. "And I'll take care of her from now on."

"You can't go against Amber's wishes. We're both on that paper. That gives me as much right to keep her here—blood family or not." Stubbornness glinted in her eyes, and her jaw jutted forward. When she tipped her chin up and gave him that glare from their high school days, he forced himself to look away before he could give in to the emotions ricocheting around his insides.

He stepped closer, forcing her to bend her head back to meet his gaze. "My sister," his voice grumbled, "thought we would be married when she signed this." He shouldn't be so petty, but it felt good. "We'll see what a judge thinks." He refolded the papers and tucked them into his back pocket. "I'm going to see my niece now." Without another word, he yanked open the screen door and stepped inside.

Voices drifted in from the kitchen, Jade's childish laughter cutting through his belligerence and hammering home the truth. His sister was gone.

Grief sliced him. He heaved it aside and forced his lips into a smile while crossing the living room.

The door slammed behind him, and Tenley's presence filled the room. It had always been that way for him. He'd loved her. Man, how he'd loved her. And losing her had nearly destroyed him. If not for the job in Chicago and his work with K-9s in the police force during those early years...he didn't want to think about where he might've ended up.

Then he'd found Laura, and the future brightened. They'd had three years of marriage together before she passed, and the years of grief in between didn't prepare him for losing his sister.

Nothing—absolutely nothing—prepared him for seeing his high school sweetheart for the first time in almost seven years.

He waited for her to speak, but she seemed content to loiter behind him. No doubt she had her arms crossed and wore a frown that didn't fit her always congenial expression.

Shaking away the thoughts, Mac eased toward the kitchen. He paused at the entryway and leaned his good shoulder on the doorframe.

Jade sat at the kitchen table, a plate of cookies inches from her hand.

Peter and Margaret sat on either side, half-drunk glasses of milk lining the center of the table.

Peter winked at Margaret. "I don't know, dear. I think she's won." He tapped his fingers on the arm of his wheelchair. His gaze skimmed Mac, then settled on Tenley. Tight lines fanned from his mouth as he frowned, but he quickly schooled his expression and returned his attention to Jade.

"You think so?" Margaret tilted her head from side to side and dropped her hand to Jade's arm. "The goal was to see who could blow the most bubbles in their milk." She hiked one eyebrow into an arch. "I count five in mine."

"I had seven." Jade scooted to the edge of her chair and grabbed her glass of milk. She eyed it, the look of disdain so like Amber that it clenched Mac's heart into a vice grip. "One popped when I set it down. But it still counts, right?"

"What do you think, Mac?" Peter rolled away from the table and waved a hand for Mac to join them. "Do popped bubbles count?"

"They never did when I played." Pain skirted around his shoulder and sent twinges into his fingers. He tucked his hand into his pocket before they could see him flex the pain away.

Jade's glass hit the table with a clatter, and she stared at him, mouth hanging open. "You played?"

"Sure I did." He gave her a lazy grin. "No one could ever beat me. That's why they had to make rules about popped bubbles." He jerked his chin in Tenley's direction, the memory washing over him too fast to toss aside. "She used to pop my bubbles so she'd win."

"Did not." Tenley's voice held a smile despite her outward scowl. She cuffed his arm, the touch light as a feather but no less potent than napalm.

She breezed past him, leaving behind the combined scent of horse and the coconut shampoo she'd used for as long as he could remember.

Jade ran around the table and skidded to a stop in front of Tenley.

Mac dragged his gaze away from the unlikely pair and focused on Peter and Margaret. They looked well, older, a bit more worn, but they both smiled at him. Tension knotted in his throat at the glint of something brewing in Peter's eyes. He'd counted the man like a father when his own died during Mac's high school days. Losing Peter after the wedding debacle pained him more than he cared to admit.

Jade twirled, holding out her arms and asking Tenley to

dance. Like the rowdy youth he remembered, Tenley joined in. Joy shone from her face, along with a peacefulness that he'd not seen in years.

Lord, why? Mac staggered over the force of worry gnawing at him. Why him and this awful situation that put him within Tenley's grasp again? She pulled him into her world without even trying.

"Going to be in town for a while?" Peter tapped his fingers on the arms of his wheelchair, keeping time with Tenley's whirling steps.

Mac glanced at Tenley. "Depends."

"On?" Peter pressed, and only his respect for the man kept Mac from saying something he'd regret.

He breathed deep, letting the air expand his lungs, and counted to five. "Got some business to take care of."

Jade and Tenley's laughter rang out clear and strong, and the sound did something to Mac's heart. An ache built, and he pressed a fist to his sternum to keep it contained.

He blinked away the vision threatening to cloud his mind. One where Tenley danced in their kitchen, with their little girl. A dream that would never be realized.

"I think we all know why I'm here. I'd like to not discuss it in her presence." He motioned at Jade but realized that his mood currently included Tenley too.

There had to be a way out of this predicament.

"She'll stay here tonight, and we'll sort everything out once you've had time to digest what's happened." Peter's voice made the order direct and final.

Mac considered arguing when realization dawned. "She knew that we shared custody?" He couldn't say her name out loud. It hurt too much.

Margaret laced her fingers together under her chin and watched him with a hooded expression. "She found out right after…" Tears filled her eyes and her chin wobbled.

He looked away from the sight of her grief. Margaret and

Peter had been like parents to him, Amber, Callie and so many others through the years. They gathered them up like a hen did chicks and gave them a safe place to call home. He'd forever be grateful for their hospitality to him and Amber all those years ago, but he couldn't allow that to cloud his judgment now.

He pushed away from the table. "Jade." The girl spun in his direction, her face wreathed in smiles.

She ran to him, arms wide with the same love and abandon her mother had showed. "Are you staying forever?"

He shook his head once, and her smile morphed into a frown. "I have to leave, but I'll be back tomorrow." Like Peter, Mac made his words into a promise.

He hugged Jade tight and stood.

Tenley fiddled with the edge of her tattered shirt, her mouth flat with disapproval.

Mac escaped to the front porch and patted his leg, indicating Zeus should follow. The dog lay on his back in the dirt path that led from the porch to the driveway. Flowers poked through the ground on either side, evidence of Margaret's love of gardening.

The dog eyed Mac from his upside-down position, tongue lolling out. The pup bounded around Zeus, nipping at his tail and doing his best to get Zeus to engage.

A snort of laughter slipped out before he could stop it. Mac crossed his arms despite the pull and sharp jab of pain in his shoulder. "Don't tell me you like that mangy pup?"

Zeus flipped over and barked. His tail swished in the dirt. It was the most animated movement the dog had made of his own free will since he woke from the surgery that removed a sniper bullet from his side. Maybe Mac's captain was right. Maybe Zeus should be retired. He cuffed a hand over his cheek and strode toward his truck. He'd worry about that problem once he figured out how he was going to raise a little girl all by himself in Chicago.

CHAPTER TWO

THE NEXT DAY, Mac waited outside Leonard's office. At a quarter past nine on a Friday morning, the lawyer's office should be open, but when Mac pulled the door, the lock held fast. He palmed the back of his neck and scoured the street. Shops lined the road on either side, a few of them showing their age with peeling paint and haphazard signs.

Zeus sat at his side, head up and ears pricked forward. Mac put a calming hand on the canine's head. "Easy." Zeus whimpered and looked up, then licked his lips before returning his attention to the shop directly in front of them.

The door to Granny's Diner stood open as a couple exited, allowing tantalizing aromas out into the open air. Mac inhaled, and his stomach rumbled loudly. Through the plate glass windows, he watched people dining and considered abandoning his stakeout for a plate of gravy and biscuits. No one made biscuits and thick, rich gravy like Granny.

Zeus pressed his nose against Mac's leg and let out another whine.

Mac reached into the truck and retrieved Zeus's collapsible bowl and a bottle of water. He poured a healthy portion into the bowl and set it on the sidewalk. While Zeus lapped at the water, Mac checked the dog's vest. He wasn't actively working, but Zeus's police dog career was long and the vest kept curious people from running up and trying to pet him. Most of the time. Mac kept an eye on the foot traffic moseying up and down the sidewalk. A couple jaywalked a dozen feet away from him, but he paid them no mind. This was Tamarack Springs, proud owner of one stoplight—that almost never worked—and not a single crosswalk. They were more of the throw-your-hand-up-in-thanks-and-jog-across-the-street-while-cars-stopped-for-you kind of town.

Leaving here for Chicago had been a massive culture shock. And now, being back, he scarcely knew where to begin.

Seeing Tenley had hit him harder than he'd expected. He'd put all that behind him years ago. Or so he'd thought. One look. One touch from her, and it all unraveled. All the years apart threatened to collapse and drag him back to when things were good and he felt whole. He picked a flaking paint chip from the side of his truck. He'd lost so much over the years that this, seeing Tenley and knowing nothing could bring back what they had, shouldn't kick him in the gut with enough force to stop his breath.

He'd suffered the loss of his parents, Tenley's love, his wife and now his sister. He and grief were well acquainted. But he still had Jade, and he'd do anything and everything within his power to take care of her. He'd sworn to keep her safe on the day she was born, and he'd uphold that promise. Even if it meant taking her away from Tamarack Springs. From Tenley. The woman he'd given his heart to, only to have it crushed under her boot heel.

Never again.

Tenley didn't deserve the chance to protect Jade. She'd given up that right when she jilted him, proving herself untrustworthy, and all she'd do was end up disappointing him again—or worse, disappointing Jade. He'd suffer if it was just him at risk. But he refused to put Jade through that loss.

She loved Tenley. He'd seen it in the way they danced in the kitchen last night.

A stout woman dressed in a paisley apron shuffled out of Granny's. "Malcolm Mitchell, get in here and eat your breakfast." Granny glared at him, her wispy white hair curled in a halo around her head. She brandished a wooden spoon in his direction, eyes eagle-sharp as they raked him over. "Come on. Not telling you twice. Got your food in your booth. And something for the pup too."

Mac opened his mouth.

Granny arched an eyebrow and pointed her spoon at him. "Breakfast is getting cold. Cold gravy never did nobody no good." Old-fashioned Southern charm at its finest, the double negatives thick enough to make even Mac take a moment to appreciate Granny's adept use and the deep drawl that spoke of home.

She yanked the door open with more strength than he thought possible for a woman her age. Granny's Diner had been around longer than Mac had been alive. She was a staple of their little town. Everyone paid attention when Granny spoke, and even though he no longer considered himself part of Tamarack, he knew better than to say no.

He motioned for Zeus and followed her into the diner. Familiar sights, sounds and smells surrounded him. Granny stopped at a table and chatted with the man and woman sitting there before she angled her steps toward the open kitchen behind the long counter. Granny didn't believe in "keeping up with the times" as she called it. Which meant the diner looked exactly the same as it had when he was a child. Same square tables marching in a line down the center of the diner. Same cracked red coverings on the booths.

"Isaac, get another batch of hash browns ready." Granny slipped behind the counter and disappeared.

Mac's feet moved on instinct, carrying him to a booth left of the door. Sure enough, he found a plate piled high with gravy and biscuits waiting for him, along with a cup of steaming black coffee and a bowl of kibble for Zeus. Mac's brow puckered. How…? Why did Granny have dog food in her diner? He shook his head. The woman was a mystery that no one had ever figured out.

He set the bowl of food on the floor for Zeus and motioned for the dog to eat. Zeus sniffed the bowl before chowing down.

Mac bowed his head, but prayer eluded him. Words tumbled together as though in a race to reach God first, and all he could do was allow his heart to open and let God hear the cry for Himself. Mac grabbed his fork and cut into the flaky biscuit, releasing a puff of steam.

Granny appeared when he reached for the pepper shaker.

He eyed her from the side while shaking pepper onto his sawmill gravy.

She puckered her lips but didn't comment on the blasphemy of seasoning her food before he'd even had a taste. "Who you looking for out there?" She jerked her head toward his green pickup, parked midway between her diner and Leonard's law office.

"Who says I'm looking for anybody?" He eased a bite of piping hot biscuit and gravy into his mouth and sighed as his eyes sank closed. He chewed slowly, relishing the buttery biscuit and peppery gravy. When he opened his eyes again, a delighted smile wrinkled Granny's face.

She lowered herself onto the bench seat across from him, her short stature ensuring he could still see the door and everyone around him over her head. She gave him a knowing look that was equal parts annoyance and happiness. "Nobody stands outside my diner, sniffing and pining but refusing to come inside, unless they're waiting on somebody mighty important."

Mac ate a second bite while he considered his options. Most likely half of the town population already knew his business, but he'd rather not instigate any new rumors. He sipped his coffee and grinned. "Still serving nothing but coffee, I see."

Granny harrumphed. "You want water, you go to the kitchen and get it yourself. Breakfast goes best with coffee." She leaned forward, her smile widening. "And I'm still smart enough to know when someone's trying to distract me."

Customers sat all around them, their voices rising and falling as conversation flowed thick as the honey Granny bought from Bill, their local beekeeper. Heads turned in his direction. People he'd known his whole life offered grins and nods but didn't interrupt. No one interrupted Granny once she'd taken it upon herself to join someone.

He saw the curiosity, and the knowing.

"Point taken." Mac took another sip and waited for a woman carrying a full breakfast platter to pass by his booth. Once she was out of earshot, he spoke. "What time does Leonard come to work?"

"That old coot?" Granny tipped her head back and laughter rolled out. Her shoulders shook. "Honey, you're better off looking for him at home than at the office. Old Leonard don't come in unless it's an emergency."

"I see." Mac resumed his breakfast, though the biscuits now sat hard as lumps of coal in his gut. The flavor though, the flavor made it worthwhile. Had he considered it an emergency when he couldn't get hold of Mac? Was that why Jade stayed at the ranch with Tenley? After Mac's abrupt departure from the office yesterday, Leonard was probably more than happy to wash his hands of Mac and Tenley's predicament.

Shared guardianship. The words tasted sour in his mouth and turned him away from the rest of his breakfast. Pushing the plate aside, he wrapped both hands around the coffee cup and leaned his elbows on the table. "Guess I'll need his phone number. Or address."

Granny snorted. "Thought you were smarter than that, Mac." The use of his nickname softened the anger curling his stomach into a tight knot. Granny leaned across the table and patted his forearm. "Sorry about your sister. Know it doesn't help but can't let you get out of here without saying it anyway. She was a delightful girl. Came in every Saturday morning for breakfast. The three of them." She met his gaze, her own full of grief. "Take care of that girl."

"I will." He forced his throat to work, to push the words into existence and will them into truth. Jade was all that he had left in this world. He couldn't lose her too.

Zeus poked his nose into Mac's leg, his whine drawing attention.

Mac ruffled the upright ears and rolled his shoulders to loosen the tension. He'd almost lost Zeus to a bullet, and now might lose him to retirement. He didn't want to start over with another canine partner. Or another human one, if he was being honest. Pain sliced through his shoulder when he shifted, reminding him of that night. Of all the things he'd done wrong, all to save his partner's life, and he'd gotten both Zeus and himself shot in the process. His captain used the injury to put Mac on administrative leave without making it obvious. Mac broke protocol that night, and almost seven years of playing by the book didn't undo this one night where it all went sideways.

"You still with me?" Granny peered at him over the rim of her glasses.

Mac released his death grip on the coffee cup and resumed patting Zeus, who'd begun inching toward Granny.

She looked at Zeus, then at Mac. "That dog of yours looks almighty worn out."

He felt the statement all the way to his bones.

"Seems his owner is too," she continued.

"Zeus isn't mine." Mac drained the coffee. "I'm a K-9 handler in Chicago. Zeus and I work together."

Granny harrumphed. "Honey, I'd love to be a fly on the wall the day you try and tell him that. Better yet, I want to watch if anyone is ever fool enough to try and take him away from you. Don't care what your job is. That dog is yours. He's accepted you as his human. End of story."

Mac glanced at Zeus, who stared back at him with that searching look. It was true. Zeus hadn't connected with any of the other K-9 officers until Mac. He'd been on the verge of early retirement since he refused to follow orders. It had taken Mac a week to earn the dog's trust, and they'd been inseparable since. He followed all the rules about keeping Zeus. He wasn't a pet. He wasn't a family dog. He was a working partner. Something Laura and he had argued over more than once. She'd wanted to make a pet out of Zeus, but Mac had stood firm.

His thoughts turned foul, and he heaved them into the darkest corner of his mind before they took root and grew. "Thanks for dragging me in for breakfast." He changed the conversation without bothering to sugarcoat his rush to leave.

Granny narrowed her eyes at him. "Why don't I let Leonard know you need to see him? He'll be at church Sunday. You can talk to him then."

Mac ignored the built-in insinuation that he'd even go to church. He grabbed Zeus's leash and stood. "Monday morning is soon enough. Tell him I'll be waiting at 8:00 a.m." He slid two twenties under the edge of his plate.

"You take that money and put it to good use." Granny poked a finger at him.

Mac grinned back. "I just did." He sauntered away, feeling lighter now that he had a plan in motion. Monday morning, he and Leonard would sit down and iron out all the wrinkles Amber's will left behind. In the meantime, he needed to get back to Jade. He'd promised to come back, and he'd keep his word, even if it meant seeing Tenley.

TENLEY TURNED A slow circle, keeping Jade and Freckles front and center in her line of sight. "Good, Jade. Keep him moving forward. Use pressure from your knees. Good."

Jade's grin broke through like the sunshine after a rainstorm. It overtook the clouds that had become the girl's expression for far too long. Not that Tenley blamed her. Jade had every right to scowl and grieve and want to lie in bed all day with her stuffed animals. But Tenley didn't deny the burst of joy singing through her heart at the sight of that proud smile.

Freckles continued his steady walk around the corral. He'd been trained to listen to voice commands but also to feel for his rider's wants through the reins and leg cues. Right now, Tenley wanted horse and rider to work together. Jade was an established rider, and knew how to guide her mount even at her young age.

Jade sat easy in the saddle, the reins relaxed in her hands and her feet firmly in the stirrups. She stared ahead, her body language letting Freckles know which way she wanted to go. "Can I ride with the class tomorrow?" Jade cast a look at Tenley, then looked ahead again.

"Sure." Tenley kept turning. Her hat brim shielded her from the worst of the sun's glare but reminded her yet again of how nice it would be to have a covered arena like the one at Daniel Wells's riding school. She tried not to feel inadequate with her single arena and barn. Tried to stuff the jealousy down. Daniel would offer the use of his arena in a heartbeat if she asked. Not that she ever would. This was her dream, and she'd accomplish it her way, on her terms.

Enough of that. She sounded like her brother Brody.

Boots scuffed nearby. Goose bumps prickled the back of her neck, and she knew who stood at the rail behind her without turning around. Mac. He'd come back, just like he'd said he would. Good ole Mac. Reliable as the day was long. Never backed down from what he believed was right. Willing to jump into any mess for those he loved when they needed saving. And always true to his word.

Spots danced in front of Tenley's eyes, a harsh reminder to stop holding her breath. She gulped air and tried not to shiver when his gaze landed between her shoulder blades with the intensity of a laser. No one else ever made her feel this way.

Jade rode toward Mac, forcing Tenley to turn. She did, as slow as possible, while wrangling her face into anything other than the regret that bubbled up in his presence. He deserved an apology for what she'd done. To him. To them. He deserved the truth. A truth that he'd asked her family for when Tenley disappeared. But her shame trapped her, and Mac knowing the real reason for their failed wedding felt like it would tip her over the edge of an unscalable chasm. So, they'd stood by her request not to tell him about the alcoholism, and he'd hightailed it out of her life—probably as hurt and confused by the blockade erected from Mom, Dad and Brody, people he counted as family—before she had a chance to come to terms with her overnight stint in jail and subsequent months in rehab.

Barking erupted from the barn, and a ball of white fur bounded toward the corral.

Tenley groaned in time with the puppy's playful yips.

Mac looked over his shoulder, giving Tenley a reprieve.

"Rascal." Jade called the puppy, her tone scolding even though she laughed.

The puppy hurtled toward Freckles, darting under the fence's lower railing and giving Tenley a wide berth like he knew she'd keep him from reaching the horse.

"Get that dog out of there." Mac's voice shook, and Tenley didn't know which was heavier, the anger or the fear.

Jade and Freckles kept moving forward. Rascal raced around Freckles, pretending to nip at his fetlocks. His teeth snapped together on Freckles' tail.

Mac hissed through his teeth and squeezed between the rails. He ran toward Jade, face set and jaw tight. "Why aren't you doing anything?" He glared at Tenley as he raced past. "I knew this would happen. You never think, Tenley."

What? Her spine snapped into a straight line and her hands landed on her hips. "Freckles, stop." The gelding halted in his tracks.

Mac didn't pause his headlong rush toward Jade.

Jade frowned. "Why'd you stop him?"

Mac yanked Jade from the saddle amid her protests and held her tight. "I can't believe you'd put her in danger."

"Jade, go put your dog in the stall. Like I told you to do before the lesson started." Tenley matched Mac, glare for glare. "While I explain to your uncle why he should never, ever enter my arena and approach the horses without my permission."

Jade wiggled. "Put me down, Uncle Mac."

Rascal never stopped bouncing. He zoomed past Mac, ran under Freckles' belly, and back out of the corral.

Mac lowered Jade to the ground, but he kept hold of her like he might snatch her up and run away at any second. His fear made no sense. Mac grew up here, riding the same horses she'd ridden. He knew Tenley would never put a child in danger. Didn't he?

Jade sighed, the sound older than a girl her age should know how to make. "I did put him in the stall. I promise I did."

"He must have dug his way out. Again." Tenley resisted the urge to rush into an explanation. "Go on. See if you can catch him."

"That dog—"

"Wait." Tenley interrupted Mac. She jutted her chin toward Jade. The girl let out a groan and trotted off after the pup. Tenley rounded on Mac. "In what world do you think it's okay to come in here, interrupt my lesson and jerk Jade around like she's a rag doll?"

Fury rolled through her, and a matching look seared her from the depths of Mac's brown eyes. He took a step forward. "In what world do you allow that little girl on a horse while a dog runs around out of control?"

Tenley sank her teeth into her cheek to keep from blasting him with the harshest words that came to mind. She paused long enough to cleanse her thoughts and lowered her hands to her pockets. "I'm going to say this once, out of respect for you and your role as Jade's co-guardian. Freckles is a therapy horse. He's been trained to deal with any and every situation with one reaction. Nothing."

"You're not putting Jade's life in danger on someone else's word." Mac all but crackled with the furious anger drawing his eyes into narrow slits.

"It's my word, Mac, mine. Not someone else's."

Mac splayed his hands in a so-what motion, and Tenley swallowed her retort. He'd never listen. Her words and promises meant nothing to him, not after what she did.

She could tell him all day how many hours she'd put into verifying Freckles'—and all the other horses'—ability to handle any situation. Time Mac would never give her. Not that it would matter. But maybe if he took half a second to stop panicking and focus, he'd know that for himself. She also didn't have time to delve into why Mac was panicking in the first place.

She motioned at the gelding standing still as a stone and took a step toward Mac with more bravado than she felt. "And I'll say this once as well. Never talk to me that way again. I don't care if you hate me. Don't ever speak that way in front of Jade. I may not deserve your love or forgiveness, or even your respect, but you won't force your prejudices on to Jade."

Mac's jaw could smash concrete into submission. When he ducked his head, his gaze pulling away from hers, she forced herself back into his line of sight. "I promised Amber that I'd take care of Jade. That means something. Whether you believe it or not," she said.

He inhaled deeply, no doubt brewing up a storm of arguments. Before he could utter a word, Jade loped back into the corral with Rascal in her arms. "Uncle Mac, will you help me train Rascal? You know about dogs, right?"

He shook his head and took a step away from Tenley. She noted the sudden haggardness in his eyes and the way he continually rubbed his shoulder while wincing.

"Wait." She didn't mean to plead and stopped before she said more. One word. A single syllable, but it stretched across the years separating them and offered the tentative bridge of hope she desperately needed. From the looks of Mac, he needed it too. She used to be able to read him. Way back when, she'd have known in half a second what he was thinking. Not anymore. He'd learned how to guard himself against her.

Her stomach lurched and tightened. She'd loved him more than she thought possible. Or healthy. What he considered the ultimate betrayal she knew to be the only way to set him free from a lifetime of regret. Regret he had no idea he'd managed to avoid.

Jade grunted at Rascal's weight and lowered the pup to the dusty ground. "Uncle Mac?"

He spun to face Jade, his last look at Tenley full of all the things they'd never said. A breath hissed between his teeth when he dropped to a knee, bringing himself to Jade's level. "Of course, I'll help you train your puppy."

While Jade grinned and hugged Mac, he glared at Tenley over his shoulder.

Jade pulled away. "I'll go put him up, then you can watch the rest of my class." Her nose wrinkled. "That's okay, right, Aunt Tenley? Long as he doesn't come into the corral again?" she said respectfully.

"That's fine." She answered before Mac could say a word.

He faced her once Jade walked out of earshot. "She's not going to keep riding."

"You try telling her that. Freckles is part of Jade's equine therapy program. The grief counselor from the Department of Family and Children Services recommended it, and she signs off on all Jade's paperwork. You'll have to take it up with her." Tenley shrugged even though her heart drummed hard and fast.

Mac ripped off the ball cap covering his dark hair and scrubbed a hand over his scalp. "Fine. Then, she's not allowed to ride unless I'm here."

Tenley couldn't help it. A bark of laughter shot out. She crossed her arms. "She rides when she's scheduled to ride. If you want to be here, that's fine. I'll give you a copy of her riding times once we're finished here." She held up a hand. "But if you're not here, that's on you. She rides anyway. I'm not responsible for you."

"Yeah, you washed your hands of that a long time ago." Mac's voice lowered to a growl. His expression was drawn tight, lines fanning out from his eyes and narrowing them to slits. "If you have something to say to me, say it now. Get it over with."

"Oh, there's plenty I want to say to you, but not here. Not now. I have a class to teach." She stalked over to Freckles and gathered up the gelding's reins. The horse followed her to the mounting block near the gate. Tenley spoke to Mac over her shoulder. "Right now, you need to get on the other side of the fence."

"And if I don't?" He dared to lean against the railing and cross his arms.

Tenley gripped the reins until her fingers cramped. What could she do to convince him? "You're not qualified person-nel."

"So, if I'm in here, then Jade can't ride?" He smirked and crossed his arms. "I think I'll stay."

"What happened to you?" The question shot out before she could stop it. "Where's the uncle that Jade always talks about? The one who promised to take her on a trail ride the next time he was in town?"

Mac reeled back like she'd struck him. He pushed off from the rail and palmed open the gate without saying a single word.

Jade walked out of the barn, and they both went silent.

Tenley regretted trying to break into Mac's past. She kept an eye on him while Jade hopped in the saddle. Mac had lost so many people in his life. Their names flashed through her mind. She hesitated on one. Laura. His wife.

It surprised her that Mac had fallen in love so soon after leaving. Amber had been sure that Mac still loved Tenley, but Tenley had known better. Tenley had felt immeasurable grief when she heard of Laura's passing. With Amber gone, Mac was alone except for Jade. She didn't blame him for wanting to cling tight to his last thread of family.

For the remainder of the class, he stood with his arms atop the rail and a deepening scowl pulling lines from his mouth.

Tenley did her best to ignore him, but it was like trying to ignore an approaching storm. The small hairs on the back of her neck prickled. She could all but smell the burnt ozone coming from the lightning strikes Mac sent her way.

It took enormous effort to keep her body relaxed and her tone even, but she managed. *Lord, help me get through this.* She tried to hold on to the sliver of peace the prayer offered, but it eluded her. Mac coming back into her life churned up the past she'd tried so hard to bury.

CHAPTER THREE

TENLEY LET A breath of relief escape when the time came for class to start and Mac hadn't arrived to hover, but then she felt bad for Jade, who continually scanned the arena and whose little shoulders deflated when it became obvious he wasn't coming.

Tenley waved at her two additional instructors. Carl and Julie had come highly recommended, and Tenley loved working with the married duo. She also loved Saturday classes when all the kids rode together.

Carl nudged his hat up with his thumb and glanced at his watch. "Ready when you are, boss."

Tenley swallowed the lump of disappointment she told herself was for Jade and clapped her hands. It was ironic that she'd wrought such turmoil in Mac's life, and here she was mooning over him. She didn't deserve a second chance, even if her subconscious quietly hoped for it. Still, seeing him stirred up old embers she thought had gone cold.

She gave herself a little shake. Back to business. "Alright, we'll begin with a walk. Jasmine will lead today. Jas, stop at the gate after the third round. Okay?"

"Got it." The girl bobbed her head. Being the leader was a privilege that changed every class. Today was Jasmine's first time, and from the way she sat up straight in the saddle, she planned on taking it seriously.

Her class of six kids sat quietly while she stepped between Carl and Julie.

Cody, a scrappy tow-headed boy who was also one of the younger kids in the group, was here for grief counseling like Jade. His dad had pulled Tenley aside upon their arrival to mention Cody's anxiety had improved though his grief ebbed and flowed. Cody leaned forward and patted his horse's neck. She was one of the tallest horses they stabled, and even though little Cody looked outmatched on her, Tenley had her reasons for the pairing. The gray mare didn't move, standing as she'd been trained until given the signal.

"Lead on, Jasmine." Tenley lifted her hand and let it fall.

Jasmine nudged her horse into a slow walk. The others moved one by one, falling into a line, one horse length between each horse. Smiles broke out, a sight Tenley never tired of. She could watch kids ride all day every day, and each time they broke through whatever trauma or distress that made them feel trapped, she knew she'd made the right choice in opening an equine therapy center here on the ranch.

She turned on her heel, keeping her kids in sight. The small, covered arena wasn't as nice as the one at Wells Riding Academy, but it worked for Tenley and her groups. Someday, she'd expand.

Jasmine continued her slow walk, her horse's sorrel coat contrasting with the white fence behind the mare. Parents sat in a row of bleachers near the gate where the riders mounted and dismounted. The barn connected to the covered arena via a short, roofed path that led straight to the gate and gave the riders a feeling of freedom while also maintaining safety.

"Good job, Cody." Tenley praised the young boy when he gently nudged his horse back in line after the mare weaved closer to the rail than the others. She lost her footing a little, but Cody didn't overreact. He'd started out so afraid, but now he handled her with skill and more confidence—well, most of the time anyway.

"Tenley." Mac's voice brought her head around, distracting her. He yelled her name a second time and motioned for her to join him. He waved a set of papers at her like they were on fire, and she had to take them or he'd get burned.

The nerve.

She shook her head in a negative motion. Now wasn't the time. "You're doing great, kids."

That's when she saw silent tears running down Cody's face. She'd been about to join Mac to put him in his place, and almost missed them.

Tenley frowned and walked toward the little boy and his big horse. "Everything okay, Cody?"

The boy nodded, but his chin wobbled and he clutched the reins in both fists. "I don't want to stop. I want to keep going, but I'm afraid."

She kept pace with him. "It's okay. Can I walk with you? You can keep going. I'll be right here."

He sniffled and nodded. "Yeah."

Losing his mom at his age had turned the once-confident boy into the anxious quiet one before her. It was a normal grief reaction for such a young child, and one they could help him work through. His happy self was still in there, but grief made him afraid. Learning to ride a muscled, tall mount like Tank, along with regular counseling sessions, was helping him overcome some of those fears.

"Nice and easy. Let's keep it at a walk for a few more laps. Can you tell me what's making you afraid?"

"I... I think she might buck me off. I don't want to fall." Little sobs escaped. *The wobble earlier at the fence, that's what did it*, Tenley thought. She'd turn it into a lesson. His mother had died from a fall, though not from a horse.

"Has Tank ever bucked before?"

"Uh-uh." His head shook.

"You've been to class, what, five times? Has Tank always been gentle? Have you always been safe on her?"

"Mmm-hmm," he said, seeing where this was going.

"I think Tank hit her hoof earlier. Like when you stub your toe. When you trip over your feet, does it make you mad?" Tenley made her best mean face.

Cody giggled, "No!"

"So is your thought a good, helpful thought or a bad, unhelpful thought?"

"Bad!" he yelled, getting excited.

Tenley matched his pitch. "And what do we do with those bad thoughts?"

"We flush them down the toilet!" It wasn't exactly a horse analogy, but the kids didn't care. The other students shouted it with him again, this time louder, and they all laughed.

Mac watched with quiet curiosity, and put aside the bundle of papers.

Some of the tension bled out of his expression as they passed him, one of the kids cracking a potty joke that had nothing to do with therapy. Mac lowered his hands to his hips and gripped his belt. He tried to hide the ghost of a smile creeping free. He wore jeans and another T-shirt with what looked to be a pair of brand-new cowboy boots. The soft brown gleamed in contrast to her own battered and scarred boots.

She motioned for Julie to take over when she thought Cody was okay, then made the slow trek over to a waiting Mac.

Memories shot through Tenley. Images of Mac in his sheriff's deputy uniform right after he'd completed his training flashed through her mind. He'd stood just like that. Tall and proud, gripping the belt like a rodeo champion would a prize buckle. Smiling that same smile. The full one though. A lot of hard work went into earning the right to strap the utility belt on.

She looked over at the kids, finding healing in her therapy school. Tenley's throat worked as tension gathered in her shoulders and pressed down on her heart. This school wouldn't have existed. And all his hard work wouldn't have meant a thing if they'd gotten married. Maybe she wouldn't have gotten help. Maybe her next accident would have been her last one. Maybe her arrest would have stalled his career if anyone ever found out a deputy's wife was an inebriated road hazard?

She'd spent weeks coming to terms with her problems and the potential fallout of a deputy's wife getting arrested. Didn't matter what for or that it happened before the wedding. Tamarack Springs had a long memory when it came to juicy gossip. But her downfall had happened in Bridgeport, far enough away from their sleepy little town's gossip mill. Still, she was afraid her problem would follow her back then.

So many what-ifs, and here he was, stirring them up like horses swatting flies with swishing tails.

Behind her, her co-leaders directed the group back to dismount. Class was over already? With Mac watching, everything sped up double time.

Jade had beat the group to the punch though. She'd already dismounted and removed her saddle. She called to Mac while rushing toward the tack room. "I'm almost done. We can train Rascal together."

The look Mac gave Tenley said he'd rather be doing anything other than working with that rambunctious pup, but he didn't argue. A promise was a promise, to Mac.

Tenley grimaced.

"Where's Zeus?" She'd meant to ask the day before but lost track of the question after their argument.

"He's at the house with your parents." Mac lifted one eyebrow. "Didn't want him down here getting into trouble around the horses like that pup."

"I'm sure he'd be fine." Tenley shrugged.

Mac laughed, the sound cold and cruel. "You would think that. Troublesome Tenley." The old nickname shot out of his mouth like a snake spitting venom. "Always thinking that everything will work out. Never prepared for reality."

She snapped her teeth together with a click, trapping angry words behind them. How dare he? They both knew the casualties that came with living. Her father's accident was the single worst thing that she'd ever experienced aside from leaving Mac. He used her moniker as a weapon, knowing she despised it. Yes, she'd been the one always getting into trouble as a kid. She claimed middle-child syndrome, though there was more to it than that.

It wasn't like Mac to be cruel. Even if she deserved it.

"What happened to you?" She asked the same question from the day before. He'd changed so much more than she'd anticipated. Gone was the funny and lighthearted man who'd stolen her heart. In his place was this jaded and cynical person she hardly recognized.

"I grew up." Mac thrust the papers he'd been cradling at her, like they were a bomb. "And I brought these."

GRANTED, MAC KNEW printing the "Voluntary Surrender of Rights" form from an internet lawyer's website was a risk, but one he was willing to take. Getting ahold of old Leonard to do the deed himself was a harder task than running down a drug dealer—in hiding—on purpose. It made him wonder if the old lawyer had something to hide, or some nefarious matchmaking plan concocted by Granny, or if it was just that the man was so old he spent more time napping than working these days.

Now, if he could only get Tenley to sign it and be done so he could get back to Chicago—with a six-year-old. He swallowed the lump forming in his throat and ran a hand down his face. Calling Tenley *troublesome* wasn't going to help his case, but she was a burr in his side that he couldn't help scratching hard.

Tenley eyed the papers, her eyes snapping fire at him. She took a giant step back. "I'm not signing that."

"It's what's best for Jade." Mac hit her with a low blow, and he knew it. He had to try. He'd done enough waiting for Tenley. "I'm done here. Sign the papers and let me take Jade home."

Tenley's expression morphed so quick he almost missed it as she hid her anger between one blink and the next. She closed the distance. "Jade is home." She jerked her head toward the barn. "And she'll be headed this way in about three minutes, so you'd better put those away and get ready to train that dog."

Mac was the one who could use some training. Or a crash course in raising a little girl. How was he supposed to do this? He folded the papers and thrust them in Tenley's direction. "You know this is what's best." He pushed because that's what he was good at. He'd built a career on being the guy who followed the letter of the law. He never wavered. Never backed down. He'd beat this thing with Tenley if it took every last breath. Breath that grew shorter the longer she stared at him without moving.

"I'm not a criminal you can scare into doing what you want." She crossed her arms and took another step closer. If not for the fence between them, she'd probably have tried to haul him away. "I have Jade's best interests at heart. You're just anxious to get away from me, and you'll end up hurting Jade because you can't stand the heat." She dared him to contradict her.

Mac swallowed the first retort that came to mind. Even Tenley didn't deserve to have those words thrown at her. She was right. He was running scared and trying to drag Jade along for the ride.

Tenley was a contradiction to the woman he used to know. Still bold and full of fire, but this one had a tenacity and grit that he'd only seen in people who'd suffered.

What experience did Tenley have with grief and agony?

Tenley moved with lightning speed. She snatched the papers from his hand and ripped them to shreds then threw the pieces into the air.

Mac watched the bits flutter in the breeze until they landed on the ground and lay still.

"I will do everything in my power to protect her." Mac stooped, ready to duck under the rail and gather the scraps. "Jade is the last of my family. She's everything to me."

Tenley flinched like the words were a physical blow he'd dealt her.

Tough. He had every right to say the truth.

Childish laughter spilled out from behind Mac. He straightened. "Jade doesn't need to know about this."

"Of course." Tenley spat the words at him. "I'm not the one trying to ruin her life by taking her away from everything—and everyone—she knows and loves."

That's not what he was doing.

Jade skipped toward him, hand in hand with Cody, the little boy who'd been struggling earlier.

Tenley wore a smile bright as sunshine. The sight pinched and poked at Mac. She'd make a great mother. The kind of mother he'd wanted for his kids. Now those dreams were shot to bits no bigger than the pieces of paper Tenley had left behind.

CHAPTER FOUR

TENLEY COULDN'T BELIEVE Mac's audacity. If Jade hadn't interrupted, she might have tossed her cowgirl hat at his feet and showed him what her boot spurs could do—if he didn't run away fast enough.

Lord help me, she prayed, and took a deep calming breath. *Lord, help me show Mac that I've changed. For his own sake, not mine. Let him see the damage he could do to Jade by taking her away. And if it's better for Jade to leave, then help me see that as Your will.*

Jade tucked her small hand into Mac's giant one and grinned up at him. Her grin faltered, no doubt feeling the tension, and she looked back at Tenley with such anguish that Tenley's heart broke into a thousand little pieces.

"You ready, Uncle Mac?" she said quietly. "Rascal is at Molly's with Luke."

Mac's steps hesitated when Tenley started walking with them. "I don't need help training the dog." The words were halting, almost like he didn't quite mean them.

"Didn't offer any. You demanded to watch Jade ride, I demand to watch you train Rascal." She infused strength into her spine and strode alongside. Two could play this game he'd made up with rules no one else understood.

Tenley hung back while Mac and Jade approached her sister Molly's house. The log cabin–style home shone with love and attention. The front porch was swept clean and the windows sparkled.

Jade thundered up the steps and banged her fist on the door. "Luke, come on. We're going to train Rascal."

The door burst open. Five-year-old Luke and Rascal spilled out onto the porch in a tumble of arms and legs. Luke's dark blond hair stuck up in every direction. He rolled to his feet and grabbed Rascal's collar before the pup took a nosedive down the steps.

"Grab his leash." Mac's shoulders shook with what appeared to be repressed laughter.

Luke's nose scrunched as he frowned. His freckles shone bright in the sunlight, the adorableness diminishing his growing scowl. "Who're you?"

"Luke." Molly admonished her son from the open doorway. Wisps of hair that matched Luke's fanned around her face. Red splotches covered her cheeks, a sure indication she'd been baking. Molly wiped her hands on a dishcloth. Her gaze skipped over Mac, then came back to rest on him. Her mouth opened in a vivid display of shock. "First, Callie. Now you. Which other long-lost residents will come back next?"

She didn't seem to want an answer to her question, so Tenley didn't offer one. Her sister had a point. Callie had come back after ten years. Mac after almost seven. Tamarack Springs hadn't seen this many prodigals returning in its whole history as a town.

That adage "you can never go home again" had been true for a long time, but Tenley understood that anyone could come back from the darkness. If she could, then anything was possible.

Jade joined Luke, the two of them wrestling with Rascal. "What do we do first?" Jade held the wriggling puppy with both hands around his middle.

Molly passed Luke a leash, which the boy clipped to the collar. Mac took the leash from Luke and the dog from Jade. "First, let's get some of this energy out."

"Never going to happen," Tenley whispered under her breath.

"I heard that." Mac grinned as he passed, then seemed to remember who he was talking to. He paused, and for a fraction of a second, he looked like he might apologize.

Tenley moved out of the way, then fell in line behind the kids when Mac moved on. They walked in Mac's footprints, laughing and falling into each other when his strides lengthened and they couldn't keep up.

Jade giggled. "You walk too big." She leaped from one step to the next but lost her balance on the landing and tumbled to the side.

Mac turned around in time to see what they were doing. He paled enough that Tenley almost reached out a hand to steady him.

Rascal chose that moment to leap from Mac's arms and pounce on Jade. He licked her face and wiggled all over, his tail fanning the dirt track Mac followed, which led from Molly's house to their parents' house.

Mac dropped into a crouch and helped Jade sit up. Luke mimicked Mac's posture, and his scowl.

"How long have you had this dog?" Mac zeroed in on Tenley.

She met him look for look. "Couple weeks."

"Have you taught him anything?" The look he gave her—well, she'd seen it before. The accusations in Mac's glare were far too memorable.

Everything that came from the man's mouth had bite. Was there anything left of the old Mac inside? Sadness swamped her, and she forced down the automatic, inflammatory response. She was not the same girl he thought he knew. She'd grown up, matured. Yes, the Troublesome Tenley nickname stuck around tighter than burrs in a horse's tail, but she was handling it. She could handle this too. And honestly, she was sad for him "No. I haven't had time."

"You don't get a dog if you don't have time to train it properly."

Tenley gave a hunch of her shoulders.

"Don't be mad." Jade threw herself at Mac's back and wrapped her arms around his neck. "I begged and begged. Cried too."

Mac rocked forward with a grunt and a wince. His breath came in short bursts and sweat broke out along his jaw. He was in pain. Concern bolted through Tenley, and it was all she could do not to throw herself on the ground beside him and offer to help. He wouldn't appreciate her interference though. Even before the wedding fiasco, Mac never knew how to ask for help. He had that in common with her and her siblings.

Rascal barked and bounced high enough to lick Mac's chin. He nudged the dog aside and patted Jade's leg. "I'm not mad."

Jade waited several seconds before she slid from his back. "If you're not mad, then you can go trail riding with us tomorrow." She skipped around in front of Mac.

"I can't."

"You promised." Jade's green eyes sparked with enough fire that even Mac seemed taken aback. "Last time in Chicago, you said you'd ride with me the next time you were here. You're here. Now you ride." Tiny arms crossed and her jaw stuck out in a mirror image of her mother, frankly with a whole lot of Mac too. It took Tenley's breath.

Mac's jaw worked side to side. He looked at Tenley, probably hoping she'd refuse to let him go. She held up her hands in a show of surrender. "This is between you two. You made that promise. Not me." And they both knew not to trust her promises. Or Mac thought he did, based on the way his eyes sought hers before skipping away. But Mac's promises were usually a sure thing.

"Okay. Alright." He ruffled Jade's hair. "I'll go trail riding with you."

MAC APPROACHED HIS sister's house the same way he'd enter an interrogation room. Shoulders back, chin up. He all but dared the house to offer the slightest hint of a confrontation when all he wanted was a confession. Silly, really, considering it was just a house. He motioned for Zeus to sit at the bottom step and waited for the dog to follow through before he put his boot on the pressure-treated wood.

He couldn't believe she was gone.

The two-bedroom ranch home glared back at him, challenging him through twin windows on either side of the front door. He stomped across the leaf-littered porch and twisted the knob. Locked. He took a step back and tipped over one of the empty flower planters while craning his head around in search of a key. Surely Amber had left a spare somewhere. She was always forgetting hers since she and Zack almost never bothered locking the door at all.

It was the only thing they'd ever argued about as adults. Every time she came to visit him in Chicago, he brought up the house, and she called him out for letting Chicago ruin his memories of small-town life.

No one in Tamarack Springs had been robbed for as long as Mac could remember. Didn't matter. That one-in-a-million chance was enough to drive him to distraction. Their tiny town also hadn't suffered a major vehicle accident since Tenley's father was involved in a hit-and-run nearly eleven years ago either. Didn't stop his sister and her husband from a fatal crash.

Stop. Just…stop. Mac gripped the concrete flower pot with both hands and forced out a breath. Spending the morning helping Jade with her pup had loosened the knots and let him breathe freely for the first time in months. He treasured those moments, every second spent with his precious niece. The thought of taking her away from here ate at him night and day, but what choice did he have? His life, his career, everything was in Chicago. Not to mention the sight of Tenley threatened to knock him to his knees.

The *whoop-whoop* of a police siren dragged Mac's attention away from the front door. He spun around and watched as the police car rolled up in Amber's driveway. The white-and-black sheriff's vehicle stood out in the overgrown grass.

Mac moved down the steps, out of the shadows and into the sunlight peppering the ground, turning the trees golden. He kept his hands within sight and his body relaxed.

"Well, I'll be." Sheriff Dodge Hanks opened the car door and smacked his palm on the open window. "I knew it. I told Martha there weren't no way somebody'd try to break into this place. Minute I heard you were back in town, I knew it was you." He unfolded his lanky frame from the car and stood to his full height. Gray threaded through the dark brown hair, and lines creased the sheriff's cheeks. The years had made quite a difference.

Mac didn't bother keeping back a smile. He covered the ground between them and held out a hand. "Sheriff. Good to see you."

The sheriff shook Mac's hand, his grip as strong as ever. "Been a long time, son."

Mac felt the years unspool. This man had taught him everything he knew about police work. Had given him a place within the department without hesitation and helped Mac learn the ropes. Then, when things fell apart with Tenley, the sheriff hadn't batted an eye when Mac said he needed to leave. That he couldn't stay in the same town, seeing her day after day.

It was the sheriff's recommendation that got Mac's foot in the door in a small precinct in Chicago. He'd earned his way from there.

And now they'd come full circle. Mac let his hands fall to

his sides and eyed the house over his shoulder. "Just came by to check on things."

"Yeah? Not moving in?" Sheriff Hanks scrubbed one knuckle over his cheek. "Well, suppose that might be tough, but what with you caring for little Jade, I thought you might not want to sell."

Mac's entire body stiffened. His pulse was a rabid thing, racing and erratic. "What are you talking about?"

"Huh?" Sheriff Hanks stared at Mac.

Zeus barked, and both men looked over.

The tension bled out of Mac, and he snapped his fingers. "Zeus, come."

"The mighty Zeus." Sheriff Hanks whistled appreciatively. "Heard a lot about him. How's he doing since the accident?"

"Is that what they're calling it?" Mac snorted a laugh.

Sheriff Hanks's expression didn't change, but a muscle ticked twice in his jaw. "You'd call it something else?"

"Yeah. I call it a rookie move made by a seasoned cop who knew better than to break protocol." He paced up and down the sidewalk. "I knew better. I knew what to do but ignored the rules."

"You saved your partner's life," Hanks said. A breeze rippled through the oak tree leafed out in the front yard. Its limbs rattled together as though in agreement.

"He never should've been in danger." Mac grabbed Zeus's collar when the dog paced alongside him. Soulful eyes locked on to Mac, and Zeus pressed in tight to Mac's leg. He'd gone into protection mode, sensing Mac's distress, and was doing his best to figure out what it was that Mac needed.

Sheriff Hanks put a hand on Mac's shoulder, stilling his furious steps. Zeus shoved his body between Hanks and Mac until Hanks lowered his arm. "Son, I understand your frustration. You did a decent thing, and you and your dog were shot. You did what you thought was right in the moment to save a man's life. There's no wrong in that."

"I missed my sister's funeral." He hadn't meant to say that, but being here, at her house with memories falling through him faster and faster, they refused to be denied. "I should have been here. Jade needed me."

The world closed in around him, suffocating. It was all too much.

He had to get away. He had to figure out how to get Jade away from Tenley's guardianship and get her back to Chicago where he could protect her. He was *not* going to lose someone else he loved.

"You're here now. Make the most of it." Sheriff Hanks waved toward Amber's house. "And now that you own this place, maybe stay awhile. Get your bearings back. Taking a shot like that does things to a man." He brushed a hand across his abdomen, and Mac remembered that Hanks had been shot years ago in a situation much like Mac experienced. If anyone understood, Hanks did.

Mac finally realized what else Hanks said. "What do you mean, I own this house?"

"Leonard didn't tell you? That old coot. We need a new lawyer in town." Sheriff Hanks scooped his black ball cap from his head and ruffled his graying hair. "All this confusion with Jade would never have snowballed if the man could still make it through a single court case without falling asleep. Guess the cat's out of the bag now though. No sense trying to put it back in." He heaved a breath and replaced the cap. "Amber left this place to you. Her husband had no family, so it seemed like the logical thing to do. Mortgage insurance paid off the deed free and clear. Least, that's what I heard from Leonard. The man still knows how to gossip, I guess."

Was everyone talking about his sister's life and death? A raw mixture of hurt and betrayal threatened to overwhelm him.

"No." The denial came immediately, without his thinking about it. He did not need one more thing trying to keep him here in Tamarack Springs.

Sheriff Hanks cocked his head to the side. "I suppose now's not the right time to tell you that I'd love to have you back in my department?"

Mac took a step back and held up both hands. Zeus followed Mac's lead, walking backward but keeping his body between Mac and Hanks.

"Definitely not." Mac forced everything down. He couldn't think. Couldn't breathe. Things were coming at him from every angle. He had no place to go that felt safe.

Least of which his dead sister's home.

CHAPTER FIVE

TENLEY MANAGED TO keep it together through church and the ride back to the ranch on Sunday morning. Jade chattered from the back seat, her voice rising and falling in equal parts. The one-sided conversation consisted mostly of Jade's excitement over Mac coming to ride with them today. Tenley sank her nails into the steering wheel as her pulse skittered quicker than a nervous colt.

The man had been gone nearly seven years, and she couldn't spend a single day without him by her side.

She'd love to sidestep this whole day. Or flat-out run away. But her bolting days were over. Tenley glanced at Jade in the rearview mirror. She loved taking care of Jade even if the circumstances that had led them to this point were anything but ideal. You couldn't help but love the girl, and love her Tenley did.

Seeing Mac at church had started something she didn't know how to stop. Their past planted a wall between them. A wall built of her indiscretions and her refusal to fully reveal herself to the man she'd loved.

Relegating Mac to her past took more effort than she'd anticipated. In typical Mac fashion, he blew up any opposition that dared stand in his way. He was a trailblazer on a mission to take on his responsibility. He loved Jade, Tenley knew that as well as she knew her own name. But did he see Jade, truly see her, in the way that she needed? That question kept Tenley awake at night and dug her heels in when it came to Mac ripping Jade away from this place and the people who knew and loved her.

They reached Tenley's house and Jade leaped out. "I'm going to get my boots and hat." She raced into the house, Tenley following behind at a slower pace.

Mac's truck rumbled up behind hers. He killed the engine and stepped out, still wearing his jeans and pressed blue shirt from church. He reached into the truck and retrieved the black ball cap he'd worn every day since he walked back into her life.

"Give us five minutes." Tenley called over her shoulder while following Jade. She closed the door behind her, an obvious dismissal and refusal to allow him into her house. Her mother would be ashamed, but Tenley had precious few moments to preserve her sanity from Mac, and if rudeness was what it took, then, she'd close a hundred doors in his face.

Jade ran back out of the room where she'd been sleeping these last months, her new tan Stetson clutched to her chest and her boots peeking from her too-long jeans. "Can I show Uncle Mac around the barn?"

"Wait for me." Tenley held up a hand to stop the argument brewing. "You can sit on the porch, but do not go to the barn without me."

"Okay." Jade groused, but her bad mood didn't last long once she whipped the front door open and spotted Mac sitting in one of Tenley's rocking chairs.

Tenley made quick work of changing from her pink, flowy skirt to her favorite pair of jeans. She carried her boots outside and sat on the top step to yank them on.

Mac and Jade stood in the middle of the porch, waiting with matching frowns.

"You two keep making that face and one day it's going to

get stuck like that." Tenley stood and grinned as her mom's words came out. Once upon a time, she'd believed it and had spent hours trying to make her face stick in one expression. Those lessons had come in handy later when she needed a mask to wear when she was deep in her alcoholism.

Jade cocked her head to the side. "Really?" She eyed Mac, tiptoeing to see his face. "Wow, Uncle Mac. Yours must already be stuck."

Mac startled. The frown deepened, a groove appearing between his eyebrows.

Tenley reached out and smoothed her thumb over the deepening line. Her breath stuttered at the look Mac shot her way. Equal parts shock and memory. "Smile, Mac." She forced her own lips to move. "Like this. See? Easy."

Mac grinned back in a knowing sort of way. Maybe the damage wasn't completely done, and besides, he looked rather adorable with the wrinkles of additional years.

Jade clapped and then grabbed his hand. "Let's go."

Thankfully, all thoughts of how well Mac had aged fled under Jade's enthusiasm. Tenley chuckled and followed the pair. Jade skipped alongside Mac's long strides and talked a mile a minute all the way to the barn.

Luke shot out from his and Molly's house, one hand holding his hat on his head and the other waving frantically. "Wait for me."

Molly hurried out onto the porch.

"I got him." She joined Molly, the steps creaking when she jumped up.

Molly put a hand to her throat. A flicker of unease raced across her face. "You sure you don't mind?"

"Luke is always welcome to ride with us." Tenley gripped her sister's arm in a quick squeeze. "We'll be back in a few hours."

Molly nodded but didn't return to the house.

Tenley jogged to catch up with Mac and the kids at the barn

door. Both Jade and Luke stopped at the line where light met shadow. Their toes brushed the dark interior of the barn, but they didn't move inside.

Mac lifted his eyebrows and glanced at Tenley. "Thought we were riding."

"They know they're not allowed inside the barn unless they're with me or Brody." Tenley smiled at the upturned faces. "Good job, guys. Thanks for following the rules. It would've been easy to assume that you were allowed to go in with Mac since he's an adult, but thank you for waiting."

They shot matching smiles at her, the looks tugging at her heart. They could be brother and sister standing there.

Mac huffed a sound that might've been appreciation but sounded an awful lot like annoyance.

Tenley stepped into the barn, the kids on her heels. "Mac, do you need help with your horse? How long has it been since you rode?"

"I'm fine." One side of his mouth quirked up in a semblance of a smile. At least he was trying. Clearing his throat, Mac rubbed a hand over his forehead. The cap shifted on his dark hair before he tugged it back in place. "I haven't forgotten how to ride. Just point me at which horse I can use."

Tenley paused on her trek down the barn aisle. Horses greeted them from both sides, several stretching their noses toward Tenley in hopes of getting a treat or a pat. "Jade, you can take Snowflake today."

"And I'm riding Ranger." Luke stood in front of his horse's stall. He held out his hand and Ranger—the black-and-white paint that Brody found for Luke's last birthday—nudged Luke's palm.

"Right. You can bring your horses out and start brushing them."

"Is that a good idea? Letting them take care of their horses by themselves?" The pleasant wrinkles in his face deepened, carving trenches between his eyes. But it wasn't anger or frustration. Was he afraid?

Tenley grabbed his sleeve and pulled him farther away from the kids. "They're safe with their horses, Mac. I've been riding with these kids since they could climb on a horse. I've taught them well and I'd never put them in a bad spot."

He flinched away at her touch but sighed, sounding resigned. "You and I both know that horses can be unpredictable. It's been years. I don't know who you are anymore. Maybe not even back then." The sadness coming off his voice pulled at her heart.

"Six years, eleven months, ten days, five hours." Tenley rattled off the exact numbers since she'd broken Mac's heart. The hours since she'd hit rock bottom and knew that she had to let Mac go...for both of their sakes. The months since she'd checked into rehab and sobered up. "But who's counting, right?" She gave a careless shrug and pivoted on her heel. "You can ride the black mare." Tenley pointed at the stall. "Her name's Midnight."

"You keep track?" His question burrowed deep and offered a quiet reprieve.

"Of the worst moment of my life?" She kept her back to him, afraid of what she'd see if she turned around. "Yeah, Mac. I keep track."

"You're not what I expected." The sound of his footsteps told her Mac had moved to the stall door.

Tenley gave herself a moment to collect her thoughts and turned. "Mac?"

He tensed, his body turning rigid.

She continued before she lost her nerve. "I'm not asking for you to forgive me, but can we at least put aside the animosity long enough for the kids to enjoy this ride? I don't want to be your enemy. I never wanted that."

"What did you want?" Mac ran his hand over the mare's coal-black face and his eyes softened when he caught Tenley watching him. "You left me, Ten. You shut me out and I still don't know why."

The sound of the nickname he'd given her in middle school gutted her. While everyone else labeled her troublesome, Mac called her Ten as a way of easing the hurt. Brody and Molly picked up on it later and it had carried over even after Mac took off for Chicago.

The answer to his unasked question perched on the tip of her tongue, the facts that would push him away for good. A boulder lodged in her throat, and she took a step back. "Because you were too good for me. I'd made too many mistakes, Mac. Mistakes that I've finally forgiven myself for and put behind me."

He shoved the cap back and ran a hand across his head. "What does that mean?"

"I—"

"Can we saddle the horses now?" Luke's voice carried down the barn aisle.

Tenley spun away from Mac, her heart hammering like she'd been caught with her hand in her mama's cookie jar. "Sure. I'll help you."

She spent the next several minutes helping Jade and Luke put their saddles in place while her heartbeat slowed toward normal. She tightened cinches and double-checked the bridles were on properly. All as a means of avoiding Mac and the conversation she knew they needed to have. Was it selfishness or self-preservation that had her unwilling to reveal the facts of that night, to wait and postpone watching the last of the light dim from his eyes when he discovered what she'd done?

Mac led his horse from the barn behind Luke and Jade. He paused beside Tenley and threaded the reins through his hands. "I'll watch them while you get your horse."

"Thanks." Unlike Mac, she had no qualms about putting the kids' safety in his hands. She tried not to rush through brushing and saddling Romeo, the bay gelding she usually rode on these trail rides. She led him from the barn and blinked to clear the sudden glare of sunlight from her eyes as she settled her Stetson on her head.

Mac stood with his back to her. Jade and Luke sat on the fence railing in front of him, seemingly mesmerized by whatever Mac was saying. Tenley crept forward on silent feet until she stood close enough to knock the cap from Mac's head. She did so with enough enthusiasm to send the hat spinning through the air.

She didn't know what had come over her.

Mac whirled around, eyes blazing.

Tenley's laugh rang out. She held up the battered brown cowboy hat she'd hidden behind her back. "You're not going out with us without the proper attire." She gripped the hat's brim and stood on her tiptoes to slide the Stetson onto Mac's head.

His gaze locked on to her face. As quickly as the tension gathered, it released in a shared breath.

Her fingertips grazed his ears. The pulse in his neck jumped, and her heart joined its beat. She jerked back and nearly stumbled into her horse.

"My old hat." Mac's voice was throaty and deep.

Did the memories flow through him as easily as they did her?

"I found it in the office." She lifted one shoulder. "Thought you might want it back." She remembered the day he'd left it there. The day after the wedding debacle. He'd come here demanding answers, and she'd denied him that then, the same as she did now. She'd watched from her room, pausing from packing her bag for rehab, to see him stomp into the barn. He came out minutes later, appearing disgusted and hatless.

Brody had never told her what transpired during those few minutes. She hadn't been strong enough back then, or in the years since, to ask.

Putting her foot in the stirrup, she swung into the saddle.

Luke and Jade jumped from the fence and led their horses over to the mounting block.

Mac stood back, watching. He waited until they were both safe in the saddle and standing alongside Tenley to swing into his. He gathered up the reins. "Where should we ride to?"

"The ridge." Luke stood in his stirrups and pointed at the small path leading deep into the woods. It started near Brody's house, the line of oaks, maples and hickories causing the trail to disappear unless you knew where to look.

"Yeah," Jade agreed with a whoop.

Tenley eyed Mac, noting the way his jaw tightened. He didn't argue, merely dipped his head in a nod. "Let's go, then."

His tone was less than enthusiastic. Tenley let it go. She no longer had the right to call Mac out on his moods. She could ask all the questions she wanted. He didn't owe her any answers. Not after the way she'd ended things.

Luke and Jade rode side by side, chattering like magpies.

Tenley envied the ease between them. "Is it too much to ask for us to be friends?"

"I think it's best if we aren't." He settled into the mare's stride with the years of muscle memory taking hold, though he held the reins with a stiffness she didn't remember.

"We share guardianship, Mac. Jade deserves for us to at least try not to shoot daggers at each other every time we're in each other's sight." She tried to keep the desperation from her voice but failed.

"We share it *for now*," Mac said meaningfully. He patted his mare's neck and glanced over at her. The heat of his gaze tore away the layers created by years of distance and left her cut to the bone. "I'm only staying until the end of the school year. Once I talk to Leonard and get this mess sorted out, Jade comes back to Chicago with me. I'm her blood. You and I know the court's going to rule in my favor. It's the only way to resolve this—" his left hand pawed the air "—whatever *this* is."

Mac moved away, his body taut and eyes holding a smolder of something she didn't recognize. The loss pained her, all the way to her bones. What happened to put the look of doom in the depths of his eyes? She opened her mouth to ask, but it was written in every conversation they'd had recently. Mac had lost everyone he loved. If she didn't know better, she'd think he felt guilty.

Tenley locked the words away in a vault. Mac's past belonged to him. If she tried to find her way in, she risked losing herself to his charm.

They stepped into the shade of the overarching trees. A shudder rippled down Tenley's spine that had nothing to do with the sudden change in light and temperature and everything to do with the man riding at her side. She was going to lose Jade.

After everything she'd done to him, Mac had found a way to exact his revenge.

MAC REGRETTED HIS HARSHNESS, if not the words themselves. Tenley poked at him, prodding his old wounds, tearing them open, exposing them to the light of a new day. He couldn't start over with her, not now and not ever.

Tenley rode alongside him. She faced forward, her spine arrow straight and her gaze on Jade and Luke. The kids never stopped talking, a fact Mac was thankful for. They didn't need to hear any of his and Tenley's troubles.

Oak leaves dotted the ground, their purled edges showing streaks of brown and gold, left over from the previous autumn. No trace of stress marred Tenley's face. She sat relaxed in the saddle, wrists crossed over the saddle horn. She dipped her chin toward him. "Been a while."

For so many things. He relaxed into the horse's stride. "I missed this in Chicago."

"What? You mean you didn't demand a spot on the mounted police force?" Her nose crinkled. "That's a thing, right?" A laugh bubbled out of her, edged with sadness she couldn't hide from him.

"Yeah." His laugh joined hers before an avalanche of grief cut him off. "I wanted to be known as more than the country cop."

Hooves struck dirt, the steady thud-thud excavating the pain. Mac pushed hair from his forehead, tucking it under the hat brim, and breathed in the smell of horse and leather. They fell into old habits too easily. Confronting each other one minute and able to laugh the next.

"Did you make it?"

"Make what?" He'd lost the conversation, distracted by Tenley's quiet presence and the swish of horses' tails.

She sent a glance his way. Thoughtful in her perusal. "Were you more than a country cop in the big city?"

"Yeah." And look what came of it.

"What was Chicago like?" She ducked under a low-hanging branch. It snagged her hair, pulling the ponytail taut.

Mac reached over and freed her but didn't let himself revel in the moment. In the softness of her hair and the fact that she didn't pull away from him. Spinning the green-and-brown twig by its stem, he focused on the colors whirling. He contemplated his response.

"I loved the constant action. They put me with an older officer, let him show me the ropes." He tossed the stick aside. "I married Laura. Lost her. Then nearly lost my partner. Lost Amber. Came back here to get Jade."

The years between his leaving and recent return condensed into a monotone announcement that held none of the anger and shame. His life was not a storybook for Tenley to read late at night.

Tenley's face registered shock. "I'm sorry." Tenley threaded her fingers through her mount's mane and turned her face away from him. "Amber told me about Laura."

A peculiar note in her voice tugged at him. Jealousy?

Anger? Neither made sense. Tenley hadn't wanted him. He deserved to find happiness wherever he could, and Laura had made him happy.

"Don't you think Jade deserves the chance to have us both in her life?" Tenley's question was soft. "She's lost her parents. I know you're probably right—" she choked over the words "—about the court. But please don't take her away from everything that she knows."

Mac tightened his grip on the reins, then relaxed it before his tension traveled through to the horse and made her anxious.

"Maybe that's exactly what she needs. A fresh start in a new place."

Tenley scoffed. "Like you." She scrubbed a hand over her face. "Sorry. That was rude."

"I'm not the one who quit, Tenley. You did." He nudged his horse closer, until their knees almost brushed. "You left me first, and I couldn't stay in this town another minute knowing that I might run into you and have to see that dead look in your eyes that said you'd stopped loving me."

"I never..." She trailed off and lifted her head to the sky. Sunlight caught the curve of her chin and deepened the lashes fanning out across her cheeks. She rode with her eyes closed, trusting her horse in a way that was pure Tenley. It ripped away the last of the bandages covering his scabbed heart and exposed him to the light.

Mac's pulse skipped. "What?" He ground his teeth together. The need to hear her answer shouldn't hook straight into his heart and draw him around. But it did. After all this time, after all he'd done to put her aside, it always came back to Tenley.

A grunt of dismissal left him. He'd loved Laura. He'd fought the cancer alongside her, every step of the way. When she wasn't strong enough to fight on her own, he put in enough to carry them both through.

Still, one look at Tenley and he felt like a teenager all over again. She twisted him up inside unlike anyone else.

"You never what?" He forced out the question, desperate for an answer that might alleviate the pounding in his head and the constant drive for peace when he thought of her.

She met his gaze head on. "I never stopped." She shook her head, a sad look entering her eyes. "What I did, I did for your own good."

"Funny how I can't believe that." He reined his horse sideways, putting space between them. Her response fueled more questions. "I never wanted to come back here." He rolled the stiffness from his shoulder.

"So why did you?"

"Jade." His niece's name rolled from him like thunder through the sky. "She's all I have now, and I'll protect her with everything I have."

"Even from me." Tenley looked at him, then ahead where Jade rode. "I'm not some monster you need to protect her from. I love her like she's my own. I've been here the whole time, part of her life since she took her first breath."

Mac fought to keep himself in check. It did neither of them any good to keep rehashing these same topics. He locked his jaw tight. "I'm going to ride with Jade." He urged his mount into a trot and caught up with Jade's white pony. Schooling his expression, he grinned at her. "Hey, kiddo."

Jade beamed at Mac, bouncing in her saddle. "Wait till you see the ridge. It's so pretty. Tenley says it's her favorite trail."

"Is that so?" Mac resisted the urge to look at Tenley. They used to ride this trail together all the time. He'd proposed at the top of the ridge that overlooked Tamarack Springs. Would Tenley take him back there after the harsh words they'd spoken?

Luke leaned forward and patted his horse's neck. "Uncle Brody says it's a good spot for finding God." He wrinkled his nose. "I keep looking, but I haven't seen Him yet. You think we might see Him today?"

The simplicity of Luke's question battered Mac's heart. He'd gone to church for as long as he could remember. He'd trusted

God with every piece of himself, until it seemed God didn't want him anymore. His heart had been crushed and torn apart. Laura sewed the pieces back together and he'd thought maybe God was there then. Until it all came apart at the seams. Everyone he'd ever loved, God took away.

Mac swallowed hard as he rode alongside Jade. Tenley appeared in his peripheral. *God, please. Don't take them too.* Them. He tugged his hat lower over his forehead and breathed in slow and steady breaths until his heart settled back into a normal rhythm. He didn't love Tenley. They were past all that.

Weren't they?

"I think you can find God no matter where you are." Tenley spoke up from behind Mac. She reassured Luke when Mac couldn't. "Some places make it easier to open up and see Him, but all it takes is a willing heart."

Luke continued patting Ranger's neck.

They rode with nothing but birdsong and the horses' thudding hooves as background noise. Each of them lost in their own thoughts. The ridge appeared, slowly at first. A hint of open sky through the trees. Greens of every variety mingling together and swaying in the breeze.

Mac emerged first, followed by Jade and Luke. They lined up at the edge of the path, facing the deep valley. Tamarack Springs appeared in flits of color that dotted the landscape. The red roof from the Langleys' Bed and Breakfast where he'd been staying. Tan and white from the library sitting in a little corner away from the main center of town, which was concentrated on diners and shops. And Leonard's office.

Mac rested his wrists on the saddle horn and let the mare lower her head to sniff the ground. Tomorrow, he'd learn what his options were. Whether he had a chance of cutting Tenley out of Jade's life. It hurt him to consider how Jade might react to that. Later. He'd deal with that later.

Tenley leaned over and whispered to Luke, her voice too low for Mac to hear.

Luke nodded at whatever Tenley said and wiped his eyes. Jade scooted sideways and patted Luke's back. Their easy friendship reminded Mac of him and Tenley. They'd always known when the other needed comfort or when they needed space to work things out by themselves.

Until they didn't. Until Tenley walked away without a backward glance.

She shot a look at him like she felt his gaze on her now, and he snapped his head around to the view. His mare snorted and lifted her head. Mac tightened his grip on the reins and eyed the terrain. "You should have a fence up here. It's dangerous to let riders be able to get this close to the edge."

"I'll let Brody know you don't approve." Tenley's spoke sharply, her tone cutting. She reined her horse around. "We should head back."

Surprisingly, the kids didn't argue but spent most of their time looking from Tenley at the front of their little parade to Mac taking up the rear.

Jade looked at Luke and shrugged.

"Aunt Tenley, can we race back?" Luke asked with a sideways glance at Jade.

"Oh yeah. Let's go." Jade urged her pony faster.

Mac rode closer to Jade. "Hold up. You can't go faster than a trot on these trails."

"He's right. You both know the rules." Tenley agreed with what sounded like begrudging respect. She caught his gaze and lifted an eyebrow in a clear challenge. "What about it, Mac? The trail from the trees to the barn was always our racetrack. Care to see if you can beat me?"

She was goading him. No surprise, really.

"Please, Uncle Mac?" Jade folded her hands under her chin. "Pretty please? We'll be careful."

Sure. Galloping at full speed was being careful. Past races with Tenley nudged at him. He remembered the first time he'd raced her down that trail. They'd barely been Jade's age, and her dad had laughed as he ran alongside them on his own horse. Mac closed his eyes, attempting to hold on to the joy he'd felt then instead of the aching emptiness he endured.

His eyes snapped open. "Let's do it."

A trio of whoops filled the air. Tenley's smile was the stuff songs were written about. It filled her face with such absolute joy that it took his breath.

She reined around and waited for him. "Luke, you and Jade go first. Mac and I will be behind you. Ride toward the round pen. Once you pass the last fence, slow your horse."

"I know." Jade bounced in her saddle. "Let's go, Luke."

"On three." Tenley held her gelding back, coming alongside Mac. "One. Two. Three."

On three, both ponies launched forward. Laughter rang out, the kids' giggles floating on the wind. Ranger and Snowflake raced along, nose to nose.

Mac gave himself permission to enjoy the moment instead of worrying over the what-ifs. Jade and Luke sped past the last fence, then slowed their mounts.

Tenley glanced at him. "Ready?"

Not in the least. He nodded anyway.

"Let's see what you remember, cowboy." Tenley tapped the brim of his hat and laughed when he scowled. "Just like old times."

That's what he was afraid of. She counted them down and bolted on three, with Mac reacting a half second later. They thundered down the dirt path, his bones jarring with every stride. The mare smoothed out, stretching her neck and straining forward.

Tenley sped alongside him, her hands deep in her mount's mane. They pulled ahead, and Tenley shot him a smile of victory.

"Oh no you don't." Mac urged the mare faster, bringing her back in line with Tenley's gelding. The mare crept ahead by a nose, then a head. By the time they flashed past the fence,

Tenley's gelding's nose was behind Mac's stirrup, making him the undisputed winner. He reined back to a trot, then a walk.

Tenley thwacked his hat again, knocking it down over his eyes.

Clapping sounded from Mac's left. He propped the hat up and scoured the area to find Margaret, Peter, Brody, Molly and a woman he vaguely recognized standing in the shade under the barn's sloping roof.

Mac stopped the mare and dismounted.

Brody approached, a sly grin showing as he slapped Mac between the shoulder blades. "About time you won a race against Tenley."

"Just wait until I get Shadow running." Tenley groused from the side. She dismounted and patted her gelding's neck. "No offense, Romeo."

"Shadow?" Mac returned Brody's back-slapping hug. They'd been friends long before Mac and Tenley became a thing, and Brody was another person Mac had left behind for a life in Chicago. It seemed only fair. Brody was Tenley's brother. Of course he had her back when Mac's world came crashing down.

Brody answered for Tenley. "Tenley rescued Shadow from the auction last month. Been trying to train her, but she's not having any part of it."

Tenley led her gelding into the barn. "I'll get through to her. She just needs time to learn to trust me."

Molly helped Luke with his horse, while the familiar woman helped Jade.

Brody stepped forward. "Mac, you might remember Callie. She spent summers with us as kids."

"And now she stays with us all the time." Tenley added. "They got married a few months ago."

"Wait." Mac shook his head to clear it. "Callie." He snapped his fingers. "I remember. You left to ride in the rodeo. Barrel racing, right?"

"Yep." She pulled Snowflake's saddle free and headed toward the tack room. "Came back when my horse went blind. Brody helped me retrain her." And they'd picked up where they left off? There was more to this story than he was being told. But he remembered the devastation that rocked Brody all those years ago when his dad was in the accident that paralyzed him and Callie left after Brody proposed.

Whoa. Mac scuffed a hand over his cheek.

Talk about small-town life.

Talk about forgiveness.

Callie was back. Mac was back.

But not for good, he reminded himself. *No, sir.*

Few more weeks and he'd return where he belonged.

CHAPTER SIX

MAC LEFT LEONARD'S office on Monday morning with enough weight on his shoulders to send him to the ground. He fought to straighten his bones and shore up his muscles to bear the responsibility anchoring him to Tamarack Springs. Sheriff Hanks was right. Amber had left her house—and her daughter—to Mac. He refused to allow Tenley to keep her temporary position in Jade's life. He was being harsh, but it was for Jade's own good.

He slid into his truck and leaned his forehead on the steering wheel. "What were you thinking, Amber?" He understood giving him guardianship of Jade. Giving it to Tenley too was what kept coming back to him. Amber couldn't have known that this would happen to her and her husband. No one could've known. It was a worst-case scenario. How often had he seen that play out during his years in Chicago? Too many. Thank goodness Amber and her husband had a will. Otherwise, Jade might've ended up in foster care until he recuperated enough to bring her home.

He wasn't ready for what lay at the end of Amber's paved drive. For the house he'd need to empty and sell before returning to Chicago. He pinched the bridge of his nose. This meant he could leave his room at the B and B and move into

Amber's house in the meantime. Zeus would appreciate the fenced-in backyard.

What about Jade? The question pummeled him into cranking the truck and heading toward Amber's. He'd do what he could with the house until he could talk to her. Which meant seeing Tenley again.

She'd showed up in his dreams last night. Flashes of memories, times long past when one look from her sent Mac's heart into overdrive. He'd loved her so deeply that losing her was like losing half of himself. Their ride together had stirred him into remembering better times. Times that he ought to leave well enough alone.

Hours later, he rolled up to Tenley's house amid a flurry of activity. Molly and Luke hurried past. Luke waved at him. "Where's Zeus?"

"Resting." He'd left Zeus in his crate for an afternoon nap. The dog was sleeping more lately. Mac chose to take it as a sign of Zeus's healing.

Mac stepped out of his truck and popped the hat Tenley had returned to him onto his head. It fit as snug as ever, yet another reminder of times gone by. "What's going on?" He shot the question at Brody when the man rushed from the barn.

Brody spun on his heel. "Hey, man. Been trying to call you since yesterday. We decided to have an impromptu anniversary dinner for Mom and Dad tonight. They wanted you to come."

"Me?" He palmed the back of his neck.

"Doesn't matter how long you've been gone. You're still part of the family as far as they're concerned." Brody waved in a hurry-up motion. "Come on. They'll be excited you made it."

"I need to talk to Jade." Mac picked up the pace until he was jogging alongside Brody.

"She'll be at the house. Saw her and Tenley headed that way a bit ago. Probably decorating or something. You know how Tenley loves to spruce these parties up."

A memory came unbidden. The night before the wedding.

He'd been exhausted, nervous, excited. And Tenley. Man, Tenley just kept going. She fussed with every flower and shifted every tablecloth. He'd tried to get her to leave it alone and go home to rest. She'd ushered him out of the reception hall with assurances that she was almost done.

He'd offered to stay, but she said it was something she wanted to do herself. He remembered watching her from the doorway for a few minutes. Noted the dark shadows around her eyes and how she leaned on the tables like she needed their support. She'd dragged a hand down her face and bowed her head. And instead of going in to ask what was wrong, he'd left, assuming the nerves he felt were the only problem between them.

How wrong he'd been.

Mac followed Brody down the rutted drive and nearly pitched straight into Brody's back when his boot landed in a hole. He staggered upright and nudged his hat from his eyes. "You ever regret staying?" He didn't know why he asked, or what answer he expected.

Brody leaped over the porch steps and pulled open the screen door. He spared a glance at Mac before heading inside. "Used to, sure. But not now. I'm right where I'm supposed to be."

Callie met Brody in the middle of the living room and embraced him.

A pang of jealousy shot through Mac before he could control it. Jade skipped into the room, ribbons trailing behind her. She held up the spool of bright red. "Help, Uncle Mac. I can't reach to put this on the door."

He swept Jade into his arms and lifted her to his shoulder. "Your wish is my command."

Her giggle drove away the lingering sadness. They worked together to drape the ribbon over the arched entryway separating the living room and dining room. The cozy space where he'd crashed after football games and weekends wrapped around him. Everything looked the same, from the hardwood floors to the tattered brown sofa.

Margaret, Molly, Tenley and Callie moved around the kitchen. Molly slid a cake onto the counter at the same time Brody bumped into Tenley, who took a step back and knocked her elbow into Molly's side.

Mac lunged, lowering Jade and throwing out a hand to stop the cake from sliding off the counter. His palm hit the cardboard under the cake and his fingers slid into the icing. The cake wobbled but remained on the counter.

"Nice save." Brody clapped Mac's shoulder. "Just like the old days on the football field, huh?"

"Glad I didn't try to tuck it under my arm and run to the end zone." Mac snorted and reached for the towel Tenley extended to him without saying a word.

He eyed the cake, where he'd left a hand-shaped imprint behind. "Sorry, Molly."

She waved a hand. "No biggie. I can fix that. It hitting the floor would've been a different story."

"Just call me saving-the-day Mac." He laughed while wiping icing from his hand.

A look crossed Tenley's face. One that begged a million questions. None of which he could ask here in front of everyone. She pursed her lips and turned away before Mac could do something foolish like reach for her.

The bottom layer of Molly's cake was a square, while the layer atop that was a circle. White icing swirled with hints of blue and gold spun around the perimeter of both layers. A banner hung across the top, with Peter and Margaret's names written out in cursive letters that twined together so that he couldn't tell where one ended and the next began. Molly had always had a gift, but this was next level. Maybe some things had changed?

The Jacobs family piled into the dining room. Before Mac realized what happened, the only chair left was next to Tenley. She eyed him, the look almost challenging, daring him to ask for a different seat.

Not happening.

He firmed his resolve to keep his emotional distance and accepted the seat. Jade sat on the other side of Tenley, and he stretched an arm behind Tenley to tweak Jade's ponytail.

She squealed and smacked at his hand.

Peter bowed his head, a prayer ready.

Mac ducked his own head, realizing then that he'd invaded this dinner with his presence. He didn't belong here anymore. Before he could stand and get away, Peter's low timbre drew him into the peace and comfort the Jacobs always gave him.

It wrapped around him, as real and tangible as an embrace, pinning him to his seat.

Mac rolled his shoulders, attempting to rid himself of the feeling. He didn't deserve it, and he couldn't let himself fall into the trap of thinking that anyone wanted him here.

Tenley's hands clenched in her lap.

Mac watched her through lidded eyes as she twisted the napkin between her hands, wringing it into a knotted mess. He gripped her wrist, having moved without thought to offer comfort.

Tenley's hand spasmed under his, and her head jerked in his direction.

Mac squeezed again, then released.

Heads lifted around the table, and in typical Jacobs' fashion, chaos ensued. Conversations swirled around Mac, many of which he didn't understand. Jade chatted with Luke across the table, and Tenley focused on her plate like it was the most interesting thing in the world.

Mac let everything roll over him, doing everything he could to keep his heart from engaging.

Once the meal finished, Mac followed Jade and Tenley out onto the porch.

Jade climbed into the porch swing. Tenley put it into motion with a gentle push before sitting down in one of the rocking chairs that matched the pair on her own front porch.

"Tenley, I need to talk to Jade." Mac tucked his thumbs into his belt and gave the front door a pointed look. "Alone."

"No." She shook her head. "Anything you need to say can be said in front of me."

"You don't trust me with my own niece?" Indignation drove his voice into a growl.

Tenley crossed her arms. Her chin jutted forward in that stubborn tilt he knew achingly well. She'd made up her mind and nothing would change it now. It reminded him of Brody and years of arguments between the siblings. Arguments he'd mediated to the best of his ability, even when they involved his best friend and his girlfriend. Never a good place to be, by his reckoning.

Mac scrubbed a hand over his head and stopped the swing long enough to settle in beside Jade. She scooted next to him, tucking herself into his side and looking up at him with gem-green eyes. "What's wrong, Uncle Mac?"

"Nothing." He fought back a rush of grief. "I stopped by your house today." He waited to see how she'd react. He needed to know her feelings before he proceeded.

Jade dropped her gaze to her lap and twisted the hem of her shirt around her thumb. It hit him with a jolt, how often he'd seen Tenley do the same thing when she was nervous.

He shot a look at Tenley and found her watching them with inscrutable eyes.

"I miss home," Jade admitted in a whisper.

Mac's breath rushed out. "Well, that's what I wanted to talk to you about. Your mom and dad gave me the house." He cleared his throat of a boulder when Jade whipped a look at him so full of hope and love that it near to choked him. "I'm thinking about staying there, if that's okay with you?"

She nodded, her chin quivering.

Mac ignored the deep gasp from Tenley and plunged ahead. "And you can stay with me. If you want to."

Jade swiveled from his face to Tenley's and back. "What about Tenley? And the horses? Can I bring Rascal?"

"We'll work something out." Mac made the promise with all the assurance he could dredge up. He'd work everything out. That was his job now, to protect Jade. She was all he had left.

"Jade, I think Molly's about to cut the cake. Why don't you grab a piece and eat with Luke." Tenley stood and held open the screen door.

Jade slid from the swing, Mac forgotten in the anticipation of sugary sweets.

Tenley closed the door behind Jade and faced Mac with her arms crossed. The only word that came to mind when he looked at her was *furious*. She was absolutely furious with him.

He couldn't say that he blamed her. "She belongs with me."

"She's not a possession you can cart around from place to place. She needs stability." Tenley crossed to the swing and poked a finger at him. "You didn't tell her about Chicago. You made it sound like she'll be staying home forever. You have to tell her the truth, Mac."

"And what's the truth, Tenley?" He stood, peering down at her. "The truth is that I'm never going to stay here. Tamarack Springs isn't home anymore. I'm moving back to Chicago as soon as school's over. I thought you'd accepted that." Not true. He'd known she would fight. He recognized the instincts kicking up in Tenley from the minute he walked back onto the ranch. He pinched the bridge of his nose and rolled the stiffness from his shoulder. "Let's not make this any harder than it has to be."

"I'm not the one who's using a child as leverage for revenge." She sniffed and tears sheened her eyes. "Don't do this, Mac. Please. Don't take her away." There was more to the plea than the simple words spoken between them.

"You asked what happened to me." Mac didn't know why

he pushed now, when they were so close to touching that he felt her breath rush across his cheek. He needed to see her reaction. He needed to understand her the way they used to be, before she gave him the heave-ho without a thought.

Tenley's gaze roamed his face, then tracked to his shoulder that he gripped tight to still the aching.

"I lost my parents, you, Laura and then Amber." Saying it out loud wrenched his heart like it was the first time. "I can't lose Jade too. I won't lose someone else that I love." He tightened his grip on his shoulder and straightened. "I'll stay until school's over, then we're leaving. I've already talked to Leonard about sole custody. He's going to talk to the judge."

Tenley backed away from him, her hand clasped tight around her throat. "You can't..." She trailed off and then shook her head, weaving side to side in slow motion. "I'm sorry, Mac. I'm sorry I never explained why I couldn't marry you."

"It doesn't matter." He slashed a hand through the air. "It's in the past. Let's just move on. Jade is the only thing I care about now."

Tenley tensed but didn't speak. The heartbreak in her eyes ripped through him. She spun on her heel and raced down the drive. She left him standing there alone, and though she no longer loved him, the feeling of abandonment tightened his gut.

Mac watched her go until she disappeared into the barn. Was he making a mistake? His heart twisted, begging him to reconsider the decisions he'd made since coming home. No. This was no longer home. It would never be home.

He didn't belong in this place of peace. Scrubbing his palms over his eyes, he opened the door and stepped back inside. He'd let Tenley get to him yesterday during the trail ride. She'd given him a glimpse of what they could have been, and his heart couldn't take the beating of loving her again just to have her toss him aside. Better for him and everyone else if he guarded himself against her and the feelings he'd spent years learning how to cage.

TENLEY HEAVED. HER stomach roiled against Mac's angry words. She'd had a chance to tell him the truth, about her, about the past and the wedding, and she'd chickened out. Because once he knew, he'd pack up Jade and leave. He wouldn't wait another day, much less another week and a half while Jade finished school.

She pushed tears from her eyes and opened Shadow's stall. The mare backed away and tucked her body into the corner farthest away from Tenley. Crooning, Tenley latched the door behind her and squeezed her eyes shut.

"God, I've made a mess of it all." She slid down the wall and drew her knees to her chest. Her sobs mingled with her muffled words, creating a cry only God could understand. She had to fix this. Somehow. "I can't do this alone." She gripped her calves and lifted her head, banging it on the wooden wall.

The mare shuffled her hooves and snorted a low breath in Tenley's direction.

"Sorry, Shadow." Tenley stayed curled into herself while the mare adjusted to her presence. She'd made great strides this week in training Shadow. The mare still didn't quite trust her, but they were getting close.

Tenley picked up a handful of hay, shredding it into tiny bits. "I've changed too, you know. I used to hurt everyone who got too close. I knew that I'd do the same thing to Mac. So I pushed him away in the only way that I knew he'd never forgive." What a mistake. If she was a stronger person, she would've told him everything years ago.

Now it was too late. There was no moving forward for them.

Footsteps sounded down the aisle. Tenley's heart leaped in hopes that Mac had come after her.

Instead, she heard Brody's voice calling her name.

"In here." Tenley stuck her fingers over the stall door and wiggled them. She could've ignored him, but, like her, Brody was too stubborn for his own good. He wouldn't leave the barn until he tracked her down.

"Right where I thought you'd be." He draped both bronzed forearms over the door and tipped his head at her.

Tenley avoided his gaze. "Here to tell me you were right? That I should've left well enough alone?"

Brody opened the stall door and nudged her with his booted toe. "Scoot over."

She did as he ordered, sliding through the shavings until he had enough room to close the door and sit. He grunted while stretching out his long legs. "I know I've not been the best brother over the years. But I'd like to think that I wouldn't rub your nose in your mistakes."

Tenley harrumphed. The mare startled at the sound, and Tenley made gentle shushing sounds until Shadow settled. "Until Callie came back, you delighted in trying to manage me and my life. Along with everyone else. You took on the responsibility of the whole ranch, Dad's medical bills. Everything. And heaven forbid anyone try to help."

Brody removed his hat and slid a hand through his hair. He nodded, a muscle feathering his jaw. "You're right. I did all that. Until I couldn't anymore. It nearly broke me, Ten. I don't want that for you."

"I can't let Mac take Jade away." She tightened her grip on her legs, digging her fingers into her calves until they ached. "He's going to try and contest the will. Take my guardianship away."

Brody whistled through his teeth. "Then we'll fight. Together." He squeezed her shoulder. "You don't have to do everything alone either. Mom, Dad and Molly will all stand with us on this. Jade is part of the family too." He gave her a long look from the side. "We both got extra doses of stubbornness. I personally blame Dad."

Tenley managed to grin at the running Jacobs' family joke.

"I made a promise to you years ago, that I'd stand by your side. I'm here. Whatever you need." He gripped her shoulder and pulled her into a side hug.

"You never agreed with my decision to cut Mac loose." Tenley muttered into his shoulder.

Brody's arm tightened across her shoulders. "I wanted you to tell him the truth. About the alcoholism. About rehab. I still think he deserves to know, but that's your choice."

"It ruined your friendship with him. I ruined everything."

"Stop." Brody leaned far enough away to meet her gaze. When she tried to look away, he ducked his head, forcing her to see him. "You're forgiven. For all of that. Don't let yourself get trapped in that spiral of regret. You did what you had to do to get better. You're stronger than you know. Stronger than I am."

Strength. What did that mean exactly? She didn't feel strong. She felt weak and helpless. And like a failure.

But Brody had a point. She'd pushed back against her alcoholism, and with God's help, she'd won. Almost seven years sober. A fact she never wanted to take for granted.

"Callie's been good for you." Tenley poked Brody in the shoulder.

Brody's laughter rang out, loud and long. "No kidding. Wasn't a picnic reaching this point though. We both know that anything worth having is worth fighting for."

"So, what you're really saying is I need to stop hiding out in this stall and make a battle plan." If only she knew where to start.

Brody rocked his head side to side. "Never said that. Hiding has its merits. Sometimes. Other times, you have to cowboy up."

"Get back in the saddle after getting bucked off." Tenley rolled her eyes. "That's the metaphor you're going to use? Really?"

He tugged her ponytail. "Whatever works, little sister."

"I need to find Mac. If he's going to take Jade back to her house, then we should figure out some sort of schedule." She stood and brushed hay from her jeans. The mare shuffled forward a step, then another. Her low breath huffed over Tenley's arm, and she bumped her nose into Tenley's elbow. Tenley raised a hand to the swirl of hair in the center of the mare's forehead. "It's okay. You're safe here too. Even if you don't realize it yet."

"I think she's figuring it out." Brody stood and unlatched the door. He held it open for Tenley and closed and locked it behind them both. "I'll see you up at the house."

"Thanks, Brody." Tenley hugged her brother.

He didn't often allow displays such as this, but tonight, he held her tight, rocking them side to side. "Jade's fortunate to have you, and Mac will do what's right. He's hurting. Don't forget that he lost someone too."

Tenley stuffed the tears back to keep them from falling. Brody was right. She'd let her own emotions run rampant without real thought to how Mac must be feeling. She hurried from the barn and almost ran smack into Mac.

He reeled back, his hands gripping her arms to keep them from falling.

"I was just coming to find you." His voice held a gruffness that might mean anything.

Tenley let herself relax into his touch, knowing it wouldn't last.

Sure enough, he blinked once and then dropped his arms back to his sides. "Feel like arguing some more?" He said it with a hint of a teasing lilt. One side of his mouth quirked up, and he thumbed his hat back. Dusk had fallen an hour before, leaving the yard decorated in shadows.

Tenley bit back the immediate retort and focused on the darkness ringing his eyes, the way he constantly seemed to need to move. He rolled his shoulder again, the same one from before, and winced. The signs were obvious now that she took the time to look. Mac wasn't sleeping well. Grief sat on him with a crushing hold.

"I think it's good that you want to spend time with Jade at

her old house." She let a beat of silence slip between them. "We can work this out, Mac. There are more options that neither of us have considered. You could stay here. Mom and Dad have a spare room."

He shook his head before she finished. "The whole point is to get to know my niece away from everyone else. I won't have your parents to lean on once we get to Chicago."

"Stop saying Chicago like it's the golden trophy at the end of the football season." She gripped the sides of her head and breathed in slow through her nose. "You've never taken care of Jade on your own. Maybe it would be an easier transition if you had people around to help at first." She wasn't giving into his idea of leaving Tamarack Springs, but she had to attempt to get him to see that there was more involved than he'd considered.

His lips puckered into a frown.

Tenley forged ahead. "Why don't you let her stay here during the week? We already have a schedule in place that gets her to school on time. She can stay with you from Friday after school until Sunday night. As long as you bring her here for her riding classes on Friday and Saturday, and church on Sunday."

"You make it sound like we're parents splitting custody after a divorce."

She winced at the tone and the implication but kept her mouth shut tight.

Mac needed time to consider her proposal. She knew him well enough to remember that he hated feeling pushed into anything. He considered every angle. He did things by the book. He did the right thing even when it was hard. Even when it hurt him. They were alike in that regard, even if he didn't know it.

He angled his head to the side, peering at Tenley as thoughts scattered across his expression like pieces of broken glass. She'd done that to him, broken him and left him to put the pieces back together on his own.

"Okay." His voice was a mere whisper. He took off his hat and tilted his head to the stars appearing overhead. "I'll be here every day after school. Every lesson. If she's not at school, I'll be with her. I'll pick her up on Friday."

"And bring her for her lessons?" Tenley reiterated her demands.

Mac nodded. Lines fanned out from his eyes when his expression tightened. "And church on Sunday."

Tenley held out her hand.

Mac looked at it like he expected her to slap him, but soon enough his callused palm slid against hers. He shook it once, then let go and stepped back.

Tenley curled her fingers together as the memory of his touch lingered.

CHAPTER SEVEN

MAC PICKED UP Jade after her equine therapy session Friday after school and took her straight to her old house. She lingered on the edge of the porch, her unicorn backpack slung over her shoulder and a frown tugging her mouth down as she sank her teeth into her lip.

"It's okay." Mac held out a hand. "Take your time." He should give her an out. Tell her that she didn't have to go inside, but he hesitated. What if she refused to stay? How was this going to work? He'd never spent time alone with Jade unless it was a couple hours while Amber and her husband went out to dinner, while Jade and Mac vegged out in his Chicago apartment, watching TV.

Zeus pushed his head against Jade's other side. She gripped the ruff around his neck with her free hand and lowered her head.

Mac waited. He knew how to be patient when it really mattered. Tenley shattered his senses, but patience remained for Jade.

Jade's grip tightened around his fingers. She gulped and took a step forward. Zeus moved with her, keeping pace with his head pressed tight to her stomach. He took up the protective stance that he usually only awarded to Mac.

The dog was one in a million. Mac let Jade set the pace. They stepped into the house and he blinked to let his eyes adjust. After spending the last few days cleaning and restocking with essentials, he knew what she'd see. The small living room held a couch and a recliner nestled along the back wall. A small TV was mounted on the opposite wall, and a rectangular coffee table was pushed into the middle of the room.

The kitchen lay on the other side of the living room, a straight shot from the front door. Jade glanced that way before angling her steps to the short hallway to the right of the front door. The hallway led to two bedrooms and one bathroom. Jade's old room came up, the first door on the left.

She stopped in the open doorway. The buttery yellow walls melded into the soft pastel pink of Jade's bed, with its matching nightstand and toy chest. Pictures of horses and puppies hung haphazardly on the walls with strips of tape.

Jade's hand spasmed, and Mac watched her grip and release the thick fur on Zeus's neck. The dog scoured the room, searching it for any hint of danger. The instinct Mac had honed in the dog refused to rest, even now.

It's what made them such a great team…until he'd gotten them shot. His shoulder ached as though to remind him of what happened when he didn't follow the rules.

"Where's my stuff?" Jade let go of his hand and moved toward the bed. Her steps slowed, and she ran a hand over the freshly washed cover. "My stuffed animals are missing."

"They're in the basket in your closet." Mac pulled open the sliding door, revealing the pink laundry basket stuffed to overflowing.

Jade shook her head. "They don't go there. They go on the bed. Mama…" She sniffed and wiped her nose with her sleeve. "Mama always kept them on the bed for me." She lifted her chin and spared Mac a glance before grabbing the basket. She grunted and hauled it toward the bed.

Mac's heart faltered, pain piercing deep.

"Do you want me to help?" He clenched and unclenched his hands. He longed to leap in and do it for her, but the jut of her chin and the sudden glint of stubbornness warned him away. He still couldn't resist asking.

Jade grunted again and pulled the basket while walking backward. "I got it."

Zeus whined while keeping up his position beside her.

Mac ran a hand through his hair, feeling the way the buzzed sides had grown out since he came back. "Okay. I'll go make us a snack, then." He backed into the hallway still watching, feeling helpless. "Call out if you need me."

"'Kay." Jade managed to drag the basket all the way to the side of the bed. She grabbed a stuffed dog from the top of the pile and placed it right on top of her pillow. She reached for another, and a tear trickled down her cheek. She sniffed it back and shoved the stuffed lion beside the dog. Her movements turned jerky, almost angry, as she moved one stuffed animal at a time.

He was in over his head. He knew that now. He'd expected the house would have an impact on Jade. He'd expected a few tears. He'd not considered that Jade hadn't yet reached the anger stage of her grief process. Not that grief was in any way a linear process. Did children even work through anger the same as adults? That was Tenley's specialty. He'd seen her in action with that little boy, Cody. He shook his head, worried. Jade might've processed her anger, only for her old home to bring it back when she confronted the familiar space. Maybe he'd been right when he told Tenley that Jade could use a fresh start in a new place.

He crossed to the foot of Jade's bed and sat down on the floor. She might want to do this on her own, but that didn't mean he had to leave her to go through this by herself. He'd stay as long as she needed. Mac stretched out his legs and crossed his ankles. Jade shot him a look but kept up her frenzied pace of returning every stuffed animal to the bed. He'd not known what to do with them. When he first came into her room, they'd been strewn around the floor, the bed rumpled with sheets and blankets tossed aside, like Jade had left in a hurry.

He should ask Tenley what happened that day. His throat convulsed. He knew the basics of Amber's crash, but not the minute details. He knew Jade was not in the car with her parents. Had she been here? With who? Tenley? Why? The questions kept coming, piling up on him until he couldn't bear the weight anymore.

Jade finished her mission, returning the gray-and-white stuffed horse last. She tucked it into the pile and stroked its mane. "He's the last one. Daddy bought him for my birthday." She sniffed again. "He said he'd buy me a real horse when I turn eight." Her chin lifted. She dragged her hands down her cheeks, scrubbing away the last of the tears. "Can we have spaghetti for supper?"

"Sure." He'd agree to almost anything at this point. He pushed to his feet and held out his hand. Her resilience humbled him.

Jade chewed on her bottom lip, then grabbed the stuffed horse from the bed and hugged it to her chest with one arm while she grabbed hold of his hand with the other. "Can I feed Zeus?"

"Absolutely. And after dinner, we'll take him into the backyard and play fetch." He squeezed her hand. "Would you like that?"

"What about Rascal? Can we bring him here too? Zeus likes him, and I want to show him the house." Her green eyes pleaded with him. She'd lost so much in her short life.

How could he ask her to give up more? Which meant he'd be taking a little girl, her rambunctious puppy and his old man, Zeus, home to Chicago. Throat tight, he dipped his chin to his chest. "We'll bring him back tomorrow after your riding lesson."

Jade let go of his hand and walked ahead of him. She climbed onto a kitchen chair and crossed her arms on the tabletop.

What was he doing here? Mac faced away from the curiosity burning in Jade's eyes. He dove into preparing the meal, like making spaghetti was the most important mission in the world. Right now, it was. Nothing else mattered except helping Jade get through this. One meal at a time, if that's what it took.

He worried about the other details as he cooked pasta and mixed up a quick recipe for homemade sauce. The day-to-day of raising his niece felt real after they finished eating and she helped him clear the table. His hours with the Chicago PD were a complication he'd put aside. He needed someone to watch Jade while he worked. Someone to keep her safe when she wasn't at school in the summer and when he worked weekends. Sheriff Hanks popped into Mac's thoughts. The sheriff had mentioned a job. That he'd like to have Mac back at the department.

Staying in Tamarack Springs solved so many problems. All but one, really. But that one—the one that took up a Tenley-shaped space in his heart—couldn't be overlooked.

Mac carried their empty dishes to the sink and wiped his hands. "Come on. We'll go outside while there's still light." He'd worry about dishes—and everything else—once Jade fell asleep.

They stepped out into a brisk May wind. An approaching storm tinged the air with hints of rain. Fading sunlight dappled the yard and filtered through the many oaks that lined the far side of the picket fence. Mac handed Jade a tennis ball. "Why don't you throw it for him?" He made a hand motion at Zeus, but the dog already had his attention riveted on Jade and the ball in her hand.

Jade raced to the middle of the yard and hurled the ball toward the back of the fence.

Zeus streaked after it, belly low to the ground. The exercise was good for him and would keep him in shape for when he returned to work. *If.* If Zeus returned to work. Mac looked the dog over with a critical eye. He still had a few years of police work in him, if his captain agreed.

That was the crux of the matter. Mac still hadn't heard back about his administrative leave being lifted. When the captain asked if Mac thought he'd made the right call, while he lay in the hospital bed bandaged and sore to the very marrow of his bones, Mac didn't have an answer. He still didn't.

Maybe that was the problem. He spent his life following the rules and controlling every aspect of his life. Until the moment when he knew his partner was in danger and he'd flung all his training aside to save the man's life.

It was only by God's grace that Mac and Zeus had lived through the assault.

And he couldn't bring himself to be sorry for breaking protocol. A fact his captain must've recognized when he asked Mac to walk him through what happened. Weren't rules sometimes meant to be broken when the outcome of that choice seemed less than perfect?

Given the same choices, Mac would do it all again.

Thunder rumbled overhead. Tree branches swayed, the wind whipping them into a frenzy. Jade stiffened, her shoulders drawing up to her ears. She bolted for the porch and threw herself at his legs. "I want to go home."

"You are home." He patted the back of her head. "Are you afraid of the thunder?"

She nodded once, her entire body trembling.

Zeus raced around the yard, barking at the darkening sky. Lightning zigzagged through the clouds in brilliant purple streaks. Mac narrowed his eyes against the glare. Thunder cracked nearby, and Jade screamed.

Zeus ran for the house and slammed into Jade. He planted his paws on her feet and pushed his head into her side.

"Let's go inside." Mac held the door for Jade.

She loosened her grip on his leg and wrapped her arms around Zeus's neck. They hurried into the house. Jade hesitated at the kitchen table, her eyes darting around fearfully. "Can we go back?" Her voice quivered.

"Back where?" He spread his hands as confusion overtook him. "We're safe inside. The storm can't get us here."

As though to argue with him, the house shook with the next boom of thunder. Lightning crashed at the same time, illuminating the kitchen in a blinding flash.

Jade clapped her hands over her ears. "I want to go home."

Mac dropped to a knee, bringing them eye level. "I don't understand. Jade, you are home."

She shook her head and threw her arms around his neck. "Not this home. Tenley's home. I want Aunt Tenley."

He scooped Jade into a hug, and her head dropped onto his shoulder. "I won't let anything happen to you."

"I'm scared, Uncle Mac."

"I know, baby." He was too. Not about the storm. He loved the crispness of the air during a good one. The raging, untamable power that surged and seemed to fill the sky. He saw God in the wildness. He kissed the top of Jade's head and stood, carrying her to the couch where he settled in with Jade tight to his side. "Why are you afraid of the storm?"

He didn't remember her being afraid before. She used to sit with him in Chicago and watch it rain. Though the storms there were nothing like this.

Zeus stretched out across Mac's feet, his head on his paws. Jade nestled in close, her hands cradled under her chin. She implored Mac with her gaze. "I don't want to stay here." The quick plea broke Mac's heart.

He couldn't deny her. What kind of monster would he be to insist that she stayed?

"Let's make sure Tenley is home. Okay?" He pulled his phone from his pocket and tapped Tenley's contact button. Thank goodness he'd thought to get the information from her earlier.

Tenley answered on the first ring. "Everything okay?"

He wanted to lash out that he was perfectly capable of taking care of Jade. But was he? Really? He'd managed a handful of hours before Jade wanted to go back to Tenley. Maybe it was just the storm. But what if it was more? Mac gritted his teeth until he gained control. "Jade wants to come back to your house. She doesn't like the weather."

"If you leave now, you should be able to stay ahead of the rain. The front door is open." Tenley spoke quickly and without admonishment or scorn. "I'll be waiting for you."

Those last five words punched straight through him, hitting harder than the bullet that ripped through his shoulder and punctured his lung. He couldn't breathe for several heartbeats as her words settled around him. He'd told her that same thing the night before their wedding. He'd held her close and kissed her until nothing else mattered but the two of them and the hopes of forever.

He ended the call without saying goodbye, then patted Jade's back. "Grab what you need."

She leaped from the couch and sprinted toward her room. Mac was still pulling on his boots when she returned with her backpack over one shoulder and two more stuffed animals in her hands. "Zeus too?"

"Yep. We'll bring him too." Mac whistled for Zeus, and the dog lumbered to his feet with a long stretch and a yawn. Mac checked the weather through the living room window. "Okay. It's not raining yet. You go straight to the truck while I lock the door."

Jade sank her teeth into her bottom lip. "Zeus will go with me?"

"Of course." Mac pushed the front door open against the howling wind. Any other time, he'd avoid driving in weather like this. It wasn't safe. But Jade's mental state couldn't handle that argument. He hurried to lock the door and followed

Jade to the truck. He helped her inside, then closed the door behind Zeus.

The drive to Tenley's passed quickly, the wind pushing them from behind, rocking the truck. Mac kept both hands on the wheel and his jaw locked. Jade held on to Zeus with a white-knuckled grip until they pulled up in front of Tenley's little house on the Jacobs' ranch. Her pumpkin-orange door stood out in the darkness, a beacon of comfort to the dreary night.

Tenley opened the door and stood limned in the brightness behind her. She ran for his truck. Jade fumbled with her seat, once Mac killed the engine. He heaved against the wind and hurried around the truck, shielding Tenley from the gusting breeze.

Jade leaped into Tenley's arms, wrenching a new knot in Mac's heart.

"Come on." Tenley grabbed a fistful of his shirt and pulled, hauling him toward the house.

"I should go." He dug in his heels.

"No." Tenley and Jade shouted together amid a long rumble of thunder.

Jade pleaded over Tenley's shoulder. "You have to stay with me."

The knot in his throat threatened to strangle him right then and there. Tenley kept hold of his shirt, pulling him forward despite the sudden woodenness of his legs.

He followed her into the house, Zeus at his heels. The dog stopped inside the threshold and eyed the new space. Mac palmed the door shut as another gust came howling down the mountain.

Lightning flickered and danced through the windows. Mac blinked to clear his vision and to adjust to the brightness. Tenley had every light blazing. Lanterns lined the counter in the kitchen to his left. They were unlit but ready, along with four flashlights.

"I made hot chocolate." Tenley scraped her long, dark curls

from her face after lowering Jade to the floor. The sight of her hair undone from its usual braid or ponytail pulled at his attention. She smiled, and Mac noted the tightness around her eyes. "It's going to be okay, Jade. Rascal is in the laundry room. You can let him out if it's okay with Mac and Zeus."

Zeus whined while looking at Mac like he understood the words, then padded quickly toward a white door.

"I think Zeus would like that." Mac scrubbed his palms along his thighs to rid them of the longing to reach out for Tenley.

She still held his shirt in one fisted hand. When she took a step toward the kitchen, the sudden pull of resistance snapped her head around. She flushed bright red and snatched her hand back. A quick shake of her head and she rubbed her thumb across her palm. "Sorry." She cleared her throat and took another step backward. "Want some hot chocolate?"

No. He wanted her. He wanted to rewind the years. He wanted to know what had happened between them. He wanted a second chance to be her forever. That last one rocked him onto his heels as he realized the truth digging past his resolve. It snapped and crackled brighter than the lightning outside.

Something had gone horribly wrong seven years ago. Could he forgive what she was so unwilling to reveal? The secret her family staunchly protected too? Or would it harden his heart against her—against them—like she so feared?

He followed her into the kitchen, still reeling from the epiphany pulling him back and forth. Tenley poured three cups of hot chocolate from a pot on the stove. She passed him one and took the other. "I'll let Jade's cool for a bit. The dogs should keep her busy."

"Why doesn't she like storms?" Mac sipped the blistering hot beverage, scalding his tongue and keeping him from asking the questions battering against the walls he'd erected around his heart.

Tenley's heart-rending sigh and the sudden shine of tears in her eyes completely brought down his defenses. What had he unbottled with that question? He lowered the cup and reached for her. His body moved with the aching quickness of muscle memory. The need to comfort her rose above all others. She settled into his embrace, and it was like the pieces that shattered years ago snugged back into place.

"We found out about Amber during a storm. They were coming home from a dinner date in Bridgeport." She whispered the tragedy between thundering booms.

Mac's body tensed and relaxed in waves. "The report said they wrecked after hitting a deer."

"They did." Tenley nodded, her cheek scratching the thick cotton of his shirt. "The storm came after. It's why it took so long for anyone to notice the accident."

His cheek landed on top of her head. He held her tighter, rocking them both side to side as grief welled. It ebbed and flowed, rushing through him in a torrent. Outside, the thunder abated, but his tears finally flooded free. The thunder and lightning rolled into the mountains after lashing the windows with rain. It fell now in soft sheets that peppered the tin roof overhead and created a gentle symphony.

Storms in the mountains were like that. They blew in, furious and bent on destruction, only to calm and beguile with rain-tinged air.

"I'm sorry, Mac." Tenley cried into his shirt too. Her arms snaked around his waist and gripped the back of his shirt. "I'm so sorry."

He heard more than one apology in the agony of her voice. "Me too." It was the best he could do. After another heartbeat of the blessed torture of holding Tenley, he let go.

Jade scampered into the kitchen. Zeus and Rascal bounded behind her, ears flopping. Zeus sat and eyed Mac, his head tipped to the side. Rascal copied Zeus after giving the older dog a quick look. Rascal's oversize white ears stood straight up, turning his expression comical when the pup opened his mouth and his tongue lolled out.

"Here." Tenley held out Jade's hot chocolate, sniffing back tears. "Sit at the table and drink this. Then we'll get you ready for bed."

Mac checked the clock, surprised to see the lateness of the hour. Adrenaline continued to pump through his system, and he knew he wouldn't sleep much tonight.

He stood back and let Tenley take over Jade's care. She didn't seem to mind their obvious tears. Maybe they'd been doing a lot of crying together, which was probably a good thing. He felt better than he had in months.

He finished his drink and poured another from the pot, then topped off Tenley's cup while she ushered Jade down the hallway. Their voices filtered out, both quiet and Jade seemingly calm now that the storm had abated.

It might no longer flash outside, but Mac felt it start up again inside him. The storm gathered and surged through him. Try as he might, he couldn't escape the gravity of what lay ahead. The decisions to be made. The reality of having a little girl. The responsibility he bore to his sister. Jade couldn't even make it through the night without Tenley. Maybe it was the storm. Maybe not. What would happen if he *did* take Jade to Chicago? Tenley couldn't save him then.

Suddenly, leaving all this behind a second time didn't appeal as much as before. He'd settled back into this place. Chicago never felt like home. The closest he'd come was when he married Laura. Without her there, it was just another place.

Tenley returned, her arms burdened down with blankets and pillows. "You can sleep on the couch." She pointed her chin at the plush brown couch that curved around the corner of the living room.

"I should go back to Amber's." He couldn't call it home. If anything, this place—Tenley's place—felt more like home than anywhere he'd been in a long time.

"Don't." Tenley sighed and tossed the blankets onto the couch behind him. "Jade made me promise that you'd be here when she woke up." A disconcerting look crossed her face. She hugged her elbows tight over her abdomen. "I need to go to the library in the morning for Saturday's book reading. Jade wants to stay here with you."

"Did you promise that too?" His voice came out too harsh. Old habits died hard when confronted with one of Tenley's promises.

Tenley pushed her fingers into her eyes and sat on the coffee table. "No. I said I'd ask you." She motioned at the door. "If you want to leave, go ahead. I'll explain to Jade in the morning." Her shoulders rounded, with what he couldn't say. Disappointment. Frustration. Fatigue. Any manner of things might weigh on Tenley. Things he no longer had the right to ask about.

But he wanted to. He almost asked her right then why she'd walked away. Earlier this week, in the barn, it had felt like she wanted to explain. Maybe it was time he found out the truth. If he heard her say the words, heard her say she'd stopped loving him, then he could move on.

Except she'd said on the trail ride that she'd never stopped loving him. Confusion warred within him.

He dropped onto the edge of the couch and leaned his elbows on his knees.

Zeus sat pressed into Mac's leg. Rascal raced around the coffee table. He zipped left and right, happiness radiating from his puppy face. He ran himself into exhaustion, then collapsed on Tenley's socked feet. She ruffled the pup's ears, and he thought he heard another sigh before she lifted her head. "Mac." His name whispered between them, drawing him into the lullaby sound of her voice.

He lurched to his feet. "I'm going to check on Jade." Almost running, he retreated to the room where he'd seen Tenley and Jade go.

Jade lay on a twin bed, a pink blanket pulled under her chin and her stuffed animals in a row along the wall.

He dropped to his knees beside the bed and started to take Jade's hand. She grunted and rolled over, her frown and the whoosh of a quiet cry threatening to ruin the tiny morsel of peace he'd taken from this place. He rolled to his feet and brushed a kiss over the top of her head before backtracking to the living room where Tenley sat in the same position.

She didn't look up, barely moved. She remained so still that he wondered if she'd fallen asleep.

He angled his steps toward the kitchen, and Tenley's quiet steps followed him. They sat across from each other at the kitchen table, the harsh fluorescent light highlighting the hollowness of Tenley's cheeks.

He drummed his fingers on the table, the sound echoing the quiet rainfall pattering against the windows.

"I'm sorry. For everything." How many times would it take hearing her say "I'm sorry" for him to believe her? Tenley knotted her fingers together on the tabletop. Her gaze skirted his, never landing on anything. "If you want to hear it, I'll try and explain why I did what I did."

His heartbeat picked up the refrain between needing to know and refusing to allow Tenley any quarter. She already took up too much space in his thoughts. "Will it change anything between us now?"

"Probably." Tenley winced. "If by change you mean make things worse."

His heart fell.

Worse. "I can't handle worse, Ten." The nickname came against his bidding. It slipped into the quiet between them. Mac propped his head up in his hands and closed his eyes. "I'm barely making it day by day. I don't know what to do about Jade. My job. Chicago. I had a plan, and now I don't know what to do." He allowed the truth freedom to roam. Tenley made it easy to confess his insecurities. She always had, because she never judged him for them. She helped him understand himself in a way no one else ever had.

"Have you prayed about it?"

The question surprised him, and his head jerked in response. "God and I are not exactly speaking to each other."

"On the contrary, I don't think He stopped talking to you. Maybe you quit listening." She unknotted her fingers and stretched out one hand toward him. "God doesn't run away when we throw a temper tantrum."

"You think that's what I'm doing? You think I'm a toddler who's pitching a fit over the fact that he's lost everyone he's ever loved?" He scoffed, the sound lodging between them.

Tenley took his hand. The shock of it slammed into him. His fingers curled around hers despite his orders to let her go. His head and his heart fought each other, and his heart won when his hand tightened. The grip had to hurt, but Tenley never flinched. She simply wrapped her other hand over his and held on tight.

"You didn't lose everyone." Her throat convulsed in an audible swallow. "I'm still here."

Was she saying what he thought?

He couldn't handle that either.

"I need to focus on Jade and what she needs. Everything else—" he waved between them "—all this. It will have to wait. Our past has waited this long. It can wait a while longer. Jade is all that matters. I have to do what's right by Jade."

"Then, stay." Tenley pursed her lips and blinked furiously. "I'm sorry." She lifted her chin. "Wait. No, I'm not. This is what Jade needs. This place. The people here. She's comfortable here and is surrounded with people who love her. What will she have in Chicago?"

"Me." He forced aside the guilt and focused on the woman across from him. She'd grown up. His fiancée Tenley loved arguing, but she was reckless. This version had a wisdom that he'd never expected. "You think I'm not enough for her?"

"Don't put words in my mouth." Tenley shot him a look that pierced him to the bone. "What about your job?" Tenley's grip on his hands never faltered. "We have a system here that works. Jade is always with someone she knows. She has her therapy here, the horses."

Mac pulled his hands free of Tenley. "You're not the only one who loves her. And you're not the only one who can take care of her." He took a slow breath to steady his pulse and his racing thoughts. Everything Tenley said made sense. Was he being stubborn out of a need to hurt Tenley? Was he that far gone?

He searched his heart, and for the first time, he saw all of his actions since coming back with a clarity he'd been missing. He'd thwarted Tenley at every turn because he didn't want to trust her with Jade. She'd hurt him, and he wanted her to feel that pain.

He stared into the abyss of his heart and didn't like what he saw waiting for him there. He saw loneliness and a desire for revenge. Tenley had pegged him from day one.

His lungs tightened, constricting his next breath. Mac ran a palm down his face and groaned.

Tenley shifted, almost rising before he stopped her with an upraised hand. She settled back in her seat. "You'll think about what I said?"

The fact that she read him so easily after all these years should be disconcerting. He shifted in his seat and massaged his forehead. "I'll think about it."

She stood and moved around the table. Mac tensed in preparation, but she merely patted his shoulder and moved on. "I'll see you in the morning."

He wanted to collapse right here on the kitchen floor as the fatigue slammed into him. Instead, he shoved to his feet and stumbled to the couch where he removed his boots and kicked them under the table. He tossed a sheet over the couch and face-planted onto the stack of pillows while dragging a blanket over his shoulders. He expected to stay awake, his thoughts in turmoil, but seconds after his head hit the pillow, the gently tapping rain lulled him to sleep.

CHAPTER EIGHT

CHILDREN GIGGLED AS Tenley gathered them into a loose semi-circle for Saturday Book Nook. Tamarack Springs's local library believed in helping kids read, and Miss Williams, the librarian, welcomed the parade of readers from her place behind the curved desk where she'd been librarian for as long as Tenley could remember. The rambunctious children's voices were enough to make Tenley offer her an apologetic smile.

Tenley had left Jade with Mac at her house—a house that, last night, Jade had called *home*.

Tenley swallowed and focused. "Who's ready for a story?" She slipped around the edge of the group, grinning at the upturned faces. "I thought we'd read one of my favorites."

"Me." Their voices chorused together, creating a unique blend that Tenley adored.

Cool air ruffled hair on several small heads, and hands clapped intermittently when Tenley picked up her dog-eared edition of *The Tale of Peter Rabbit*.

"Will you do the voices?" Angelina popped onto her knees.

"She aways does the voices, Angewina." Peter's lisp swapped *l*'s for *w*'s. His head cocked to the side, reminding Tenley of a cocker spaniel when brown curls drooped over his ears.

Mattie threw his arms around Peter. "Will you be Peter? You're such a good hopper."

The seventy-year-old Miss Williams shook her head at Mattie and Peter, but a smile teased the edges of her stern expression. Fast friends since the day they met last year, the two boys loved interactive story time.

Tenley sat in the oversize red rocking chair as a dozen pairs of eyes locked on to her. Opening the book with reverence, in a low, mysterious voice, she began. "'Once upon a time, there were four little Rabbits...'" When she reached Peter's name, the human Peter hopped around the group, eliciting a round of giggles and clapping.

For the next hour, Peter and the others alternated acting out bits while she read. Before she knew it, parents arrived to pick up their littles. Miss Williams stood and braced her hands on the desk. "Excellent reading, as always. Same time next week?"

Every Saturday morning for the last year, Miss Williams ended story time with the same question. Tenley smiled at the blessed routine. She'd started coming here after her first year of sobriety, a way to make amends or to help in some small way.

"Sure thing." Tenley tightened her grip on her bag. "I'll see you next week."

"I've been meaning to talk to you about a summer program." Miss Williams nudged her glasses up her nose, rattling the silver chain that allowed them to dangle around her neck when not in use. "All of the elementary school is participating in a reading program, and I wanted to ensure that Jade will be joining her class."

Tenley gulped air and tried to force words through the sudden tightness in her throat. She didn't dare mention the situation between her and Mac. Her stomach knotted. She still had time. If she could get him to fall in love with Tamarack Springs again, maybe moving back to Chicago would lose its luster. If they could be friends, maybe she wouldn't have to lose Jade too. Her hands clenched into fists. A week of being face-to-face with Mac shouldn't have her feeling this strongly about him. But wishing he might fall in love with more than the town was the most wishful of thinking.

At least he'd implied he'd try to be friends. That had to be enough. Nothing more. She could never run the risk of hurting him like that ever again. He deserved better.

Slinging the bag crossways over her chest, Tenley pulled the door open. "I'll do my best to make sure Jade is here."

Miss Williams held the door behind Tenley. "It's a good thing you're doing for that girl. Not everyone has someone willing to step in when they're needed."

Tenley resisted the urge to argue. She was doing her best for Jade. Even though it felt like nothing she did was ever enough to make up for the mistakes in her past. God had forgiven her. And she'd done her best to forgive herself. Even Brody, Molly and their parents held no ill will against Tenley. None they mentioned, though she felt their assessing looks following her around the ranch every time she fell into a foul mood. Like she might bolt at any moment. There had been a few close calls in those early years, but not in a long, long time. She had all the tools to keep her sobriety, and a million reasons to never fall back into that pit.

Enough.

Tenley pushed the thoughts aside and focused on the next task. Brody had texted her on her way into town, asking if she'd help him with a new project involving the horses. She needed to get back to the ranch before he changed his mind or did it himself. Brody asking for help was another new development in her brother since Callie's return. Gone was the reticent cowboy who snarled at everyone who offered to ease the burdens he carried.

Tenley liked this version of her brother. He was still gruff and tough, but with a softer side that she'd not seen since they were in high school. He was proof people could change.

First, work with Brody and the horses. Then an afternoon with Mac as he hovered while Jade rode. Tenley shook her head at Mac's obstinacy. Why did he struggle with releasing even a smidgen of control?

If she wanted the brainpower to work through that mess, she needed breakfast.

She left her car parked outside Granny's. An empty sidewalk boded well for a quick sit-down. Inside the building, Tenley wove her way to the booth she'd shared with Mac throughout the years. She settled in and scanned the room before turning her attention out the window.

Pink and orange streaks spread across the sky in a fan of color among the dark clouds, their rays reaching with broad beams toward a small, nondescript building hunkering between two elaborate structures. With clapboard siding and an old green metal roof, it looked like the last century had forgotten the quaint structure. A closer look revealed stained-glass windows. Windows that had kept her busy for hours as a child. She'd imagined the building to be a castle, with a princess and a dragon. The windows were the key to a puzzle and only the bravest knight would earn the right to enter.

A longing to collapse onto a pew and trace the patterns of light with her fingertips seeped in and drowned out the cafe's noise, until Granny's voice sliced through the daydream. "Mercy, girl, you're as lost in thought as snow in Hawaii."

Granny bounced onto the seat across from Tenley and patted her hands. "Tell Granny what's got you staring at that old church."

"Who made the windows?" Okay. That wasn't what she wanted to know. "I mean, if I went over there, are the doors locked?" Open mouth. Insert foot. Tenley forced her mouth to remain shut.

Like Miss Williams, Granny gave Tenley a quiet look that read and assessed a wealth of information, all while making her feel like a misbehaving child. "That place ain't never locked. You go on and visit anytime. If ole Vernon gives you any trouble, you tell him Granny said it's okay."

"I don't have time today." Tenley fiddled with the napkin on the table.

"Everyone always in such a rush." Granny huffed. "Take it from an old woman, nothing changes by hurrying through life." She waved a hand. "Pish. Listen to me scold you like you're one of my own. Comes with watching you grow up here." She patted Tenley's hand again. "Things have a way of sticking around here. People too. Just give them a chance. Remind them of the good."

Was she talking about Mac? Tenley's cheeks burned, and she knew they had to be bright red. She looked away from Granny. "Some people can't change the hurt they caused."

"No. But the good Lord says we ought to forgive them. No one is the same today as they were years ago. We age, we change. Sometimes, those changes are for the better." She stood with a creak of old bones and held out her arms. "Give me a hug and I'll get your breakfast."

"You sure know how to bribe your customers." Tenley complied, allowing the comfort offered to do its job.

"Oh, child. You get as old as me, you learn a thing or two about people." She waved her hands around her head. "Most of them are so busy, they don't know which way they're going. The rest so still and quiet, the world passes them right by and they never notice. You got to learn to live in peace. Move forward and don't look back. Keep your eyes on God and He will make sure your path goes the right way."

Tenley cast a glance out the window, an undeniable tug drawing her back. No time today for a visit. She had a lesson to teach and horses to train.

MAC APPROACHED THE round pen with cautious steps and peered through a gap in the vertical wooden slats. An obstacle course obstructed his view, the gates and poles not making sense to his untrained eye. He shifted to the side.

Tenley stood on the back of a horse, her arms spread wide.

Mac staggered to a halt, afraid to make a sound or movement. If the horse spooked... It didn't bear thinking. What was Tenley thinking to put herself at risk like this? His own conscience pricked. He had no right to judge her actions. Not after the way he barreled through his job, throwing himself into every dangerous situation like it didn't matter if he lived or not. Until Amber's death, it hadn't mattered.

Brody shuffled his boots in the dirt and led another horse into the ring. He lined the new horse's nose up with the tail of Tenley's mount. "Go ahead."

With the grace of a ballet dancer, Tenley stepped from one broad back to another. She spun, dancing her way from saddle to saddle before ending with one boot on either horse. Neither horse moved.

Mac's muscles relaxed when she jumped to the ground and praised both equines.

Brody cracked a smile and gave Tenley a nod. She beamed in response, a smile brighter than sunshine.

"Take her through." Brody handed her the reins to his horse, a blood bay. The horse tossed its head and chomped the bit.

Tenley swung aboard and clucked her tongue.

The first obstacle, a simple gate, presented no problems. But the second, a narrow beam that required patience and trust, caused the mare to halt and paw the strip of wood. Tenley sat relaxed in the saddle and asked the mare to move forward.

Hoof by hoof, the horse responded until they clomped off the other end. The mare gave a little buck. Tenley laughed and patted her neck.

They finished the course without further incident. Once Tenley started back toward Brody, Mac eased through the gate.

Tenley waved at him as she dismounted and jogged over. "Sorry. We're running a little late."

"You're helping Brody." Captain Obvious returned for another round. Mac rolled his head, dislodging the thought, and hoped Tenley didn't notice the tightness in his voice.

She unleashed the power of her smile. "He didn't intend for me to help. He asked Molly first. But she couldn't because she had to make a wedding cake. He let me, even though he wasn't happy at first." A glance at her brother, and her brows pressed over her eyes. "He might not be happy now, but he hasn't been a total brat."

So it was one of those days between the elder and middle siblings where they bantered with an underlying current of tension.

Brody stroked the other horse's nose. "I never said you weren't welcome. I asked if you were sure you wanted to help."

"Same difference." Tenley crossed her arms. The mare shoved her nose into Tenley's back, knocking her forward.

"You need me to come back later?" Mac turned to leave.

Tenley grabbed his sleeve. "Why don't you help us? We could use the extra hands, then I'll help you work with Rascal before Jade's lesson." She scrunched her nose. "He's started chewing all my shoes."

Mac laughed. He couldn't help it. "He's a puppy. He needs lots of activity and stimulation to wear him out. Bored dogs create chaos. Especially dogs like him who're meant to work." He motioned at Zeus sitting outside the gate. "It took years to train Zeus. Nothing good comes without hard work."

Her sigh slipped between them. "Point taken." She tugged on his sleeve again. "Will you help? I want to bring Shadow out and start some groundwork. It'll be good for her to have exposure to more humans. And Brody has a few other horses to take across the obstacle course."

He wanted to ask why he should help her. It was a selfish thought, but it lingered. He'd taken Jade up to Peter and Margaret's house when Margaret asked for Jade's help packaging meals for a local elderly couple. She'd promised to have Jade back in time for her therapy session with Freckles.

The last thing he wanted to do was go back to Tenley's and wait. He'd woken up this morning disoriented but with a sense of homecoming that he still hadn't shaken. Being here ignited too many memories. All of them good, except the last, the day he'd left and sworn never to come back. Never say never.

He should've packed Jade's stuff the minute he woke up and took the girl back to Amber's house. It would have saved him this problem of getting close to Tenley again. She dragged him in, one hesitant step at a time. He'd watched her train horses before. He knew her powers of persuasion over the equine mind. He'd just never expected her to have that same power over him.

He took in a ragged breath and shoved a hand across his stubbled cheek and caught Brody's eye. "You're not planning on putting me on a wild horse, are you?"

"Would I do that?" Brody's grin spoke of years of pranks and made zero promises.

Mac tucked his thumbs into his belt. "Yes."

Brody guffawed. "Maybe when we were kids and I knew you could handle it." He strode over and clapped a hand to Mac's shoulder. "You're in good hands. All the horses I'm working today are in need of fine-tuning. Sale prospects for the ranch. I need them to be kid-friendly and game for anything the trail might throw their way."

Mac released the knot of tension gathering between his shoulders. "Okay."

"Great." Brody handed Mac the reins to a dun gelding. "This is Pepper. He's been around the course several times, but it's been a few weeks since I've ridden him. Just take him over all the obstacles. He's not a fan of the pool noodles." Brody waved at the contraption that looked something like a car wash with pool noodles sticking out on either side of a narrow tunnel. "Take it slow."

Mac gathered up the reins, checked his girth and lowered the stirrups to the length he needed, then swung into the saddle. Pepper snorted and shook his mane. "My thoughts exactly." Mac patted the horse's neck and clicked his tongue. The gelding responded and carried him forward across the wooden seesaw, barely hesitating when the structure shifted under the weight.

He heard Tenley and Brody behind him but focused on the horse. Pepper's steps shortened, his agitation showing in the way he pranced without making any real movement forward. The gelding eyed the pool noodles and sidestepped.

Mac kept pressure on with his heels, urging the horse forward and offering encouragement with continuous murmurs and pats to his neck. "Come on. You can do it. I know it looks scary. Looks like it might gobble you up, but it's safe. I wouldn't ask you to do anything that would hurt you."

Hadn't the pastor preached on something similar last week? That God was there through every trial, even when it felt like He'd abandoned His children. Mac's grip on the reins tightened, and the gelding responded with another sidestep.

"Easy now." Mac guided him back to the tunnel and waited. "Hey, Tenley." He called softly over his shoulder.

"Yeah?" She jogged over.

"Do me a favor and walk through there." Mac nudged his chin at the tunnel. "Let him see what happens. Better yet, lead that other horse through first."

"You got it." Tenley hurried away, her steps sending puffs of dust billowing up to sparkle in the sunlight. She came back within seconds, leading the bay horse. She never slowed as she walked into the tunnel. The horse followed without a fuss.

Pepper's ears flicked, swiveling from Mac to the horse and back.

Tenley reappeared at the other end.

"Now, lead him back through, coming toward us." Underneath Mac, Pepper shifted. The tightness eased from the gelding's muscles when his friend came back through the tunnel unscathed.

Tenley stopped the horse nose to nose with Pepper. She glanced up at him, a smile brimming. "Go on, Pepper."

Mac nudged, and the horse responded, walking between the rows of pool noodles like he'd done it every single day. Mac repeated the path several more times, until Pepper didn't hesitate at all.

Tenley watched from the edge of the round pen, her arms crossed with the reins looped between them. She propped one booted foot on the wall behind her. "You should consider training horses with Brody."

"Not my job experience." He swung from the saddle and rubbed Pepper's forehead. "I just know what it's like to face a path that seems impossible and know that you have no choice but to go through it. Even when it looks like you'll never come out the other end unscathed."

"Mac—" Tenley started his way.

Mac held up a hand to stop her. "It's okay. You did what you had to do. I survived." Seemed like he kept surviving. He wished he knew why. What was God's plan? What was the end goal in all this? This pain? What purpose did it serve? "Now I have to do what I need to do, and I need you to give me the space to find my way."

She pursed her lips and kept silent. It stretched between them, taut as a barbed wire fence. "I understand what you're saying. But you also don't have all the details. You don't know all the pitfalls that were laid in your path. When you're ready…" She took a shaky breath. "If you want to know why I did it, I'll tell you."

"Soon." Mac promised while leading Pepper away. "Not yet, but soon." He couldn't believe all the answers he wanted were a breath away, and yet his heart railed against hearing it.

He'd have to deal with the truth sooner or later. No matter how painful it might be. But fear had an iron grip on reasoning.

When it first happened, he'd been too hurt and angry. He'd demanded answers, and when she didn't give them—didn't answer his calls or even come to see him—he'd left it all behind. But like most things, the not knowing ate at him. For every time he said it didn't matter, that Tenley did what she did and he'd gotten over it, there were moments when all he wanted was the truth.

Why had the woman he'd loved with his entire being pushed him aside like yesterday's garbage? He'd promised from the day they met to protect her. He'd never expected that he'd need to protect himself from her.

CHAPTER NINE

TENLEY WALKED ALONGSIDE MAC, her arms swinging loosely by her sides. He stared straight ahead. She'd expected a lot of anger from him after his arrival, and he'd fulfilled that. And more. But this felt like something else.

A weight had settled on him that wasn't there before. Every step seemed to be harder than the last. Tenley tried to shake off the feeling that it was her fault, but she knew the truth. All of this *was* her fault. Her dad's accident. Mac leaving Tamarack Springs. Even Amber's accident could be laid at Tenley's doorstep. She'd been the one to insist Amber and her husband needed a date night. She'd been the one to put it all together so the couple could enjoy dinner and a late movie while she watched Jade. The ache of that secret was hers alone to bear.

Her decisions were toxic to those she loved. Even decisions made while sober hurt those around her. How could she be trusted to take care of Jade when she continually hurt everyone?

She recoiled from the truth and forced her gaze ahead. Just because she wasn't worthy didn't mean she'd let Mac take Jade to Chicago. Jade deserved to make a life here, at a place she loved. Selfish. Tenley was being selfish. She didn't want to give up her one link to Amber after losing Mac.

Mac lengthened his stride, and Tenley hurried to catch up. His reaction to the obstacle course in the round pen haunted her. His words swirled around, mixing with her guilt.

"What you said earlier, about the path not hurting..." She trailed off, uncertain what she really wanted to say.

Mac didn't slow. If anything, he sped up. His lips flattened into a thin line.

"I feel like everywhere I turn, I get hurt." Tenley forged ahead, feeling her way into the conversation. "No matter what I do, people I love get hurt." She winced against the painful words. Mac didn't care about her troubles anymore. She was just Troublesome Tenley, the middle Jacobs' sibling. The one everyone overlooked in favor of Brody the Brave and Molly the Magnificent. Okay, that was going too far. Tenley had no one to blame for her actions but herself. She knew that, but blaming her problems on other people was so much easier.

It hurt to know that she'd allowed those thoughts to drive her all those years ago. Back in high school when teachers compared her to her siblings, always with a tone that said Tenley was lacking. It stung. And it pushed her to be different. Only she'd chosen the wrong way to put an end to the pain of never measuring up.

Mac didn't respond, but she didn't expect him too. Mac took the idea of a "man of few words" to heart. Unless he was angry with her, which seemed to be always, he kept his thoughts captive.

"I asked you to stay because I wanted Jade to have a semblance of a normal life. But I also wanted to prove to you that I'd changed." She shoved her hands into her pockets and averted her eyes. Sunlight sparkled on the trees. Horses grazed in the pasture on her left, their coats shining with health. Shadow lifted her head from her small paddock near the barn. Tenley had turned her out for a few hours after their lesson, and they were supposed to be on their way to train

Rascal, but Mac's steps angled them toward the fence instead of the house.

Jade raced out of the main house, Zeus and Rascal at her heels.

Tenley's time alone with Mac dwindled with every step. She had to get this out now, before she lost her nerve or he cut her off. "I'm sorry. I'm sorry I wasn't at the church for our wedding. And I'm sorry that I never told you why. I was ashamed."

"We were supposed to be a team." Mac spun to face her. "I told you everything. We promised never to keep secrets from each other."

"I didn't want to hurt you." She folded her arms across her stomach and hugged her elbows tight. "I was trying to protect you."

He took a step back. They stopped walking and now stood face-to-face. "From what? What was so bad that you couldn't tell me?"

It was time to tell him everything. She knew that, but her stomach clenched and her legs shook.

Jade ran toward them, and her approaching shouts carried on the wind.

Tenley had time for one confession. The one that started her downward spiral. "Dad's accident was my fault. I called and asked him to pick me up."

"Ten—"

The softness in his eyes and voice, the way he held out a hand to her, threatened every wall she'd built to keep them apart. All she had to do was tell him the rest, and he'd be gone from her life for good. And so would Jade. He'd never allow Jade to come back here once he knew the depth of Tenley's betrayal.

She took a step away from Mac, from the comfort he offered, and tightened her grip on her elbows to still her shaking hands. "I left before he could pick me up. Decided to go out with a few of our friends. When he couldn't find me, he drove around town. That's when another driver hit him." She shuddered her way through the confession. The accident should've woken her up to her toxic habits, but it only sent her spiraling deeper.

It wasn't until she spent her wedding day in the neighboring town's jail that she wizened up to the truth about herself and her future. There'd have been no keeping it quiet if Sheriff Hanks knew about Tenley's overnight visit.

The past was a gulf between them. No bridge or road could connect their hearts ever again. She'd only hurt him.

Jade skidded to a stop, her hair flying wild around her face. She shot a smile at them both. "Time to train?"

"Yep." Mac dropped his hand to his side. He let out a loud whistle, and Zeus came streaking across the yard.

The dog leaped over ditches and slid under fences until he reached Mac's side.

Jade's jaw dropped. "Whoa. That's so cool. Can Rascal learn how to do that?" She attempted to whistle and ended up spitting and spluttering.

Mac chuckled and ruffled her hair. "We'll teach him."

As though he knew they wanted him, the pup ambled along in Zeus's wake. His ears perked up straight, and he trotted over to Zeus before plopping onto the ground with a huff.

"Jade, if you think Zeus is impressive now, you should see him and Mac work together." Tenley nodded at Mac, a sly smile emerging. She'd only seen them in videos that Amber recorded when Mac trained, but it was enough to raise chill bumps on her arms. "Why don't you show her?"

He held up both hands in defense. "That's not necessary."

"Oh, but I think it is." She cocked her head to the side, daring him. When he refused to relent, she wagged her head at him. "Come on. Please?" She pushed aside the heaviness of their earlier conversation and focused on adding a teasing tone to her voice. "I've never seen him work in real life. It's always fascinated me how Zeus understands your commands."

"Yeah, please, Uncle Mac." Jade danced around him, grabbed his hands, and pulled. "Please. Please. Pretty please."

He shot a glare at Tenley, but it didn't hold the usual venom. He almost seemed proud at the chance to show off. "Well, since Zeus might not be my partner for much longer, I suppose it won't hurt to have one last training session. Should keep him in shape in case the captain lets him stay on the force."

With that news hanging rent-free in her head, Tenley gaped at Mac. "Zeus is retiring?"

"What's retiring?" Jade asked.

"Nothing." Mac scrubbed his hands over his face. "Forget I said anything. It's not important." He took a step away from them and snapped his fingers in Zeus's direction. "You two stand by the fence, and I'll take Zeus through a few exercises."

Jade took Tenley's hand and led her to the split-rail fence. Tenley helped Jade climb onto the top rail and settled a hand on her knee to keep the girl steady.

Mac met Zeus's eyes. He made a hand motion, and Zeus trotted to Mac's side. Tenley tried to understand the movements that Mac made, but she lost track of them in the beauty of their partnership. Zeus settled by Mac's side and looked up. His gaze never wavered. It was as though they were connected through thought alone.

Mac strode across the field with Zeus planted firmly against his leg. Then the dog moved to stand between Mac's knees. With every step Mac took, the dog kept pace. Mac dropped to a crouch, and Zeus sank to his belly. When Mac stood and pointed, Zeus zipped off in a blur of legs.

Mac whistled, and Zeus whirled, coming back to rest in front of Mac. They were in sync, tuned into each other in a way Tenley had only seen with Callie and her mare, Glow. It was the kind of connection Tenley longed to have with Shadow. The mare wanted comfort from Tenley but little else. It was a small improvement in a long journey of overcoming the mare's fears.

Mac gave Zeus another signal, and the dog lay down on the ground and belly crawled forward a dozen feet. Mac crept to the dog's side and patted his back. When he held up a tennis ball, Zeus leaped to his feet and waited for Mac to throw it across the field.

Jade clapped wildly, almost pitching off the rail from her enthusiasm. Mac grinned and bowed at the waist. Tenley joined Jade in clapping loudly and let out a whistle.

Mac blushed beneath his cowboy hat, turning his cheeks rosy. Tenley's own face scrunched in a grin at the sight. She'd never expected him to be self-conscious of his work with Zeus or to dislike performing for them. She found it endearing for the always confident cowboy to have a flaw.

He trotted back to them and held out a hand.

Jade slapped her palm to his and scooted from the rail. "Show Rascal how to do that."

"We will. But he needs to learn a few basic commands first. Start with the small stuff. Let him gain some confidence before we ask him to do the big things. Even puppies need confidence if you want them to become well-adjusted dogs." Mac tweaked Jade's ponytail and her grin widened.

Huh. Tenley let that rumble around for a minute. It made sense. They did the same things with horses. She or Brody never asked a horse to carry a rider before they were comfortable with a saddle and bridle first. They wouldn't ask an untrained colt to go through the obstacle course. Confidence. That's what Shadow needed.

Mac spent the next half hour showing Jade ways to teach Rascal. He showed the puppy how to sit and stay, with Zeus helping. Every time Mac gave an order, Zeus completed it, then looked at Rascal like he was saying, "See? This is what you're supposed to do."

By the time they finished, Rascal had the sit command

down pat but still lunged after Jade every time she tried to back away while he was in stay position.

Jade huffed and put her hands on her hips. "You're not listening."

"He'll get there." Mac's calm reassurance caused Jade's forlorn expression to clear.

She hopped through the thick grass like a rabbit. "Will you come to the fair?"

Mac's eyebrows winged upward. "The fair isn't until August."

"It's the end of the school year. Homecoming." Tenley plucked a blade of grass and rolled it between her fingers until it blurred. "They moved the date up a few years ago. August is too hot, so the city council decided to mix the school's field day with the homecoming and make a huge event over at the fairgrounds."

"Ah." Mac scratched the back of his neck and then rested his right hand on his hip. "I guess I could put in an appearance. For old times' sake."

"Yay!" Jade barreled into his legs, almost knocking him down.

Tenley stifled a laugh.

"Jade?" Luke shouted from across the pasture. He stood on his front porch, hands cupped around his eyes like binoculars.

Jade popped up from the grass and waved her hands overhead. "Can I go play with Luke?" She looked at Tenley first, then faced Mac.

Indecision warred on Mac's face, and Tenley let him take the lead. He needed to understand the full brunt of what he was taking on.

"Isn't your riding class about to start?"

Tenley checked her phone. "In an hour."

"So I can go?" Jade bounced from foot to foot. "I want to show Luke what Rascal can do." The pup leaped up at the sound of his name and raced around Jade's legs, yipping on every bounce.

Zeus yawned and stretched out for a nap.

Mac moved closer to Tenley, a question brewing in his eyes.

She twitched her shoulders, refusing to let him persuade her. This was his call.

Luke looked over his shoulder, nodded, then jumped off the porch and ran a few steps. "Mama says we can play in the backyard. Can you come?"

Jade settled into her pleading position, hands clasped under her chin and eyes wide as saucers.

"Yeah. Okay. Stay in the backyard with Luke until I come to get you for class." He huffed like one of the horses but softened when Jade squealed and threw her arms around his legs in a tight squeeze.

She shot over to Tenley next and repeated the move. "I can't wait to ride today. We're going to trot!" She bolted before Tenley could answer.

Mac's easy expression dropped into a glower.

Tenley held up a hand to stall him. "It's a trot, Mac. You've already seen her ride at a gallop. Freckles trots like a little old man. She's perfectly safe."

He seemed about to say something, but nothing emerged.

Tenley tightened her ponytail and turned on her heel. "I'm going to work with Shadow for a bit before class."

The last thing she expected was for Mac to fall into step beside her. He kept quiet until they reached the mare's pasture. Then he looped his arms over the rail and tipped his hat up. "Why did you rescue her?"

The question took her by surprise, and Tenley answered without really thinking it through. "Because I could. She needed me. No one else at that auction saw what I did."

"And what did you see?" He peered at her from under his hat brim, genuine curiosity burning in his eyes.

"I saw a horse that had never been given a chance. She was

scared and skinny. She needed help that no one else wanted to give." Tenley gripped the wooden rail until splinters pierced her palms.

Mac continued staring, looking at her, through her, to something she couldn't fathom. "You saved her." He nodded, his assessment complete. "And the equine therapy? What's that about?"

"When Dad…" Tears clogged Tenley's throat, surprising her. She stopped and blinked rapidly, pushing back the onslaught of emotion. "After Dad's accident, I felt lost. Out of control. The only place I felt safe was in the barn with the horses."

"You never told me that." Mac's voice was quiet and without censure. He didn't blame her or ask for a reason, he simply stated the obvious.

Tenley held on tighter to the railing. "There were a lot of things I didn't tell you back then. I wish I had. Maybe things could've been different." She whispered the last almost too low for him to hear. The urge to ask for a second chance flared bright, but she stuffed it down where it belonged.

He'd gotten over her. Married Laura and had a life of his own in Chicago. There was no more Mac-and-Tenley and never would be again.

"Why didn't you come to the funeral?" The question popped out before she knew she planned on asking it.

Mac jolted back and hissed between his teeth. Zeus looked up from where he lay on Mac's boots. He gave the area a serious perusal, then lowered his head to the dirt. Tenley never even heard the dog approach or come to rest with Mac.

Mac took off his hat and settled it on the fence post. Sweat dampened his hair, curling it at the edges and plastering it across his forehead. It shouldn't look as good as it did. Tenley curled her fingers into the rail to keep from reaching over and brushing the hair back.

"A few days before the accident, my partner and I found

ourselves in the middle of a sticky situation. We were on a call." He paused and pinched the bridge of his nose. "I broke protocol. I had a gut feeling that my partner was in danger, so I abandoned my post and ran after him. Shoved him to the ground when I thought I saw one of the guys pull a gun."

Tenley's heart lodged in her throat. She read the rest of the story in his expression, in the way he'd moved. His admission upon arrival that Zeus was injured. And moments ago when he said the dog might not return to active duty. "You were shot." She made it a statement, but he nodded to confirm.

She lifted a hand to her mouth, covering the shocked inhale and quelling the sudden urge to throw herself into his arms.

"How bad?" She spoke through her fingers, muffling the words.

Mac ran a hand along his ribs. "Lucky shot. Went under my vest and chipped my shoulder blade. Punctured a lung."

Words failed her. He spoke about getting shot like it happened every day. Like it didn't matter. "And your partner? He's okay?"

"He's fine. Zeus took the second bullet while protecting me. Cole got the guys." Mac grabbed his hat and jammed it onto his head. "You told me once that I had a savior complex. That saving people wasn't just what I did, but that I'd made it my identity." He nodded toward Shadow. "Maybe you were right. But maybe you have the same complex."

"I'm no one's savior." She laughed off the idea.

Mac faced her, eyes inscrutable. "No? Then, why did you open an equine therapy center? Why do you spend day after day saving kids from the pain wreaking havoc on their lives? Why did you save a horse that no one else wanted?"

"Because I know what it's like to be them." She shoved away from the fence. "I know what it's like to be drowning in grief and guilt and feel like there's no place to turn. I know what it's like to look at your family and have them stare back at you like you're a stranger. I know what it's like to think that if I'd only made a different choice, then my life would be better." The floodgates tore open, spewing her thoughts with every breath. "I forced you to walk away from me because I knew it was only a matter of time before I ruined you too. You were better off without me. You just couldn't see it."

She darted between the rails, cutting off Mac before he could reply.

And then she ran.

The same as always. Because she couldn't face seeing the truth once it came to Mac. She couldn't face knowing she'd almost lost him. Almost seven years in Chicago and he'd never been injured. Until now.

Tenley ran hard and fast down the packed dirt trail the horses had created through years of tromping across the field. It led her into the woods, where sunlight stopped and gloom ruled all.

"Does your dad know you blame yourself?" Mac's voice penetrated the woods.

She startled. She hadn't heard him following behind.

He approached from the side, hat askew and not the least bit out of breath.

He'd followed her. Because of course he would. This was Mac. He'd obviously not changed. Even now, when she pushed him away, he came back for more punishment. He eyed her, and his eyes flashed with what looked like concern. "You never told him. What about Brody and Molly? Does anyone know you're carrying around all this unnecessary guilt?"

"Unnecessary?" She glared at him from her spot under an oak. Bark dug into her shoulder when she shifted, but she held her ground. "You want to talk about unnecessary? *You* blame me." She waved a hand at his incredulous expression. "Ever since you came back, *you've* been on my case. *You've* been hurtful and mean. Which in Mac speak, means you blame me. I get you despising me for jilting you. I do. I'd have a hard time forgiving someone for that. But acting like I'm going to hurt Jade? Making my classes sound like I'm practicing high-speed sporting events on horseback without any training? What's that about?"

She launched the diatribe at him, hoping and praying it would make him go away. Every word scored her heart and gouged at her peace of mind. It was the truth but spoken with a spite that she never felt toward Mac.

Mac put his back against an oak tree directly in front of her. He hooked his thumbs in his belt loops and crossed one ankle over the other. "Go on." He caught her gaze and held it. "The only way we're getting past this is to get it all out in the open."

"What if I don't want to get past it?" she asked.

"You're the one who begged me to stay in Tamarack Springs." He lifted a shoulder. "Co-guardianship, right?"

He was messing with her. He had to be. Sure, he'd said he'd think about it, but this wasn't merely thinking. This was actively asking for a possible solution. Her anger dried up as fear took over. "You're not moving back to Chicago?"

"I don't know." He rolled his shoulder and offered her a rueful smile. "Getting shot, spending days laid up in a hospital bed. Missing Amber's funeral and finding out about you and Jade. It all overwhelmed me, Ten. I've just been trying to survive. Every time I come up for air, there's something else there ready to push me back down."

She understood that. That feeling of drowning had chased her for years.

"When Laura died, I said that was it." He made a slashing motion through the air. "I wasn't going to love anyone else ever again. It hurt too much. I'd lost too much already."

A breeze slipped between them, fluttering Mac's sleeves and dragging Tenley's ponytail into the tree's bark. She lost her voice, her thoughts, her heart, as Mac revealed the hurt burrowed deep down inside. He'd always held things close. Sometimes she forgot just how good he was at burying his emotions. Now they were on full display.

"When I found out about Amber. About Jade. I lost it. I've been living on autopilot since then. Seeing you again, being here where all our memories collide, it's ripping me apart." He turned away from her. "I don't know if I can stay. Or if I can get past what happened between us. But I think I have to try. And if I'm going to try, then you do too. Starting with talking to your family about the accident."

He strode away, leaving her heart a twisted mess that might never beat right ever again. He'd always been able to do that, twist her up in knots and make her think.

And he was right. She had to confess to her family. She should've done it years ago.

And sometime soon, she'd have to tell *him* the rest.

CHAPTER TEN

A TWINGE OF homesickness hit Mac when he pulled into the fairgrounds. People mingled, laughing and enjoying the bright May morning. It felt odd having this many people rushing around this early on a Saturday morning. But that was Tamarack Springs. An event like this was one of the highlights of the year, and the whole town turned out for it. School had ended and the whole town wanted to celebrate.

He'd managed to spend the last week going back and forth from Amber's house to the ranch with Jade without any more meltdowns.

They were making progress, and with school over, he could work toward a new routine.

He stepped out of his truck and released Zeus. The dog stayed glued to Mac's leg even with the leash attached to his brand-new collar. No vest today. Mac patted the dog's ribs. "Enjoy yourself. This may be the only time you ever get to see this." He expected a phone call from his captain any day. No matter whether Zeus went back to work or not, he hoped he'd get to keep the dog once he went into retirement. The department would put him into a conditioning program centered around conditioning police canines into becoming family pets.

"Mac." Sheriff Hanks waved from a blue-roofed tent tucked in the corner of the fairway.

Mac made his way over, people giving way to him and Zeus with barely a glance.

"Good to see you." Sheriff Hanks pumped Mac's hand, then gestured over his shoulder. "You remember Bricker and Smith."

Mac grinned at the two deputies he'd worked alongside while training for a position as one of Tamarack's own deputies. Before...well, before he and Tenley fell apart. "Good to see you both." He shook their hands and motioned at the crowd. "Quite a turnout today."

"Just wait." Bricker took off his black baseball cap and wiped sweat from his hairline. He resettled the cap and rested a hand on his hip.

Mac took note of the positioning. Bricker's hand grazed the grip of his firearm in a relaxed manner.

It was the same move Mac found himself making time and again. He'd left his gun behind until his administrative leave ended. If it ended. Even after a month off duty, he kept reaching for that assurance. It felt wrong to have his trust in a weapon. A weapon hadn't saved his life when he shoved his partner out of the way.

"Got a minute?" Sheriff Hanks's question tugged Mac away from his thoughts.

He nodded. "Sure."

Hanks jerked his head toward the back of the tent, where traffic was less congested. "You boys man the table."

Bricker snorted and crossed muscular arms. He nudged Smith with an elbow. "You remember that time Mac hit back-to-back home runs?"

Smith whistled. "Now, that was a sight." He winced and shook his head. "Sure wish we had someone like him on the team today. We'd beat those Bridgeport city cops without a lick of trouble."

"You need another man?" Mac played into their game, letting them feel like they were in charge. It was an old ploy. One they'd used when he was a wet-behind-the-ears greenie who didn't know a thing about being a deputy but knew he wanted to help people. He lifted his shoulders in a casual shrug. "Haven't played in a few years. Might be rusty."

Smith and Bricker eyed each other. Bricker gave way first, his grin crawling out until it forced his eyes closed. "Six o'clock. Don't be late."

Mac tapped the brim of his cowboy hat and followed Hanks to the open area behind the tent.

"Glad to see all of you getting along." Hanks palmed his chin. He looked everywhere and nowhere, his posture appearing nonthreatening. Mac knew it was a ruse. The man could strike out in any direction at a moment's notice. "Been meaning to talk to you again. Never seemed like a good time. Probably no better now, but this has been weighing on me something fierce, and it's time I get it off my chest."

"I'm all ears, Sheriff."

"I mentioned it before and you shut me down pretty hard." Sheriff Hanks tilted his head to the side and scrutinized Mac from head to toe. "I was serious about that job offer. Stick around and come back to work for me."

Mac's mouth dropped open. Zeus pressed his head into Mac's hand, and he snapped his teeth closed.

Hanks watched through narrowed eyes. "I don't know your situation in Chicago. Maybe you're happy there. Maybe you're not. But if you're looking to come home, the position is yours."

"Sheriff." Mac thumbed the spot where his gun would be if he wore his uniform. The missing weight tugged on him. "I'm a mess. I can't say if I'm coming or going." A yearning hit him with a full-on body blow. A need to stay here where he knew the people walking down the street. A place where people greeted each other with smiles.

Was this the answer he'd been praying for?

"What about Zeus?" He motioned at the dog sitting on his foot. "I don't know what's going to happen with him. My captain is considering retiring him."

Sheriff Hanks eyed Zeus and then the fairgrounds that were steadily growing busier. "That's up to you. Adopt him and bring him with you. If he's capable, we'll consider adding him to the force with you. Maybe he's not up for running down drug dealers, but he'd be handy for sniffing out Bricker's candy stash." The sheriff rubbed his palms together and wiggled his eyebrows. "Hunt down rogue hamburgers at Granny's."

That easy?

Mac gave in and grinned. "I'll think about it." The simple phrase had become his mantra since returning to Tamarack. Everything he'd ever wanted out of life was still here, in the only place he'd ever called home. "I need to find Jade." The arena sat atop the hill, beckoning him closer.

Tenley would be there, along with Brody, Callie and Jade. His pulse ratcheted up at the thought of seeing Tenley again. Ever since she told him about how she blamed herself, she never strayed far from his thoughts. What else had she hidden from him? They'd always said no secrets. He'd meant it, and from his side, he could say that he'd never kept anything from her. But now he wondered just how much of their relationship had been real. The last thing he'd expected was for Tenley to withhold information from him. Especially something as big as blaming herself for her father's accident, which happened four years before their disastrous almost-wedding.

Four years that turned into a little over a decade. How much strength had it taken to carry that burden alone?

It was time he stopped hiding from the truth in his past. Tenley had offered to explain why she'd jilted him at the altar. He hadn't really wanted to know. Out of desperation or some sense of self-preservation, he'd asked her not to tell him.

No more. No more hiding. Time to clear the air and see where their lives might go from here.

FUNNEL CAKES AND apple pie. Two of Tenley's favorite smells. Now that she was here, she didn't mind Brody roping her into helping with the pony rides. Tamarack Springs's annual end-of-the-school-year and homecoming fair was not to be missed. The only thing weighing on her today was knowing whether Mac planned on staying. They hadn't spoken since the confrontation in the woods. Mac kept his distance while still showing up for Jade's classes. The space felt unnatural, but Tenley appreciated the way it helped ease the tug-of-war in her heart every time he was there.

They could do this, coexist and still take care of Jade. There were no rules or laws that said they should revisit the idea of being a couple. They could raise Jade into a healthy adult this way. She believed that, even if the idea of more with Mac left her gazing up at the mountains long after night fell as dreams of a different future played out.

But it wasn't meant to be. She'd thought maybe they had a chance. Mac insinuated as much. Getting past what happened was one thing. Having a second chance with Mac was another, and it was completely out of the question.

Someone shouted her name, drawing Tenley's attention back to the present.

The fairgrounds burst with every color of the rainbow. All along the edge, colorful canopies kept the sun from frying people as they sold their wares. Everything from hand-sewn quilts to books, even a booth filled with cookware, covered the grassy embankment. Patrons took advantage of what little shade they could find, fanning their faces and enjoying glasses of cold iced tea or lemonade.

Food vendors lined the opposite side, Molly smack in the middle. Luke ran around the table. A smear of icing along his cheek spoke all too clearly of eager energy. His teacher approached Molly and made several hand motions. Molly nodded and Luke took his teacher's hand before they skipped over to the bounce castle.

Anything a person could dream of could be found here. Even deep-fried Oreos. Her stomach rumbled at the scent, and she headed toward Patrick's food truck. He'd painted it since last year and added Brewsters in fancy block type. Tenley stood on tiptoes to peer over the people in front of her.

Patrick greeted each customer by name, the same as he did in his coffee shop, located beside Granny's. He caught Tenley's eye, and his smile broadened. "How's my favorite Jacobs doing today?"

"Fine and dandy." She took a step closer as the line inched forward. "Off to find that brooding brother of mine."

"He'd better get over that." Patrick gave an exaggerated eye roll. "I might have something that'll sweeten his disposition." Patrick disappeared from the truck's window, and a woman took his place.

By the time Tenley made it to the front of the line, Patrick returned with a cup carrier loaded down with four drinks and a stack of donuts. "There you go. No charge."

"Nope." Tenley waved her money. "I can pay."

"Never said you couldn't. Consider this a thank-you for those lessons you've been giving my nephew. Never seen him happier than he is after his Saturday ride." Patrick pushed the carrier closer. "Take it. I won't hear otherwise."

Tenley stuffed the money into her pocket. "I'll get it back to you somehow."

He chuckled. "I don't doubt it. But not today. Today, it's my treat."

Tenley hefted the drink carrier and stepped out of line. She spun the cups around, looking for her own, when Mac's name in a heavy scrawl stopped her in her tracks. That sneaky man. She bit the inside of her cheek and resumed her trek up the gravel drive leading to the arena, where Brody and Callie would soon arrive.

She worked her way through the crowd, nodding hello to

those she knew and stopping to talk when someone waved her over.

Winding her way around a cluster of kids waiting in line for a train-shaped bounce castle, someone shouted her name. Tenley was surprised she heard them amid the children's clamor and the general noise created by half of the town crammed together on the same five acres. Turning toward the sound, Mac waved at her from under the Tamarack Springs Sheriff Department's tent. Seeing him there in his casual clothes amid a slew of blue uniforms ignited something in her midsection.

Mac never caused butterflies. No. The feeling he evoked felt more like a herd of buffalo stampeding across the plain.

Apprehension tickled her spine. The emotions he set loose said that being with him could be detrimental to her emotional boundaries. Her sobriety took all her effort. Adding a rekindled relationship with the man whose heart she stomped broke all the rules.

He ran to her.

The buffalo in her gut stampeded again. Mercy but the man looked good.

"Where are you headed?" He nudged his hat up and peered at her from under the brim. "Can we talk?"

"I'm on my way to help with the pony rides." She lifted the drinks in the direction of the arena and didn't bother hiding her annoyance at his sudden appearance. "Patrick sent this for you." She turned the cup carrier where his drink faced him.

Mac grinned and took the cup. "Good man, that Patrick. I was in need of a caffeine boost." He took a slow sip. "Need help with the horses?"

No. Sweat trickled down her spine. "I can manage."

"Which means you don't want me to help, not that you don't need help." He fell in step beside her, aiming them at the gate.

Brody had the trailer backed in and the gate down. He and Callie led the horses out, one by one, while Jade watched from outside the fence.

Tenley resisted an eye roll in Mac's direction. "I can't stop you."

"Good." Mac's smile appeared genuine. It faltered after a few seconds. "I'm playing baseball tonight with the Sheriff's team. Can you stay? We'll talk afterward."

Stay and watch him play like old times? It might be her last chance to see him as the Mac she knew and remembered fondly. Not the hardened version he'd showboated around earlier. The one she barely recognized. Maybe the old Mac was making a comeback.

"Sure. I'll stay. I'll bring Jade so she can see her uncle hit another double home run." She smiled when he ducked his head.

"Been a long time since I played. Not sure I have another double in me."

She squeezed his forearm before ducking between the rails. "I believe in you." She hurried toward Brody and Callie. "Hey, hold up."

"Is this a stick-up?" Brody's smile creased his cheeks.

Callie's laugh caught Tenley by surprise, and when Brody joined in, Tenley grinned and held up the drink carrier. "I was going to give you these. Patrick made them special for you." She turned away. "But if you're going to crack jokes, then I'll drink them myself."

Brody cut in front of her, blocking her exit with his body and horse. "Oh no. You're not getting away with my coffee." He grabbed the cup and lifted it to his nose. After a deep inhale, he frowned at Tenley. "You didn't put salt in it, did you?"

"First of all, that was an accident." Tenley held up one finger, then another. "Second, would I really sabotage a Brewsters coffee?"

"Yes." Callie and Brody said simultaneously.

Tenley chuckled at their gaping expressions. "Yeah. Okay. I would. But I didn't." She reached for Brody's cup. "You want me to take a sip and prove it to you?"

"No thanks." Brody tucked the cup close to his chest and

thrust the lead rope at her. "Can you take Pepper over to the rail with Spirit? I'll get the next one unloaded."

She took the lead and nodded once. "You got it, boss." Their laughter followed her as she turned and walked the horse to the white rail.

A line of kids formed behind Jade as they approached the horses, reminding Tenley of ducklings. She wiggled her eyebrows at Mac, doing her best to remove the strain from earlier.

Jade climbed onto the rail beside Spirit's head, stroking the gelding's mane.

Tenley hopped up beside her. "Hey, you. How was the ride over with Brody and Callie?"

"Great." Jade beamed. "He let me watch the horses on his camera."

"Sounds fun." Mac stepped in. "He mentioned last week that he wanted cameras installed in the trailers. I didn't expect him to get it done this fast."

"That's Brody. He's never one to sit still." Tenley chuckled and slid back to the ground. She checked over the horses. Once they were all geared up and settled in a line, Tenley motioned for Jade to hop into Pepper's saddle. "Mac, you have Jade. I'll grab the next one. Two laps around the arena, then switch."

He tapped the brim of his hat with one finger in his version of a cowboy salute. It warmed Tenley to see him slowly breaking through that wall and coming back into the Mac she knew...and loved?

She forced a smile into place and untied Spirit while motioning for the little girl next in line to come up. "Hi, I'm Tenley. What's your name?"

"Becky." The girl bobbed her pigtails and smiled, showing a gap where her front teeth should have been.

"Well, Becky, would you like to go for a ride?"

Another nod.

Brody and Callie each took a horse and formed a line behind Tenley and Spirit.

Tension melted away under the kids' scrutiny. Tenley adjusted the mounting block and rested her hand on Spirit's neck. "Step right up there and into the saddle." A couple stood by the rail, faces wreathed in anxiety. "Mom. Dad. Do you want to walk with her?"

Relieved breaths expelled and smiles took over.

Motioning them forward, Tenley gave gentle directions. "Why don't you each take a side? You can rest your hands on the saddle if you like. And let's walk on."

Spirit took a step, and the woman gasped. Becky laughed, the sound bright as the sunlight. "I'm riding. Look. I'm riding."

"You sure are." Becky's dad spoke up while her mom remained tight-lipped.

Mac winked at Tenley across the arena, sending a blush soaring into her cheeks. How did he do that? Why, after all these years, did he still affect her this way? She turned her attention to Becky. The girl struck up an animated conversation, telling all she knew about horses. This one had the horse bug, reminding Tenley of herself at that age. She'd never outgrown it. Unlikely Becky would either.

After two rounds of the arena, Tenley helped Becky dismount and nodded at her parents. "I would apologize, but I think it's too late."

The dad chuckled. "Pretty sure I see a horse in our future."

While the mom frowned, Becky squealed and pirouetted.

"My brother trains horses. Brody Jacobs. If you decide to buy, look him up." She slid a card toward the man, who took it with a smile.

THREE HOURS OF walking kids around the ring in the sweltering heat and Mac was ready to dive headfirst into an ice bath. Or a river. Whichever he found first.

Maybe then he'd be in the mood to play baseball. Right now, the idea of any activity other than sitting with a cool drink in his hand felt like torture.

Zeus lifted his head from where he'd been napping in the shade and yawned. He'd been patient all morning. Mac had let a few of the kids pet him but kept an eye on Zeus to ensure the dog didn't mind the attention. *He didn't*, Mac thought with a laugh.

Brody and Callie had stayed with them for the first two hours. Once the line slowed, Tenley had told them to go enjoy themselves. They'd taken Jade with them so she could enjoy time with her friends. Tenley had tried to drive Mac off too, saying she could handle it herself.

Despite the heat, he found himself enjoying chatting with the kids and walking them around the arena. Their awe and delight brightened his day. It reminded him of years gone by. He'd grown up riding horses with Tenley and the others. The sense of awe had become normal at some point, and he wanted that back.

"I need food." He tied Snickers—a pale brown horse with a single spot on his rump and a salt-and-pepper mane and tail—in the shade beside a pail of fresh water, and for half a second considered dunking his head in the five-gallon bucket.

"You always need food." Tenley rolled her eyes. Sweat glistened on her neck and arms and dampened the dark hair framing her face. She'd pulled it back earlier, but tiny wisps escaped and stuck to her cheeks.

He itched to brush them away. Mac patted his stomach and groused. "I'm a growing boy."

Tenley gave him a slow perusal, her eyes lingering over his shoulders. With a shake of her head, she started removing Spirit's saddle. The gelding pushed his nose into the water bucket and swirled it around, sending a waterfall onto Tenley's calves. "Nice." She shook out one foot.

"They'll dry in no time out here." Mac took off his hat and wiped a trail of sweat from his face. "I'm turning into a raisin. Or a dry husk of corn."

"Stop complaining." Tenley threw a rag at him. "You sound worse than a toddler who's lost his binky."

"What's a binky?" He rubbed the rag over Snickers' coat, drying sweat while the horse groaned, cocked a hind hoof and relaxed.

Tenley lifted Spirit's head and wiped a clean rag over the sweat-dampened hide. "A pacifier. Have you never been around babies?"

Except for the few times he'd attended a birthday party for one of his partner's kids, or when Amber brought Jade to visit, no. Mac leaned into the work, hoping his extra effort covered the sudden discomfort. "Work in Chicago is different than here. Not much time for kids. By the time I got to people, it was usually too late." He clamped his teeth before he set loose more words.

"I'm sorry." The somberness of Tenley's tone brought his head up. She couldn't understand, not really, but the way she looked at him, with sadness and empathy in her eyes, she showed sincerity.

Snickers nudged Mac's pocket, a soft whicker shivering through the horse's body. No doubt he wanted a treat after all his hard work. Mac fished one from his jeans and let the horse lip it from his palm.

She kept her back to him, but her movements lacked her usual smooth grace.

"How about a trip to the dunking booth?" Mac tossed the dirty rag into the grooming box and dusted off his hands. "I could use a cooling off."

"Let me call Molly. She wanted to drive the horses home. The last text she sent said she'd already sold out of all her baked goods. She left the tent up so people could come by and talk, but I think she's about reached her limit of socialization for today." Talking about her sister put the light back in her eyes.

Mac tracked her movements as she paced up and down in

front of the stands, phone to her ear. Doubt niggled the back of his mind.

Coming to his side, Tenley rubbed her hand over Snickers' mane. "It's all set. Molly and Luke will take the horses home, but she'll come back for me when I'm ready to go."

"There's no sense in that. I'll drive you home. You said you're staying for the game." He narrowed his eyes when she protested. "Let Molly enjoy her night. I'll drop you and Jade off."

"Only if you let me pay for your dinner."

Unnecessary…but Mac took a long look at Tenley, from her fidgeting hands to her toes tapping in time with the band on stage at the bottom of the hill off to the right. "Fine. If you can dunk me, you can pay for dinner."

"Deal." Glee emanated from Tenley, drawing light to her eyes. Sweaty, dirty and tired, she still looked beautiful to him.

They loaded up the horses and waited for Molly and Luke to climb into the truck and pull away. Then he grabbed Zeus's leash and they left the arena.

They weaved through the crowd, the shouts and shrieks coming from every direction. Passing a blue tent, the smell of funnel cakes caused Mac's mouth to water. Tenley shook her head. "Not yet. There's a water tank with your name on it."

He let her lead him away, his stomach grumbling a complaint.

A soggy man pulled himself from the tank as they approached.

"Hey, I'll take the next one if you don't care." Mac held Zeus's leash out to Tenley.

She took it from him and moved away.

The man slapped Mac on the shoulder. "Water's cold. Have fun."

"Yeah, Ten, have fun." Mac sent her a grin while he removed his shoes and climbed the four ladder rungs and settled onto the narrow platform. Dropping his feet into the lukewarm water, Mac waited. A line, several kids deep, cheered when Mac waved.

The first kid he remembered seeing around town. Travis, senior in high school. Deputy Smith's oldest kid. Travis hurled the sandbag, nicking the circle's edge. He groaned.

Mac slapped his knees. "Come on, Travis. You can do better than that."

Travis squinted at the target and wound up for the pitch, sandbag tight in his palm. He released, the bag slamming into the red paddle and sending Mac into the water.

He came up with a smile. In this heat, he welcomed any form of liquid.

Tenley smirked from her place in line, her smile widening each time a kid sent him under. Reaching the front of the line, she picked up a sandbag and tossed it up and down in her palm. "Having fun, Mac?"

"Absolutely. Give it your best shot."

She squeezed the bag and eyed him from the side. "Remember you said that." Her eyes brightened, and before Mac could reply, Tenley launched. The bag slapped the bullseye.

He fell with a plop and a splash and came up spluttering.

Tenley laughed and handed a bag to the next kid in line. "You forget, I don't like losing. Dinner's on me." Zeus gave Tenley an adoring look and followed her as she walked toward the funnel-cake truck.

He'd missed this. The easy camaraderie felt familiar yet brand-new.

CHAPTER ELEVEN

TENLEY SETTLED ON the wooden bench closest to the dugout and shaded her eyes with her hand. Jade sat beside her, clapping and cheering. A ring of blue circled her mouth from the cotton candy Tenley bought on their walk to the baseball diamond.

Mac's long strides ate up the ground as he crossed to the dugout with Zeus at his side. Deputy Darren Smith pulled Mac into a hug, the two men talking and gesturing wildly like no time had passed.

Annoyance bit deep. Why did Mac get the homecoming of a lifetime while she was ignored? Except for the side glances shot her way, like now, from a mom and dad huddled around their two children as though Tenley's past could rub off on them.

Sure, she'd been a bit chaotic as a teenager, some of those times spent with the people who now gave her the side eye. They'd grown up, and so had she. Couldn't they see she'd changed?

Or maybe that was her insecurities rearing their ugly heads. Turning away, Tenley ignored them.

Mac picked up two bats, swinging them in easy arcs. Darren popped up at his side with a helmet in his hand. Mac swung, and Darren ducked. "Whoa, Mac. Take it easy. Save your energy for the game. I'd like to keep my face where it is."

"Sorry." Mac took a step back and dropped one bat. He gestured over his shoulder.

Darren caught Tenley's eyes. He nodded and Mac jogged her way. The opposing team filed onto the field.

"You still keep up with the games?" Mac curled his fingers into the fence, his hair—still damp from the dunk tank—curled under the cap he'd taken from his truck. "I could use your help if you do."

Her thoughts scattered. Put her up against a twelve-hundred-pound horse and she never batted an eye, but ten feet from Mac and a simple question and all coherent thought fled.

She shook off the feelings and met him at the fence, placing her fingers over his. "See the guy with the yellow cap? Watch out for him. He's got the best swing on the team." Tenley let the familiar smells of sweat and dirt rewind the years. She used to attend every one of Mac's games.

"Thanks for the warning."

Her breath caught, stomach churning as past and present collided. "Play your best game. No regrets. Leave it all on the field."

The smile he gave her—the sweet, innocent grin that had once told her how much he loved her—threatened to be her undoing as it rattled the cage where she kept memories of him locked away.

He slipped a finger out and hooked it around her thumb, but he didn't say the words to complete the ritual. *As long as I have you, there are no regrets.* That's what he was supposed to say. The lack of them hovered, as solid as a jail cell. The cage stopped rattling. Memories of what they'd been would never compare to the hurt. It didn't ease it and couldn't take it away.

Tenley nestled that core of pain against the traitorous beat of her heart that still yearned for Mac. For what was and could never be again.

What looked like regret flickered in his eyes before he turned and walked away.

Tamarack Springs' team, the Rangers, had a man on second and another on third, with two outs before Mac came up to bat. He stepped up to the plate and nearly took a pitch to the head. The umpire shouted, "Ball," and Mac readied for the next pitch. With runners on second and third, Mac settled in, his concentration on the pitcher.

Tenley chewed a fingernail, tension curling through her, as the pitcher wound up and released a fastball.

Mac connected, the crack of bat on ball sending Tenley to her feet with a shout. The ball sailed toward the outfield. Mac raced toward first. His foot slapped the base seconds before his teammate raced over home plate.

He hit second, while Darren raced home. The other team had the ball, winding it toward Mac as he lowered his head and barreled toward third.

Tenley jumped up and down, arms waving. "Slide, Mac!"

Jade joined her, screaming and jumping on the bench.

He glanced back and picked up speed before throwing himself into a slide that carried him safely to third base. Jumping to his feet, he whipped off his cap and waved it at the crowd as the stamping and shouting increased.

She clapped and cheered along with everyone else, the years falling away and taking her back, despite her attempts to stay. It was after one of Mac's games that Tenley had first tried alcohol. A little in the beginning, then more, until it overshadowed everything else in her life.

And after this game, she'd tell Mac all of it. The confession was a long time coming.

The next batter struck out, and Mac jogged off the field. He grabbed his glove and took up the shortstop position. His favorite. Not everyone could handle the intensity. He'd once told Tenley that he loved the constant action, knowing that other people depended on him. A hero complex in the making.

Her mind whirled with questions. Evidence of his heroism leaked out with everything he did. Protecting Jade. Saving his partner. Where did she fall in his circle of protection? Did she want to be there?

The man that Tenley had warned him about stepped up to the plate. Mac pounded his fist into his glove while shooting a look at Tenley. He rocked his weight left to right, ready to move in any direction. She'd seen him in action too many times to doubt his ability.

Darren let loose from the pitcher's mound. The batter swung and missed, a disgusted expression on his face. He pointed his bat at Darren, who threw his head back and laughed.

"Coming for you, Smith." The batter taunted.

Darren rolled his head from side to side. "Give it your best shot."

These matches were all fun and games. Though the competition and rivalry excited the crowd, they were all friends joined in the same cause. This year's fundraiser went to the Tamarack Springs Fire Department.

The teams were made up of police, firemen, EMTs and volunteers until they wrangled enough people for four baseball games. While the homecoming along the square boasted an arcade, bounce castles, food, music and games, known four counties wide, the real attraction came from the baseball diamond.

Sweat trickled down Tenley's back. She rolled her shoulders to ease the tickling sensation and sipped from her water bottle.

Jade grabbed her pink tumbler from the bench and gulped, then dragged the back of her wrist over her mouth. A streak of blue smeared her hand.

Mac swiped his face on his shoulder, leaving dirt and sweat on the white uniform.

Darren released another pitch. The batter connected, and the ball hurtled toward Mac.

His glove snapped in front of Mac's stomach, the slap of the ball meeting leather sending Tenley's heart into her throat.

Mac's face didn't change, but she knew what catching that ball cost him. The speed and power behind the swing, coupled with the smack and Mac's single step back with the glove pressed against his stomach, told her more than he'd ever admit. The impact had hurt him. But it wasn't in Mac to show his pain. Or to quit.

Like the time he'd broken his hand in football practice and not told the coach. He couldn't stand the idea of letting his team down and had played through the pain. They'd won that night and Mac had run off the field. Straight for her.

She needed to stop these trips down memory lane. No more ball games. She had to quit pretending things between them could go back to the way they were. She thought she'd managed, but being here, watching him, it brought it all back. She had to let him go.

Until she could look at him without so many mixed emotions, it would be better for them both if she backed off. She couldn't put Jade at risk. Which is what would happen if Tenley gave in to the love hurtling around inside and begged Mac for a second chance. She'd keep to the plan and tell Mac everything tonight. Then she'd have no choice but to let him go.

MAC TIGHTENED HIS grip on the wheel, wincing when his palm reminded him how long it'd been since he caught that many hurtling baseballs. They'd won the game, putting him on cloud nine until he walked off the field and been unable to find Tenley and Jade. He finally checked his phone and found a text message that she'd be waiting for him at the truck.

Tenley hadn't spoken a word since her shout for him to slide during the first inning. Her aloof posture and closed-off expression pulled at his heartstrings.

They'd had such a good day together.

She punched buttons on his radio, brow furrowed, until

she landed on an oldies rock station. Not good. Tenley only listened to oldies when she wanted to forget. It was funny the things he remembered about her. Little quirks of personality that he'd figured out over the years.

Like the fact that she owned enough Converse shoes to fill a closet but rarely wore them. When she did, the color she chose made a statement about how she felt that day.

Red when she wanted to be brave.

Purple when she was hurting.

Yellow when she was excited for a new adventure.

And oldies on the radio when she felt sad.

Leaning back with her hands pressed together between her knees, she stared out the window. Her reflection bounced back at him under the streetlights. Jade tucked her head against the back seat and closed her eyes. They'd discussed dinner, and since Tenley demanded he uphold their bargain that she owed him a meal, they'd settled on eating at her house. Then talk after Jade fell asleep. Nervous tension gripped him, and his left foot bounced against the floor.

He kept his eyes on the road but glanced occasionally at Tenley. "You okay?"

She lifted one shoulder, her expression aloof. "Fine."

Liar. "Music says different." He sent her a smile, but she refused to look his way.

"So, change it." The acidic barb hooked deep, no doubt as it was meant to. He never messed with her music. He knew how much she needed the relief that came from finding the right beat to express her mood.

This one was angry, yet somehow also sad. They rode without speaking, empty streets flashing by, child sleeping silently, until the road changed from country town to country road and trees encroached on the edges of the roadway.

Mac bumped down the drive and hooked a right toward the little cabin where Tenley lived with Jade. He put the truck in

Park, and she slid from the seat. She opened Jade's door and scooped her up before Mac could protest.

Zeus whined from his spot beside her.

Tenley marched toward the house while Mac released Zeus.

Let her go or confront her? Confront was too strong. They'd agreed to talk, and if she was as nervous as him, it was no wonder she stomped away. Following her up the steps, the fine hairs on the back of his neck stood at attention. A seam of light highlighted her open front door. He reached for Tenley to stop her, his arm going around her waist.

"Mac, wha—"

"Shh." He stuck a finger to his lips and dipped his head close to her ear. "Did you leave your front door open when you left this morning?"

Her eyes widened.

Good enough answer. With his arm still around her waist, he hauled her backward, one slow step at a time, until they reached his truck. Could someone have broken in? "Stay here." He motioned for Zeus, and they started forward.

"I probably didn't pull it closed all the way," Tenley hissed behind him.

Mac kept his focus on the door. "I'm not letting you take that chance." Not with Jade, and not with herself. *Lord, please help me keep them safe.* His throat convulsed on a tight swallow. This time when he prayed, it wasn't lip service. He'd stopped trusting God to protect him and those he loved. Maybe it was time for that to change.

Where had unbelief gotten him?

His shoulders knotted with tension. Would he be able to protect Jade? If only he knew where the threat would come from first. Tenley? Or something else?

He approached the house with Zeus at his side. His fingers inched toward his belt before he remembered he didn't have his gun. Probably for the best. "You and me, big guy." He patted Zeus and sent the dog inside.

They cleared the house room by room. Zeus never alerted to danger, and Mac didn't find anything out of place. Still, his nerves jangled and the space in his heart where Tenley lived ached.

When Mac stepped back onto the porch and motioned for Tenley, she ran straight for him and gave him a swift punch to the arm—but it wasn't the angry kind. She held Jade on one hip and gripped the back of his shirt as she followed it with a hug. "Don't ever scare me like that again."

"I wasn't worried about me. I had Zeus." He played it off as nothing more than an exercise.

Tenley didn't buy it. She leaned back and glared at him. "You might not care what happens to you, but I do." She poked his shoulder for added emphasis.

"Can I go to bed now?" Jade yawned and scrubbed her hands over her eyes before lowering her head to Tenley's shoulder.

Tenley's eyes flashed to him. She took in a shuddering breath and seemed to search for words. "You want to tuck her in? I'll fix us something to eat. She ate during the ball game, so she should sleep all night."

Mac carefully took Jade and walked ahead of Tenley into the house. They parted ways in the living room, and by the time Mac tucked Jade in and returned, Tenley had steaks sizzling in a pan.

She frowned, and her shoulders bowed forward. Her body language screamed her weariness.

"These are almost done." A grin flashed. "How many stories did you read her?"

"Two." Mac sat in a kitchen chair and propped his head on his clenched fist with his elbow on the table. "Do you want me to help?"

"I'm good here." She flipped the steaks. "You can grab us some plates."

He stood and made his way over to the cabinets. They fell

into an easy rhythm, one they'd developed over time and fell back into without hesitation. Tenley slid the steaks onto matching plates and spooned carrots alongside while Mac grabbed the rolls from the oven and dropped them into a basket.

They moved to the table and sat across from each other. Tenley bowed her head, and her lips moved in a silent prayer. Mac gripped the plate and tried not to let the nervous energy send him reeling backward.

"Do you want to eat first, or talk?" Tenley slid her napkin into her lap and watched him beneath lowered lashes.

He felt her gaze, every second of it tightening the coil in his gut. "I don't think I can eat." Shameful as it was to let the steaks go to waste, he nudged his plate away.

Tenley did the same. "You can take it with you. If you want." She'd removed her hat before cooking, and now her hair curled around her face. She ran her hands over her head, laced her fingers together behind her neck and leaned back. It was meant to be a casual stance, but the harsh lighting cutting across her cheekbones and the way her arms trembled gave her away.

"Just tell me, Tenley." He leaned forward. "Tell me why."

"I wish it was that easy." She sighed and slipped a hand into her pocket. A coin glinted in her hand, and she gripped it in a tight fist before placing the coin on the table and pushing it toward him.

Mac picked it up. A gold tree of life stretched bare branches across the top of the coin. A purple six glinted in the center of the tree's trunk. Underneath the tree was the inscription To Thine Own Self Be True. "What's this?"

"There's no easy place to start." Tenley retracted her hand and tucked it into her lap. "I'm an alcoholic, Mac."

He reeled back as a hundred thoughts crashed in on him at once. Denial hit the forefront, and he shook his head. "No, you're not."

"Yes. I am. I'm sober. That's my six-year coin. I'll get my

seventh-year token soon. On what would've been our seven-year anniversary."

The implications hit him harder than a thousand baseballs to the stomach at once. His heartbeat stuttered and his vision wavered. He pulled in a deep breath to clear the black spots dancing before his eyes. How...how had he not known?

"Why?" He choked on the question.

Tenley's brow furrowed. She dug in, her face falling into an expression he didn't recognize. Anger? Fear? It combined into a new version of Tenley.

"I started drinking in high school. Didn't take me long to become addicted. When Dad had his accident, I tried to stop. The accident really was my fault. I was going to try to go home that night, but I didn't..." She shook her head and lowered her eyes to the table. "It gets worse," she said under her breath. "I went drinking the night before our wedding. Got arrested in Bridgeport. That's..." She started to cry. "That's why I missed our wedding."

The words were clipped and short. They said everything with succinct power and no frills. Words had become weapons, and these tore him apart.

"And after? You never called. Refused to talk to me. Your family turned me away for three days straight before..." His leg bounced up and down.

Tenley pulled her left leg under her and crossed her arms over her stomach. She twisted the hem of her shirt around her forefinger, her nervous tell from years ago. "I begged them not to tell you. I left for rehab on the day you showed up here. No phone and no visitors the first week."

"So you were here that day, and you didn't talk to me?" He leaned forward and put his head in his hands. "Brody and I argued in the barn. I knew he was holding back, but nothing I said convinced him to tell me where you were."

There was more to it than she was admitting. Mac knew that, yet he couldn't bring himself to ask the questions. Betrayal sucker punched him and sent him clambering to his feet. "You never told me." He paced, hands going up in the air. "You drank for four years and never said a word? How did I not know? I knew you," he said loudly. "I thought I knew you," his voice quiet.

She shook her head, shame twisting her features. "You didn't need my problems weighing you down." Her voice was quiet, but he heard the intensity in the words. The excuses.

He pointed a finger at her, and even though it shook, his voice remained even. "We promised each other forever. Marriage meant in sickness and in health. I was willing to make that commitment."

"You were willing because you didn't know what a mess I was." Tenley stood but didn't approach. "I never told you because it wasn't your problem to solve—and I was ashamed."

"I would've helped." He pressed his palms into the sides of his head, trying desperately to relieve the pressure building inside him.

"You would've tried to fix it." Tenley's tortured gaze met his. "Love means letting go when you know you're going to destroy. I was on a path that would've taken you down with me."

"That's ridiculous." He scoffed, but a thread of truth lingered in the back of his mind.

Tenley continued like he'd not spoke at all. "You were a brand-new deputy in the smallest town around. I was on the brink of a major disaster. If we'd gotten married, only God knows how long it would've taken before I fell hard enough to go to rehab."

"I could've helped." He hated the pleading note cutting through his voice. "You meant everything to me." Mac's breath whooshed out. Blood roared in his ears. It wasn't true. It couldn't be true. He'd never seen Tenley touch a drop of alcohol.

"I know." She lifted her head, showing the slim line of her throat. "And I would have destroyed us. Best-case scenario, you'd have pulled me over and been forced to give me a DUI. Worst case, we'd have kept going until I eventually ended up being the one causing a wreck like Dad's, like the one that put him in that wheelchair, or worse, Mac."

"But you didn't."

Tenley spun around. "No. And I thank God every day that He helped pull me out before then." She took a slow breath. "This isn't about me. This is about you understanding what I did." He shook his head, but she kept going. "I know you. Maybe better than you know yourself. You think it's your fault. No doubt you found a way to blame yourself and ran off to Chicago. You go somewhere and hide until the pain is manageable. I look at myself in the mirror every day and know that I'm the reason you left. Don't put this on me. I don't have the strength to carry it all."

"I'm trying to understand. But you're part of this too."

"No. You're trying to protect yourself. Life happens, Mac. Grief and love and death and joy. They're all part of it. You don't get one without the other. Do you know how many times I've looked at Dad and wished it was me in the car that night? I'm the one who should be paralyzed. I'm the one who made all the mistakes." She rubbed the cuff of her sleeve over her eyes, the movement angry as she dashed tears away, her hands shaking.

"That isn't your fault." He had to get her to understand that.

Zeus whined from his spot under the table but didn't emerge. The sound reminded Mac that Jade slept just down the hall. Jade. His blood turned cold. "You didn't tell me this before. Why?"

"Because you were looking for any reason to take Jade away from me. Telling you this is the proverbial smoking gun." She looked as tortured as he felt. "I loved you enough to drive you away. You got along fine without me." A rueful smile tipped her lips.

"That's what you think?" He let his arms fall to his sides.

"Nothing has ever hurt me more than losing you." Not even Laura's death. He felt abominable over that, but it was the truth. He'd loved Laura with his whole heart, but Tenley was first, Tenley was now, always Tenley. She was his one and only. "Maybe things would have turned out the way you say." He brushed a hand down his face, dragging in a ragged breath. "But you didn't trust me enough to let me try."

"Alcoholism isn't a problem you could fix for me." Tenley pursued the same line of thought with dogged determination. "It was my battle. My choice. I had to want it, Mac. And with you there offering help at every turn, I knew I'd never quit. There was no reason for me to give it up as long as you were there."

"You didn't let me protect you." The crux of the problem rushed out of him. His shoulder throbbed as though he'd been shot all over again. His throat constricted. "That's all I ever wanted. To love you and protect you for the rest of my life."

"Sometimes, we have to protect ourselves." Tenley took a step toward him. Her hand lifted like she might touch his face. A tortured look entered her eyes, and she moved away. "I understand if you still want to take Jade to Chicago." Her voice dropped to a whisper. "I won't fight you on it. You're right. I don't deserve the chance to take care of her."

"You're giving up?" He scoffed. The bitterness in the sound echoed around the kitchen. "You fought me tooth and nail. You insisted that we could work this out. Now you're quitting?"

She lifted one shoulder to her ear and let it drop. "I love her enough to make sure she has the best life possible. Who wants an alcoholic as a stand-in mother? Amber wouldn't want that."

"Don't." He held up a hand. "Don't you dare say what my sister would want." Indecision warred inside him. "Did Amber know?"

Tenley flinched, and Mac had his answer.

"I'm a fool. Everyone knows. Everyone but me." His head fell forward, chin thumping against his chest. "The one person who you should've been able to trust is the one you pushed away." He spun on his heel. "Well, you don't have to worry about it anymore. I understand now." She'd never trusted him with her whole heart, with all her fears and her troubles. She'd withheld those pieces of herself and only given him the side she thought he could handle.

It was too much betrayal. He didn't know where they were supposed to go from here. When he first came back to Tamarack Springs, it was with the sole purpose of getting Jade back to Chicago. The longer he stayed, the more he remembered why he loved this place and the people who lived here.

For a few brief flashes, he'd remembered why he loved Tenley, and the desire to push her away had waned. It returned now in full force. He'd never asked anything of her, except that she love him. And she couldn't do that. She pushed him away and chose to suffer through her troubles alone.

Longing filled him. More than a desire to care for Jade and protect Tenley. More than a need to save. This need split his heart wide open. A need to be loved.

"Take care, Mac." Tenley's voice sent a shot of adrenaline through his veins.

He spun to face her, taking in her neutral expression and hands shoved deep into her purple hoodie. His gaze traveled down to her feet. Purple socks. He'd missed it before but saw it all clearly now.

Sadness sat in the room with them, filling the air with a gummy feeling that clung to him like cobwebs.

Mac nodded, forcing himself back to the conversation. What now? The ache intensified. It used to be easy, knowing what to say to Tenley.

The chasm between them yawned deep and wide. One step and he'd fall in, never to be seen again. Loving Tenley was fraught with peril. This time, he'd be going in with a full arsenal of equipment to keep him safe.

Love was never safe.

Exciting. Terrifying. Never safe. Not for him.

"I'm sorry for being blunt." Tenley had retreated behind a mask of indifference.

He stood frozen in the center of her kitchen. "You said what you needed to say."

Tenley ran her hand down his arm and grasped his fingers. "But I have something to say now that I couldn't say then. I love you, Mac. Always."

His breath rushed out, leaving him empty for a flash of time before a shining light took up residence in his chest and bloomed outward. "We can't, Ten. Too many obstacles, remember?" But, oh, how he wanted to believe it could happen.

"The only thing standing between us is the past. A list of wrongs I committed and the pain I caused." She pressed something hard into his palm. "I'm not going to chase after you and beg. But I'll be here. If you can forgive me, you know where to find me."

He stepped away, choked back a sob he was sure Tenley's parents could hear from their house. Tenley's face—her beautiful face—crumpled.

He cleared his throat, rubbed angry fists across his eyes, stalked across the living room, slapping his leg for Zeus to follow. "I have an appointment with Leonard on Monday. We'll sort this out then, but I'm taking Jade with me." If he stayed here one more minute, he didn't know what he'd do.

Keep telling her she'd made a mistake.

Say something he couldn't take back.

Kiss her until the world stopped spinning.

Everything he'd thought he knew about them, about their love, was false. How did he come to terms with that?

Tenley followed him into Jade's room and stood in the hallway while he scooped the little girl up and held her close. She muttered in her sleep but quieted when he told her where they were going.

Throughout the walk from the house to the truck, he waited

for Tenley to argue. She remained silent as stone. Giving up. It made no sense to him that she'd fight so hard only to quit now. Maybe because she knew she'd never win if he contested the will. *When*. When he contested the will.

He'd wanted to trust Tenley with Jade's well-being, but she'd broken his trust too many times.

Once Jade was buckled in his truck, he pried his fingers open. Resting against his palm, he found the wedding band she'd bought for him. The black titanium band glinted in the moonlight, the softness of the color contrasting the strength of the material. Like Tenley. Like himself and the riotous feelings for Tenley that always resided in his heart.

CHAPTER TWELVE

CONFESSION WAS SUPPOSED to be good for the soul. So why did she feel so bad? Tenley rubbed her fists into her eyes, grinding out the scratchy feeling left over from the hours of crying. Her phone trilled her alarm for church, eliciting a groan. She rolled over and covered her head with her pillow. She didn't want to leave the house, much less explain to her family why her eyes were red.

That was the easy part.

She had to tell them about Jade. She and Mac were probably well on their way to Chicago by now. He'd said he wanted to talk to Leonard on Monday, but she knew that once he took a second to think, he'd decide to leave Tamarack Springs.

They were both too good at running away.

Tenley's phone shrilled again, this time with a text message. She groaned and rolled over, grabbing the phone and scanning the message before thumbing off a response to Mom that she'd not forgotten about dinner after church. She considered feigning an excuse not to go but rolled to her feet and resigned herself to the inevitable.

She managed to get through church without any problems other than a few concerned glances. Brody caught her elbow on the way out the door. Tenley tugged her arm free once they reached the parking lot. "Sheesh. Does Callie let you man-handle her like that?" She frowned at her brother.

"What's going on?" He leaned in close, his concerned gaze almost undoing her control.

She puffed her cheeks full of air and let it out in a slow exhale. "I can't talk about it here." She angled her head toward the crowd of curious onlookers.

Brody glanced back and nodded once. "We'll see you at dinner."

Not a question but a demand. She was surrounded by stubborn men who wanted to protect her. Good grief. Was she really going to complain about that?

Yeah. Kind of.

An urge to grin caught her by surprise. Tenley coughed to cover it and slipped into her truck to follow the rest of her family back home.

By the time they'd all gathered in the kitchen around plates of pot roast and root vegetables with fresh sourdough bread on the side, Tenley's stomach was a writhing mass of tangled knots.

Brody caught her eye. Under the table, his boot thudded against her calf.

Tenley scowled at him. "Mom, Brody's kicking me."

"Brody." Mom admonished with a wry twist to her lips.

"Tenley has something to tell us." He cocked his head to the side. "Don't you."

Again, not a question but a demand.

Tenley tightened her grip on the hem of her shirt.

Callie looked back and forth, her eyes wide. "Oh, this can't be good. Last time Tenley made that face was the day Brody put a frog under her hat."

Molly snickered into her napkin. Luke's gaze bounced from adult to adult. "Where's Jade?"

Tenley's heart lurched in her chest. She gave Brody a pleading look as tears welled in her eyes. She choked them back, but not before Brody fully understood what was about to happen.

"Jade's with Mac." Brody smiled at Luke, then shot a look at Molly that she understood right away.

Molly scooted her chair closer to Tenley and took her hand.

"I told Mac everything." Tenley forced her throat to keep working. "I'm not sure what happens next. He said he'd talk to Leonard tomorrow." But he'd not shown up at church, which was a big red flag. He'd promised to bring Jade to church.

She couldn't look at her family and see the disappointment. She scooted away from the table, her chair scraping the linoleum in a harsh screech. Her legs wobbled as she stood and made her way to Dad. She fell to her knees by his side and put her forehead on his arm. "I'm sorry. It's my fault. If I'd never called you that day, none of this would've happened. It's my fault you were hit." She might be a different person if not for that one choice.

"Don't." Dad put a hand on the back of her head and stroked her hair. "Don't you dare blame yourself for any of this. You made your mistakes, and you paid the price for them."

"That doesn't mean I shouldn't suffer the fallout. You're in that chair because of me. Amber went out that night because of me. Mac's leaving, or is already gone, because of me." And he took Jade with him. She didn't say that part, not with Luke listening in, but they all understood the implications.

"Mac's angry." Brody spoke up. His voice carried a weight to it, an understanding. "Once he has time to think things through, he'll come around." The assurance might've worked if Brody didn't reach for Callie's hand and squeeze like his life depended on it.

"If you're asking me for forgiveness, then you have it. You've had it all along because I never blamed you." Dad put a finger under Tenley's chin and lifted her head. "I love you. No matter what. Everyone is responsible for their own decisions. You couldn't know what would happen, and I would do it all again if it meant keeping you safe."

"But I was safe. I called you, then I changed my mind and went to the party anyway." Tenley sniffed back tears. "If I'd just stayed. If I'd waited for you to get there."

"Then we both might've been in the car when the driver crossed the yellow line." Dad kissed the top of her head. "The world is full of what-ifs and maybes. You can't play that game, Tenley. It's one that everyone loses. Make peace with yourself, forgive yourself, and keep moving toward God."

Keep moving toward God. The words hit a sweet note in her heart and resonated.

Small arms wrapped around Tenley's neck. Luke hugged her tight. "Love you bunches, Aunt Tenley."

"I love you too, squirt." She patted his arms and did her best to let go of the past that had hounded her every step for the last ten years. She'd tried to make up for it. The equine center became part of that, but it also felt like the thing she'd always been meant to do. She pushed to standing, grabbed Luke's feet, and carried him up with her.

Luke laughed and squeezed tighter.

Tenley bounced him a few times before detaching his arms and returning him to his chair. She eyed her family. "I'm going down to the barn." Her throat worked in a hard swallow. Tears blurred her vision, and she bolted.

Her breaths turned ragged by the second step down the long driveway. A sob worked its way up her throat and slipped out against her will. Dad forgave her. He'd never even blamed her. The weight she'd carried for ten years lifted. Tenley released it with a gulp of honeysuckle-scented air and stumbled into the barn.

Horses shuffled, a few of them poking their noses over the doors to watch her. Tenley scratched foreheads and patted sleek necks on her way down the aisle. She slipped into Shadow's stall, breathed deep through her nose and buried her face in

Shadow's neck. The mare chuffed and ground hay but submitted to her affections.

"Tenley?" Brody stopped at the stall door, his eyes hidden beneath heavy brows.

"I'm sorry." She combed Shadow's mane with her fingers. "I understand if you can't forgive me."

Brody's long exhale lasted a full ten seconds. "I'm sorry too. I was so angry with Callie that I missed it. I didn't see that you needed help. I didn't want to look too hard at what you were doing. Growing up, you were always the pesky sister tagging along, begging to do everything I did."

Yep. She'd been like that. Her lips quirked at the memory. "And Molly spent all her time in the kitchen, learning how to bake."

"Well, you quoted lines from books all the time. I guess we all have our own quirks." Brody shifted his weight and cleared his throat. "When I figured out you were drinking, I told myself that it was nothing serious. That you'd outgrow it once you realized it was wrong. I had no idea you'd been drinking for years."

The knot in her throat swelled. "Then Dad got hurt and Callie left." She stepped away from Shadow and angled toward her brother. "I wish I'd made different choices." A shudder twitched her shoulders. Shadow nuzzled the middle of Tenley's back as though to offer comfort. "I should have been here to help you that night. I should have done a lot of things different."

"I knew you'd been invited to a party." Brody removed his hat and whacked it against his leg. "I'm as much to blame as you. I should've stepped in and made you come home. I thought maybe you'd choose your family." The words were caustic, but his soft tone said he meant them with earnest hope. "I wanted my sister back. The one who rode horses with me and nagged me every day because she was fearless in ways I wasn't."

"I'm beginning to think fearlessness is not a desirable trait for me."

"It is when it means you're not afraid to go after what you want." Brody looked at her, long and hard. "You still love Mac."

"It's too late for me and Mac." Her heart raced, the pitter-patter of adrenaline kicking in among the unfurling anger. "He doesn't trust me."

"Neither did I. Not for a long time after you came back from rehab. But you never stopped trying to prove you were worth trusting. Don't stop with Mac either." He offered a sad smile. "And I'm not mad at you. I've never apologized for all the things I've said over the years, or the way I treated you. I was mad at myself for not seeing it sooner."

"Seeing what?" She leaned against Shadow's shoulder and let every breath bring a release to the pain.

Brody settled his forearms on the stall door. "That you had a problem. I was so focused on my life, on keeping the ranch going, that I neglected you. I let you fend for yourself instead of offering a lifeline."

"It wasn't your place to save me." Just like it wasn't Mac's. Something the men in her life never seemed to understand. "I had to reach my own breaking point. I had to want sobriety for myself and no one else." She focused on talking through the pain cinched around her heart. "The responsibility was never yours to carry, big brother."

"Maybe Dad's right on this one."

Big words for Brody. He'd been the epicenter of anger around which Tenley revolved. Realization settled in. She'd wanted his approval the way she wanted Mac's trust. With acceptance came loyalty. With loyalty came love. With love came an end to the torment.

"How do we forgive?" The question tumbled out. "The person who hit Dad and then ran? I've tried to forgive them, but it's even harder than forgiving myself."

Brody stared down the barn aisle, a crease between his eyes. "I don't know. But I think we should try."

"It's a decision you'll have to make a thousand times over." Molly bounded into the barn, her sunshine heart spreading waves of love through the chill in Tenley. Molly had suffered the same as the rest of them, with the added pain of losing her husband the year Luke was born, yet she never lacked a restorative spirit.

"And you've done it. Just like that?" Curiosity drew Tenley closer to her younger sister. "You've forgiven them." *And me?* Tenley left off the last bit. Now wasn't the time to bring the conversation back to her and her troubles. This was the first time they'd discussed forgiveness for Dad's accident. Ever. She wasn't about to ruin it with her own insecurities.

"I'm trying." Molly scrunched her nose and shrugged. "I was angry, but then I realized that my anger doesn't affect them. It only makes me more miserable. I can't afford more misery. Luke has enough instability in his life. I won't add more."

Short and sweet, Molly's argument silenced the older siblings. Tenley glanced at Brody, who stared at Molly as though she were a different species. "I have the weirdest family."

Tenley tossed Molly's words around, examining them from every angle. She'd heard similar before, about forgiveness not being for the person who'd done wrong but for the one wronged. The Bible said that a person should forgive not seven times but seventy times seven. That didn't sound right. How did a person just keep forgiving? Tenley frowned and twisted her cuff. If she forgave, who received the bigger gift?

Pressure built behind her eyes, and she scrubbed the gritty feeling away with her palms. Bitterness and anger led to hatred. Hatred helped no one.

Now she was getting somewhere.

What difference might she feel if she let go? Tenley offered a tentative prayer for relief, while making a conscious decision to make the next few minutes free of thoughts of revenge.

An image of her mornings at the library flitted through, of the kids who tromped in and out every Saturday. They were young, with all of life ahead of them. Mistakes were part of life. Some of them would choose to take the wrong path. They'd need forgiveness. Everyone needed forgiveness. God gave it freely.

"What do you want out of life?" Molly joined Brody at the door. "Do you want to keep going with this hovering over your head, or do you want to give it up and let go?"

What did she want? What woke her up each morning and was her last thought before bed at night?

Peace. The word drifted on a cloud, too high to reach. But she wanted it. Oh, how she wanted peace.

Shadow nudged Tenley's back. Her shuffle brought her head around to Tenley's chest, where she butted her nose into Tenley's stomach.

Brody hitched up his jeans. "I'm going for a ride." His swagger carried him away at a rapid clip. "Got some thinking to do."

"Yeah." Tenley stroked Shadow's neck. "Me too."

Molly held out a hand to Tenley. Tenley gripped her sister's fingers. "Thank you." Her voice broke.

Molly nodded and smiled through a glint of tears in her eyes. "Mac will come around." She cleared her throat. "Don't give up. You tried that once. Maybe this time you fight for Mac like you fought for your sobriety."

Did she dare?

MAC SAT ON the back porch with his legs stretched down the steps and his heels resting on the ground. Jade ran across the backyard, Zeus at her side. She'd asked about Rascal, but Mac hadn't been able to bring himself to drive back to Tenley's to collect the pup.

His thoughts ran ahead of him, and no matter how many

times he brought them back, he couldn't corral them into anything that made sense.

He felt betrayed by his sister and the entire Jacobs family. Tenley especially. That hurt worst of all.

"Got a minute?" The deep baritone came from the gate to Mac's right. He wheeled and found Brody sitting astride a horse, his wrists crossed over the saddle horn.

Mac considered denying Brody entry, but he knew it wouldn't do any good. Like Tenley, Brody had a tenacity that meant he'd sit there all night if he had to. Better to let him say whatever he'd come here to say and get it over with. He stood and opened the gate.

Brody dismounted and looped the horse's reins around one of the posts that anchored the picket fence. He followed Mac to the porch and waved at Jade, who ran over and hugged Brody's legs before loping off again.

Zeus gave Brody a cursory look and sniff before following Jade.

Mac sat and let the silence stretch. Best interrogation technique he'd ever learned. The guilty despised silence. Not that he wanted to interrogate Brody. Much. Questions about Tenley pinged around. He'd skipped church this morning to keep from coming in contact with her or her family. That hadn't stopped him from pouring out questions to God in prayer. Questions that were still unanswered.

"You leaving again?" When Brody finally spoke, concern carved a groove between his eyes. He removed his hat and settled it on his knee as he lowered to the step.

Mac stared across the yard. "I don't know."

"Fair enough." Brody settled in, and the sudden quiet surrounding them reminded Mac of why he and Brody had become natural friends. They knew when to leave the other to their thoughts and when to push. Brody plucked a blade of grass from the yard and twirled it between his thumb and forefinger. "Sorry I never told you."

"Family comes first." Mac let the weight of the words carry across the distance. "You were trying to protect her. I might not agree with what you all did, but I understand it." He shook his head. "That's not true. I'm furious. With Tenley. With all of you. You were my best friend aside from Tenley. Why wouldn't you tell me what she was going through?"

Brody frowned and leaned back, anchoring his elbows on the porch and stretching out his legs. "When Tenley came home the day of your wedding, she was a mess. Not just from the alcohol, but from realizing what she'd done. I've never seen her like that before. Not just the crying but the pure devastation. She was adamant that no one talk to you."

"And you agreed?" Mac snorted, disbelief evident in his tone.

"No." Brody met Mac's gaze, his own hard as steel. "After you left the barn, I drove Tenley to rehab. Stayed with her as long as I could. I was going to tell you when I got back. By then, you were gone." There was an accusation there, but Mac brushed it away. Brody drummed his fingers on the porch, the rapid beat revealing the tension he'd kept under wraps until now.

"We all made mistakes that weekend." Mac managed to admit.

"Well, maybe Tenley's stronger for having made this one." Brody stilled. "Took her a long time to hit the bottom and decide she wanted to claw her way out."

"And she wanted to do it without me." Mac sent a pointed look at Brody. "But you all were allowed to stay. You all knew. My sister knew."

A bark of laughter shook Brody's shoulders. "I see why you're in a knot now. Yeah, Amber knew. Not at first. Tenley told her about the same time you proposed to Laura. By then, Amber decided it was best if you didn't know. Said you'd found happiness finally."

"Yep." Mac squinted into the fading light and watched Jade throw a ball for Zeus. The pair were inseparable now.

What kind of relationship would they have if Tenley refused to let him help her? He wanted her to need him. As a partner throughout the rest of their lives.

Brody knocked his bootheels on the ground, the expression on his face growing serious. "Tenley has a hard time admitting when she needs help."

Did that mean she needed help now and wouldn't admit it? Much as he tried to stop it, Mac's chest tightened. Would he always feel this way? Worried that the next words out of someone's mouth would be to warn him that Tenley was drinking. He'd known for all of a day and the worry threatened to drown him. He held his breath and waited.

"What is with you two and not breathing? Tenley nearly turned purple this morning when she told us you'd taken Jade and left." Brody shook his head. "Don't make me jab you, because I will. Y'all are worse than toddlers, holding your breath like it'll change things. I just wanted to tell you that she still needs you. Don't know if you're interested in sticking around, but you're welcome to."

Mac released his breath with a deep sigh. "Your parents don't mind?" He chuckled. "Why'd that sound like I was asking if they'd let me take Tenley out on a date?"

"One has nothing to do with the other. But no, they don't. They're thrilled you're back. They just worry. Parental rights, I guess. Tenley is happier when you're around." He bumped his shoulder into Mac's. "And I've missed having my friend." He held his hand up, thumb and finger pressed together. "Just a little bit. We've had precious little happiness lately and there have been more smiles since you came home."

Mac stood.

Brody's next words stopped Mac cold. "Callie told me something last week, and it really stuck with me."

"Yeah? What's that?"

"It's the people we love the most who hurt us the most." Brody lurched to his feet, and he strode away, leaving Mac with his mouth hanging open.

He loved Tenley. Had never stopped loving her. But this love went deeper and had grown stronger since his return. What did Tenley need from him? Would it be better if he left it alone and let her move on? He thought maybe he understood Tenley better now. He understood why she might think letting him go was the best answer. But Mac could not restart this relationship with Tenley unless he felt absolutely certain he could be there for every hurdle.

Loving Tenley meant risking himself. His heart belonged to her, but did he have the strength to offer his trust after everything she did?

If she didn't answer his calls one night, would he immediately leap to conclusions and accuse her of drinking?

He was so afraid of losing her, of losing another person he loved, that he couldn't think past the panic. Brody's tack jangled as he mounted up and rode away.

"Uncle Mac, I can't find my stuffed horse." Jade's wheedling tone caused Zeus to whine.

Mac raised his head and found Jade standing in the middle of the yard. "Where did you have it last?"

Her face scrunched into a frown. "I was throwing it for Zeus since I lost his ball." She shrugged. "I didn't see where it went."

Mac stood and stretched. "I'll help you look."

"Can't Zeus find it?" Jade motioned at the dog lying in the grass nearby.

"Zeus isn't a tracker. He doesn't find things." Mac held out his hand to Jade "Come on. We'll look together."

"I wanted Zeus to get it." Jade pouted. "Zeus, find the horse." She mimicked one of Mac's hand motions, the one that sent Zeus away. He'd used it that night when he'd thought someone broke into Tenley's house.

Jade must have been awake and seen him.

Zeus lifted his head and whined. He licked his lips and sat up, attention riveted on Mac.

"Look, he wants to help." Jade tried again. "Zeus, find."

"He doesn't understand." Mac squeezed her fingers. "Zeus's specialty is protection."

Zeus stood and nosed the ground. His tail swished high in the air and he spun in a circle then streaked toward the fence.

"He'll find it." Jade gave a decisive nod. "I believe in him."

Oh, the faith of a child. Mac pressed his lips tight to keep from saying anything that might hurt Jade's feelings.

He wouldn't hurt her for the world.

You know where to find me. Tenley's voice ricocheted through his head, giving him freedom to move. He knew what he needed to do, but it would take time. It felt wrong to leave without saying goodbye, too much like a repeat of the past or an attempt to teach Tenley a lesson. It was neither.

He needed to prove that he was in it for the long haul. Words were not sufficient for that.

Jade squealed. "He did it!" She jumped up and down, pulling on his arm.

Mac squinted at the dog racing toward him with a fuzzy stuffed animal in his mouth. The dog ran to Jade and sat.

"Drop it." Jade pointed at the ground.

Zeus opened his mouth and the stuffed horse hit the ground.

"Good boy." Jade threw her arms around Zeus's neck and loved on him. "See. He just needed me to believe in him."

THE NEXT MORNING, Mac settled Jade into the seat beside him. Leonard sat across from them, his gnarled hands knotted together atop the desk. His gray suit was rumpled, and his tie hung slightly crooked, but his demeanor was all business. "You're sure about this?" Leonard reached into a side drawer and removed a file. "Last time we spoke, you wanted a reason to change the current situation." He eyed Jade meaningfully. "Took me a while, but I found this."

Mac took the proffered folder and flipped it open. Images of Tenley's arrest record stared back at him in black-and-white. Lank hair hung around her face, and a dazed expression lingered in her haunted eyes. He didn't recognize this Tenley. She was a stranger to him. His stomach knotted. Until this moment, he'd been able to tell himself that it didn't matter. Maybe it was even a ruse from Tenley to push him away. He couldn't deny it any longer. He had undeniable proof. Mac scanned the document that listed Tenley's infraction as drunk-and-disorderly, snapped the folder shut and handed it back to Leonard. "We don't need that. I've made up my mind."

Leonard's weathered and worn face creased into a smile. He patted the desk with both hands. "Well then. Let's get on with it." He retrieved a stack of forms and grabbed a pen.

Jade fidgeted in her seat as boredom settled in. Mac watched her from the side while he answered Leonard's questions and then signed the paperwork.

Leonard held out a hand to Mac. "If it means anything, I think you made the right choice."

Mac let his own grin match Leonard's as he shook the older man's hand. "Coming from you, that means a lot."

Leonard held up a hand to halt them when Mac stood and reached for Jade's hand. "Before you go, I have something for Jade." He removed the lid on a crystal candy dish, revealing an assortment of mints.

Jade flashed a questioning look at Mac, then grabbed a green peppermint when he nodded. She popped the candy into her mouth and spoke around it. "Can we see Tenley now?"

Mac winced slightly. "Not yet. There are a few more things to take care of." He snuck a look at his phone and the unanswered calls from his captain in Chicago. They were increasing in frequency, and Mac knew he walked a thin line, ignoring the calls.

Once they were in his truck and headed toward the Jacobs' family ranch, Mac tried to relax. Everything was moving as it should. According to Brody, Tenley was at the Wells's ranch with Callie. Which meant Mac and Jade could visit Margaret and Peter before they left town.

Jade bounced in her seat. "Are we going to take Rascal with us?"

"Not this time." Mac drummed his fingers on the wheel. "Tenley will take care of him until we get back."

Jade puckered her lips in a grimace but didn't argue. She waited for him to stop the truck before she unsnapped her seatbelt and grabbed for the door handle.

Mac followed Jade up the steps and rapped his knuckles on the front door.

Margaret answered with a smile and pushed open the squeaky screen. "Come on in. You don't have to knock, Mac." She swatted at him with a kitchen towel. "You're family. Same as always." Mac followed Margaret into the kitchen, where Peter sat at the table working on a saddle. He glanced up when Mac entered and grunted a hello. "Almost done, Mac. Brody needed these fenders replaced weeks ago, but he's not had the time."

"No rush." Mac took a seat and waited.

Jade scampered over to Margaret, her chatter filling the kitchen.

Peter poked the leather strap of a new fender through the saddle tree and pulled. The leather slid home with a snap, and he picked up the stirrup from in front of Mac. "Brody gave us the rundown on what's happening." He lifted one bushy eyebrow. "Sounds like a good plan." A beat of silence, then, "Not sure of your motives."

"Sad fact is, I'm not sure of them either. But I know I have to go back to Chicago. Wrap up things that need tending." He tugged the old saddle fender out of Peter's way and ran his hand along the ragged edge of leather that would've snapped soon. Only a matter of time. That's what it all came down to. Time. "I need to clear my head. Make sure this is what I want, but this place—" he made a vague motion with his hand "—this town, it gets to you, you know? I'm too close."

"I get that." Peter buckled the hobble strap around the fender and scrubbed a knuckle over his cheek. "Can you look me in the eye and tell me you're not running off without telling Tenley as some way of punishing her? Of punishing us in asking that we keep this from her?"

Mac met the older man's gaze. "Peter, you've been like a father to me since high school. I'd never ask you to hurt Tenley. I'll be back." The truth of it landed between them. He was coming back. Back to Tenley. Back home where he belonged.

Peter's gaze followed Mac when he stood. Once full and jovial, the older man's cheeks were now sunken, the cheekbones sharp.

His smile never changed, and it appeared now as a rainbow after a storm. "That's the Mac I remember. Sit and talk a while."

How did he keep positive? Mac sat, lowered his hands to his knees, and pressed his back into the chair. "Sorry I didn't come back sooner." The response came without thought, but Mac realized as it left his lips that he meant it.

"I'm not going anywhere." Peter chuckled at his own joke before growing serious. "Tell me, son. What do you want from Tenley?"

Restitution. Forgiveness. Tenley. Each word battered harder than the one previous. Had he come back for her? He'd not thought so. Not when he first arrived. He'd come back for Jade. But he knew, deep in his heart, he knew that a part of him had hoped for reconciliation.

The moment Tenley walked into his life, things shifted. She became the center of his life. Her gravity hauled him in and put him in orbit so that he saw her. Only her. He broke away from the black hole of Tenley's grasp.

"Jade." Mac spoke past the lump in his throat. "I came back for her. To make sure she had a good life." And that she'd not be in Tenley's life. "I'm sorry I left the way I did. When Tenley and I—"

Mr. Jacobs shook his head. "There's no need for you to apologize for that. You had to protect yourself. I know it. Tenley knows it. She doesn't care to think about it, but she knows it." He cleared his throat and blinked away tears. "She's a strong woman, Mac. Stronger than any of us truly know. When she's taken with something, nothing will stand in her way."

How well he knew. Even when she chose to focus on the wrong thing.

"Do you think she'll ever forgive me?"

"I think she already has. I saw how she looked at you. That girl loves you."

A memory of Tenley curled into all the empty places in his heart. He'd missed her. Every waking moment during their years apart. Her presence righted his trajectory. But could he trust her? Did he have the strength to love her again, knowing each day was a precipice, a knife edge, between her and sobriety?

The amount of trust required sapped his strength. *This is why cops don't marry criminals.* Unfair though it was. Divorce rates among cops were sky-high. Tenley might be a criminal in the milder sense of the word, but deep in the archives of Bridgeport's police department, a file with her name on it and a list of infractions remained.

He'd seen it for himself, and even now, doubt tried to wiggle its way in.

Mac slammed the door on his fears and stood. "Let's go, Jade. I'm going to need your help in Chicago."

CHAPTER THIRTEEN

TENLEY WANTED TO hug the early morning sunshine. One week with forgiveness for herself clashed with missing Mac and Jade. The conflicting emotions overwhelmed her, growing stronger every day. She needed this run more than ever. She hurried through a series of stretches before setting out in a ground-eating trot. Knowing she'd regret the pace, she pushed her legs faster. Maybe, if she ran fast enough, she could out-run the past...and the pain.

She'd messaged Mac to no avail. Voicemails went unanswered. She'd driven over to Amber's house, but the windows were dark and the front door locked. Mac's truck gone from the driveway. He'd retreated to Chicago, leaving her with little more than a quick note that he'd be in touch.

Thundering heartbeats slammed against her ribs. Dappled rays of sunlight flecked the trail, creating highlights of light and shadow, a masterpiece of color bouncing off thick tree trunks and beaming through the green leaves. Lungs burning, she passed the one-mile marker standing upright in the shade, a picket of success. Pine filled her nose with every breath, soft evergreen needles cushioning each pounding stride.

Clicking the timer button on her watch, she kicked the pace up another notch.

An ache settled below her right lung. *Breathe, Tenley.* In. Out. Repeat.

Pain seared her chest, lancing through like a thunderbolt as memories assailed her vision. Dad crumpled in a heap amid the wreckage. No sign of the person who'd crashed into his car. The doctor's prognosis and the paralysis. Mac's leaving. Never seeing Jade again. She bit her tongue to keep from screaming and increased her pace.

Another marker flashed by.

She ignored her watch. What did it matter? Time held no quarter here. It did not ease the agony.

A flash of color by her side wrestled her attention from the past. Mac. He nodded, mouth in a flat line, eyes bright. Brown hair flopped with every footfall. Tanned arms pumped in rhythm with her own. Their feet landed in sync, legs eating up the miles.

"Hi," he said simply.

Athletic shorts and a blue tank top said he'd meant to be here today. Looking for her? He couldn't possibly know that she'd be here, running the trails at the ranch. Unless he'd planned it. Which meant that he'd talked to her family.

Confusion warred with a feeling of elation. What was he doing here?

She gauged his breathing. Steady. Exerted, but no worse than her own.

He inclined his head, giving her permission to set the pace. They were already blistering their way down the trail, but Tenley accepted the challenge and kicked into her last gear as easily as a racehorse nearing the finish line.

Mac's back. Her footfalls landed in a jarring tempo that matched the refrain. *Mac's back. Mac's back. Mac's back.* Her heart soared. He wouldn't come here like this if he meant to break her heart. She'd told him that he knew where to find her, and now he had.

Mac raced beside her, never faltering or falling back.

Even though she wanted to be alone, she couldn't deny the security of long-ago friendship, giving her a glimmer of hope. How long since she'd allowed hope to sneak into her life?

He swiveled his head in her direction, switching between watching her and the trail.

Tenley read the concern in his expression. She'd never been one for exercise, but with sobriety on the line, she needed an outlet. Running gave her that. An escape, and an endorphin rush.

A slow grin spread across Mac's face. He eased a step ahead, a challenge. His warm acceptance traveled the length of her bones, spreading a heated glow that had nothing to do with exercise. Tenley shut it down and cranked out another gear. They didn't need words. It was enough that he was here. At her side.

Two miles later, the dirt path changed to grass, and Tenley checked her pace, dropping her speed every few feet until they reached the trail's peak. Tenley slowed to a fast walk until she reached the rock ledge jutting out over the valley.

Coming to a stop, she nodded a thanks at Mac. Questions bombarded her. Why had he come back? Did he want to stay? She longed to ask. Not yet, though his running with her today put in solid groundwork that might be built on if she allowed it. Did she want to allow it? A month ago, an adamant no would have burst out. After a week without him, a definitive yes crept in.

Side by side, they strolled to the edge. Rock crumbled beneath Mac's feet and fell into the void. A deep valley spread out below the ridge, a forest of trees proudly showing off bright green foliage. Wind howled over the break, whipping Mac's shirt against his chest and causing Tenley to slap a hand on her ball cap to keep it from flying away.

Tenley dropped to the ground and dangled her feet over the edge. "I never get tired of this view."

"Or of giving me heart palpitations every time you do that." Mac rubbed his chest.

Patting the rock beside her, Tenley grinned at him. "Come on. You don't have to put your feet over, just sit here with me. You won't fall."

"You underestimate how much I'm shaking in my shoes right now. I'd vibrate right off the edge like a Slinky on stairs." He held out a hand to prove he wasn't kidding. His fingers spasmed and jerked.

Her laughter filled the air. "Sorry. It isn't funny."

Mac slipped off a backpack that she hadn't noticed and unzipped it. He pulled out two water bottles. Condensation trickled across his knuckles. He handed her one and cracked the seal on the other. After taking a long drink, storm-filled eyes locked on her. "You plan on setting the same pace going back?"

Laughter slipped out before she could stop it. "Maybe."

"We need to talk first."

Pure, unadulterated fear pressed a hard ridge against her spine. He'd seen her past, lived part of it with her, but the darkest parts, the bits that chased her, always looking for a way back into her life, those she could not let him see. Her past impeded their ability to coexist. "Okay."

She saw their chance at reconciliation slipping away. She reached for it. "I'm sorry I never told you. If I'd shared my struggles with you, maybe things would've turned out different."

"You used to tell me everything." He crushed the bottle in his hands, the plastic emitting a protest. "At least, I thought you did."

Step eight of the twelve-step program darted through her thoughts. *Made a list of all persons we had harmed and became willing to make amends to them all.* She was willing. The list under her pillow attested the fact. Step nine, though. That one made her grind her teeth. *Made direct amends to such people wherever possible, except when to do so would injure them or others.*

She'd apologized to him. Her explanation weighed the air between them. Even after their talk last week, she didn't feel like she'd properly explained herself. Not that it really made a difference, but she had to try.

Standing, she put a hand on his forearm. "I thought I was doing the right thing. I see now that I was selfish. I wallowed in my pain and kept it from you. I put on a front to the one person I knew I could trust with my whole heart. I pushed you away." She shook her head and tucked the water into the crook of her elbow so she could take Mac's hand in both of hers. "I wanted to save you from me, from the person I'd become."

His callused fingers wrapped around her wrist and squeezed. "Loving you was the only thing I ever wanted. We both made mistakes. If you'd told me about your alcoholism, I would have tried to save you. Like you said. Maybe we needed to go through this valley of trials."

Movement in the trees throughout the valley snagged Tenley's attention. "Like the seasons change, so too do the seasons of the heart." She firmed her resolve and met Mac's eyes. "I want a second chance, Mac. Let me prove to you that I can be worthy of forgiving."

"You don't need to earn forgiveness." Mac ran his thumb across her knuckles.

What did he mean? Was he not even going to give her a chance? "People change. Molly says that things about people change, even if the whole person is the same. This is something about me that has changed."

Giving her a look that said he wasn't going to back down, Mac sat on the overhang, either to show he'd overcome his fear or to prove her point about change, and patted the left-over space. "Talk to me."

Tenley took a breath and joined him. "I'm still in love with you." There. She'd said it. The words were out there, wild and free. Mac could do what he wanted with them. Maybe this time he'd listen.

She shot to her feet. It hurt too much to stay still. She needed movement, the slap of feet on packed dirt. The rush of air over her face and the pounding tempo of an exerted heart. Not this bludgeoning pain ripping her apart from the inside out. Does one ever recover from betraying family? So far, the answer was no. Though she'd not been the one behind the wheel, she could have been. It should have been her who took the injuries. Molly touted forgiveness as the key to moving forward.

How could Tenley forgive a stranger for ruining Dad's life when she couldn't forgive herself for the pain she'd inflicted on Mac?

Mac took her elbow, grounding her with him, here at the ridge. Every heartbeat drummed in her ears, the whoosh drowning out his words.

He peered into her face, then pulled her into his arms.

Home.

It felt right, being here again. And that's why she couldn't stay. Tenley pulled away and bolted down the trail. He'd come back, but she wasn't worthy of a second chance.

Seconds later, Mac set his stride to hers and they ran together. Each step took her deeper into the past, dredging up history she'd rather stayed buried.

When she reached the edge of the forest and their old meeting place came into view, Tenley skidded to a halt and leaned over, planting her hands on her knees. Her breaths wheezed in and out. She'd not meant to come here. It hurt to stand in the place where the past saturated the heady air and know they didn't have a future. Not one that included the other. Mac still hadn't acknowledged her proclamation. She waited with bated breath.

"Ready for breakfast?" Mac stretched, bending his leg back in an arc. Unlike her, his breathing could barely be called labored. He looked ready to go again.

Tenley did her own stretches, her legs feeling more like wet noodles with each minute that passed. "You'd eat after a run like that?" Her heart fell. Here she'd offered him her everything and he was thinking about food.

Mac shrugged. "You keep running away every time we try to talk."

"Hey. You bolted after the homecoming." Tenley felt the need to point that out even as Mac smiled at her.

"Okay. So we're both good at running away." He stretched his other leg. "What if we both agreed to stop pushing the other away?"

MAC CHUCKLED AT the indignant expression Tenley gave him. He stretched his left arm across his torso, twisting at the waist, then repeated the movement with the other arm. "Join me?" He motioned at the bench.

The backpack scratched his skin through the thin shirt. A lump burned in his throat when Tenley shot him a disbelieving look. "Please. You took off before I was done talking."

She huffed but settled on the stone bench that he'd built during their senior year in high school.

Mac slid the backpack from his shoulders and dropped it onto the ground before moving to sit beside Tenley. He stretched out his legs, attempting to relax the jumping muscles.

Tenley rolled her head from side to side, then stretched her arms over her head. "What did you want to say?"

His grin returned. "You're just as impatient as I remember."

She punched his shoulder. "I said I still loved you, and you didn't answer. Then you packed up Jade and left town. I said it again and you ignored me. Forgive me if I'm not in the mood to kid around." She looked out over the valley. A sigh parted her lips. "I haven't been here in years."

"I remember the last time we sat here." Mac reached into the bag with one hand while draping his other arm across the back of the bench. Nerves attacked, and his fingers clenched around the papers he withdrew from the bag.

Tenley pinched her eyes closed. "You proposed here. We planned our wedding here. Our future. But all that's over now." She shifted sideways and drew her leg underneath her. "Please, Mac. Don't draw this out. If this is some kind of punishment, please know that there's nothing worse you can do to me. Get it over with. Tell me you want to move on."

"Is that what you want?" He stilled as a cold chill washed down his spine. Had he waited too long? It had taken longer than he thought to get everything together.

No. She said she still loved him. He trusted the raw emotion in her voice and the pure terror in her eyes when he didn't respond. If he could go back, he'd react differently, but she'd surprised him.

"I'm glad you left." Each word Tenley spoke drove the wreckage deeper into his chest.

He fought for air. Mac kept silent. Waiting, hoping for forgiveness. For abandoning her when she needed him most.

"You're the one person I didn't destroy." Tenley placed a shaking hand on his arm. "I couldn't see it then. How much my drinking hurt you. I refused to see how it impacted Brody and Molly. Mom and Dad. It wasn't until I came home from rehab that the veil lifted and I could see the trail of damage behind me. When I left, I was a mess. I had no idea what to do. I told myself for years that I made the right choice in driving you away."

Mac settled his hand on the back of her neck. "I want forever with you. That's all I've wanted since the day we started dating."

She blinked furiously. "I'm willing to fight for happily ever after. But only if you're willing to give me a chance. You said I can't earn your forgiveness. I understand that."

"You misunderstood me." Mac traced the curve of her jaw

with his forefinger. "I said you didn't need to earn forgiveness. Because you already have it."

"Oh." She breathed the word into the narrow space between them.

Mac pulled the papers from behind his back and pressed them into her lap.

"What's this?" She eyed the tri-folded papers like she would a snake. Her expression flickered from worry, to panic, to hope and then to resignation. Moving cautiously, Tenley unfolded the notarized will and testament and began to read.

A hand came up to cover her mouth. "Is this real?" She ran a finger across the gold seal and the notary stamp. "Why would you make up a will?" Her eyes widened. "Mac?"

"If anything happens to me, I want you to have sole guardianship of Jade." He tapped the pages. "If you're willing to give me a chance to make up for leaving you when you needed me most."

Her chin trembled. "I'd give you a hundred chances."

"Good." Mac gave a decisive nod. "I'm moving back to Tamarack Springs. Sheriff Hanks offered me a spot with the department. Jade and I packed up my apartment in Chicago." He brushed a tendril of hair over her ear. "That's why I was gone. I needed to clear my head, away from the influence of this place and all the memories here. And I needed to get the papers drawn up."

A smile brightened her eyes, like sunshine was pouring out of her. She flung her arms around his neck and held on. "I love you."

"It's always been you, Tenley." He wrapped his arms around her waist and pulled her close. "I tried to scrub you out of my life, but you've always been there. You're rooted in my heart so deep that nothing could pull you out."

"Are you calling me a weed?" She laughed into the side of his neck.

He pulled back far enough to catch her gaze. "You're the

most stubborn weed I've ever known. You're my first love, and God willing, my last." He hesitated. "If you'll have me."

"I wouldn't have it any other way."

His lips met hers, his eyes falling shut. The thrill of love cascaded through him. This was what it meant to come home again. To find peace amid the storm and chaos that life had thrown his way. He'd thought his life and all the love in it gone forever. He'd lost everyone through the years and struggled to trust that love might be worth the threat of pain and loss.

With Tenley in his arms and their future stretching before them in a golden path studded with the memories of their past, he knew they'd make it. They were older, wiser and more willing to trust each other. The jagged pieces of their past hurts only made them stronger.

EPILOGUE

One year later.

TENLEY RODE ALONGSIDE Mac up the winding trail carving its way through the forest of oak, maple and hickory trees. She tugged her hat brim down to shield her eyes as they emerged from the path and into the sunlight rising over the ridge. The sight took her breath away as pink and purple spread over the horizon. Her white dress fluttered in the breeze and the first rays of sunlight warmed her shoulders.

Zeus and Rascal trotted on either side of Jade as she rode ahead. Mac had done wonders for the pup in the last year, most of which he attributed to Zeus's calming influence. Mac's captain in Chicago had retired the K-9 and helped Mac through the process of adoption. Zeus spent his days playing with Jade and Rascal or loping alongside Tenley and Mac on their daily runs.

Mac reined his horse closer to Tenley and took her hand. They rode like that, boots and knees brushing with every stride, until they reached the outcropping. Jade waved and bounced in her saddle. "We're here!"

Laughter joined the sound of creaking leather as her family circled around. Jade rode over and stopped alongside Luke and Molly. Her dad turned his chair to face the approaching couple, her mother standing by his side.

Tenley felt a tug on her hand and glanced down, her gaze snagging on the engagement ring winking at her.

"Ready?" Mac grinned the mischievous smile from their youth, the one that sent her stomach tumbling and her heart racing. "I think it's time."

"Yeah?" She lifted an eyebrow. "What makes you say that?"

Mac motioned at her family—soon to be his too—and cupped a hand around his mouth. "Because I don't want to spend another day without you." He leaned in close enough to whisper. "I'm ready to see you walk down the aisle dressed in white, Tenley." He winked. "Or ride beside me all the way to the altar."

"Not afraid I'll bolt again?" After the last year of healing and growth, the previous insecurities didn't bait Mac into frowning.

He nudged his horse closer. "If you do, then this time, I'll follow you. And I won't stop until you do. We're in this together."

"I'm done running away from you, Mac." Her breath hitched. She nodded at the pastor waiting on horseback amid her family and their friends. "Today would've been our eight-year anniversary."

He squeezed her hand. "Everything worked out the way it was meant to."

"Just needed a little faith, trust and pixie dust." She winked at him and cupped his cheek. "You're all mine, cowboy."

"Always was." He answered before his lips touched hers.

"You're supposed to wait till he says the words," Luke piped in. He bounced in his saddle. "They're doing it wrong, Uncle Brody."

Brody grinned at Callie and tipped his hat in Tenley's direction. "I think we'll let it slide this one time."

The pastor grinned and cleared his throat. "Looks like we'd better get started."

Tenley looped her arm through Mac's and they nudged their horses forward amid whistles and cheers from all around.

Forever might not last as long as she wanted, but right now, with Mac by her side, it was long enough.

* * * * *

A Protector For Her Baby
April Arrington

MILLS & BOON

April Arrington grew up in a small town and developed a love for books at an early age. Emotionally moving stories have always held a special place in her heart. April enjoys collecting pottery and soaking up the Georgia sun on her front porch.

Books by April Arrington

A Haven for His Twins
An Orphan's Holiday Home
A Protector for Her Baby

Visit the Author Profile page at millsandboon.com.au.

Thou art my hiding place; thou shalt preserve me from trouble; thou shalt compass me about with songs of deliverance.
—*Psalm* 32:7

For grandmas, grannies, nanas, meemaws
and all the rest: thank you for loving us!

CHAPTER ONE

MALLORY KENT NO longer believed in New Year's resolutions. In past years, she'd made them with enthusiasm at the stroke of midnight beneath a burst of fireworks, hoping to improve her future. But soon the challenges of daily life—complete with all the obligations and pain—would resume, and every year she'd been left with the same feeling of failure. The same disappointment of losing more than she'd gained.

This New Year's Eve, she'd been left with two things in life. One, she didn't want. The second was the only thing of value left in her life.

Faith.

"Are you sure this is the place?"

Mallory glanced over her shoulder at the small sedan idling behind her in the darkness. One hour ago, the car had belonged to her. Now a stranger sat behind the steering wheel and the certificate of title, signed by Mallory, rested on the passenger seat she'd just vacated.

It wasn't the loss of the car that struck a deep chord of grief within her; it was the loss of the life she'd dreamed of having. A life full of love, family and safety with a husband who would protect rather than harm her. Leaving her home, belongings and job didn't coax the sting of tears to her eyes, but the loss of her well-being, trustful nature and personal dignity made her breath catch on a sob. And being forced to abandon everyone she'd known and loved to be able to live a peaceful life hurt most of all.

Blinking hard, Mallory fastened the top button of her long winter coat and tugged the plush hood lower on her forehead. Being adrift among strangers in unfamiliar surroundings with an uncertain future was…terrifying.

"Yes," she said. "This is it."

At least she thought so.

"Doesn't look like anyone's home." The woman behind the steering wheel lowered the driver's side window a bit more and leaned her head out, concern in her eyes.

Her complexion was bright and scarless—her face, most likely, had never felt the blow of a fist. Her gaze was clear, and her tone full of relaxed confidence.

All things Mallory used to possess…and never would again.

Jealousy and pain tore through her. Oh, how she wished she could go back. How she wished she'd had some kind of warning. How she wished others, like the stranger in front of her, knew how much they took for granted. How lucky they were to have lived a life of safety and security and to never have experienced the fear and pain she had.

Strangers like the woman before her meant well. They truly cared, said the right things and always offered to help, but they did so from the inside—a place of peace and protection—looking out at the suffering of others, never truly understanding. Because to understand was impossible unless they'd suffered through it themselves.

Mallory flinched and ducked her head. It wasn't right to feel this way. To resent the happiness and health of others simply because she'd lost her own. With each passing month, she could feel herself changing, becoming someone she no longer knew and, even worse, didn't want to know.

Immediately, she lifted her head, her lips parting to deliver an apology for her thoughts, to say something nice—anything to prove to herself that the kind, caring person she'd used to be still existed, somewhere deep inside.

"It's cold out," the woman continued. "You sure you don't want me to drive you into town? We passed a motel in Hope Springs not far from here. It looked like a nice enough place to lay your head for the night."

Mallory turned and studied the small cabin in front of her. There was a low glow in one of the front windows—the flicker of firelight, maybe?—and an ornate metal humming-bird, tacked beside the front door, was just visible in the gleam of the sedan's headlights.

"No, thank you," Mallory called out over her shoulder.

Log cabin, hummingbird sculpture. Forested seclusion among the Blue Ridge Mountains in North Georgia...

This was the place. Her new hiding spot. Or, hopefully, a starting point for establishing a new life somewhere safe. Safety was her top priority now. The unwanted responsibility she'd reluctantly taken on—after months of desperate prayer— had made it so.

Cheeks heating, Mallory lowered her head again.

"Well, if you're sure?"

Mallory summoned a polite smile, faced the stranger who sat in the sedan she no longer owned and nodded.

"Okay, then." The woman smiled. "Thank you for the great deal on the car. It's my New Year's present to myself."

Mallory patted the side pocket of her coat where she'd tucked a check for several thousand dollars safely inside. "Thanks for buying it so quickly. And for the ride. I know it must've been out of your way."

"No problem. I was happy to do it. Besides, now I can show off my new-to-me car to my friends at our party tonight." The woman smiled wider—a generous, carefree smile. "Happy New Year!" Her expression turned tender as her gaze lowered to Mallory's midsection. "I wish you both the best."

Mallory stiffened. Her weak smile vanished. She stood there, motionless, as the stranger backed the car out of the long dirt driveway. The headlights swept over the dormant lawn, the thick line of cypress trees, then settled on the paved highway before it disappeared into the night.

A brisk wind cut through the trees and shoved back her hood. She tugged it forward, exhaled heavily and watched the frigid wind break up the small white cloud of her warm breath.

"Just one step today," she whispered. "I'll take the next to-morrow."

Inhaling, she adjusted the strap of her small overnight bag on her shoulder, walked up the steps onto the porch and knocked on the front door of the cabin.

There was no response.

Goose bumps broke out over the back of her neck as cold wind cut through a gap between her ear and the hood of her coat. She glanced around at the dark, wooded surroundings. It wasn't late—only around seven thirty—but the early sunset and winter temperature made it feel like midnight. She tugged the strap of her overnight bag higher onto her shoulder, lifted her fist and knocked again, more forcefully this time.

A light flipped on inside the cabin, flooding through the front windows and pooling on the wooden slats of the porch beneath her tennis shoes.

Oh, what was her name? Mallory nibbled her chapped lower lip. Jennifer? Jessica?

Heavy footsteps approached on the other side of the closed door.

Jessie! That was it. Jessie Alden. The women's shelter was named Hummingbird Haven and its owner, Jessie Alden, lived in a cabin with a metal hummingbird hung by the door—this one. Jessie was the best at hiding women who didn't want to be found, or at least, that's what Mallory had been told.

The doorknob turned, wood creaked and the door swept open. She lifted her head and smiled. "Hi, I'm Mallory K—"

Her breath caught, choking her words. She stumbled back over the top step, one gloved hand fumbling for the porch rail, her hood sliding off her head.

"Whoa there." The deep throb of a man's voice barely penetrated the roar of her pulse in her ears. A big, masculine hand drew near, reaching for her elbow. "Caref—"

"Don't touch me!" She gripped the porch rail, steadied herself and forced her eyes to meet his.

They were hazel. A rich hazel dark with concern...or was it pity? How she'd grown to hate that look over the years.

"I'm sorry." He held his hands up, palms facing out, and stepped back. "I didn't mean to scare you."

She bristled. "You didn't."

His eyes held hers then his gaze roved over her face and lingered on her left temple. The concern in his eyes deepened.

Her face flamed. "I must have the wrong place." She moved down to the second step—slowly this time—and glared at his hands, her knees bent slightly, ready to bolt, if necessary.

"Wait."

The urgent tone in his voice forced her eyes back to his. She backed down another step.

"Sorry, I didn't mean to surprise you. Here, see for yourself. I've got nothing on me. It's just me." He lifted his arms out to the side as if to reassure her he wasn't a threat, exposing the wide expanse of his chest covered with a long-sleeved flannel shirt, and parted his long legs, encased in worn jeans, a couple of inches. His boots scraped across the wood planks of the porch with his movement. "I was only trying to help. To keep you from tripping over the steps. That's all."

The deep throb of his voice was soft, steady and calm. Concern still darkened his eyes and his expression was gentle. He returned her stare and remained motionless, save for the ruffle of his thick, blond hair in the wind.

He looked harmless enough.

A cynical laugh broke free of her chest and rose to her

throat, but she clamped her lips together and swallowed hard, forcing it back. In her experience, appearing harmless wasn't a reliable measure of potential cruelty.

She had loved, trusted—and married—a man years ago who she thought was harmless, loving and kind only to discover he was the exact opposite.

"I assume you're looking for Jessie." He spoke softly. So softly, she could barely hear him over the whistle of strong wind between them. "She's my sister-in-law. She owns this place—Hummingbird Haven, I mean. I'm Liam Williams."

He lowered his arms then held out his hand. When she didn't reach for it, he returned it to his side.

"I'm in town, visiting Jessie and my brother for the holidays." He gestured to a dirt road that curved around the back side of the cabin. "She's out back at the community center with the residents, getting ready to ring in the New Year with fireworks. I told her I'd keep an eye on the cabin in case someone were to—" he gestured awkwardly toward her "—show up. I promise you, I'm only here to help."

"How can I know that?" The words burst from her lips before she could stop them. "I mean, for sure? How do I know?"

He tugged a wallet from his back pocket, opened it and held it out. "Here's my license so you'll at least know I am who I say."

She hesitated then ascended the top step and leaned forward, eyeing the license inside the open wallet under the porch light.

Liam Williams. 2971 Magnolia Lane. Pine Creek, GA.

She looked up, her eyes tracing the strong curve of his jaw beneath a blond five-o'clock shadow. "You...your brother's married to Jessie?"

"Yes. She and Holt were hitched two years ago." He flipped the wallet closed and returned it to his back pocket. "You said your name is Mallory...?"

"Kent." She licked her lips, which were now parched, the split flesh stinging beneath the moist touch of her tongue. "Jessie's having a party?"

"Of sorts. There are several women and children living in the cabins on the acres behind us. Jessie and my brother got everyone together, served a big dinner and planned on putting together a New Year's Eve fireworks display for them in an hour or so. Though with the wind blowing like it is, I doubt that'll come to fruition."

"Oh." Her throat tightened. "I don't mean to disturb the party but I need to speak with her, please. It took a lot for me to get here and I don't have a ride back, otherwise I'd never intru—"

"You're not intruding." He smiled gently. All kindness and compassion. "Please, come in." Seemingly harmless.

Mallory pressed her chapped lips together and focused on the sharp sting of pain. "No, thank you. Would you please get Jessie for me? I'll wait out here."

He hesitated, his eyes narrowing on her left temple then her chapped mouth. A strong gust of wind rocked her back on her heels and he frowned. "Wouldn't you rather wait inside?"

Shivering, she wrapped her arms around her chest and glanced over her shoulder at the darkness behind her. Then she leaned to the side and peered past him into the interior of the cabin. An overhead light lit up the living room, which had a large couch and a recliner. A fire burned bright in a stone fireplace.

"It's warm in here," he continued. "There's a comfortable couch near the fire and I just cooked up a fresh batch of soup for supper. You're welcome to enjoy both."

Her stomach growled at the tempting offer and she licked her cold, dry lips again. "Y-you're alone in there?"

"No." His smile dimmed. "My mother's asleep in one of the bedrooms."

Something in his tone had shifted. There was a heaviness to it. One of…regret?

Mallory studied his face. Sad shadows clouded his eyes. "She's not attending the party?"

"No," he said. "She's not comfortable around a crowd and if they do manage to have the fireworks show, she wouldn't enjoy them. The noise unsettles her." He shrugged and smiled again—forced this time. "As I said, it's warm inside and there's plenty to eat. Your wait for Jessie will be a lot more comfortable in the cabin rather than out here."

At her silence, he said softly, "I promise you're safe here."

Her eyes met his again, clinging, searching for the smallest sign that what he said might be true. That in this cold, violent world some modicum of safety and kindness remained and could be trusted. The thought of it—her belief in the tenuous possibility—was what had carried her here, after all.

A small, hopeful refrain whispered through her, echoing through her heart and mind. The sound of it had been her guide for months now and in this moment, she could either embrace it as she'd been doing, despite the presence of this unexpected man…or turn back and fall prey to the doubts that had plagued each step she'd taken forward.

Have faith.

Mallory glanced at the dark, empty night behind her once more, inhaled deeply and then, holding his gaze, forced her trembling legs to carry her inside.

CHAPTER TWO

SHE WAS PREGNANT—very much so—and someone had hit her.

Liam clenched his jaw, followed Mallory inside the cabin and shut the front door. He kept his back to her, his hand tightening around the smooth doorknob as he drew in a calming breath.

He'd almost missed it—her thick coat had obscured the generous curve of her belly until she walked past him on shaky legs, clutching her overnight bag and tugging her coat tight across her chest. The material had stretched and clung to her protruding middle, drawing his attention.

The dark bruise on her left temple had been much more obvious—he'd noticed that right away—along with the slight swelling and discoloration around her left eye…as though the brunt of the injury had initially been inflicted there before fading with time. And the fear in her wide blue eyes and trembling frame had been almost palpable.

He was well aware of why Jessie established the women's shelter. He knew abuse occurred and how passionate his sister-in-law and brother were about helping women and children who'd fallen victim to it. He felt the same calling—to protect. That was why he hadn't hesitated when Jessie had asked him to stand watch at the shelter's intake cabin in the event that someone arrived, seeking help.

But knowing abuse occurred was different from coming face-to-face with the evidence of it…and he hadn't expected the surge of anger or disgust that rose within him at the sight.

Clearing his throat, he faced Mallory again and gestured toward the couch. "Please have a seat." He extended one hand slowly. "I'll take your bag, if you'd like?"

She studied his hand then her gaze traveled up his arm to his face, her eyes peering into his for a moment. "Yes, please."

Still moving slowly, he stepped closer and stretched his arm out. His fingers curled around the bag's strap as she passed it to him, taking care to avoid touching hers.

She nodded. "Thank you."

"You're welcome."

The fire crackled and she startled slightly, her hood sliding off her head as glowing embers sprayed against the iron fireplace screen.

"Nothing to worry about." He offered a small smile. "That screen's effective and the fireplace is up to code. Jessie used to live in this cabin with the twins before Holt renovated one of the larger cabins on a back lot for their new family and she never neglected anything."

She avoided his eyes. "She and your brother have twins?"

The thought of his rambunctious nephews widened his smile. "Yeah. They've got a toddler, too. A pretty little girl named Ava."

Her lips trembled and her hands seemed to move absently, lifting toward her belly then falling back to her sides without touching it.

Liam carried the bag across the room and sat it on the floor, out of the way, then returned to the center of the living room. "May I take your coat, too? I imagine it's carrying some of the chill from outside and you'll warm up faster if you sit on the end of the couch, closer to the fire."

She stilled, stared at him then the fire, and nodded slowly. "Thank you."

Her fingers, stiff and clumsy, unbuttoned the buttons on her coat, then she slid it off and held it out. She wore a gray sweater, long and loose, that draped low, almost to her knees.

He took the coat from her just as he had the bag, taking care not to brush his fingers against hers, and she immediately walked away and sat on the end of the couch, nearest the fire and farthest from him.

"I'll give Jessie a call and get us some soup while we wait." He hung her coat on a coatrack near the front door. "Vegetable beef okay with you?"

She nodded and her big blue eyes widened as she glanced up at him beneath her thick lashes. Her legs, long and slender, bounced nervously against the front of the couch, and her hands, balled into fists, nestled below her belly, making the generous curve of her middle even more prominent.

She continued to steal glances at him, wariness in her eyes.

For an instant, a familiar mix of tenderness and hesitancy streamed through his veins, surprising him. It was a sensation similar to the one he had each time he welcomed a skittish mare to his farm for the first time—a warmhearted urge to soothe and reassure.

"Would you like a piece of cornbread, too?" He glanced at her belly then averted his eyes and remained motionless, allowing her to examine him openly with what he hoped would be a greater degree of comfort. "I always make it sweet—not spicy—on account of my mother's tastes." He smiled slightly. "She says the peppers give her heartburn—especially when she was pregnant with me. I'm not sure if it does that to you, but just in case...you know, on account of your pregnancy."

She didn't answer at first and the fire continued to fill the room with crackles and pops. He began to think she wouldn't answer at all but then—

"Yes," she whispered. "Thank you."

He looked up then and met her eyes. "You're welcome."

She turned away, facing the fire again.

Liam walked to the kitchen, tugged his phone from his pocket and dialed Jessie's number. She answered on the second ring.

"Liam!" Music and laughter sounded in the background. "You ready for Holt to take your place and stand watch for a while? If so, this is the perfect time." She laughed. "We've just started a round of limbo and the kids would get a kick out of seeing you try to shimmy your six-foot-three self under that low stick!"

Liam grinned. For years, he never thought his twin brother would ever settle down in one place, much less marry. A nomadic bull rider, Holt had left their family's farm when he'd turned eighteen and toured the circuit with no intention of returning home or mending the estrangement between himself and Liam. But after unexpectedly becoming a father, falling in love with Jessie and embracing God's new purpose for his life, Holt had become the strong, selfless, honorable brother, father and husband Liam always knew he could be if he put his mind—and heart—to it.

Liam thanked God every night for renewing his bond with his brother and caring, high-spirited Jessie, who had become the sister he'd always wanted. Holt and Jessie brought much-needed light and laughter into his lonely life, and they'd been pillars of support over the past two years as his mother's health had rapidly declined.

"I imagine you'd get a kick out of seeing me embarrass myself, too," he said. "And Holt would probably tell you to record it for posterity."

She laughed again. "Honestly? Yep. I would. And yes, Holt would probably ask that, too. So why don't you come on down and let Holt keep Gayle company for a while? It's time you had a break."

Liam's smile fell. He walked to the opposite side of the

kitchen, farther away from the living room, and lowered his voice. "I can't. We have a guest. I need you up here, Jessie."

The music and laughter in the background faded, and the sound of a door opening and closing echoed down the line. A rush of wind sounded and the teasing tone in Jessie's voice vanished. "A woman or child?"

"Both."

"I'm on my way."

Liam disconnected the call, shoved the phone in his back pocket and grabbed two bowls from the kitchen cabinet. By the time he'd filled both bowls with soup, sliced generous portions of cornbread, gathered utensils and poured two glasses of sweet tea, Jessie had arrived.

She knocked once on the front door then entered, her gaze sweeping the room, meeting Liam's as he stood in the doorway of the kitchen, a glass filled with sweet tea in each hand.

"Thank you for coming so quickly, Jessie." Liam carried the glasses of sweet tea to the small table in the kitchen, set them down then glanced at Mallory, who still sat on the couch in front of the fire. "Mallory Kent, I'd like to introduce you to Jessie Alden, my sister-in-law."

Mallory, her face and neck now blushing a healthy pink from the warmth of the fire, stood slowly then walked across the living room and held out her hand. "Hi, Jessie. Thank you for coming to see me so soon. I'm sorry to have interrupted your party."

Jessie shook her head, her auburn ponytail slipping over one shoulder. "Please don't worry yourself. You haven't interrupted anything and I'm happy you came." She squeezed Mallory's hand gently then smiled. "But there is one thing I don't want to interrupt." She looked down at Mallory's round belly and smiled wider. "I imagine your little one's hungry for a warm meal right now and the smell of Liam's cooking even has me salivating."

Mallory looked down and stared at her belly. Her hands

moved toward it briefly, without touching, then lowered to her sides as before. "It does smell delicious and it's been a while since I ate lunch." She glanced at Liam, her mouth curving slightly. "Liam's gone out of his way to make me feel welcome."

Liam grinned. The slight curve of her mouth—a vague resemblance of a smile—sent an unexpected wave of warmth through his chest. "Please have a seat." He gestured toward the table and the extra place setting he had arranged for her. "The soup's nice and warm. I have salt and pepper, milk or water if the tea's too sweet, whatever you might like." He glanced at Jessie. "Would you like to join us? I made plenty."

Jessie shook her head. "Thanks, but I'm stuffed to the gills. All the residents brought a dish to the New Year's Eve party. We'll have leftovers for at least a week." She walked over to the small kitchen table, pulled out a chair then beckoned for Mallory to sit. "I'd like to talk with you while you eat, Mallory, if you don't mind? I have some questions and am eager to help you in whatever way I can."

Nodding, Mallory walked over to the table and sat down. "I'd like that. Thank you."

Liam hesitated then asked, "Would you like some privacy?" He shrugged when Mallory glanced up at him. "I don't mind eating in the guest room if you'd be more comfortable speaking with Jessie alone?"

Mallory held his gaze, her eyes searching his, then returned her attention to the place setting in front of her. "No." She picked up the napkin beside her bowl of soup, unfolded it and laid it in her lap. Her hands, pale and graceful, still trembled. "Please stay. I'm the one who showed up unannounced and you've gone to a lot of trouble to make me feel comfortable."

He hesitated. "If you're sure?"

She glanced at him once more. "I don't mind if you stay. I'd hate to disrupt your meal."

He pulled out a chair, sat then propped his elbows on the

table and folded one hand over the other. "I'll say grace." He bowed his head and closed his eyes. "Dear Lord, we thank you for your many blessings and the meal you've provided for us tonight. We ask that this food nourish and strengthen us so that we may continue to serve you."

A low rumble followed his last words.

Liam cracked one eye open and glanced at Mallory. Head bowed and eyes closed, she cringed as another growl emerged from her generous belly. Pale cheeks deepening to a fiery red, she quickly folded her hands in her lap, beneath the bulge of her belly, and her cute nose wrinkled.

She was adorable—surprisingly so.

Smiling, Liam continued, "We also thank you for bringing Mallory to our door tonight—for blessing Jessie and me with the opportunity to know her and enjoy this meal together and, hopefully, allow the three of us to enrich each other's futures. Your will be done. In Jesus's name, we pray…"

When Jessie and Mallory joined him on *Amen*, he opened his eyes, raised his head and inhaled the delectable scent of the soup steaming before him. "Smells delicious, if I do say so myself." He grinned at Mallory. "I'm as eager as you. Let's dig in, shall we?"

Her stomach rumbled again.

She lifted her head and smiled—a sincere one, this time— at his teasing expression. Despite the bruise that marred her left temple and the unfortunate circumstances she'd obviously endured, a flash of delight brightened her blue eyes and the hot flush in her cheeks receded, replaced by a pretty blush. "Yes. Let's do."

Brave *and* adorable. With the most beautiful smile he'd ever seen.

Liam ducked his head and redirected his attention to the food in front of him. She was extremely vulnerable. She—and her baby—were in trouble and she'd come here for help. His focus should be on ensuring she received that help. Allowing his thoughts to roam anywhere else—however innocent the territory—would not only be inappropriate and insensitive but disrespectful as well.

"So, Mallory," Jessie said. "Where do you come to us from?"

Mallory scooted her chair closer to the table then dipped her spoon into the soup. "Eton. It's a small town near the Cohutta Wilderness. A little more than an hour from here."

Jessie smiled. "I've heard of it. Never been there, but I'm told it's a beautiful community."

Mallory lifted her spoon to her mouth and closed her eyes briefly on a soft sound of appreciation. "Mmm." Swallowing, she returned her spoon to the bowl and dabbed her mouth with the corner of her napkin. "It is. Very small—quaint—with mountains surrounding all sides." She ate another bite of soup then said, "Everyone knows everybody."

Jessie lifted one eyebrow. "Sometimes that's not a good thing. Is that so in your case?"

Mallory nodded. "My ex-husband lives there. We moved there to be close to his family five years ago. I was twenty-five at the time, had no family of my own and looked forward to settling down." She winced, picked up her glass of sweet tea and drank deeply, then added, "Starting a family."

Jessie glanced at Mallory's belly with a gentle expression. "It looks like you'll still be doing that."

Mallory's hand fumbled as she returned her glass to the table, spilling a few drops of sweet tea on the cloth place mat. "Not by choice." Voice shaking, she grabbed her napkin and dabbed at the sweet tea stain. "I didn't mean that," she whispered. "I mean, I did choose to keep the baby. I just didn't choose…" Her chin trembled and she frowned, stilling the movement as she returned the napkin to her lap. "The act of conception."

Liam froze, his fingers tightening around the spoon in his

hand, the metal digging into his flesh. His eyes shot to Jessie whose smile died as she studied Mallory.

"May I ask..." Jessie said softly. "Was it your ex-husband who assaulted you?"

Mallory nodded.

Jessie moved to speak twice before finally asking, "Did it happen before or after you were divorced?"

Mallory lifted her glass to her mouth and drank deeply again before answering. "After."

Her expression grew drawn, and the color drained from her face.

Liam put his spoon down hastily and pushed his chair away from the table. "I'll leave you two alone t—"

"No!" Her tone was sharp—so sharp it made him flinch. "You don't have to leave." She jerked her chin at him, anger flashing in her eyes. "I'm not embarrassed. Or ashamed."

"As well you shouldn't be." He peered into her eyes, facing the overwhelming pain that haunted the blue depths head-on, and silently urged her to focus on his words. To believe in his sincerity. "I only meant to ensure your comfort and privacy. I'd like to hear your story if you're still okay with me being present while you tell it."

Her mouth opened and closed silently then she nodded.

"How far along are you?" Jessie asked.

"Seven months." Mallory cleared her throat. "I'm due in early March. And when I said I chose to keep the baby, I didn't mean I'd—well, I could never..." Inhaling, she rubbed her forehead. "What I meant is that I considered adoption but after a lot of prayer, I decided against it." She looked up then, her gaze moving from Jessie to Liam earnestly. "However this baby came to be, it's a part of me and I want to try to be a good mother."

Jessie reached out and covered one of Mallory's hands with her own. "And you will be." She smiled gently. "We'll do everything we can to help. I assume you came here because you'd like to relocate?"

"Yes." Mallory turned her hand over and squeezed Jessie's hand, a pleading tone entering her voice. "I need a safe place to start over. I need to relocate, get a job…begin fresh in every way just about. But I'm a hard worker and I'm willing to do whatever is needed to make a go of things. I subleased the apartment I was staying in, so I'm free of that contract, and I sold my car tonight, so I have several thousand dollars to help with putting a down payment on a new place to stay."

"And your ex-husband?" Liam bit his lip, the angry question slipping off his tongue before he could contain it. "Is that how you got that bruise on your temple? Has he attacked you again recently?"

Mallory slipped her hand free of Jessie's and touched her face. Her fingertips grazed the dark bruise on her temple then traced the swelling around her eyelid. "It's better than it was. It's not the first—or worst—time he's hit me. He was abusive during our marriage but I stayed with him for three years, hoping he'd change. We went to marriage counseling, he took an anger management class and his parents were really good people who tried to help as much as possible. The problem was just beyond them—and me—and Trevor just got worse and worse."

She placed her hands in her lap and sighed. "I filed for divorce two years ago, got my own apartment and tried to move on, but he kept showing up all the time. At my new home, at my job—he was everywhere." A cynical laugh escaped her. "It wasn't like he was heartbroken. He just couldn't stand not having control over me anymore. I tried ignoring him, warning him, reporting him—none of it worked. He always stopped short of doing anything that would get him arrested, until he r—" Her voice broke. "When I came home from work seven months ago, he was waiting by my door. He was calmer than usual—even kind—so I tried to get him to leave on my own, but he followed me inside my apartment and…"

She looked down, her hands twisting together in her lap.

Jessie leaned forward. "Afterward, did you go to the police?"

Mallory nodded. "They tried to help but it was my word against his, though. And we were married at one time so his story was that we'd briefly reconciled. I had no visible injuries or bruises—" she touched her temple and scoffed "—like this one, and he said I invited him in. It might've been different if there'd been a witness. Someone who might've heard something and come forward, but there wasn't." She squeezed her eyes shut. "I was terrified but I didn't scream." She looked at Jessie, her eyes pleading. "I don't know why I didn't scream."

"It wasn't your fault," Liam said firmly.

She looked at him, her eyes wide and pained, but resolute. "I know. In the end, I just wanted to put it behind me."

"And when you discovered you were pregnant," Jessie prompted. "What happened then?"

"Like you said, Eton's a small community." A wry smile lifted Mallory's lips. "I couldn't hide it for long and word got back to his parents three months ago. His mother asked if we could meet and I agreed."

Liam winced. After all she'd already endured, he couldn't imagine how difficult that must have been. "How did that go?"

"Trevor's mom is a good person. It was hard for her to accept what Trevor had done and to walk away from her grandchild but she did believe me and she wanted to abide by my wishes." She sighed. "She persuaded Trevor to sign away his parental rights so I could start over on my own. I was surprised when he agreed to that but I thought that'd be the end of it. And it was for a while, but a few days ago, when he found out I was moving, he showed up at my place again. He was angry—said I'd forced his hand and that this was still his child."

She gestured toward the overnight bag Liam had sat on the

floor in the living room. "The next day, I packed a few things in that bag, got in my car and left town. I stayed in a motel for a few nights and put a for sale sign on my car. Someone called yesterday, wanting to buy it, and I gave her a good deal on the condition that she'd drop me off here after taking possession of it."

"I'm glad you came," Jessie said. "How did you hear about us?"

"My preacher." Mallory issued a small smile. "I went to him for advice and he suggested I come see you. He said Hummingbird Haven had been mentioned in several churches near our area as a safe haven and he thought you could help me get established somewhere else safely."

Jessie smiled. "I'm glad he gave you our information. It was very brave of you to come."

"Yes," Liam said. "It was."

Mallory looked at them, then picked up her spoon and resumed eating. "This is wonderful, Liam," she said between bites. "Thank you." She glanced at Jessie. "For being willing to help me, too."

"Right." Jessie rubbed her hands together briskly. "Now that I have more background information and I know what resources we're working with, I can get started on making inquiries as far as placement. Do you have a particular location in mind for starting over?"

Mallory shook her head. "I'm willing to go anywhere you say is safe. But I would like to put some more distance between myself and Trevor, if possible. Some place farther away from Eton would be great."

Jessie smiled. "Then that's what I'll search for." She pushed back her chair and stood. "I'll get started right away and make a few calls tonight. You're in need of a place to stay—the farther from Eton, the better—with access to good health care and a job that's either based at home or near local transportation. Is that about right?"

"Yes." Mallory pushed her chair back, too, and moved to stand. "I can't thank you enough for helping me, Jessie."

She patted Mallory's shoulder. "You've thanked me enough. For now, stay put and eat a decent meal, then you need a good night's sleep. When you finish eating, I'll walk with you back to my place and you can stay in our guest room for the night. We'll talk strategy in the morning."

Liam stood. "What about the fireworks? Do you need me to help Holt set them up while you get Mallory settled?"

Jessie held up a hand. "No. We decided before I came here to skip the fireworks this year. The wind's too strong. Too much of a fire hazard. They'll hold in storage 'til the Fourth of July."

"I can't help but think I've put a damper on your celebration," Mallory said. "Showing up like I have, interrupting your party—and now you can't even enjoy your fireworks on account of the weather. It's not much of a New Year's Eve celebration tonight for you, is it?"

The despondent tone in her quiet voice made Liam's heart ache. What a painful journey she'd had in life and how very vulnerable she seemed. But she'd had enough strength to travel to Hummingbird Haven and there was a reason God had led her here. Of that, he was certain.

"Tonight is very much a celebration." Liam placed his hand flat on the table, as close as he could get to hers without touching. When she glanced up at him, he said softly, "It's a celebration of a new start—a new life—for you and your baby."

"I hope so," she whispered.

"I know so," he replied. "Anything is possible. All you need is faith."

She looked up at him in surprise, the longing in her expression at odds with the wounded doubt haunting her eyes.

Liam stared back at her, wanting to reassure her that her life would be different, that she would no longer have to live in fear or defend herself or her child against violence. To prove to her that although some men did aim to hurt, other men—good men—chose to protect.

In that moment, he decided that was exactly what he was going to do.

CHAPTER THREE

LIAM HADN'T ASKED for much over the past thirty-eight years of his life but for some reason, he wanted to help Mallory find a safe place to call home. And he wanted it more than he'd wanted anything in a very long time.

"She's on her own," he said, lowering to one knee beside the bed in the guest room of Jessie's intake cabin. "For now, at least." He picked up one soft slip-on shoe from the floor, cupped his mother's left heel in his palm and slid the shoe onto her foot gently. "She's having a baby in a couple of months."

"A baby?" His mother's eyes, dazed and unfocused, strayed to the window and stared out as soft morning light slowly spread across the sky. "A real one?"

Liam smiled. "Yes, ma'am. A real one."

His mother's expression brightened. "One that cries and all?"

He slid the second shoe on her right foot. "Yep."

She clapped her hands together and laughed. "How wonderful!"

Liam sat back on his haunches and studied her expression, his smile growing at the cheerful sound she made. His mother was young—only sixty-seven—but her cognitive impairments had emerged early following a stroke and had progressed rapidly. Two years ago, she'd been an active, vibrant woman with a zest for life. Now she had difficulty performing everyday tasks independently and often forgot where she was.

Late last night, after Jessie and Mallory had left, she'd woken up and wandered off again, strolling out the front door of the cabin and into the cold night in bare feet with no sense of direction. She'd been angry when he'd caught up with her. He had walked her back inside the cabin then cleaned and rubbed her chilled feet. She'd sat upright in bed and scowled at him for over an hour until sleep overcame her.

Lately, only two things made her smile: a ten-year-old brown mare named Sugar that had recently been boarded in the stable at Pine Creek Farm, and an aloof barn cat that had taken up residence in the stable as well. Liam had named the stray Miss Priss on account of the feline's fluffy tail twitches and constant disdain for humans.

Liam chuckled softly at the memory of his mother following the stray cat around the stable, speaking sweetly and trying to pet it, while the feline turned up its nose and sashayed away. His mother had always loved animals of any kind and she still enjoyed walking to the stable every morning to feed, pet and talk to the horses and that high-and-mighty cat.

Who knows? Maybe having a new baby around to visit every morning might make her smile even more.

"Would you like that?" he asked. "Having a baby in the house?"

"Would I like it?" Her eyes, the same hazel shade as his own, returned to his face. "I'd love it." Surprise flashed through her expression. "I used to have a baby of my own once, you know? Nine pounds and seven ounces, born just after midnight. I named him Holt."

His smile slipped. "You had two babies that night, didn't you? Had a baby boy who arrived before Holt?"

She stared down at him and frowned. "No. Just Holt. I used to pick him up and rock him to sleep every time he cried."

Liam ducked his head and nodded. His mother's memory of him had faded several months ago and had yet to return, so her answer was no surprise. But the fact that she only remembered his brother's name still stung. Painfully so.

Not that it mattered. Though she could still recall Holt's name she didn't recognize his face, which did neither Holt nor Liam any good. As identical twins, they shared the same physical appearance but the similarities stopped there. Holt had always been somewhat of a thrill-seeking extrovert, a disposition that had led him to leave home at eighteen, following in their father's footsteps.

Liam winced. The memory of his father abandoning his wife and sons for another woman and a new life had been painful, but Holt's departure from Pine Creek Farm on the day they'd turned eighteen had left a hole in Liam's heart that had taken years to heal. Liam had immediately taken over management of their family farm and bed-and-breakfast, staying put in their family home after high school graduation, working back-breaking hours for years to keep the land in their mother's name and food on the table.

Even now, after reuniting with his brother and healing the rift in their family upon Holt's reemergence in his life, Liam occasionally felt the sting of resentment. Some of it was for the years of estrangement from his brother, some for the opportunities he'd missed out on in his own life as a result of staying put and taking responsibility for the family farm, and some of it—the part that shamed him the most—was for the fact that his mother, the person he'd loved and cared for his entire life, had no memory of him at all. Not even his name.

Liam didn't know who he was in her mind now. A caretaker? Friend? An annoying stranger who dragged her back indoors when she roamed, reminded to her eat and take her medicine?

There was no sure way to know.

Sighing, Liam stood and held out his hand. "It's a bit early for breakfast with Jessie and the kids but Holt always brews coffee before the break of dawn. Wanna walk up to his cabin with me? See how he's doing this morning?"

"My Holt is here?" Her expression was as surprised this morning as it had been yesterday morning and each day before when he'd delivered the same news throughout their two-week visit at Hummingbird Haven.

"Yeah." Liam took her hands in his and gently coaxed her to her feet. "He might even be waiting outside for us already. But it's cold out." He grabbed a long wool coat from the end of the bed and slipped it over her arms, one at a time, taking care to tug the material slowly over her frail arms. "You'll need all your winter gear today."

Five minutes later, with his mother bundled up in her warm coat, hat and gloves, Liam donned his own jacket and led her outside.

Holt, as Liam had guessed, was already waiting for them on the front porch, his hands thrust deep into his coat pockets, smiling wide in the morning sunlight. He'd followed the same routine every morning of their two-week stay at Hummingbird Haven for the holidays. Before the sun rose, he'd stroll down the hill from his and Jessie's cabin, lean on the porch rail of the intake cabin and wait for their mother to emerge.

Every morning, he smiled at her. But there was a heavy look in his eyes—one Liam easily recognized.

Grief.

"Morning, Mom." Holt hugged her then kissed her cheek. "I see you're up early as usual. You're on vacation. You should sleep in at least one morning."

Gayle frowned up at him. "Who are you?"

"I'm Holt. Your son." Smiling wider, he pointed at the dirt road that curved behind the intake cabin. "I'm the guy who lives up the hill a bit, just around that curve."

She blinked, her focus seeming to turn inward. "Is Miss Priss there? She needs her breakfast."

Holt glanced at Liam and lifted one eyebrow.

"Arrogant barn cat." Liam issued a wry smile. The feline, she remembered.

Holt grinned. "Oh. Unfortunately, Miss Priss isn't here. She's back at Pine Creek. But I just put on a strong pot of coffee and Jessie picked up some more of that cinnamon creamer you like." He moved closer and nudged their mother with his elbow. "So how 'bout it? Wanna take a stroll up the hill with me and Liam? Get a hot cup of joe?"

She thought it over, eyeing Holt then Liam, and sighed. "Might as well. Walks do a body good."

"That's the spirit." Holt patted her hand after she looped her arm around his extended elbow then waited as she did the same with Liam. "Cinnamon joe, here we come."

The sun was awake now. It peeked over the mountain range and stretched out its rays, the gold beams of light spearing through the canopy of evergreen trees overhead.

"It's a gorgeous morning." Holt slowed his steps to match Gayle's pace. "Colder than usual."

Liam tucked his mother's arm snugly against his and covered her gloved hand with his palm. Her steps, though slow, were steady this morning. "You warm enough, Mom?"

She nodded as she surveyed their surroundings, her gaze roving over the gritty dirt that crunched beneath their shoes then taking in the tall trees that bent in the winter breeze.

"Jessie and the kids are up," Holt said. "The boys wanted pancakes and bacon. Whatcha think, Mom? Pancakes sound good to you?"

Gayle didn't answer. Instead, she continued to study her surroundings, a small smile appearing.

"Mallory up, too?" Liam asked.

"Not yet. She was already settled in the guest room by the time I brought the kids home last night and was still in there sleeping when I left to come get y'all." He chuckled. "They had a blast at the New Year's Eve party. Ate about a pound of pizza, drank a gallon of soda then limboed and danced 'til they slap gave out."

Liam smiled. "I bet they slept good, too."

"Like rocks." Holt laughed again. "I'm surprised they got up as early as they did, but I suspect they were curious about our new guest since they didn't get a chance to meet her last night."

"Jessie mention if she'd found a place for Mallory to stay yet?"

"No. But she was working on it late into the evening. Called just about every contact we have, but she's still waiting on responses on account of the holiday and late hour."

Liam cupped Gayle's elbow, guiding her around a knotted root that protruded from the dirt path. "What about Pine Creek?"

Holt glanced at him. "Say what?"

"You heard me." Liam's neck prickled under Holt's scrutiny. He kept his gaze on the dirt path in front of them. "I could use the help and there's plenty of room."

Holt fell silent for a moment then asked, "Help with the bed-and-breakfast?"

"And Mom." Liam glanced down at her face, but she seemed uninterested in his and Holt's conversation as she continued taking in the mountain views. "I'd feel better having an extra pair of eyes and hands in the house round-the-clock rather than just for a few hours a day, which is what the home care aide's been providing."

"There's an easy fix for that. I told you Mom's welcome here anytime, for as long as you want. Jessie and I'll set the guest room up as close as we can to the room she has at the farm, and we'll take over her care. That'll give you time to—"

"Thank you," Liam said softly. "You know I appreciate the offer." He looked at Holt then, meeting his eyes over their mother's gray head. "I truly do. But she's most comfortable at the farm. Less confused. She's lived there her whole life.

That land and that sassy cat are about the only things she re-members clearly anymore."

Holt sighed, his gaze straying to Gayle. "Yeah. But I miss her."

In more ways than one.

Liam rubbed his stubbled jaw with his free hand, hearing the words in his mind even though Holt hadn't said them. His brother had reunited with their mother only a few years prior to her illness occurring, and even though they'd reestablished a close, loving bond before she'd succumbed to dementia, he could imagine just how painful it was for Holt to lose her all over again.

"The farm's your home, too, Holt. You know you, Jessie and the kids are welcome anytime. No need to call ahead, just come."

"I know." Holt lifted his chin toward the two-story cabin that drew into view as they ascended the hill. "But we're rooted here. My heart's wherever Jessie is and Hummingbird Haven is more than home to both of us. It's where God called us to do His work."

Liam smiled, his chest warming with pride. For years, Holt had worked hard to turn his life around and become a good man and now he was a loving husband and father who worked selflessly alongside Jessie to improve the lives of the women and children who sought refuge here. Not only had Holt be-come a good man, he was now the best man Liam knew.

"You and Jessie do a lot of good here," Liam said. "Maybe this is my chance to do the same."

"But is taking Mallory in what you really want?" Holt hesi-tated. "I mean, you've always stepped in for Mom and you've had more than your fair share of responsibility over the years. You'll be taking on more than just an extra pair of hands. There'll be a baby soon and the house'll be—"

"Full up," Liam said. "There'll be the baby, Mallory, Mom,

guests..." He smiled. "The farm'll be lively again. Active. And Mallory and the baby will be protected and secure."

Holt fell silent for a moment then said, "From what Jessie told me, Mallory's been through a real tough time. And the women who come here with pasts like that aren't usually looking for—or wanting—a hero."

"I'm not looking to be her hero. I only want—"

"To be less lonely."

Liam stiffened.

"I'm sorry," Holt said quietly. "I don't mean that in the wrong way or to offend you, I just..." He sighed. "All I mean is that I know how difficult things have been for you lately. How painful and scary Mom's illness is and how much you love visiting here and how much you enjoy being a great uncle to my kids. You've put your own life on hold for a lot of years to take care of Mom and the farm. That's my fault for abandoning Mom like I did years ago, and I regret that more than you know."

He's right. Liam's throat closed. He swallowed hard, ignoring the surge of grief that rose in his chest. *But he isn't completely right.* "I don't hold that against you—"

"I know. And I also know having others around is a nice distraction for you. It helps lighten the load. But bringing Mallory and her baby to the farm or filling up the house with people isn't going to take away the pain in terms of what's to come with Mom. Not to mention, what Mallory really needs right now is—"

"I only want to help. That's all. Isn't that what God wants us to do? Serve others when we can?" He met Holt's eyes, holding his gaze. "You remember how tough it was for Mom after Dad left us? Having to work and take care of us on her own? It would've been so much easier for her if she'd had a little help. Mallory's in a similar position now, and I have the resources and the opportunity she needs to rebuild her life in a safe home. If she comes to Pine Creek, she won't have to go it alone like Mom did—at least, not right off the bat."

They reached the top of the hill and Holt's cabin came into full view. Gayle's feet halted, bringing all three of them to a standstill.

Admiring the view, she said the same phrase she'd announced every morning since they'd been at Hummingbird Haven. "Gracious, what a gorgeous home!"

Liam nodded and said softly, "It's what everyone deserves. A safe place of their own to call home and put down roots. Pine Creek Farm can offer Mallory the same." He looked at Holt. "Don't you think so, Holt?"

He stared back at Liam for a moment then tugged Gayle forward into a comfortable pace, resuming their walk toward the cabin. "Yeah, well…you're gonna have to convince Jessie—and Mallory—of that."

"ARE YOU SURE about this, Liam?"

Sighing, Mallory blinked heavily and opened her eyes. Morning sunlight, pouring through sheer lace curtains into the small bedroom, casted a golden glow over the white comforter covering her. A crow cawed nearby as though it was perched high in an evergreen right outside the window.

She was in the guest room at Jessie's cabin, lying in bed, wearing a pair of flannel maternity pajamas Jessie had rounded up for her. That much she remembered—and was extremely grateful for.

It'd been dark when she'd followed Jessie down a dirt path to her home last night, but lights had glowed warmly inside the cabin when they'd arrived. Inside, framed photos of a happy family were displayed prominently with Jessie and her husband—Liam's twin, much to Mallory's surprise—smiling as brightly as the twin boys and toddler girl who were pictured with them in the photos.

Along the foyer and around the living room, children's toys

and stuffed animals and a colorful blanket were strewn about in a happy way, as though Jessie and her husband encouraged their sons and daughter to play and enjoy themselves throughout the house. The guest room was bright and inviting, and the extra down pillows on the bed had fit perfectly along Mallory's swollen belly, supporting her through the first deep, peaceful night's sleep she'd had in months.

Mallory frowned, a pang of loss moving through her. When she'd married and moved into the first house of her own with Trevor, she'd been excited to make the space a warm, inviting home. Trevor, however, had dismissed her opinions outright and had chosen all of the furniture and decor himself. Throughout their marriage, he'd expected her to keep every inch of their home according to his specifications and she'd never had a space of her own. Even her side of their walk-in closet, full of only clothes that Trevor had approved of her wearing, was required to be arranged in a specific order like the rest of the rooms in the house.

Shirts were hung on plastic hangers to the right, pants in the middle and dresses on the left. Shoes, laces folded neatly over the toes, had to be stored on a wooden shoe rack, lined from right to left in order of occasion. Formal first and casual last.

Any deviation from the norm elicited punishment.

"I mean, it's a lot to take on."

That was Jessie's voice again. Muffled but still discernable, coming from the vicinity of the front porch near the bedroom window.

Mallory shoved off the comforter, rolled over onto her bottom and dangled her legs over the edge of the mattress. A familiar ache resumed in her lower back. Moaning, she rubbed the small of her back, just above her right hip, then looked down at her protruding belly where a visible movement within delivered a sharp jab at her ribs.

She winced and curled her fists into the top of the mattress, waiting for the baby to settle comfortably again inside her womb.

"I want to help her. I don't think it's a coincidence that I was the one in that cabin when she arrived. It's as though it were planned. I can't think of a single reason why it wouldn't work."

That was Liam's voice now, sounding right outside the window. Deep and even. She recognized it immediately, her fists relaxing slightly against the mattress. It was the calmness in his tone that caught her attention. Trevor had never spoken in such a soothing way.

"I need the help as well," Liam's voice continued. "I truly do. I mean, cleaning the guest rooms for the bed-and-break-fast, boarding the horses and running the business while taking care of Mom has become almost impossible over the past few months." A heavy sigh sounded. "She's getting worse every day now. Noticeably so."

"I know," Jessie said.

Frowning, Mallory eased her bare feet to the floor and padded quietly over to the window. She slid one lace curtain back slightly, just enough to peek out at the two figures standing on the front porch. Jessie and Liam, bundled in warm coats, were both leaning against the porch rail, holding cups of hot coffee in their hands.

She hesitated and glanced back at the bed, guilt from eaves-dropping prompting her to consider slipping away from the window as quietly as she'd approached.

"I could use an extra pair of hands and eyes when it comes to taking care of her," Liam continued. "She's up at all hours now. Last night, she fell asleep early and slept soundly for about three hours but not long after you and Mallory left to come here, she was up and about again." He frowned and rubbed his forehead. "She even went outside, starting walking through the woods before I woke up and noticed she was gone. If I hadn't fallen asleep on the couch and the cold air from the open door hadn't woken me...there's no telling what might've happened to her."

Curiosity got the better of Mallory. She tugged the curtain back a bit more and leaned closer to the window, pressing her uninjured temple against the cold glass. They were speaking about Liam's mother, who had been asleep when she'd first arrived the night before. He'd mentioned she wasn't well and that noises like fireworks made her uncomfortable. Could she be suffering from dementia?

"I don't know how you've handled things on your own for this long, Liam," Jessie said.

"I wanted to." His calm, even tone had changed, and his words had grown heavy.

Mallory tilted her head and squinted against the sunlight streaming over the mountains at their back for a better view of his face.

But he looked down at his boots, his muscular build and broad shoulders blocking out the sunlight, somewhat cloaking his handsome features in shadow as he dragged one hand over his stubbled jaw, then lifted his coffee mug to his lips. He drank deeply, the strong column of his throat moving as he swallowed, then he lowered his mug and cradled it in his big hands.

"I want Mom with me," he said. "In her own home where she feels safe and comfortable, for as long as possible."

"I understand," Jessie said, running a hand through her long hair. "But, Liam, there'll come a time when—"

"Yes, I know." Liam pushed off the porch rail and straightened, his tone firm again. "But we're not there yet and right now, I need extra help at home. Mallory's in need of a soft landing. I can give her that. She'll have free room and board, a better-than-average salary to help her save financially and the ability to work from home. In exchange, I'll be able to focus on work when I need to while knowing Mom's in capable hands.

Getting work done faster on a regular basis means having free time again. Quality free time that I can spend with Mom."

Jessie looked up at him. "And the baby?"

Mallory looked down at her middle and cringed. The curve of her belly blurred as tears filled her eyes.

"I'm renovating one of the guest rooms in the main house already," Liam said. "I can easily turn it into a nursery. That way, Mallory can stay put in one place for a while after the baby's born. She'll have everything she and the baby will need, and she'll be able to continue saving for a place of her own when she's ready."

"Liam..." Jessie said quietly. "Have you considered how Mallory will respond to your offer?" She spread one arm to the side. "I mean, she's had a very traumatic history, and she was clearly uncomfortable around you last night. Not to mention, you live hours from here on an isolated farm in the middle of nowhere. I don't know that she'd take to packing up and moving out to the country with a strange man."

She's got that right. Mallory dragged the back of her forearm over her wet lashes and frowned. Just the thought of moving into a house in a strange place with a strange man was enough to make her shudder. And she wasn't a charity c—

"It's not the middle of nowhere," Liam said. "It's my family home in peaceful countryside down south. It's not as cold there as it is here right now and spring'll be here before you know it. You know how beautiful it is there in the spring. Even though she'd be assuming a caretaking position, Mallory might find Mom is good company when she wants it. Outside of that, I wouldn't crowd her. I'd give her all the space and time she needs. She'd have fresh air, sunshine and room to breathe."

Mallory stilled. The benefits Liam described sounded overly generous considering the going rate for caretaking positions. She wasn't a charity case and didn't need another man bulldozing into her life! But, oh...

Room to breathe.

How wonderful that sounded.

"She may still turn you down, despite all that," Jessie said.

Liam nodded. "Maybe. But I don't think she will. She's too brave to turn down an opportunity for a fresh start out of fear."

Mallory's gaze shot to his face. He moved, his broad shoulder shifting as he lifted his face into full view of the sunlight and stared back at her, his eyes meeting hers through the window, his gaze gentle but steady.

"She made it this far on her own," he said softly. "She's strong enough to take the next step."

Mallory dropped the curtain back into place and stumbled back from the window. Gracious! How long had he known she was there?

Lifting her trembling fingers to her lips, her gaze darted around the room, taking in the clean, comfortable surroundings and the soft, rumpled bed she'd slept in so soundly. Her breathing began to slow as she turned his words over in her mind.

Fresh air, sunshine...room to breathe.

It sounded like a dream. The same kind of dream she'd had for months now. One of living a peaceful, comfortable life. Sleeping soundly at night and living her days free of fear. And his words: *All you need is faith. Take the next step...*

Those couldn't be a coincidence, could they?

She looked up at the ceiling, imagining the cold, clear sky beyond, trying to peer beyond the doubts that still clouded her mind. "Is this it? Is this the direction I should take?"

She couldn't afford another mistake. Couldn't afford to let her guard down and put her trust in another man who would hurt her or let her down...especially now.

A strong kick to her ribs made her flinch and her hands automatically reached for her belly, her fingertips brushing the firm mound before she could stop them. She closed her eyes and forced her palms to press gently against the warm swell of her belly for the briefest of moments, then she crossed the room, grabbed her coat and tugged it on.

Holt's deep voice, the sounds of children's laughter and the clink of utensils emerged from the kitchen as she walked down the hallway, but she didn't stop. Instead, she kept moving, taking one step after another in her bare feet until she reached the front door, opened it and stepped out onto the porch.

"Do you promise?" She stood there, clutching her coat together over the bulge of her belly, as her eyes met Liam's, urging him to answer.

He hesitated, glancing briefly at Jessie, who stared at them with surprise, before returning his attention back to her. "Promise what?"

"That there'll be fresh air, sunshine and room to breathe." Mallory shivered as a cold wind rolled over the porch and her toes grew numb against the wood planks. "That you won't crowd me? That you're offering me a legitimate caretaking job where I can earn my keep and that I won't be seen—or treated—like a charity case?"

He nodded, glancing down at her bare feet before meeting her eyes again. "I promise. Pine Creek's a safe place where you can start over in whatever way you choose."

She looked at Jessie, her heart pounding heavily as she searched the other woman's expression. "I know you're married to his brother and that you'll probably be biased, but I've also been told that you're honest—almost to a fault." She licked her lips, the tender skin already drying in the winter wind. "Can I trust him?"

Jessie smiled. "Yes, Mallory. You can trust him."

"Or…" Mallory fell silent then dragged in a trembling breath and held out her hand. "I can at least try."

Liam stared at her hand as it dipped slightly beneath a strong push of frigid wind. Then he set his coffee mug on the porch rail, moved closer and slowly closed his hand around hers.

Mallory tried to adjust to the feel of his big hand enveloping hers, forcing herself to focus on the warmth of his palm against her cold skin rather than the sight of his muscular wrist. "Th-thank you for your kind offer, Liam. I accept."

"You're welcome, Mallory," he said softly.

She stood there, his hand covering hers, while a strong surge of fear and uncertainty urged her to break free and run. But this stranger—this man—standing in front of her thought she was brave...something she'd never truly felt before in her life. She hoped, with every fiber of her being, that he was right.

CHAPTER FOUR

GAYLE WILLIAMS WAS LOVED.

"And look at that right there." Gayle, shifting in the front passenger seat of Liam's truck, pointed at a snowcapped mountain in the distance. "That's snow, isn't it, young man?"

Liam's big hands moved over the steering wheel as he navigated a sharp curve in the road. "Yes, ma'am. January's much colder up here than back home. Before long, that snow'll make its way down the mountain and Holt's yard will be covered in it."

Gayle shivered. "Oh. I hope he has a coat."

Liam nodded. "He does."

"And gloves?" she asked.

"Yes, ma'am."

"And a hat?"

"Yes, ma'am."

"And…" Gayle's attention drifted to the other side of the winding road and she gasped. "Look at those trees! So very tall. Right to the sky, wouldn't you say, young man?"

Liam nodded. "Yes, ma'am. Right to the sky."

She patted one of his hands as it moved over the steering wheel. "Take care, sir. You're not going too fast, are you?"

"No, ma'am."

"These curves are sneaky," she said. "You're being careful, aren't you?"

"Yes, ma'am."

"I hope so," she said. "My Miss Priss is hungry and we need to feed her first thing when we arrive. You remember that, don't you?"

A muscle ticked in Liam's strong jaw but his expression remained patient in the rearview mirror as he recited his answer. "Yes, ma'am."

Mallory smiled. Seated in the back seat of the extended cab, she'd listened to Liam's conversation with his mother for over twenty minutes now, ever since they'd left Hummingbird Haven and begun the long drive down to Pine Creek Farm. Though she really couldn't call it a conversation since the vast majority of the talking had definitely been one-sided.

Gayle had spoken almost nonstop since they'd left Jessie's place, asking dozens of questions about the landscape—repeating many of them more than once—and frequently cautioning Liam as he drove, never once referring to him by his name.

It'd been clear to Mallory yesterday, after accepting Liam's job offer and meeting his mother, that Gayle had no memory of Liam. Gayle had looked at Liam the same way she'd looked at Mallory when Liam had introduced them to each other—with the same curious gaze of interest in a stranger.

Having lost her parents at a young age, Mallory knew how painful the loss was but could only imagine how difficult it must be for Liam to see, talk to and care for his mother every day, knowing she no longer knew him. And today, after they'd said goodbye to Jessie and her family, settled into the truck and started the journey to Pine Creek, Gayle had continuously referred to Liam as *young man* or *sir*, an impersonal reference Mallory knew must hurt him. But despite this, Liam had remained patient, polite and kind throughout every mile they'd traveled.

"Who's Miss Priss?" Mallory asked.

Liam met her eyes in the rearview mirror, one corner of his mouth lifting in wry amusement. "A stray cat."

"*My* cat." Gayle shimmied in her seat, reached back and patted Mallory's knee. "She's just beautiful—has thick, striped fur and long, luxurious whiskers." Her voice lowered to a whisper. "Miss Priss doesn't care for this gentleman next to me. She doesn't take to him at all."

"She doesn't take to anyone," Liam said, lifting one blond brow as he glanced at Mallory in the rearview mirror. "Gives Mom a run for her money every time she tries to pet it, turns her nose up at the food I give her half the time and claws my shins every time I walk in the stable. That cat's the most uppity creature I've ever run across."

"Well, now." Gayle faced forward again, tidied the collar of her thick coat then folded her gloved hands in her lap. "That wasn't a very nice thing to say. It was quite rude, actually. I think you owe Miss Priss an apology."

Liam broke then. Rolling his eyes, he leaned his head to one side and issued a long-suffering sigh.

"And now…" Gayle said, lifting her chin. "You owe me an apology, too. You should never roll your eyes at someone whether you disagree with them or not. It's disrespectful. Didn't your mother teach you that, young man?"

Liam looked at his mother. He moved to speak then stopped before facing the road ahead and reciting, "Yes, ma'am. I apologize for offending you."

Gayle nodded. "Accepted. And you'll apologize to Miss Priss?"

The muscle in Liam's jaw ticked again. "Yes, ma'am."

"Good." Gayle smiled and rubbed her hands together. "I can't wait until we get to the farm." She frowned. "These curves are sneaky. You're being careful, aren't you, young man?"

The one-sided conversation began again, interrupted only by Liam's refrain of "Yes, ma'am."

Mallory smiled wider. Liam definitely loved his mother.

She settled back in her seat, stretched her legs as far as they could go in the back of the extended cab—which was much roomier than she'd anticipated—and looked out the window at the scenery as it passed.

Liam was making good time. From what he'd told her yesterday, Pine Creek Farm was a little more than three hours away from Hummingbird Haven. There had been little traffic on the highway thus far, and the Blue Ridge Mountain ranges soon gave way to gentler slopes and hills. The light layers of snowfall were soon behind them and the sun's rays grew stronger as they traveled, lending extra warmth to the truck's cab, creating a cozy cocoon.

Her eyes grew heavy and she blinked, trying to envision the farm Liam had described. As inviting as Jessie's guest bed had been, it had been difficult to sleep last night, knowing that the journey to Pine Creek Farm would begin today. She'd spent most of the night tossing and turning, imagining how Liam's family home might appear based off how he'd described it.

Peaceful countryside. Fresh air, room to breathe. A main house with multiple guest rooms.

It sounded so wonderful. Like a pleasant gathering place. It sounded like…a home. Something she hadn't had in a very long time.

A yawn overtook her and she wiped her watery eyes, refocusing on the passing landscape as Gayle continued asking Liam questions he'd already answered ten miles back.

In the end, it didn't matter if the place didn't live up to Liam's hype. Whatever Pine Creek Farm turned out to be, it had to be better than what she'd left behind. Any place far removed from Trevor that offered her a way to make a living and start her life over was a step in the right direction.

But, oh, she hoped it turned out to be exactly as Liam had described. *Peaceful countryside. Fresh air, room to breathe…*

"Mallory?" Something big and warm nudged her shoulder gently. "Mallory, we're here."

Her eyes popped open, and she looked up at Liam as he stood beside the open door of the truck's cab, then glanced down. His palm was curved lightly around her shoulder.

He removed it and stepped back. "I'm sorry. I hated to wake you but it's too cold to nap out here." He grinned. "I promise you our guest room will be more comfortable than the truck."

The sun was much lower in the sky than before and the truck was parked at the end of a long, paved driveway, surrounded by open fields.

Fumbling, she unbuckled her seat belt and scrambled upright. "I missed it."

"Missed what?"

"Everything." Rubbing her eyes, she shifted her legs to the side and scooted closer to the open door. "The ride into Pine Creek, the drive up to the farm, everything. I wanted to see it all when we—"

"Hey," he said softly. "Slow down. The farm's not going anywhere and there's still some sunlight left. I can show you around a bit before we go in, if you'd like. But please be careful getting out of the truck. It's a steep drop and it'd be easy for the two of you to take a tumble."

She frowned. The two of…?

Oh.

She looked down at the bulge of her belly, her cheeks heating.

"Here." Liam's hand lifted into her line of vision. "I'll help you down, if you'd like?"

She drew in a deep breath and placed her hand in his, leaning on it as she slid out of the truck's cab and stood on the paved driveway. "Thank you."

"Sure thing." He released her hand as soon as she was steady on her feet then shut the door behind her. "Did you have enough room back there? I was hoping you'd take me up on my offer to sit up front because the seats back there are a bit tight."

"It was fine." She tugged the hood of her jacket onto her head, blocking the wind's chill against her ears. "I had plenty of room and I felt better knowing Mrs. Gayle's routine wasn't changed on account of me joining you."

"Thank you for thinking of her. She's anxious to—"

"Excuse me, young man!" Gayle stood at the front of the truck, bundled up in a warm coat and hat, wringing her gloved hands together with an excited expression. "Miss Priss is hungry and I can't wait on y'all forever."

He smiled. "Yes, ma'am." He glanced at Mallory, his smile growing. "As I was saying, she's anxious to introduce you to Miss Priss. And I gotta say, better you than me. I've had my fill of that cat."

Mallory smiled back. "And from what I hear, you owe it an apology."

He winked. "So it seems."

There was a dimple—a small one—in his left cheek. It was barely visible but appeared when he smiled wide as he did now. Liam Williams, it seemed, could very easily be perceived as charming…if a woman allowed herself to notice that sort of thing.

Trevor had been charming, too. In the beginning.

She looked away and shoved her hands into the pockets of her coat. "You said you'd show me around a little before we go inside?"

"Of course. Mom's anxious to see that cat so we'll visit the stable first. It's this way."

She waited, her eyes still staring at the pavement beneath her shoes, until his heavy steps receded then lifted her head and followed, deliberately lagging behind a few paces.

Liam looked over his shoulder as he walked, his hazel eyes concerned as they studied her face. "You all right back there?"

"Yeah. Just taking in the view." She turned her head and

surveyed their surroundings, her steps slowing even more at the sight of the winding driveway lined with beautiful white fencing that seemed to go on for miles. "2971 Magnolia Lane."

"What's that?" Liam asked.

"Magnolia Lane," Mallory said louder. "That was the address on your license, right?" She pointed at dozens of trees with bare branches that had been planted in perfect lines along the white fencing. "Are those magnolia trees?"

Liam nodded. "You've got a good memory. And yeah, those are magnolias. They bloom every year sometime in March. Mom helped my grandfather plant those when she was a little girl. They're her favorite part of spring."

"I bet." When blooming, they were probably a sight to behold. That was something she could look forward to. "There are so many fields. How much land is yours?"

"Everything you can see and then some." Liam cupped Gayle's elbow as she stepped off the paved driveway and onto the dormant grass, then walked toward a large white stable with a black roof. "Around seventy acres in all. We board horses and give trail rides, so the extra acreage comes in handy."

"How many horses do you have?" she asked as they drew closer to the stable.

"Nine right now," Liam said, opening the stable door and stepping back to allow Gayle to enter first. "Our stalls are full and I'm looking into investing in another stable, but that depends on this year's revenue."

"Do you grow crops or is this strictly a horse farm?"

"We have a substantial vegetable garden and sell those crops locally, but the horse side of the business took off a few years ago, so we've gravitated toward that. If I've learned anything from running this business over the years, it's that change is the only constant and the best thing to do is welcome it." He gestured for her to enter. "The stable's newly renovated. There are nine stalls, two wash-and-groom stalls, a tack-and-grain room and an office. Take a look around."

She walked inside and strolled slowly down the center of the stable. The floors were comprised of gray rubber pavers and the ceiling and stalls were white with black trim. Tall, healthy horses of various colors stood in each stall and the air was comfortably warm.

"It's beautiful," she said. "And squeaky-clean. How do you manage that with white stalls?"

He grinned. "Lots of washing and scrubbing. We've got a small—but great—crew of hands that do the bulk of the work. Takes extra pay and effort to keep everything sparkly but it's worth it to keep the bed-and-breakfast side of the business going. When our guests visit, they're looking for a peaceful, country retreat and this type of appealing atmosphere lends itself to that. We try to make Pine Creek Farm feel like a home away from home for them."

Mallory nodded. "It's certainly impressive." She walked farther into the stable, scanning the horses in each stall. "Are any of these horses yours?"

"Three of them, yeah. I lead guests on trail rides around the property with them." He eased around her and walked toward the last stall on the left. "Sugar's a favorite. She's a sweetheart. I think you'll like her the b—"

His voice broke and a strangled growl left his throat as a big ball of striped fur wrapped around his boot and four sets of claws dug into his jean-clad shin. He lifted his right leg and shook his foot, but the more Liam shook his leg, the more the cat writhed on his shin and boot.

"Get off, cat!" Liam said.

A yelp burst from his mouth and Mallory grinned. It was a sight—this big man balancing on one leg, at the mercy of a cat.

"Miss Priss!" Gayle, who'd been searching the stable for the cat, clapped her hands together and grinned. "See—all that thick fur and long whiskers. I told you Miss Priss was beautiful. She's telling us hello, aren't you, sweetie?"

"Mom." Liam winced and kicked harder. "Her claws are so deep, she's hitting bone."

Mallory stilled, her smile dissipating and her heart pounding in her ears. Her hands lifted automatically. Liam was taller than Trevor—probably stronger, too—and the cat was so small. The deeper his frown grew, the harder his muscular leg jerked. One hefty kick of his leg, a bit stronger than before, and the cat's grip might dislodge, causing it to sail through the air and slam into the hard wood of a stall.

The cat's claws dug deeper as it released a low, panicked moan.

Let go. Trevor's voice hissed through her mind. The memory caught her off-guard, as usual. It burst forth, stealing an otherwise light-hearted moment—twisting it into something dark and sinister.

She could still feel the muscles of his forearm flex beneath her fingers as she'd tried to loosen his vicious grip on her hair. Even her scalp stung at the memory. His weight had been so heavy—too heavy to move.

Let go, or it'll be worse.

She opened her mouth but no sound emerged, a high-pitched plea lodging in her throat.

"Okay, okay." Liam stopped kicking his leg and lowered his boot to the floor. "I get it—you're scared, huh?" His voice grew quiet as he spoke to the cat, his words slow and tone low. "Hang out for a while. Have a go at the other leg, too, if you'd like."

After a few moments of stillness, the cat's tense posture relaxed and it inched back down Liam's shin and onto his boot, blinking up at him with wide green eyes.

"Good girl." Liam bent and eased his hand, palm upward, towards the cat's nose. "I'm not so bad, you know. You might like me if you give me a chance, huh?"

The cat stared, unblinking, at his hand then sprang off Liam's boot and darted away, scurrying out of the stable.

"Now look what you've done." Gayle straightened and put her hands on her hips. "You've scared her."

"I scared her?" Mouth twitching, Liam pressed his palm to the center of his wide chest. "*I* scared *her*?"

Gayle walked out of the stable, frowning at him over her shoulder. "She's hungry. But I can't feed her now since you ran her off."

Liam shook his head as Gayle left, calling after her, "She won't go hungry. The hands have fed that ornery cat every day since we left. Believe me, they've called me more than once to complain about it." Chuckling, Liam rubbed his injured shin then glanced at Mallory. His smile slowly faded as he studied her face and hands. "Mallory?"

She blinked and lowered her hands to her sides, eyeing his leg as her heart rate slowed. Her cheeks burned and she shoved her hands in her pockets to keep from covering them. "Are you okay?" Could he hear the awkward tension in her voice? "I don't see any blood."

"I'm fine," he said softly, still studying her expression. "The jeans kept her from maiming me." He shrugged. "I have no idea why that cat has such an affinity for attacking me but she does it every time I walk in here, so I should be used to it by now."

Mouth dry, she swallowed hard. "You held your own, at least."

"I guess." A small, uncertain smile returned to his face and he asked gently, "Mind if we put off meeting Sugar 'til later? My pride's taken a hit and if I don't go after Mom soon, there's no telling where she'll get off to."

Mallory nodded. "Of course."

He left the stable and she followed on stiff legs, staying a pace behind.

Sure enough, Gayle had wandered off toward the magnolia tree–lined driveway, her long gray hair billowing behind her in the winter wind. Liam caught up to her though and before long, he'd ushered her to the main house, which turned out to be a white two-story with a wraparound porch. After Gayle sat on the couch in the living room, Liam picked up a quilt that lay on the back of a recliner, draped it over her legs then turned on the TV.

"You okay here while I show Mallory around?" he asked.

Gayle focused on the TV program, her eyes growing heavy.

Liam smiled. "We'll be back soon, Mom." He joined Mallory in the foyer. "Kitchen's through here." He led the way past a large dining room and into a large kitchen with an island and stainless steel appliances. "Fridge is always stocked with fresh fruit and vegetables and there are several casseroles in the freezer that can be popped in the oven and ready to eat in a half hour. You're welcome to anything you like and if you want something that's not there, just let me know and I'll get it for you."

"You do all the cooking yourself?" Mallory asked.

"Yeah," he said. "But the frozen casseroles are dropped off once every other week by Pam Marshall. She heads up a ladies' group at our church. They like to visit Mom and always bring a couple dishes when they come."

Mallory smiled. "That's nice of them."

"Yeah. You'd like Pam. She's real down-to-earth." He stepped back and motioned for her to join him. "Follow me. I'll show you the guest rooms then we'll go upstairs and see your room."

Downstairs, there were four guest rooms. Two contained king-size beds and two queen beds were in the others. One bathroom with a large walk-in shower joined the two guest rooms on the left side of the hall and a second bathroom with a smaller shower and large garden tub joined the other two guest rooms. All rooms had floor-to-ceiling windows with spectacular views of the expansive fields or stable and paddocks. Liam also informed her that there were three small guesthouses on the property, each with a small bedroom, kitchen and bath-room that guests booked for more private visits.

Upstairs, there were three rooms and two bathrooms. The largest room, directly opposite the stairway, belonged to Gayle. A room to the left of the stairs was empty save for a mahogany dresser covered with clear plastic.

"This used to be my room but I'm renovating it and stay-ing downstairs now," Holt said. "I'd planned to turn it into another guest room at some point but I think it'd be a perfect location for your nursery."

Mallory frowned. "Oh, please don't change your plans on my account. I don't want to inconvenience y—"

"Not at all." He smiled. "From this point forward, every-thing upstairs belongs to you and Mom." He walked across the landing and opened the door to another room. "This one's yours."

She joined him then walked into the room, glancing around. There was a large queen-size bed decorated with fluffy pillows and a handwoven quilt in the center of the room, and floor-to-ceiling windows were opposite, offering another stunning view of the property—this time of the front yard and fenced driveway. There was an en suite bathroom as well.

"Do you like it?" he asked.

She stood with her back to him, motionless for a moment, admiring the comfortable bed, large dresser and walk-in closet. "This is for me?"

"Yes."

"All of it?"

"Yes." He fell silent then added, "I thought it'd be easier for you to help Mom at night if you were next door to her room. And she gets up a lot at night, so it'll be easier for you to hear her moving about. If the bedding's not comfortable, we've got a closet full of comforter sets downstairs you can choose from and if you don't like anything there, we can shop in town for whatever you want. If you don't like the way the sun hits in the morning, we can get new curtains or rearrange the furniture however you want."

"I... I can change it?"

"Yes," he said. "In whatever way you'd like. And—" he gestured toward her middle "—if the stairs become too much for you, we'll just switch things up. I'll move back upstairs and you can choose a room downstairs instead."

This room was hers. A space all her own. To do with as she pleased.

"If you don't like it," he said hesitantly, "I can—"

"No." She faced him then, seeking his eyes, hoping he could glimpse in hers at least a fraction of the gratitude that swelled within her. It flooded her heart and spilled onto her lower lashes. "I love it."

He smiled, tenderness in his eyes, and the sight of it filled her heart even more. "Good." Clearing his throat, he walked to the door then said as he left, "I'll bring up your bag so you can settle in."

Mallory stood there, listening as his heavy steps descended the stairs, then walked across the room and sat on the bed. Outside the wide windows, the sun began to set, dipping low against the horizon, painting the sky a soft pink, and—despite the winter chill outdoors—flooded the room with a warm glow. It was quiet here. Peaceful and calm. She closed her eyes and warm tears poured over her cheeks.

LIAM LEANED BACK, closed his eyes and sighed.

Some years ago, behind the main house at Pine Creek Farm, he'd built a stone firepit and patio. The space had become his favorite place on the farm. It was serene, sitting out here under the starry night sky, a fire blazing and fields stretching out as far as the eye could see. But it wasn't the starlight, flicker of flame or glow of the winter moon that inspired such a peaceful feeling within his heart.

It was the fact that out here, with nothing separating him

from the sprawling heavens above his head and hard earth below his boots, he felt closest to God. There was something about it—the fresh, open air between his heart and the heavens above—that made him feel as though God heard his prayers more clearly.

And, more importantly, he could sometimes hear God more clearly.

For the past hour, he'd sat out here by the fire, sprawled in an Adirondack chair, staring at the stars above, asking God for guidance on how to help Mallory.

Hours earlier, after he'd shown Mallory to her room, he'd gone to his truck, unloaded his, Gayle's and Mallory's bags and carried them inside the house. He'd taken Mallory's overnight bag upstairs to her room, eager to help her settle in. But when he'd arrived, she'd been sitting on the edge of the bed, her hands flat on the mattress, her eyes closed and tears streaming down her cheeks. Unaware of his presence, she'd remained motionless and pensive as though in silent prayer or deep self-reflection.

Either way, he'd been hesitant to interrupt her. He'd placed her overnight bag on the floor just outside the open door and returned downstairs, taking quiet steps to avoid distracting her. He'd gone about his routine chores as usual, checking on the horses in the stable, paying various invoices online to vendors in his office and answering inquiries related to guest reservations for spring via email. Prospects looked good for Pine Creek Farm. As it stood, he'd booked visitors for all three guesthouses on the property from the day the bed-and-breakfast opened for the spring season until the last day of summer. If the fall season stayed as busy, Pine Creek Farm's bed-and-breakfast would generate more revenue this year than in the past two years, and with Mallory caring for his mom, he'd be able to offer an additional trail ride to guests each day, garnering more income.

Pleased at the good news, he'd returned to the main house

and checked on his mom, who'd fallen asleep on the living room couch, then walked to the kitchen—a pep of cautious optimism in his step—and began cooking dinner.

Throughout it all, Mallory had not emerged from her room. But sometime later, when the rich aroma of lasagna began to waft around the house, she'd emerged from upstairs and walked into the kitchen, tears gone and a polite smile on her face as she asked if she could help him prepare the meal.

She'd set the table while he'd baked the garlic bread and by the time dinner was ready, Mallory had woken Gayle, assisted her to the dining room table and had made sure she was seated with a full glass of sweet tea before taking her own seat at the table.

The meal had been pleasant. Gayle had asked several questions about how Liam had prepared the lasagna and had complimented his culinary skills—something she used to do often but had done less as of late. Mallory had thanked him again for her room, telling him how much she liked it, and had asked several more questions about the guesthouses, the grounds and the schedule she would undertake when caring for Gayle.

He'd filled her in on his mom's most pressing needs—Gayle had briefly argued with him on a few points—and soon, he and Mallory had created a schedule with which his mom begrudgingly agreed. Mallory would serve as a live-in caretaker and companion throughout the day. She'd help his mom dress and bathe, prepare and ensure his mom ate healthy meals and snacks on a consistent basis, and stay close at hand in case his mom wandered off.

As expected, he'd earned a scowl from his mom at the mention of her wandering and "needing a babysitter," as she'd dubbed it. And she'd reminded him, in no uncertain terms, how she felt about him.

"You may be handsome," Gayle had said, "but you're annoying."

Liam's face had heated and a soft laugh had escaped Mallory. She'd tried to hide it, ducking her head and taking another bite of lasagna, but he'd noticed, and the sound of it had made him smile.

In the quiet lull between conversations, they'd eaten in comfortable silence and Liam had glanced at Mallory occasionally, hoping she wouldn't notice him scrutinizing her expression as he'd searched for a glimpse of the distress he'd seen in her eyes earlier in the stable.

He'd scared her. Of that, he was certain.

It had been unfortunate that the cat had attacked him the moment they'd arrived at the stable, but not unexpected—Miss Priss had made a habit of such a thing. But for some reason, the event had affected Mallory in a much different way than it had him or Gayle. Instead of his irritation or his mom's cheery indulgence of the cat's antics, Mallory had looked terrified. Her hands had lifted in front of her, as though shielding herself from unseen danger, and an expression of terror had appeared on her face.

The fear in her eyes had struck a deep chord of concern within him.

He closed his eyes tighter and leaned his head back against the chair's headrest. His stomach churned at the thought of what she may have endured at the hands of her ex-husband, and he could only guess at the depths of pain she hid...and the fear she probably carried for men, in general. He'd wanted to reassure her that she was safe at Pine Creek Farm...and safe with him.

At the time, he'd fumbled the moment, unsure of what to say or how to approach her. And when he'd called her name, she'd quickly redirected the conversation back to the cat's antics. He'd followed her lead, had not asked any more questions and had carried on with the tour of the farm. But after seeing her sit motionless on the bed in her room with tears streaming down her cheeks, he'd been unable to shake the urgent need to find a way to connect with her. To assure her that she could share her fears, thoughts and emotions with him without judgment. That, somehow, he could find a way to help.

Women with pasts like that aren't usually looking for—or wanting—a hero.

Liam opened his eyes as he recalled the comment Holt made during their talk at Hummingbird Haven. He'd resented the sentiment as soon as his brother had made it, but at the moment—and to an extent, even back then—he also wondered exactly how true it was.

Was that what was driving him to seek a closer connection to Mallory? Was he trying to be her hero rather than simply serve her in a time of need?

He hoped not. Helping Mallory shouldn't be about him or his own wants, it should be about—

"Mind if I join you?"

He sat upright then stood as Mallory strolled across the stone patio and stopped beside the empty Adirondack chair beside him. "Of course." He gestured toward the empty chair. "Please have a seat."

"Your mom's fast asleep," she said, placing her hands on the armrests of the chair and easing into a seated position. She was wearing her long coat, and when she settled in the chair, it pulled across her middle, emphasizing her swollen belly. "I think she's getting used to me." A small smile curved her lips. "She let me sit with her for a while after she got in bed. She asked a dozen questions about me—what's my name, where am I from—and was in the middle of asking another when she fell asleep."

Liam laughed then sat back down in his chair. "Did she ask you to read to her?"

"Ephesians, chapter two." She smiled wider, her eyes teasing. "She said she liked my voice better than yours."

Liam laughed again and leaned back in his chair, stretching out his legs. "Thank you for volunteering to get her settled tonight. And for loading the dishwasher. I didn't expect you to hit the ground running the moment you arrived, but I have to say, it was nice to eat a good supper then come out here and relax while my stomach settled instead of jumping to the next task."

"That's why I'm here," she said. "It's my job. I'm happy to help however I can and the sooner Gayle and I get to know each other, the better we'll get along."

Liam nodded. "Well, I appreciated it. More than you know." He held his hands out, absorbing the warmth from the fire. "Are you warm enough? I could grab a blanket for you if—"

"No, thank you. I'm good."

They fell quiet for a few minutes, watching the flames flicker against the backdrop of the night sky and listening to the crackle and pop of wood as it burned. He snuck a couple glances in her direction, but she had her hood on and the bulky material obscured her face.

"Why are you helping me?"

Liam stilled. Her soft voice seemed to echo into the cold night air surrounding them. He moved to speak then hesitated before answering. "Because it's the right thing to do."

He wasn't sure why, but the weight of disappointment settled over his chest as he said the words aloud.

"I'm sorry for the way I've…" Her voice trailed away and she fell silent again.

He listened to the fire crackle for a few moments then prompted, "For the way you…?"

Her coat rustled and he looked in her direction, his gaze meeting hers as she looked at him earnestly.

"I have a lot of bad memories," she said. "And I have no control over when they come." She blinked rapidly and lowered her gaze, her cheeks flushing beneath the glow of the fire. "It's embarrassing, but…it just is."

One of his hands lifted, reaching toward hers, but he stopped the movement and gripped the armrest of his chair.

"You have nothing to be embarrassed about. I'm only sorry for what you've been through."

She met his gaze, her eyes searching his, then turned away and faced the fire. Her hood hid her face again.

"Have you...?" He shifted awkwardly in his seat. "Have you spoken to someone? About the memories, I mean?"

Her hood shifted as she nodded. "It just takes time. A lot of work." She sighed. "And a lot of prayer."

Liam looked at the fire, too, watching the flames spit embers into the sky. They floated up, small red flashes amid the velvet night sky and sparkling stars. "You remember the ladies' group I mentioned? The one from my church?" At her nod, he added, "They meet often and Pam Marshall's a great leader. And a great listener. I could introduce you to her, if you'd like?"

"Yes. I'd like that very much." Voice strained, she curled her fingers around the armrests of her chair. "And I... I have another favor to ask, please?"

"Of course. Anything."

Her coat rustled and he turned his head, meeting her gaze again. "Before we left Hummingbird Haven, Jessie made an appointment for me to see a doctor in Pine Creek." She briefly motioned toward her belly. "For a checkup, you know? My appointment's tomorrow but I don't know how to get there." She laughed, her mouth twisting. "And I don't have a car anymore."

"Not a problem," he said. "I'll drive you into town tomorrow."

"I need to go by the bank, too, please. I'd like to open an account with the money I made from selling my car, if you can spare the time?"

He smiled. "Not a problem. The bank's right around the corner from the health clinic and a coffee shop's nearby. Mom loves her lattes and always enjoys going into town. We'll help you check in for your appointment then grab a coffee and come back and pick you up." He winced. "Although... Mom likes to shop in the craft store next to the coffee shop, so if we run a little behind getting back to the clinic, don't worry. It'll depend on how bossy she gets when I tell her it's time to leave."

Her smile returned. It transformed her expression, brightening her eyes and easing the tense lines that bracketed her mouth. A brief glimpse of the happy, carefree woman he suspected she might've once been.

He wished he could give her that. Make her smile forever.

"She's definitely got a stubborn streak," she said, laughing. "But I think she's earned it."

She turned away and adjusted the hood on her head. Silence fell between them, save for the crackle of the fire and the whistle of winter wind as it swept over the open fields surrounding them.

"I was wrong," she whispered.

Liam glanced at her again but was unable to see her face. "About what?"

"It's not quiet here. Not at all," she said softly. "You hear that? The chorus of the fire and the wind? Even the stars seem to whisper."

He closed his eyes again and a tender longing spread through his heart. One that urged him to imagine what it might be like to enjoy each peaceful evening out here by the firepit beneath the stars with a woman he loved by his side. And how it might feel to be loved by her in return. "Yes."

"It's like a peaceful song," she said. "The most beautiful one I've ever heard."

CHAPTER FIVE

THE NEXT MORNING, Mallory stood, legs trembling, beside Liam at the check-in desk inside a health clinic within the town limits of Pine Creek.

"Mallory Kent, right?" The receptionist, a young blonde with kind eyes and a bright smile, picked up the clipboard that lay on the desk, eyed Mallory's signature then nodded with satisfaction. "Jessie Alden called us yesterday to remind us that you'd be coming today. She asked Dr. Harper to take great care of you."

Mallory tried to smile but her mouth trembled. Instead, she shoved her clammy hands into the pockets of her coat and nodded in return. "Jessie told me Dr. Harper was the best obstetrician in Pine Creek."

"One of only two obstetricians," the receptionist said, giggling. "Not that that makes her any less of the best. Her primary practice is in Dalton—that's about an hour from here—but she and Dr. Martin Zendall, our other visiting obstetrician, come to Pine Creek once a month to take care of local patients. Being a rural town, Pine Creek doesn't have the population to serve a full-time obstetrician and we're grateful to have them."

Mallory released a small sigh of relief, thanking Jessie silently in her head again for having the compassionate foresight to arrange the appointment with the female physician. Being cared for by a female doctor rather than a male wouldn't silence the turmoil inside her at the thought of being examined, but it would at least help.

"All I need is your state-issued ID and health insurance card, please," the receptionist said, holding out her hand. "Then I'll have you fill out a new patient packet."

Mallory dug around in her coat pocket and withdrew her license, but hesitated before handing it over. "I have my ID, but I don't have any insur—"

"I'll be serving as the guarantor for Mallory's account," Liam said. "Is there a place for me to write down my information so you can bill me for the visits?"

The receptionist's eyes widened with surprise as she smiled at Liam. "Of course, Liam." The receptionist picked up another clipboard with several sheets of paper attached, removed one page and handed it to him. "Here's the payment form from the new patient packet. You can jot down your information there, although I already know where to find you." She winked. "My sister and brother-in-law are bringing their kids for a visit on spring break. I told them they better get with you quick if they want to book one of the guesthouses at Pine Creek Farm again."

Liam smiled. "That's a good idea. We've gotten a lot of reservations for spring already." He tapped the paper in his hand. "Mallory's my newest employee. She's caring for my mom and helping with the bed-and-breakfast."

The receptionist smiled at Mallory. "How wonderful! Pine Creek Farm is so beautiful in the spring! You'll love it."

"Thank you," Liam said. "And you'll be sure to send any invoices for Mallory's care to me?"

The receptionist turned to a desktop computer and began typing on the keyboard. "I'll make a note of it in the system now."

Mallory reached for the paper. "Liam, you don't have to do that—"

He pressed the paper to his chest and grabbed a pen from the desk. "I know. But we haven't discussed health benefits yet so consider it part of your salary." He smiled. "I'll get this filled out and everything'll be taken care of. You just focus on taking care of yourself."

Mallory shook her head. "But, Liam—"

"Oh, magazines!" Gayle, who'd been strolling around the waiting room, picked up a garden magazine and sat down in a comfortable chair by the window. "Now, if I just had a cup of coffee, I'd be set."

"Welp," Liam said, "that's my cue. After I fill this out, I'll take Mom next door to the coffee shop, grab a latte then we'll come back to pick you up." His eyes, concerned, narrowed as he studied her face. "Unless you'd like us to stay and wait for you here?"

Mallory bit her lip, wanting to ask him to stay. But why, she didn't know. So far, she'd attended all her checkups alone and this one was no different.

Only, it had felt different walking into this clinic today, chatting with the receptionist and filling out paperwork with Liam by her side. She'd felt less alone—almost as though she had a friend or teammate, cheering her on and wishing her well, ready to catch her if she were to fall. And looking at him now, studying the concern in his eyes and his patient expression, she found herself admiring his selflessness and generosity all the more.

So far, Liam was nothing like Trevor. Liam had been so calm and kind. So caring and understanding. If he were genuine—if he didn't turn out to be too good to be true—any woman would be lucky to have a man like him as a friend.

But Liam wasn't aiming to be her friend, was he? And this baby wasn't his responsibility. What was it he'd said last night by the fire? About why he decided to help her?

Because it's the right thing to do. Nothing more, nothing less. She was a good deed for a good man.

"No." She forced the word out between stiff lips, wanting to take it back as soon as she said it. "I'm okay. Thank you."

The concern in Liam's eyes deepened.

A door beside the check-in desk opened and a middle-aged woman with glasses and a topknot called out, "Mallory Kent?"

"I..." Mallory dragged her hands from her pockets and rubbed her clammy palms down the side of her pants. "I'm Mallory Kent."

The woman smiled and propped the door open a bit further. "Nice to meet you, Mallory. I'm Dr. Harper. Would you like to come on back and get started?"

Hesitating, Mallory glanced at the clipboard on the receptionist's desk. "I haven't filled out the new patient paperwork yet."

Dr. Harper smiled. "No worries. You can bring it back with you and we'll go over it together."

Mallory nodded but stood in place, trying to calm the tremors that still coursed through her legs.

"I'm happy to stay, if you need me," Liam said quietly.

Mallory stared up at his face, studied his encouraging smile and wished she could borrow his strength if only for a moment.

"It's okay, Mallory," Dr. Harper said. "You're my only patient for today. If you're not ready to go back yet, that's fine. I can catch up on some paperwork and you can let me know when you'd like to start. Take all the time you'd like."

"No, thank you." Mallory picked up the new patient packet and walked toward the door. "I'm ready now." She glanced over her shoulder. "Thank you for your offer to stay, Liam, but I'll be fine. Please take Gayle for her latte." She smiled. "I wouldn't want her to have a reason to get upset with you."

Some of the concern in his eyes faded, a teasing light taking its place. "You're right. That wouldn't be good for any of us." He smiled gently. "We'll be back soon."

The exam room was small but comfortable and Dr. Harper took great care to help Mallory feel at ease. She spoke in soothing tones and asked questions in an unintimidating manner, waiting patiently as Mallory filled out the new patient packet, described her family's health history and spoke of her new job at Pine Creek Farm. Dr. Harper even managed to slip in a few jokes here and there, coaxing a laugh from Mallory when she least expected it.

"And when was your last checkup?" Dr. Harper asked.

Mallory, now lying on the exam table, stared up at the ceiling. Someone had taped a poster there. The scene was a serene landscape with a field of flowers. She traced each bloom with her eyes. "Last month."

"All was well, I take it?" Dr. Harper asked.

"Yes."

"Take a couple deep breaths for me, Mallory." Dr. Harper waited as Mallory did so, then said gently, "We'll take this slow, okay? At any time, if you feel uncomfortable or need a break, just let me know."

Mallory inhaled deeply again then released a long breath, feeling her heart rate slow slightly. "Okay."

Dr. Harper was gentle and quick and soon, the worst was over.

"All seems well now, too," Dr. Harper said, removing her gloves and pushing her stool back from the exam table. She stood and walked to Mallory's side. "Would you like to see your baby today? We received a grant last year that allowed us to purchase a new ultrasound machine. Our equipment's in-house and we can do a 3D ultrasound, if you'd like?"

Mallory closed her eyes briefly then refocused on the flowers. "Sure."

It didn't take long for Dr. Harper to set everything up and before long, a rhythmic heartbeat filled the room and the small monitor to the left of the exam table showed a baby's image.

"There he is," Dr. Harper said gently as she moved the transducer over the gel slicked across Mallory's belly. "A healthy baby boy."

Mallory, her mouth trembling, glanced at the screen once then stared at the flowers again. "Yes."

"Have you chosen a name?"

"No."

"Well, there's no rush. You still have several weeks before your due date. Lots of time to think about it."

Think. Mallory narrowed her eyes as she stared at the flowers. Thinking about her pregnancy was something she didn't want to do. Avoiding it as much as possible was less painful. But she no longer had that luxury, did she? Not if she wanted to give this baby—her son—the best life she possibly could.

Son. *My son...* How strange that sounded.

Mallory forced herself to look away from the flowers and face the monitor again. The baby's face was visible now—his small nose and parted lips clearly visible. His hand, delicate fingers curled, rested against his chin. He looked healthy and content. Peaceful.

"Could I..." She cleared her throat and blinked as a sheen of moisture gathered in her eyes. "May I have a picture of him, please?"

Dr. Harper smiled. "Of course. I'll email you this batch, but I think we can print at least one copy for you before you leave." She moved the transducer over Mallory's belly again, pressing a few buttons on the machine as she asked, "I'd like to ask you something a little more personal, if that's okay?"

Mallory nodded jerkily.

"How do you feel about the baby?"

A knot formed in Mallory's chest. It tightened then swelled, constricting her throat. "I—I don't know."

Dr. Harper remained silent.

"You know how this happened, right?" Mallory asked. "Jessie told them what I asked her to when she made the appointment, didn't she?"

"Yes. She filled us in on what she knew, but from this point forward, I'm here for you, Mallory. For whatever you'd like to tell me. And you don't have to share anything that you're not comfortable with."

"I'm keeping him," Mallory whispered.

When she didn't elaborate, Dr. Harper asked, "Have you met with a counselor, Mallory? Have you spoken to someone about what's happened to you?"

Mallory nodded. "It helped but…"

Dr. Harper waited a moment, then asked, "But what?"

Mallory didn't answer. She couldn't. The churn of her stomach and increasing pressure in her chest was overwhelming.

"You know," Dr. Harper said quietly. "For some of my patients, they find comfort in journaling. Sometimes it helps to write your thoughts down. To get them on the outside. It can have a way of helping you reconcile your past with the future and help you find the strength to face it."

"I'm keeping him," Mallory repeated. "And I won't change my mind. I want to be a good mom, but sometimes…"

After a few moments, Dr. Harper covered Mallory's hand with her own and squeezed gently. "Write that thought down and try to finish it. See where it takes you. Then list the reasons you've decided to keep him. In time, you might find you're able to start a new list. One where you can explore the ways this baby might potentially bring you joy."

Mallory swallowed hard and repeated a soft refrain that seemed ingrained in her core. "I'll try."

LIAM RETURNED TO the health clinic from the coffee shop and had been waiting with his mother in the waiting room for over an hour when Mallory finally emerged from the door beside the reception desk. Dr. Harper was with her, cupping her elbow and pointing at something Mallory held in her hands.

Liam glanced to his right where Gayle sat on a couch, a magazine open in her lap, her head rolling onto her left shoulder as she began to doze off. Apparently, the large caramel latte she'd ordered at the coffee shop had failed to fend off her late-morning fatigue.

"Mom?" He touched the back of her hand. "Mom? It's time to go."

Blinking, she sat up on the couch and looked around the room. A familiar expression of confusion appeared on her face as she studied her surroundings. She looked down at her lap and patted the magazine as though offering herself reassurance. "I'm reading."

Liam smiled. "I think you stopped reading some time ago. You got a good nap in while we waited." He stood and held out a hand for the magazine. "Mallory's all finished. It's time to go."

Gayle frowned, her eyes widening with fear. "Who's Mallory? Where am I?"

Liam sighed as a fresh wave of grief swept through him. He was used to this—the repeated questions and easily forgotten answers from his mother—but each time she asked something she'd already been told or had experienced firsthand, he was reminded of how rapidly her cognition had begun to decline. And being in a doctor's office, well, that was another painful reminder of the frequent medical appointments she'd had in the past and the many more that awaited her in the future. All of it was a reminder that his time with her was growing shorter.

"You know Mallory," he said quietly. "She's here to help us out. She read to you last night and helped you get settled in bed." He smiled. "She said you told her that you liked her voice better than mine."

Gayle frowned deeper, her brow furrowing as she tried to recall the information. He could see from the blank look in her eyes that the knowledge had failed to come to her.

"You're safe and sound, Mom. I promise." Liam reached down and removed the magazine from her lap then returned it to the table nearby. "Now, it's time to go."

He cupped her elbow and helped her to her feet, waiting for her to get her bearings for a moment before leading her across the waiting room to join Mallory.

"You're Liam, I'm guessing?" Dr. Harper looked at him, her brows raised.

"Yes," he said. "Liam Williams." He held out his hand. "It's nice to meet you. Thank you for helping Mallory today."

Dr. Harper smiled and shook his hand. "I was happy to. And I'm glad to meet you as well. I wanted to make sure Mallory had a ride home." She glanced at Mallory, who stood motionless, looking down at the item in her hands. "I'm afraid I wore her out with a ton of questions today—not to mention all the poking and prodding." She laughed. "I'm hoping I didn't scare her away from our next appointment."

Mallory looked up then and smiled, but her eyelids were pink and puffy as though she'd been crying. "Oh, no. I appreciate all you've done. Thank you, Dr. Harper."

"Remember to call me if you need anything," Dr. Harper said, before saying her goodbyes and returning to her office.

Liam led the way out of the clinic and into the parking lot, stepping back and holding the door at the exit, gesturing for Gayle and Mallory to precede him outside. "So, how'd it go?"

Mallory didn't answer. Instead, she continued taking slow steps behind Gayle, a small piece of paper still clutched tightly in her fist.

"Mallory, are you o—"

"Where am I?" Gayle, who'd walked ahead of them, stopped in the middle of the sidewalk and looked around urgently, a worried gleam in her eyes. "Where's my house? Where are the magnolias?"

Liam, hastening to reassure her, jogged a few steps to catch up with her and placed his palm on her back gently. "It's okay, Mom. We're in town. We came to the doctor's office where Mallory had an appointment and had a coffee while we waited." He pointed at his truck, which sat a few feet away in the parking lot. "There's my truck, see?"

"I want to go home," she said, her eyes wide and fearful as they met his. "I want to go home right now."

Liam hesitated and glanced over his shoulder. "Mallory said she needed to go by the bank on the way—"

But Mallory was no longer there.

He scanned the sidewalk and the surrounding area, glancing back at the front doors of the clinic, sweeping his gaze over the empty benches that were positioned outside the building and visually sifting through the people who strolled in front of the building. Finally, he noticed her standing near the bushes on one side of the building. Her back was to him, and she was doubled over, her shoulders heaving.

"Oh no," he whispered. "Mom, let's get you in the truck. I need to check on Mallory."

He ushered Gayle along the sidewalk and to the truck, helped her into the passenger seat then shut the door and jogged back to Mallory. By the time he reached her, she had straightened and stepped away from the bushes, one hand covering her mouth.

"Are you okay?" he asked.

She sure didn't look it. The color had drained from her face, leaving her cheeks pale, and despite the winter chill in the air, sweat had beaded on her forehead and along her temples beneath her hood.

"I—I'm okay." Her fingers, pressing a tissue to her lips, trembled as she spoke. "I just got sick all of a sudden. Too fast to make it back inside to the restroom." A bright red flush flooded her cheeks as she glanced up at him. "I'm so embarrassed."

"You shouldn't be," he said, issuing a wry smile. "I've heard it happens from time to time during a pregnancy." He dug around in the front pocket of his jeans then both of his back pockets before glancing over his shoulder at his truck. "I've got some clean napkins in the glove compartment of my truck. Give me just a second and I'll round you up a bottle of wa—"

"It's a boy."

He faced her again. Her fingers still touched her lips, muffling her words.

"I haven't told you that, have I?"

He shook his head.

"I've known it for over a month now, but I still haven't chosen a name." Tears welled onto her lower lashes. "I decided to keep him rather than give him up for adoption and I won't change my mind, but most days I don't want him. Most days, I don't even want to think about him." The tears broke free and poured unheeded down her red cheeks. Her eyes were full of anguish, so much so it broke his heart. "What kind of mother does that make me?"

Liam remained silent for moment. His fists clenched, a surge of anger rolling through him at the reminder of how she ended up in this position. He couldn't fathom how any man—especially one who professed to love a woman—could turn violent against her. It was no wonder she had difficulty trusting him.

The wounded vulnerability in her gaze prompted his fists to unfurl. His arms ached to wrap protectively around her, hug her close and tuck her head beneath his chin.

Instead, he stepped closer, reached out and eased the small piece of paper from her free hand. It was an ultrasound picture, the baby's face clearly visible. He blew out a heavy breath as he imagined her in Dr. Harper's office, facing the image of her future child—and the weight of her past—alone.

"Considering all you've been through?" he said. "I'd say it makes you human."

A small sob escaped her. She looked up at him, some of the pain receding from her eyes, then she shoved the tissue she held into the pocket of her coat, wiped the tears from her cheeks and nodded.

It was a long, quiet drive back to the farm. Gayle, exhausted from the morning's events, had fallen asleep in the passenger seat, her head leaning against the headrest. Mallory, seated in the back of the cab, stared silently out the window, lost deep in thought. Neither of them had been eager to visit the bank after leaving the doctor's office, so he headed straight home.

After arriving at the farm, Liam assisted Gayle and Mallory out of the truck then led Gayle upstairs and helped her into bed, removing her shoes and socks and covering her with a warm quilt before shutting the door quietly behind him as he left. He found Mallory in the empty guest room across from her bedroom. She stood in the center of the room, her hands twisting together below her protruding belly as she gazed about the room.

"I don't know what I'm doing," she whispered.

Liam entered the room and stood beside her. "Not many of us do."

"I mean, I don't even know where to begin," she said.

He smiled. "You could start with the walls."

She glanced up at him, her blue eyes wide with surprise. "The walls?"

"I know blue is the usual color people pick for a boy's nursery," he said softly. "But there's no rule about it. We can paint the walls whatever color you like. Yellow might be a good choice for a boy. Or we could paint them green, leave them white or go with patterned wallpaper even. The choice is yours."

She returned her attention to the room, her eyes roving slowly over the walls, the floor and the empty corners.

"We'll need a crib," he continued. "And a bassinet, for when you want to keep him in your room. We'll need a changing table, rocking chair, or a glider, maybe. A glider might be more comfortable."

She nodded slowly.

"We can start there," he repeated. "I can give Pam a call.

Ask her and the ladies' group to come by tomorrow and help you decide on the details. It'd give you a chance to meet everyone. Have a support network when you need it. Do you think you'd be up for that?"

Her chest lifted on a deep inhale as she glanced around the room again. "Yes," she said. "I think I'm up for that."

"Good. I'll go grab you some paper and a pen and I'll bring a snack with it in case you get hungry. Mom's napping, so you can take your time. Brainstorm some ideas of things you might like. Write it down."

Her gaze strayed to the window as she whispered, "Yes. I'll write it down."

Nodding, Liam left and walked downstairs. He found a pen and notepad, washed and sliced an apple, and poured milk into a glass. It wasn't until he'd loaded it all onto a tray and began walking back upstairs that he realized he was humming a lullaby.

And he realized that when he'd made suggestions to Mallory for preparing for the baby, he hadn't said *you*. He'd said *we*.

THAT NIGHT, AFTER Mallory helped Gayle into bed and read from the Bible until she fell asleep, Mallory went back to her own room, grabbed the notepad and pen Liam had provided earlier in the day and sat on the edge of the bed. It was dark out, but the stars were shining outside the window and Liam was probably admiring them right now in his chair by the firepit behind the house where he'd gone to relax after dinner.

The house was quiet and still. It was, Mallory supposed, the best time to begin.

She uncapped the pen and scanned the words she'd written on the first page hours earlier in the guest room across the hall.

Crib, bassinet, changing table, diapers, onesies, baby wipes—

She stopped reading and looked up, her eyes peering out

the window into the dark fields beyond. Inhaling deeply, she turned the page to a blank sheet and began writing.

I want to be a good mom, but sometimes—she paused, squeezed the pen tightly in her hand, then continued writing—*I don't want him.*

A shaky breath escaped her. She lifted her head and stared out the window again for a few moments then returned her attention to the page in front of her and wrote again.

On the days that I do want him, I think of how he's not to blame for his father's sins. How innocent and how precious he is. This new life that's growing inside me.

On the days I want him, I remind myself that he's a part of me as well. But I wonder if he'll be like me. I wonder if he'll look like me or if he'll look more like Tr—

Her hand froze around the pen. Heart pounding, she left the sentence unfinished, dropped down to the next blank line on the page, and wrote again.

What color would you like the walls... Oliver?

"Oliver," she whispered. A small smile curved her lips.

Do you like that name? It was my father's name. Sometimes people called him Ollie, but only those who knew him very well.

What do you think, Oliver? Would you like me to paint the walls of your nursery blue? Yellow? Or maybe you'd prefer something more rustic, like green. A forest green, maybe? The same green that I'm sure will fill the fields here on Liam's farm when spring arrives—the same time you're supposed to be here.

You'd like Liam, I think. He's patient. Kind. Gentle. Understanding.

The words blurred and she blinked hard.

Who will you be like, Oliver? Who will you be?

CHAPTER SIX

THE NEXT AFTERNOON, Mallory took her first step toward trying to be a good mother.

Liam helped her prepare. Earlier that morning, after he, Mallory and Gayle had eaten breakfast, he'd rounded up several chairs and a folding table, carried them upstairs to the empty guest room and positioned the chairs around the table in a comfortable circle.

"For the ladies' group," he said, smiling.

True to his promise, Liam had called Pam Marshall, leader of the ladies' group at his church, the day prior and invited her and the other women to Pine Creek Farm to meet Mallory and help her brainstorm ideas for the nursery. Liam had left soon after setting up the table and chairs and had gone to work, feeding the horses and helping the hands muck the stalls while Mallory stayed indoors with Gayle. Anxious for the afternoon meeting, Mallory had busied herself with reading to Gayle and doing chores about the house while Gayle watched late morning talk shows.

By lunchtime, the ladies' group arrived with three large baskets. One basket had been filled to the brim with warm barbecue sandwiches, which they carried to the stable and distributed to Liam and the hands. The second basket, the largest of the three, held lunch for the ladies, which consisted of barbecued chicken, seasoned turnips, potato salad and warm peach cobbler for dessert. And after all the ladies finished eating, Pam Marshall gave Mallory the third basket and smiled.

"It's from all of us." Seated in one of the chairs Liam had carried into the guest room, Pam glanced around her at the other ladies, who sat around the table, then looked at Mallory. "It's only a start, mind you. We'd like to hold a proper baby shower for you closer to your due date, if you wouldn't mind?"

Wendy Owens, seated to Pam's left, scooted forward in her chair. "Oh, yes, please. We haven't had a proper baby shower in ages." She nudged her glasses higher on her nose. "All those cute decorations and baby clothes…" She sighed. "It'd be a dream day!"

Barbara Smith and Cherie Ann Little, who sat on either side of Gayle, nodded in agreement. "A dream day," they repeated in unison, then looked at each other and burst out laughing.

Mallory smiled. Liam had been right. She enjoyed spending time with the ladies' group. Pam Marshall had a cheerful disposition and spoke with a relaxed confidence and the rest of the older women were kind, easygoing and laughed often. Mallory liked them immediately.

"So," Pam said, "have you decided what color you'd like to paint the nursery walls yet?"

"There's no rush," Barbara said.

"Not at all." Cherie Ann motioned toward the big basket sitting on the table in front of Mallory. "Maybe you should open your gift first and then decide."

Mallory shifted in her seat to a more comfortable position then pulled the basket closer to her. "Thank you so much for this. I hope you know I didn't expect you to bring anything today or go to all this trouble."

"Oh, it was no trouble," Pam said. "We were thrilled when Liam called and invited us over. We always like to welcome our neighbors to Pine Creek." She glanced at Mallory's belly and smiled. "Even the smallest ones who have yet to arrive."

Mallory's smile quivered but she managed to hold it in place as she untied the bow on the white basket, peeled away the plastic covering and began removing items.

There were bibs of every color and design, several blue-and-white onesies, a pacifier, teething ring and plush blue teddy bear.

"There are so many beautiful things here." Mallory lined the items up on the table, tears springing to her eyes. "How did you manage this on such short notice?"

Wendy grinned. "When Liam called yesterday, we met up and took a trip into town."

"Liam told us you're having a boy. That's why we got a lot of blue onesies." Cherie Ann bit her lip and leaned forward, propping her elbows on the table. "I hope he was right."

"Of course he was right," Barbara said. "Liam's always right." She glanced at Gayle, who sat beside her. "Isn't that right, Gayle? I can't remember a time when Liam was wrong about anything. You raised him to be a fine man. So honorable and kind. I don't think I've met another man quite like him."

Gayle looked at Barbara blankly.

"He stayed, you know," Barbara continued, looking at Mallory. "Years ago, when Liam's father left the farm, Holt followed his dad back to the rodeo circuit, but Liam stayed here. He loved his mother too much to leave her to handle the farm on her own. Even at eighteen, he was already mature far beyond his years."

Mallory looked down and fiddled with the white ribbon tied around the plush teddy bear. "Did Liam ever leave Pine Creek Farm? I mean, for college or to explore another career?"

Barbara shook her head. "But he could have, certainly."

"Liam is one of the smartest men I've ever met," Pam said. "He could've gone to school anywhere and pursued any profession he wanted, but he chose to stay here and support his mother."

"And he never..." Mallory hesitated, winding the silky ribbon around her index finger then unwinding it. "Has he ever been married?"

"No," Pam said softly. When Mallory glanced up and met her eyes, she smiled. "Gayle shared with us once, years ago, that she'd tried to encourage him to branch out and live for himself a bit more. To maybe even leave Pine Creek for a while and devote his energy to his own pursuits. But he declined. She confided that she'd asked him once if he resented his decision to stay over the years or if he regretted the opportunities he'd missed out on." She glanced at Gayle with a tender expression. "She said he told her no. That staying with her and running the farm had been the right thing to do."

Mallory fell silent, turning the phrase over in her mind, rubbing the silky ribbon between her fingertips.

Because it's the right thing to do.

For some reason, the words settled in her belly like a heavy stone. They drew her shoulders down and made her sag against the edge of the table.

"I like the bear," Gayle said. "That shade of blue." Her hazel eyes fixed on the stuffed toy in front of Mallory and the crow's-feet beside her eyes wrinkled as she smiled. "I gave my son, Holt, one like it. He loved it so."

Her smile returning, Mallory picked it up and passed the teddy bear across the table to Gayle. "Here. Hold it. It's even softer than it looks."

Gayle held the teddy bear that Mallory passed her, cradling it in her hands gently and smoothing her thumbs over its furry ears. "It's such a beautiful shade of blue."

"Liam said we could choose any color for the walls," Mallory said. "But I do like the idea of blue for a boy." She looked at Gayle's hands, watching the older woman's ivory fingers gently smooth down the teddy bear's fur. "Gayle, I think if you and I take the bear to a paint store, they may be able to match that shade and create a custom paint for the nursery."

Gayle looked up from the teddy bear and glanced around the room. She stared at the white walls, her brow furrowing as she considered Mallory's idea. "Yes." She smiled brightly and patted the teddy bear. "This blue. The exact same shade."

"Well, there you go," Pam said. "That's one decision made already." She looked at Mallory. "Do you have a piece of paper that we can use to start writing these decisions down?"

Mallory nodded and picked up the notepad Liam had given her. She opened it, flipped to a blank page, grabbed a pen and smiled at the other women. "So which decision should we tackle next?"

They brainstormed for over an hour, discussing each item on the list of needs Mallory had made for the nursery, batting around ideas for different themes, discussing various patterns in terms of blankets and rugs, then chatted about postpartum recovery, 3:00 a.m. feedings and the many other challenges that naturally arose from having a baby in the house.

At one point, Pam pointed out how Liam could be of help by suggesting that Mallory ask him to childproof the electrical outlets and cabinets and, on occasion, change diapers, which made Cherie Ann cackle out loud. Laughter was had by all, and Mallory found herself giggling on more than one occasion, something she hadn't done naturally in what seemed like forever.

The women reminded her of her mother, whom she lost years ago, and sitting at the table, surrounded by strong, patient women who spoke with joy at the prospect of a new baby gave Mallory hope.

Hope that she might be able to be a good mother after all.

When they arrived at the last item on the list, Mallory jotted down ideas each of the ladies shared then rubbed the small of her back. A small ache had begun a half hour ago but she'd enjoyed the camaraderie with the women so much, she hadn't wanted to interrupt their conversations by leaving the table.

"Oh, Mallory," Pam said, pushing back from the table. "Here we are babbling away with you sitting in one position all this time. I imagine your back must be hurting by now."

Mallory smiled and waved away the concern. "I'm okay."

She was used to pain. The twinge in her back was simply a minor inconvenience.

The thought of her past, however brief, tugged her mouth back into a frown and she pushed her chair back from the table as well then stood. "I just need to stretch my legs, is all."

Rubbing the small of her back with one hand, she strolled across the room toward the window. It was late afternoon now, and outside, Liam led several horses and riders in a line across the front field of Pine Creek Farm, heading back to the stable.

"Liam and the hands took the horses out," Mallory said.

"Liam takes great care of those horses," Pam said. "It's chilly out there but no matter the weather, he makes sure they get their exercise and fresh air."

"And how his business has grown," Wendy said. "He told Pam yesterday on the phone that the guesthouses are almost completely booked for spring already. You must be so proud of his success, Gayle."

Mallory glanced over her shoulder and noticed Gayle gazed back at Wendy without recognition.

"She is," Cherie Ann said before addressing Gayle. "You've told us so many times over the years about how much you love him."

Gayle looked down at the teddy bear in her hands. "I love babies," she said quietly.

Cherie Ann leaned forward and patted Gayle's knee. "Looks like you'll have one around the farm soon enough. From what Liam told us, Mallory's baby boy will be here in March. That's only a couple months away."

Gayle looked up again and turned her head to focus on Mallory. Her gaze drifted down to Mallory's protruding belly as though seeing it for the first time.

"Oh, a baby." Smiling, Gayle stood and walked across the room to join Mallory at the window. She reached out and placed her warm palms on Mallory's belly. "I've always wanted a grandbaby."

For a moment, Mallory stiffened. Gayle's hands, though gentle, cradled the large swell of Mallory's expectant belly, a gesture that brought the reality of the baby into stark relief. Gayle's touch, the kind Mallory had avoided herself over the past seven months, was a tactile sensation that Mallory couldn't ignore.

Pam stood, her gaze concerned, as she studied Mallory's expression. "Gayle, Mallory's back is bothering her. It might not be comfortable for her to have others—"

"It's okay," Mallory whispered, somehow managing to smile, lift her arms and cover Gayle's hands with her own. "There's definitely a baby in here, isn't there?"

Gayle met her eyes, a look of longing on her face that made Mallory want to hug her.

"It's a boy," Mallory said.

Gayle smiled wider. "I had a baby boy once. May I hold him when he gets here?"

Mallory nodded.

Gayle glanced at the women behind them, who watched them both with soft smiles and teary eyes. "I'll be able to hold the baby." Then she faced the window again and looked out as the men rode the horses across the grounds. She pointed at Liam. "That man there. Leading them all. He's here a lot." She glanced at Mallory expectantly. "Is he your husband? The baby's father?"

A heavy sensation settled within Mallory again. She slipped away from Gayle's touch and lowered her hands back to her side. "No," she whispered. "No, he's not."

THE WINTER WIND blew cold across the grounds of Pine Creek Farm but Liam, having led the horses on a trail ride, was warm enough inside the stable to shed his jacket. He did so, setting it aside, then resumed brushing his favorite mare, Sugar.

"It's only been a few days," he said, "but I think it's going to work out."

"Sounds like it." Jessie's voice, strong and clear, emitted from the speaker of his cell phone from where it sat on the ledge of a nearby stall. "I told Holt I might drive down there this weekend and check on how things were going, but it seems like everything's well in hand."

"So far." Liam bent and brushed the underside of Sugar's belly. "The visit to the doctor yesterday was a bit rougher than Mallory expected but she pulled through it just fine."

"I was afraid that'd be difficult for her," Jessie said. "How did she react when she came out?"

Liam winced as he recalled the pallor of Mallory's face when she'd emerged from her checkup with the doctor yesterday. She'd been nervous, frightened and embarrassed by the way her body had responded to the stress she'd endured. "She did as well as one could expect."

"Has she spoken with you about the baby?"

"A little." Liam straightened and smiled as Sugar nudged him with her nose. "She's gradually getting used to the idea, I think. After the doctor's visit yesterday, we spoke a little bit about putting the nursery together. I called Pam Marshall this morning and asked her if she and the ladies' group would stop by and visit Mallory. Help her come up with some ideas for decorating the nursery and all."

"That was a wonderful idea," Jessie said, her tone brightening. "Did they come? And did Mallory get along well with them?"

"They seemed to hit it off. I didn't stick around the house long. I introduced them, helped Pam carry some barbecue sandwiches to the guys down here at the stable then went back to work." He rubbed Sugar behind her ears. "They're still up at the house now, I think, brainstorming plans for the nursery."

Or at least he thought so. When he and the hands had returned with the horses at the end of the trail ride, the ladies' cars had still been parked in the driveway.

"Good," Jessie said. "Decorating the nursery might help take her mind off her worries for a while. It might give her something positive to focus on."

Liam smiled. "She's having a boy. Had she told you that?"

Jessie laughed. "No, but what better place for a little boy to be introduced to the world than Pine Creek Farm?"

"A little boy would love it here." Liam grinned, thinking of all the fun and—sometimes—trouble he and Holt had gotten into as kids when rollicking around the farm. "By spring, there'll be grass as far as the eye can see in the fields. We can throw a blanket out and he can roll around on it beneath the sun to his heart's content. We'll show him the animals—I think he'd like the horses. Most kids do. And it'll be warmer then. We can rock him to sleep on the porch at night while the stars are shining. There's no better lullaby in the world than the crickets and frogs singing down by the pond at night."

He laughed, recalling the many times he and Holt had traipsed around the pond on a back lot behind the house. They'd spent most of each summer digging for crawdads in the mud, skipping stones across the water and catching bream.

"When he gets older," Liam said, "I'll take him out there and show him how to fish. The pond's probably stocked to the brim by now since I haven't fished in it lately. The little guy'll probably catch something as soon as he drops his cork in the water."

Smiling at the thought of teaching a little boy how to fish like he and Holt used to, Liam patted Sugar's back. It took a moment for him to realize that Jessie had grown silent on the other end of the line.

"Jessie? You still there?"

"Yeah," she said softly. "I'm just wondering how long you plan on Mallory and her son staying at Pine Creek Farm? The things you're speaking of, Mallory's son wouldn't be able to do for years. And Gayle, well…"

She didn't have to finish the sentence out loud. He already knew.

"Taking the job at Pine Creek Farm is supposed to be a new beginning for Mallory," Jessie said. "It was never intended to be an end."

Liam stilled. "I know."

As though sensing his tension, Sugar nudged his chest with her nose again.

"Do you?" Jessie asked. "Maybe it's not Mallory's baby you're thinking of. Maybe it's a son of your own," she said gently. "Having Mallory and a new baby at Pine Creek Farm may have just reminded you of what you want in life. It might have made you think of all the things you may have had to put off over the years to take care of Gayle."

Was that it? Was that what had prompted the thoughts of a boy growing up on the farm? Was the thought of Mallory's baby boy simply a reminder of the family he had once wished he'd have one day? A prospect that seemed less and less achievable as each year had passed.

He tried to envision it. Tried to picture a child—a little boy—who wasn't Mallory's son, but his own. A child who might one day belong to him and his wife.

In the past, he'd been afraid to allow himself to dwell on such wishes. He'd kept his focus on Gayle instead. And now it was difficult to imagine it. To see, in his mind's eye, a woman who wasn't Mallory living at the farm and raising a child—who wasn't Mallory's—with him.

The discomfort that moved through him at the thought of Mallory and her child leaving shocked him.

"I'm just excited at the thought of having a kid around,"

Liam said, trying to reassure himself as much as Jessie. "I just got carried away, I guess."

"It's easy to do," Jessie said gently. "I just want you to be aware of that. It's so much easier than you know to get attached to the children who you help."

And it'd be easy to get attached to Mallory, as well.

She didn't need to say that out loud either. He got the message—loud and clear.

Liam cleared his throat and patted Sugar's back. "Of course. I was just thinking out loud for a minute. Just random thoughts. Nothing necessarily tied to Mallory and her baby."

And the excitement he'd felt at decorating the nursery, that was just another byproduct of the idea of having a family. An idea he'd indulged in years ago but had packed away in the darkest recesses of his heart to focus on running the farm. Mallory's arrival had just prompted its reemergence. That was all.

He'd just have to be careful from this point forward and keep an eye out for getting too attached to Mallory and her baby.

"You're doing a great thing, Liam," Jessie said. "Helping Mallory get back on her feet and make a fresh start for herself and her baby is a wonderful thing to do. It'll change their lives for the better and they'll always remember you for it."

It was a pleasant sentiment. One he should welcome. But for some reason, the thought of Mallory and her baby moving on, leaving Pine Creek Farm—and him—behind sent a fresh wave of disappointment through him.

"In the meantime, I'm only a call away," Jessie said. "If you ever need me to come down to help with Mallory or the baby, or if you or Mallory have any questions, just give me a call. Otherwise, I'm going to give Mallory space and time to settle in before the baby comes."

Liam put the brush down, led Sugar into her stall then picked up the phone. "Thank you, Jessie. If we need you, I won't hesitate to contact you."

They said their goodbyes and Liam disconnected the call. He shoved the cell phone in the back pocket of his jeans then stood in front of Sugar's stall, rubbing the mare's forehead and allowing his mind to drift, just for moment, back to the happy images of him fishing with a little boy. A son he could help support and raise. A son he could guide through life, instilling strong values within him and showing him the ropes at the farm. A son who would grow up into a strong man and carry a little piece of Liam—hopefully, the best part—throughout his life, and pass on the lessons to a new generation.

It was a sweet dream. As sweet as it had always been. But, like most of the dreams he'd had in his thirty-eight years of life, it would likely never come to fruition.

"Liam?"

He started as Mallory's voice and soft footsteps echoed around the quiet stable. The hands, having brushed their horses and settled them in their stalls for the day, had left over half an hour ago to check the grounds and carry on with chores.

"I'm back here," he called out.

She walked into view then, rounding the line of stalls and strolling toward him. She was bundled up in her warm coat again, her hood firmly in place, as always, and she turned her head from one side to the other, smiling at each horse as she passed them.

"We saw you and the hands riding the horses earlier," she said. "Did you get cold on your ride?"

He patted Sugar's back then stepped away from the stall. "No. We've gotten used to the chilly temps and the horses enjoy getting out several times a week for some exercise." He leaned to the side, glancing at the entrance of the stable. "Did you bring Pam and the ladies with you?"

Mallory shook her head. "They left a little while ago. Gayle was getting tired so I helped her get settled in bed and then Pam and the ladies helped me clean up. They left not long after and told me to give you their regards."

Liam smiled. "I wish they'd have stopped by the stable before they left. The crew couldn't stop talking about how good those barbecue sandwiches were and ate so many they were like slugs afterward. I almost had to lay down the law to get them back up on their feet and working again."

Mallory smiled back. "They stuffed me and your mom to the gills, too. They brought quite a spread—and gifts for the baby. They're wonderful women. Thank you for introducing me to them."

Nodding, Liam shoved his hands in his pockets. "You're welcome. It's good for you to have some friends other than me in Pine Creek. That way you'll have plenty of people to lean on when you need help."

She stared back at him, blushing. "Friends?"

"Yeah."

"You've been a great friend to me already," she said quietly. "And to the baby." Her hands lifted slowly and covered her round belly, cradling it gently. "You've been the best friend I've had in a very long time."

Maybe it was the tenderness in her eyes as she looked at him or the gratitude in her smile. Or maybe it was the way her graceful hands cradled the baby she carried, her cheeks flushed and her touch gentle. Whatever it was, in that moment, she was the most beautiful woman he'd ever laid eyes on.

"I, uh..." He looked down at his boots. Tapped his right toe twice. "Would you like to meet Sugar now?"

"Yes, please."

She walked over and stood beside him at the stall, the sweet scent of her shampoo drifting in, surrounding him.

He cleared his throat. "I think I told you the day we arrived that Sugar's ten years old."

Mallory nodded.

"You been around horses much?" he asked.

"Not at all." She studied Sugar, a slow smile curving her lips. "But I'm not afraid of them."

"That's good," he said. "Sugar's gentle. Would you like to pet her?"

"Yes, please."

"Put your hand out, near her nose," he said. "Give her a chance to catch your scent and get to know you a little bit."

She hesitated, glancing at him then the mare, then lifted her right hand and held it near Sugar's nose. The mare leaned forward, her nostrils flared, sniffed Mallory's palm and then, seemingly satisfied with the introduction, nudged her fingers with her soft nose.

"Oh!" Mallory stroked Sugar's forehead and neck, laughing as the mare edged forward and pressed closer. "She's very friendly."

"Yep." Liam smirked. "The exact opposite of that cat that hangs around here. Which reminds me..." He walked over to a metal bucket that sat by the wall. "It's close to feeding time. Might as well put the food out now for when Miss Priss ambles in later."

"Liam?"

He removed the lid, grabbed a scooper and scooped up a hefty amount of dry food. "Yeah?"

"I think Miss Priss is already here."

Liam poured the dry cat food into a metal bowl and put it on the floor. "Doubt it. She would've attacked me by now."

"Maybe not."

He replaced the lid on the bucket, turned around and froze. "Well, would you look at that?"

There she was, Miss Priss, winding affectionately around Mallory's legs.

"I'm not scared of Sugar," Mallory whispered, "but this cat's another story altogether. Is it okay for me to move?"

Liam held up his hand. "No. Stay still. I don't want her jumping on you like she does me."

They stood, frozen in place, as Miss Priss continued winding around Mallory's legs. After a couple minutes, Miss Priss walked lazily over to the bowl Liam had put on the floor and, after eyeing him warily, began eating.

"Well, would you look at that?" Liam repeated.

"Oh!" Mallory jumped, her hands pressing against her belly.

Liam sprang toward her, glancing over his shoulder to make sure the cat was still eating several feet away. Miss Priss, obviously hungry, stayed put and ate despite the distraction.

He sighed with relief then looked at Mallory. "What is it? Are you okay?"

She smiled wide, her eyes bright with excitement. It was an expression he hadn't seen her make before. "Yeah." Laughter escaped her. "Oliver just kicked. I was so focused on the cat that it caught me off guard."

Liam smiled. "Oliver? You decided on a name?"

"Yes."

"It's a fine name." Caught up in the moment, he lifted his hand and stepped towards her then stopped. "If you don't mind my asking, what does it feel like when he kicks? Does it hurt?"

"No," she said, smiling down at her belly. "At least, not this time. It was like a strong nudge against my belly button."

Liam grinned. "Maybe Oliver liked having Miss Priss visit you."

She laughed and he caught his breath, savoring the cheerful sound. "Maybe so, because there he goes again."

Her eyes met his and her hand lifted, too. An expectant look crossed her face as her mouth parted. For a moment, he thought she might ask what he was silently hoping for. He thought she might reach out, take his hand in hers and place it on her belly to feel the baby's movement. To share in the moment.

But she didn't.

Instead, her cheeks flushed and she stepped back, lowering her hand to her side. "I think I've interrupted you enough." She motioned toward the cat. "I'll get out of your hair now and let you get back to what you were doing."

With that, she spun on her heel and walked away. He

watched her leave then returned to Sugar's stall and stroked the mare's back, allowing himself to imagine—just once more— what it might be like to have a son.

THAT NIGHT, BEFORE going to sleep, Mallory opened her note-pad and wrote to Oliver again.

I haven't told you about Sugar yet, have I? She's a brown mare—ten years old—and she's Liam's favorite horse. I was able to pet her today.

She smiled at the memory.

Her nose was soft and warm, and her whiskers tickled my palm when she sniffed my hand. She's so friendly and gentle. She leans against you when you pet her and when you stop, she nudges your hand with her nose to continue. Maybe one day when it's warm, after you've arrived, I might ask Liam to show me how to ride her.

She stopped writing and tapped the pen against her lips before continuing.

Maybe, if we're still at Pine Creek Farm when you're old enough, he'll teach you how to ride, too.

She stopped writing and glanced over her shoulder at the closed door. Gayle had gone to bed long ago and was sleeping soundly in her room. Liam was sitting outside by the firepit again, gazing at the stars.

Mallory began writing again.

I hope you like Liam and Gayle as much as I do. It was Liam's idea to start putting together your nursery and I think he's excited to see it all come together. A few ladies from his church visited me today and we made plans for decorations that I hope you'll like.

Gayle is Liam's mother. She's forgotten quite a lot of her past due to her illness, but one thing she remembers well is that she's always wanted a grandbaby, and even though you're not hers, she's anxious to hold you.

Mallory smiled.

I think that would make her happy. You, Oliver, will make her happy.

Mallory stopped writing. "Do you know what would make me happy?" she whispered out loud. "Do you know what I wish for you?"

She put the pen down and closed her eyes, silently answering the question with words she didn't have the courage to speak or write.

I wish you had a dad like Liam.

CHAPTER SEVEN

CHILLY WINTER WIND blew across the grounds of Pine Creek Farm for the remainder of January and throughout February. But soon the air warmed, the days grew longer and the sun shined bright. By the second week of March, the dormant grass in the fields had turned green and sprang to life. Tiny yellow wildflowers dotted the landscape and lush, healthy leaves filled every branch of the trees. But the most magnificent sight was the bounty of full blooms gracing the magnolia trees that lined the driveway leading to the main house.

"It's beautiful," Mallory said.

And it was—even more than she'd imagined two months ago when standing in the same spot on the day she'd arrived at Pine Creek Farm.

She tipped her head back for a better view of the flowery branches that towered overhead as she stood at the edge of the paved driveway. Against the backdrop of the clear blue sky, the fragrant blooms, high above, resembled thick downy feathers that danced and fluttered in the warm spring breeze.

"I told you that you would love it," Gayle said as she stood beside her.

Mallory glanced at Gayle and smiled. She and Gayle had grown close over the past two months, eating every meal together, taking long walks along the property in the afternoon and reading from the Bible each night. Though Gayle's memory had continued to deteriorate, she had grown accustomed to Mallory and though she couldn't recall Mallory's name on some days, she seemed to still recognize her face and welcome her presence on the majority of occasions.

The more comfortable Gayle grew in her presence, the more accomplished Mallory had begun to feel as a caretaker. When she'd first arrived at Pine Creek Farm, she'd been eager to earn her own way and contribute to the farm. Ensuring Gayle was well cared for and comfortable had helped her feel as though she had done just that and when the spring guests had begun to arrive two weeks ago, populating the guest houses and two of the rooms on the first floor of the main house, she was able to help even more. Every morning, she set her alarm and woke up early, joined Liam downstairs and helped cook breakfast for the guests.

Mallory pulled her attention away from the magnolia trees and gazed across the front field of Pine Creek Farm where Liam, sitting astride Sugar, led a trail ride for guests. She smiled. Mornings had become her favorite part of the day. It wasn't just the bright sun, the warm spring air and cheerful chirp of birds. It was being greeted by Liam's smile when she descended the stairs and joined him in the kitchen. It was the easy conversation and familiar rhythm they fell into every day as they cooked breakfast together that made her smile each night when she went to bed and look forward to getting up the next morning.

But despite the increasing joy she'd discovered at the farm and the recent change in season, not every day had been easy.

Mallory rubbed the small of her back where a constant ache had taken up residence two weeks ago. Oliver had grown. Each day that passed reminded her that her due date was approaching faster than ever. If the increasing ache in her legs and back, ever-growing belly and sometimes-overwhelming fatigue didn't remind her, the calendar did.

Nine days. That was it. Nine days were all that separated her from being a mother.

"What are we going to do now?"

Mallory blinked and refocused on Gayle, who looked at her with raised brows. Though Gayle had grown comfortable in Mallory's presence, she still remained on edge about each day's events. Being at home in familiar surroundings offered Gayle a tremendous sense of security, but her disorientation regarding the present day and time led her to seek frequent reassurance for what lay before her each day.

Every morning, as they ate breakfast together, Mallory would detail the itinerary of the day to Gayle and remind her throughout the afternoon of the plans she had for them, which usually included an outdoor activity since the warmer weather had arrived and the grounds were so beautiful. Sunshine, fresh air and being surrounded by the cheerful chatter of guests who strolled along the grounds always seemed to lift Gayle's spirits.

Mallory grinned. "We're going to dig in the dirt, remember? We've got several batches of Wave petunias by the front porch and we're going to start planting them today."

That was, if her body held out long enough. A sharp twinge moved through the small of her back and she rubbed the spot a bit harder.

She'd grown accustomed to the aches and pains of pregnancy over the past two months but lately—the past few days, especially—they seemed more frequent and intense. With her due date fast approaching, she'd tried to prepare as best as she could and rest whenever possible. She'd begun taking naps in the afternoon, returning to her bedroom after settling Gayle down for her daily rest, crawling into her own bed and getting as much extra sleep as she could until Gayle woke again. Lying down with her feet propped up on a pillow had become a luxury—her favorite indulgence—and she found herself looking forward to it today as well.

"It's around eleven o'clock," Mallory told Gayle. That was something else she'd learned about Gayle: knowing the time put Gayle's mind at ease so she reminded her of it often. "We'll plant petunias for an hour then go in and have lunch. After that, you'll probably be ready for your nap."

Gayle pondered this information. She narrowed her eyes and looked up at the magnolia trees again then glanced across the grounds at Liam, who led guests on a horseback ride across the field. After a moment, she nodded in agreement, spun on her heel and began walking toward the main house.

"Well, come on then," Gayle called over her shoulder as she walked. "Those petunias aren't gonna plant themselves, are they?"

Laughing, Mallory followed.

Thirty minutes later, she and Gayle had settled comfortably on the soft grass by the flower beds in front of the main house. They'd planted several petunia plants in a row and were patting the last plant into the ground before moving on to the second row.

"Getting tired yet?" Mallory asked, glancing at Gayle.

Gayle shook her head and the wide-brimmed straw hat Mallory had insisted she wear flopped over her forehead. "Got more to do," she said. "There's a whole nother row to plant."

"Yes, but if you get tired, we can always go in." And considering the achy fatigue that had taken up residence in Mallory's back, she'd welcome the rest.

"I'm fine." Gayle's eyes were heavy, but she smiled as she looked down and patted Mallory's belly. "How's the baby today?"

Mallory shifted to a more comfortable position on the ground and shrugged. "He seems content. But he's kicking quite a bit."

Gayle grinned. "He's ready to get out of there."

One of the horses walking across the grounds behind them neighed. The relaxed and somewhat playful sound echoed across the field and caught Gayle's attention.

"Such beautiful horses," she breathed.

Mallory glanced over her shoulder, smiling as Liam waved in their direction. "Yes." She waved back. "They are beautiful."

As was Liam.

Heat engulfed her face and she quickly lowered her arm to her side then returned her attention to the plant in front of her. She resumed patting damp soil around the base of the petunia, trying to keep her thoughts from straying back to Liam.

She wasn't sure when her feelings for Liam had grown but at some point over the past two months, she'd begun to take notice of and admire the many admirable traits that he possessed.

One, he smiled every morning. She knew there were mornings when he was exhausted, overworked and probably aching from the amount of physical labor he had to undertake on the farm. But no matter his physical state or mood, he never failed to greet her with a cheery disposition and optimistic outlook for the day.

Loving his mother was another great quality he possessed. No matter how busy his day might be, Liam always made time for Gayle, returning to the main house for lunch every day, answering questions repeatedly with patience and understanding on the days Gayle had trouble remembering the answers. And, most notably of all, he never failed to visit her room every night when she settled in bed to kiss her forehead and whisper that he loved her.

His hands, though big and strong, were gentle as he brushed his horses and stroked their backs, murmuring sweet phrases of praise. He'd even managed to come to some type of understanding with Miss Priss. Two months ago, after Miss Priss had introduced herself to Mallory, the cat had taken up following Mallory and Gayle around the grounds whenever they emerged outside. And the cat would follow Mallory, without fail, into the stable every evening when she would join Liam by Sugar's stall to visit with the mare. On each occasion, she'd noticed Liam smile at the sight of the cat winding around Mallory's legs and rubbing her cheek against Mallory's shoes.

"It must be Oliver," he had said once, grinning. "Miss Priss knows you're expecting."

She could still recall his expression, the gentle indulgence in his eyes as he'd gazed adoringly at her belly. It had stolen her breath the first time he'd looked at her in that way.

That may have been it. That may have been the moment that she'd begun to think of Liam differently than a friend. That look may have been what prompted her to wonder silently—but keeping her thoughts a careful secret—how it might feel to be loved by Liam. To be cared for by him in the same way that he cared for his mother. To have a kind, honorable man like him protect and support her every day and do the same for Oliver.

It was all these wonderful traits and more that had prompted her to imagine what her life might've been like if she'd met Liam before Trevor.

A slight sense of dismay unfurled deep in her belly at the reminder of her past…but at least it didn't weigh so heavily on her now as it had before. Pam Marshall and the ladies' group had been a big help, lending their ears on more than one occasion, listening to her fears, worries and concerns and offering support and advice when she asked for it. Talking with her new friends had helped and being at Pine Creek Farm seemed to help even more.

A few weeks ago, she'd taken up joining Liam by the firepit after dinner once she'd helped Gayle settle into bed for the night. It was warmer now, but Liam still built a fire, and the spring breeze was just right to make it comfortable and pleasant. Sometimes they talked, but most nights they sat in a comfortable silence and Liam would tip his head back and close his eyes as though in deep thought or prayer.

It hadn't taken her long to do the same, and she found it

was easy to talk to God in that space—to look up at the stars, listen to the rhythmic crackle of the fire and chorus of toads and crickets by the pond and listen for God's guidance.

She'd grown to love it here.

Her stomach growled and she smiled, then glanced at Gayle. "I think Oliver's hungry. How about you? Do you have an appetite today?"

Gayle stood slowly, leaning on Mallory's supportive arm, then brushed the dirt off her hands. "I'm thirsty. Do we have any lemonade?"

Mallory nodded. "I made a fresh batch last night." She placed her palm on the ground and, leaning to one side, she pushed herself to her knees then feet and brushed the soil off her hands as well. "How about we take a quick break?" She began walking toward the front steps. "I'll pour us both some lemonade and we'll sit on the porch for a while then—"

Another pain—a sharp one—tore through her, hardening her belly and streaking down her back. Gasping, she doubled over and stumbled forward, managing to grab the porch rail to prevent herself from falling.

"Miss?" Gayle's voice drew closer. "Are you okay?"

Oh no, oh no, oh no—

She still had nine days to prepare. Nine more days!

"Excuse me, miss," Gayle said again, touching her back gently. "Are you okay?"

The pain subsided slightly and Mallory straightened slowly. She turned and summoned a smile. "Yes." Her voice trembled. "But I think I'm in labor."

Gayle gasped, her eyes darting toward Mallory's belly. "My goodness! A baby," she said, as though noticing Mallory's swollen belly for the first time. "You're going to have a baby."

Mallory nodded, dragged in a deep breath and left the porch rail, taking several careful steps across the front lawn. Thankfully, the horses were still in view and Liam was still astride Sugar at the front of the pack.

"Liam!" Mallory waved her arms in the air and shouted again. "Liam!"

Sugar snorted and raised her head as Liam turned in Mallory's direction. He peered across the grounds at her as she called for him again then, sensing the urgency in her tone, urged Sugar into a gallop and raced across the lawn. He halted Sugar several feet away, dismounted and jogged over.

"What is it?" Concern suffused his expression. "Is it Oliver?"

Another painful contraction swept through Mallory and she bent forward, propped her hands on her knees and groaned softly, "Yes."

I DO WANT YOU, Oliver. I truly do. I'm just—

"Mallory?" Dr. Harper's face slowly swam into focus. "Mallory, I know you're exhausted and I know this is tough, but I need you to start pushing."

Pain ripped through Mallory, arching her back. She shoved her head back against a pillow, opened her eyes and stared up at the ceiling.

Let go, or it'll be worse.

She thrashed her head from side to side at the memory of Trevor's voice then blinked hard and struggled to focus on her surroundings. There was one chair beside the bed, a monitor that beeped, two women dressed in blue scrubs and Dr. Harper sat at the foot of her bed.

Hospital. She was in the hospital. And in labor.

Sweat streamed down her cheek, dripped off her chin and splashed onto her collarbone. *I do want you, Oliver. I do, I'm just sca—*

"Mallory." Drs. Harper's voice was authoritative now. "You've got to listen to me, Mallory. I need you to push."

How had she gotten here?

Liam's face, his hazel eyes worried and apprehensive,

floated into her mind. Oh, that's right. He'd gotten off a horse and driven her to the hospital.

Pain tore through her belly and she groaned. What was the horse's name? The pretty brown one?

Sugar. Her name was Sugar.

Let go, or it'll be worse.

"Push, Mallory."

I want you, Oliver. She bit her lip, the taste of blood hitting her tongue. *I'm just terrified. And I need—*

"Mallo—"

"Liam." She opened her mouth wider, sucked in a strong breath and whispered brokenly, "Please get Liam."

LIAM STOOD BY a window in the waiting room of the hospital in Pine Creek. It was dark outside, after midnight, and he'd never been more scared in his life.

"It's been over twelve hours," he said, pressing his cell phone closer to his cheek. "No one's come out to give me an update in over two hours now. Is that normal?"

"It's okay, Liam," Jessie said on the other end of the line. "These things take time."

Her words were low and slow as though she were still rousing from a deep sleep. He had hated to call her this time of night, but his anxiety had gotten the best of him.

"I'm sorry for waking you," he said for the third time during that conversation. "And I hope I didn't wake the kids."

"I told you not to worry about that. Ava and the boys are still sleeping soundly," she reassured him. "Is anyone there with you?"

"No. I was in the middle of a trail ride when it started. It all happened so fast. One of the hands stayed with Mom while I drove Mallory to the hospital. I called Pam once I got here and asked if she and the ladies would take turns staying with Mom until we were able to come home."

Home. How sweet that word sounded right now. And how

much he wanted to whisk Mallory and Oliver out of the hospital and back to Pine Creek Farm where he could look over them, ensuring they were safe and settled.

But Oliver would have to arrive first, and from the way things were looking, that could take quite a while.

"It wouldn't be so bad if I could see her," he said. His voice sounded rough. Almost unrecognizable to his own ears. "The last time I saw her was when I helped her into a wheelchair and they wheeled her back to a room. I haven't seen or spoken to her since."

"Take that as a positive," Jessie said. "If you haven't heard anything negative and she hasn't been asking for you, then things must be progressing rather well. It takes a lot of work to get a new baby in the world. Try to stay calm and give it time."

Liam dragged his hand over his face. "I can't help but worry. She was in so much pain. You should've seen her face."

"I know," Jessie said gently. "But pain is part of the package and Mallory's tough. I'm sure you've noticed that by now."

He had. Over the past couple of months, he'd worked closely with Mallory every day at Pine Creek Farm, cooking breakfast with her in the morning, helping her with laundry for the guest bedrooms each evening and assisting with Gayle whenever he had the opportunity to break free from work. Mallory had grown more relaxed around him and had even taken to visiting the stable every evening to pet Sugar, check on Miss Priss then walk with him to the firepit and sit under the stars until her eyes grew heavy and she retired to her room for the night.

Those evenings were Liam's favorite part of each day. Sitting beneath the night sky in peaceful silence beside Mallory had been a balm to his soul. It was easy to think and pray, sitting there beside her. And she seemed to enjoy doing the same.

He couldn't help but notice, as time had passed, that Oliver had grown, increasing the swell of Mallory's belly and causing her to move a bit slower each day. He encouraged her as much as he could to rest as often as possible, and he'd been glad to know that she had begun taking naps in the afternoon when Gayle did.

"Her ankles have been really swollen," he said. "She's been wearing flip-flops since the weather got warm and I've noticed it a lot more lately. She gets tired so fast. She sleeps almost as much as Mom does now in the afternoons. Do you think that meant there was something wrong—"

"No," Jessie said firmly. "Not at all. All of that is absolutely normal for a pregnancy." She grew quiet then asked, "You've gotten to know Mallory rather well these past couple of months haven't you?"

"Yes." He stared out the window, his shoulders tensing, feeling as though he knew what she would say next.

"This new baby will change things a lot," Jessie said.

He shoved his free hand in his pocket and continued staring out the window. "I know."

"You'll need extra help with Gayle while Mallory recovers. Holt won't mind if I come down for a couple weeks and help—"

"No." That came out harsher than he meant. He cleared his throat and tried for a softer tone. "We'll be okay. The ladies' group from my church has offered to help in any way we need them to. They'll be able to stay with Gayle for the days that Mallory needs to rest."

"Well, if you change your mi—"

"I won't," he said gently but firmly. "But thank you for the offer, Jessie."

He appreciated it. He truly did. But he knew what he'd be in for if Jessie made the drive down to Pine Creek Farm and settled in for a couple of weeks. She'd watch him close, looking for signs that he'd grown attached to Mallory and she would, no doubt, find them.

No matter how hard he'd tried to keep his distance—and he *had* tried—he'd been unable to keep Mallory from slipping into his heart. Pine Creek Farm was completely different with her there. Every morning, he had something to look forward to. He knew, without fail, that she would emerge from upstairs, join him in the kitchen and return his smile. Inevitably, they would bump into each other at least once in the kitchen while cooking breakfast and she'd laugh and say sorry for the thousandth time.

He loved her laugh. He loved…so much about her.

Love. What a surprising notion. He'd never been in love before. Was this what it felt like? Did it always sneak up unexpectedly then take hold, refusing to be ignored? He hadn't expected falling in love to be so quiet, so peaceful and so quick.

Maybe it wasn't love. Maybe it was something else…but what?

He and Mallory had become friends—the very best of friends. But what he felt for her went far beyond that. The admiration in her gaze when she looked at him, the cheerful sound of her laugh and her dedication to caring for Gayle—supporting his mom in every way possible—had taken him in.

It was, he admitted ruefully, impossible to imagine what Pine Creek Farm might be like were Mallory to leave.

"The offer stands," Jessie said. "If you or Mallory need me, I'm just a phone call away."

Liam, worried and exhausted, dragged in a deep breath. "Thank you. I really mean that."

"I know. You'll call me when the baby comes?"

Liam smiled at the reminder that there was something precious at the end of all this worry and pain. "Yes. I'll be sure to—"

"Liam Williams?"

He spun around at the sound of his name, finding a nurse, clad in blue scrubs, standing in the doorway of the waiting room. She looked at him expectantly.

"I'm sorry, I gotta go, Jessie." He ended the call, shoved his phone in his back pocket then walked across the room. "What is it? Is Mallory okay?"

The nurse pulled her mask down below her chin. "I need you to come back with me, if you don't mind?"

He froze, his heart thundering against his ribs. "The baby, is he—"

"He isn't here yet," the nurse said, propping the door open and motioning for Liam to precede her. "But I think Mallory might need your help. She's asking for you."

That was all she had to say.

Liam took swift strides down the hallway, waiting impatiently for the nurse to catch up and direct him to the right room. When he entered, his gaze darted around the figures standing around the bed, then homed in on Mallory's face.

She looked back at him, her cheeks red and fear in her eyes. "Liam?"

He moved quickly, edging between two nurses, then dragged a chair close to the bed and sat down. "How is she?" he asked the doctor, his eyes still glued to Mallory's.

"She's fine," Dr. Harper said. "But we need her to start pushing. I think she needs some reassurance and extra support."

Liam nodded and scooted closer to the bed. "Tell me what I can do to help, Mallory," he whispered. "Just say the word and I'll do it."

Her hand lifted, her fingers grasping at empty air until they fumbled over his forearm where it lay on the chair's armrest. She closed her hand around his and squeezed tightly.

He stilled, the warm feel of her soft hand against his catching him off guard.

"I'm scared," she whispered.

Immediately, he turned his hand over, weaving his fingers between hers, and leaned close, whispering back, "I know. I'm here."

"Mallory," Dr. Harper prompted from the foot of the bed, "you've got to push now. We've put this off long enough."

Mallory closed her eyes and grimaced. A fresh bead of sweat rolled over her temple and into the damp hair at her temples.

"Mallory?" Dr. Harper said again. "You have to—"

"I'm too scared, Liam." Mallory shook her head, her hair rustling against the pillow. "So scared."

There was a familiar tremor in her voice. The same one he remembered hearing on the day they'd first met at Hummingbird Haven, when she'd spoken of her past...and her ex-husband.

He leaned his elbows onto the bed, lifted their joined hands and urged her eyes to meet his. "Then scream, Mallory. Scream all you like. Just let it out."

She opened her eyes and stared back at him, then, breathing heavily, opened her mouth and yelled, the sound one of anguish, fear and pain.

Liam winced as the keening wail left her lips. It broke his heart just a bit more.

"Mallory, I know you're in pain," Dr. Harper said. "But if you're yelling and making noise, you're not really pushing. I need you to push."

"She will," Liam said firmly, scooting even closer. He brushed Mallory's damp bangs from her forehead, waited until she was silent and met his eyes again. "Now, push," he urged. "After you push, you can scream again. Scream all you want in between, so long as you push."

Her hand tightened around his then she lifted onto her elbows and grew silent, her expression twisting in pain.

"Good, Mallory," Dr. Harper soothed. "That's good. Keep that up."

The pattern continued for several more minutes as Mallory's screams and Dr. Harper's vocal urgings as Mallory pushed filled the room. But soon, another cry sounded. It was the sweetest one Liam had ever heard.

"You did it," Dr. Harper said, smiling at Mallory. "You delivered a beautiful baby boy."

There was a flurry of movement in the room as Dr. Harper passed the infant to the nurses and they went to work, cleaning the infant up and taking initial measurements.

Liam looked down at Mallory and smiled gently as her eyelids, pink and heavy, drooped low. She was exhausted. "Hey," he said, smoothing his thumb over her damp brow. "You did it, Mallory."

Her eyes closed and she didn't answer. But her mouth parted and her breaths grew slower and even.

"Liam?"

He glanced over his shoulder at a nurse who held Oliver, clean and swaddled, in her arms. "Would you like to give Mallory her baby?"

He squeezed Mallory's hand once more then stood slowly, walked over to the nurse and held out his arms.

She placed Oliver in his open embrace, the baby's slight weight settling perfectly into the crook of his elbow. Liam looked down and smiled, savoring the moment. His heart overflowed and he blinked back hot tears then, after gaining his composure, carefully returned to his chair, leaned forward and settled Oliver onto Mallory's chest, supporting him with both hands.

"Mallory?" Her eyes fluttered open at the feel of Oliver against her chest. "Here he is."

She tipped her head down, her eyes roving over Oliver's face. She pulled back the blanket a tiny bit, then pressed one fingertip against Oliver's palm and watched as his tiny fingers curled around her finger.

"He has your eyes," Liam whispered, watching as Oliver's wide gaze fixed on Mallory's face. "And he has your nose. He's the most perfect baby I've ever seen."

Mallory continued staring down at the baby then she smiled, a tired but happy smile as she whispered, "Oliver. My sweet Ollie."

The tenderness in her voice was unmistakable and Liam sagged against the mattress beneath the weight of the day. They were beautiful. Both of them. And if he had a choice, he'd stay right there, in that very moment, forever.

"Liam?" He blinked hard against a fresh surge of tears and looked at Mallory again. She reached out, cupped his jaw and drifted her thumb over his stubbled cheek. "Thank you."

YOU WERE BORN TODAY, Oliver.

It was scarier than I anticipated, bringing you into the world, but I had some help. I asked for Liam and he came. He held my hand through it all and he was the first to hold you.

I wish I could tell you how I felt when he placed you in my arms, but there aren't words for it. Not for what I was feeling.

How can I describe how it felt to have you snuggle against my chest—a tiny piece of me—the sweetest, most innocent little boy in the world? How can I tell you how it felt to look into eyes that were exactly like mine? To know that you're a part of me and that I'm a part of you?

What a miracle you are! What a beautiful gift from God.

I fell in love with you, right then and there. You stole my heart, Oliver. And you'll have it forever.

CHAPTER EIGHT

THREE DAYS LATER, Mallory brought Oliver home.

She sat in the passenger seat of Liam's truck, sitting sideways and smiling at Oliver's reflection in a small mirror that Liam had mounted to the back window of the truck's cab.

"How's he doing back there?" Liam asked, slowing the truck as they neared the turn to the driveway of Pine Creek Farm.

Mallory squirmed to the side a bit more and sighed. "He's perfect. Just like you said."

Oliver was fast asleep in his rear-facing car seat, strapped safely inside and covered with a light but cozy blanket. His hair, thick for an infant, curled adorably at the ends. His lush lashes rested against his healthy, flushed cheeks and his small mouth was parted. If she leaned back far enough and listened hard, she could just hear the rhythmic whisper of his breathing.

"I can't wait to get him home and settled in the nursery," she said, looking at Liam.

Pam and the rest of the ladies had worked hard over the past couple of months, helping Mallory plan, shop and gather materials to bring their vision for Oliver's nursery to life. They weren't the only ones though. Liam had been the one to paint the walls, taking care to get the trim just right, and being cautious about keeping the wood floors unstained and gleaming.

Barbara had come through as well. She had a friend in a local store in downtown Pine Creek who had a plethora of rugs in various colors and patterns for every nursery theme. And there had been so many blankets—blankets of all materials and styles—that Mallory had found several to match the shade of blue they'd chosen for the nursery.

Oliver's nursery was perfect and so many loving people—including Liam—had gone to a lot of trouble to make it so.

Liam glanced at her briefly and smiled. "He's gonna love it."

Mallory grinned. "He's gonna love Gayle, too."

Gayle often forgot that Mallory was having a baby, but each time she noticed, the first thing she said was that she couldn't wait to hold the baby. Oh, she'd be thrilled when Oliver arrived home!

"She's been waiting a long time to get her hands on Oliver," Liam said as he slowed the truck even more and turned right onto the long driveway leading to Pine Creek Farm.

Mallory allowed her gaze to linger on his profile, tracing the strong, stubbled curve of his jaw with her eyes and admiring his handsome features. Three days ago, she'd been fond of him, but now, after experiencing his strength and encouragement in the hospital during labor and the days after, she was afraid he'd stolen her heart completely.

Her breath caught at the thought, and she faced the road ahead as well.

It wouldn't do to jump to conclusions right now. She'd been through a lot over the past three days, so it was understandable and expected that her emotions were intense and unpredictable at times. It'd be easy to attach the tenderness, excitement and affection that filled her heart for Oliver to Liam as well. After all, he'd been there for her during the most challenging time of her life.

After he'd placed Oliver in her arms, Liam had stayed by her side in the hospital room as they'd counted Oliver's fingers and toes, and discussed how beautiful he was until the nurses took him to the nursery for the evening.

Soon after, Mallory had fallen asleep, her body exhausted and sore. She'd slept soundly and when she'd awoken, Liam had still been there.

She smiled as she recalled the image. He'd been sitting in the chair beside the bed, his long legs sprawled out, his jaw stubbled as it was now, and his head propped against the headrest of the chair at an odd angle. But when he'd stirred and opened his eyes, then looked into her own, he'd smiled brighter than she'd ever seen him smile before and his sleepy eyes had filled with joy.

Her heart had swelled. Despite a different location, their morning routine had only changed in one respect. Just as at Pine Creek Farm, Liam's smile was the first thing she saw every morning of her hospital stay. But rather than following him to the kitchen to cook breakfast, breakfast had been delivered to her and Liam by hospital staff.

"Pam called me as I was bringing the truck around to pick you and Oliver up at the front entrance of the hospital," Liam said now. "She and the ladies' group wanted to be there when you and Oliver arrived home this afternoon."

Home. A beautiful word and one she was surprised to find she preferred to use for Pine Creek Farm. She pressed her palm against her chest as she glanced to the left and right of the driveway as Liam drove, admiring the full blooms on the magnolia trees that towered above them. The afternoon sun was bright, the fields were green and the main house, with its white siding and large front porch, completed the picturesque scene.

Pine Creek Farm was perfect. As perfect as Oliver.

Mallory closed her eyes for a moment and said a silent prayer of thanks for the new baby, generous friends and the beautiful place to lay her head. She couldn't imagine anyone not feeling at home at Pine Creek Farm and it'd feel even more welcoming today, what with the ladies' group and Gayle coming to welcome—

"Did Pam mention how Gayle was doing?" Mallory asked.

She hoped her absence and the subsequent lack of predictability to each day hadn't upset Gayle too much. Mallory had asked, while she was in the hospital, if Liam might bring Gayle to visit, but Liam had thought it best not to disrupt or confuse her anymore. He said the change in routine had already upset her. Instead, he'd arranged for Pam and the other ladies to stay with her, keeping her routine in much the same way as Mallory usually did and helping with chores and assisting guests until they could return home.

"Pam said she had a great breakfast and a good lunch but that she was getting a bit tired," Liam said. "I'm glad they released you when they did, because I think we just might make it inside before it's time for her nap."

"That's it then," Mallory said, smiling. "Gayle is the first on Oliver's guest list."

She couldn't wait to see Gayle's face when she held Oliver for the first time.

When they reached the end of the driveway, Liam parked the truck beside several vehicles that were already parked in front of the house. "I see the ladies' group are already here. You should probably expect a slightly over-the-top welcome."

Mallory laughed. "That's okay. I think Oliver has earned some extra attention."

Liam hopped out of the truck first, indicating for Mallory to wait until he rounded the truck and opened her door. He helped her out then unbuckled Oliver from his car seat and carefully, oh so carefully, cradled Oliver against his broad chest as he lifted him out of the car seat and placed him in Mallory's waiting arms. His blunt fingertips brushed her forearms as he released Oliver and she suppressed a wave of affection for him, hiding the heat in her cheeks by ducking her head and focusing on Oliver's sleeping face.

"It's good he's still sleeping," Mallory said softly. "He'll wake up, ready to eat soon, and cry for all he's worth. While he's sleeping, Gayle will get to meet him when he's at his most peaceful."

Liam gently brushed the back of his knuckles over Oliver's downy hair. "Peaceful or not, he's at his best every moment of the day."

Tenderness flooded Mallory's chest at the loving gaze Liam bestowed on Oliver. What would it be like to have him look at her like that? What might it feel like to be loved by Liam? To feel safe, protected and supported by him as a wife? It was something she had begun to wonder about more and more about each day.

They walked across the front lawn, climbed the front porch steps and went inside. Liam hovered by Mallory's side every step of the way, opening the front door and cradling her hand with his beneath Oliver's head as she walked slowly into the living room.

"Oh, there they are!" Peggy, seated in a living room chair, sprang to her feet and walked briskly across the room to look down at baby Oliver. "He's precious, Mallory. Just precious."

Wendy, Barbara and Cherie Ann were there as well. They rushed over and each of them took their turn gazing with adoration at Oliver, asking questions about his weight and height, and inquiring about Mallory's health.

"We're both completely healthy," Mallory said, smoothing her fingertips over the back of Oliver's hand as he slept.

A sense of pride moved through her as she looked down at him. He was, without a doubt, the most precious person in her life.

"Mallory did an excellent job getting Oliver into the world safely," Liam said.

Mallory looked up at him then, the affection in his gaze, so similar to how he looked at Oliver, making her heart turn over in her chest. "I can't take all the credit," she said softly.

"I did have some help." She looked at the other women, who had leaned in, their wide, curious eyes moving from Liam to Mallory then back. "Liam stayed with me during labor. He held my hand and gave me a good pep talk. I don't think I'd have made it without him."

Pam was the first to speak, a slow smile curving her lips as she whispered, "How wonderful."

"Liam was the first to hold Oliver," Mallory added.

"And it's our turn now, right?" Barbara asked, clapping her hands together in glee.

Mallory laughed. "Soon enough. But Oliver already has someone very special waiting for him." She peered past the ladies and met Gayle's gaze across the room from where she sat on the sofa. "Gayle? Oliver's finally here to meet you."

Gayle lifted her head and looked at Mallory. Her eyes were heavy with fatigue but at the sight of the bundle in Mallory's arms, her expression brightened. She smiled and spread her arms wide. "My grandbaby?"

Mallory eased between the women, walked across the room and sat on the couch beside Gayle. "Yes. This is Oliver."

Gayle looked down at him and her eyes filled with tears. "He's beautiful," she whispered.

"Would you like to hold him?" Mallory asked.

At her eager nod, Mallory scooted closer and eased Oliver into Gayle's arms.

Liam was there in an instant, kneeling by Gayle's side and cupping her delicate hands with his own as she cradled Oliver against her chest. "You're a pro at this, Mom," he said softly as he tucked a wayward strand of gray hair behind her ear.

Gayle continued looking down at Oliver. "I've had my own you know," she said, smoothing one finger over the back of Oliver's hand. "His name was Holt." Tears spilled over her cheeks as she whispered, "Holt. The sweetest son in the world."

Mallory stilled, her gaze moving to Liam.

He continued to kneel by Gayle's side and murmur encouraging words, but some of the joy had faded from his eyes.

LATER THAT NIGHT, when darkness had settled over Pine Creek Farm, the stars had emerged and a full moon glowed bright above, Liam carried two thick logs in his arms to the firepit behind the main house. He stacked them on top of another log that had not quite burned completely several nights before, shoved a hunk of kindling in between them and lit a match.

As the logs began to catch fire, he walked over to the two Adirondack chairs and fluffed up a pillow he had placed in one hours earlier. He also adjusted the light blanket he'd draped over the armrest of the chair. It was warm out but there was a nice breeze in the evening air. If Mallory decided to join him, the pillow might make the hard Adirondack chair more comfortable against her back and the light blanket would keep her bare legs warm.

That was, if she decided to join him.

He glanced over his shoulder at the main house. Most of the windows were dark except for a couple lights in two downstairs guest rooms, and the soft yellow glow of porch lights pooled onto the back deck of the house. By now Mallory would be sitting by Gayle's bedside, reading to her from the Bible and helping her drift off to sleep as usual. Only, tonight there was something different in the routine.

Liam grinned. Oliver was here.

After Pam and the rest of the ladies had taken turns holding Oliver, cooing at him and complimenting Mallory, Oliver had woken and cried his little heart out, demanding to be fed. Mallory had carried Oliver upstairs to the nursery and Pam and the ladies had said their goodbyes, excused themselves and left for the afternoon.

The thought of the nursery made him chuckle. Throughout the room, happy teddy bears had taken over.

Mallory and the ladies had done an excellent job decorating

over the past couple of months. He had helped by painting the walls a soft shade of blue that matched the plush teddy bear Mallory had tucked onto a large, comfortable rocking chair that she'd placed in the room. Liam had put together a crib and changing table as well, following Mallory's direction as to which corner of the room to position each.

Teddy bears seem to have been the theme Mallory and the ladies had adopted for the nursery. There were colorful rugs with images of dancing bears of every shape and size, the sheets on the mattress and the crib were decorated the same and a mobile hanging over the crib was adorned with several smiling teddy bears that spun, dipped and twirled when the mobile was powered on.

Unable to resist, Liam had stopped by the nursery door and knocked after helping Gayle settle for a nap earlier that afternoon, then waited for Mallory to invite him in.

She had but after opening the door, he'd been hesitant to interrupt. Instead, he'd stood in the doorway on the threshold, remaining silent as Mallory, seated in the rocking chair, rocked Oliver in her arms as she burped him. Soon after, he'd slipped quietly away and returned to his chores, smiling ear to ear, already looking forward to seeing them both again at dinner.

When he knocked off work for the day and returned to the main house to prepare dinner, he discovered that the ladies' group had stocked the fridge and freezer full of casseroles, soups and side dishes. But a glazed ham caught his eye and he'd warmed it up in the oven, along with two side dishes and fresh bread, then set the table.

The delectable aroma had filled the house and, as expected, Mallory and Gayle had joined him at the dining table with eager smiles and baby Oliver had wiggled in his bassinet beside Mallory, his brief cries and sniffles mingling with the clink of their utensils against the plates.

Still smiling, Liam sat in his chair, leaned his head against the headrest and closed his eyes. How different the house had felt then, surrounded by those he loved.

Love—there was that word again. What else could he call it? The swell of tenderness within his chest grew more and more each day he spent with Mallory and Oliver. He couldn't remember how the house had sounded and felt without Mallory's presence and now he knew he'd find it hard to envision what it would be like without Mallory and Oliver...or his mother.

A heavy sigh left him, and he opened his eyes and gazed at the stars as they glittered overhead. His mom had cried this afternoon when she'd held Oliver and her tears had continued long after Mallory had removed Oliver from her arms and carried the baby upstairs. He'd sat with Gayle for some time, handing her fresh tissues, trying to distract her with news about the farm and the new guests that had arrived, but nothing had seemed to help.

He rubbed his forehead, his head aching. Her reaction to holding Oliver was another sign, another symptom of her progressing dementia. Her moods had become erratic and she had difficulty orienting herself to place and time. Only one name still remained, unchanged, in her mind, familiar and adored.

Holt.

Liam didn't resent that she remembered his brother—not at all. He loved Holt and he loved his mother, and knowing that she remembered at least one of her sons was a comfort. That knowledge would, hopefully, ease her mind a bit. Holt was someone she could reflect on when she was most afraid. She could seek refuge there, in his memory, in the reminder of someone familiar.

But despite this, Liam couldn't prevent the hurt that arose within him each time she said his brother's name and neglected to say his own. Though logically, he knew it to be untrue, he felt as though he'd never existed in her world. As though every memory of him had been erased from her mind and heart, never to return again.

And one day—more than likely sooner rather than later—he would lose her altogether.

His throat tightened and he swallowed hard, holding tears at bay. He wouldn't dwell on that now. He wouldn't think of it. The notion was too painful to bear.

"Mind if I join you?"

Almost immediately, his grief subsided as he smiled at the familiar voice.

He stood and faced Mallory as she strolled toward the fire pit, her brows raised. "You know you have a permanent invitation." He motioned toward the chair beside his own. "I brought a pillow out for you." Rounding the chair, he waited until she sat down then adjusted the pillow behind her lower back. "How's that?"

"Wonderful," she said, placing a baby monitor she held on the armrest and closing her eyes. "Thank you."

"You're welcome," he said. "It's warm but there's a cool breeze that's steady." He picked up the blanket and draped it over her knees. "This'll keep your legs warm."

"You've thought of everything," she said, smiling up at him. "But I suppose I should be used to that. You always think of others before yourself."

He didn't quite know how to react, but he knew what he wanted to do. He wanted to lean down, nuzzle his cheek against hers, breathe in her sweet scent and hug her close. He wanted to brush her soft mouth with his and savor the sight of her beautiful eyes up close.

But that wouldn't do.

Instead, he shrugged. "You do exactly the same for me and Mom." He grinned. "And Oliver."

Her eyes closed briefly at the mention of her son's name, her cheeks blushing. "He is perfect, isn't he? Just like you said."

"Yes."

"I don't know that either one of us would've pulled through

as well as we did if you hadn't been in the room with me," she added. "I don't think I've ever thanked you properly—"

"You've thanked me," he said, returning to his chair and sitting. "Besides, it wasn't so much a favor to you as it was a comfort to me. I felt better being in the delivery room, being able to see you, rather than sitting in the waiting room wondering how you and Oliver were faring."

She dipped her head, the pretty blush spreading down her neck, and her long wavy hair slipped over one shoulder. "The labor was a bit more overwhelming than I expected," she said softly. "It brought up so many things for me. Memories I didn't want and feelings I thought I had buried a long time ago."

He remained silent, studying the graceful curve of her cheek beneath the moonlight.

"They've quieted down now," she whispered tentatively. "The memories. Something's changed since I had Oliver. The moment I held him, I felt it. I was relieved that he looked like me instead of Tr—" She stopped speaking and looked away for a moment before facing him again. "But that wasn't the only reason. Seeing Oliver, holding him for the first time, I never knew you could love someone so much, so quickly."

Liam smiled. "You're going to be a great mother."

"Do you think so?" she asked.

"I know so," he said softly. "You already are."

"He's sleeping now." She glanced at the baby monitor and turned up the sound, smiling at Liam as Oliver's soft, rhythmic breaths emitted from the speaker. Snuggling more comfortably against the pillow behind her back, she continued, "It takes so little to make him happy that sometimes I think he's going to be a better son than I'll be a mother."

Liam's smile faded and he looked up again, focusing on the stars.

After a few minutes, Mallory asked, "What are you thinking about?"

He looked at the moon. Studied the light as it pooled over

the leaves in the tops of the trees. "I'm wondering if I've been that for my mom."

"Been what?"

"A good son."

"Of course you have," she said. "You've been a great one. You're a wonderful man, Liam, and you take such good care of her."

He rolled his head to the side and met her eyes. "Then why doesn't she remember me?"

Mallory frowned. Her eyes darkened with sadness as she examined his expression.

After a moment, she reached out and placed her hand over his, where it lay on the armrest of his chair. She wove her fingers between his and squeezed gently. "In her heart, she remembers."

Liam turned his attention to the night sky again, but silently savored the warm press of Mallory's palm against his own. "I wish I could believe that."

They sat in silence for a while, gazing at the stars, listening to the frogs and crickets croak and chirp near the pond, and relishing the gentle breeze as it swept across the grounds.

Before long, Liam's eyes grew heavy, and he struggled to keep them open. He must've drifted off at some point, because a rustle of movement and light touch on his right forearm prompted him back to awareness.

"In her heart," Mallory whispered near his ear, "she remembers. You're not the kind of man a woman could forget."

Before he could respond, her lips brushed his cheek in the softest of kisses then she drew away, the warmth of her presence fading as she stood and walked away. "Good night, Liam."

I BROUGHT YOU home today, Oliver.

Maybe I shouldn't call Pine Creek Farm our home. After

all, I only came here for a job. I came here hoping to start over and make a new life for us both somewhere else in the future.

But this place, you see, has begun to feel like home. Especially now that you're here, living under this roof with me. You, Gayle...and Liam.

Mallory touched her lips. It was still there, the lingering sensation of having kissed Liam, however briefly. His cheek had been warm and stubbled, and his distinctive scent had filled her senses, mingling with the faint smoke of the fire and the scent of spring wildflowers that drifted on the air surrounding them. It had felt like...

"Home," she whispered. Then began writing again.

Pine Creek Farm feels like home, Oliver. And Gayle and Liam feel like family.

I wish we could stay here forever.

CHAPTER NINE

SPRING GAVE WAY to summer at Pine Creek Farm. Full, colorful blooms opened on the petunias Mallory and Gayle had planted around the main house, dancing on the summer breeze as though in cheerful welcome to whoever approached the front steps. The sprawling fields filled in with thick, healthy grass, hummingbirds vibrated around feeders Mallory and Gayle had filled with sugar water and hung on the front porch and occasionally—if Mallory sat outside with Gayle at just the right time of day—they'd catch sight of wild rabbits springing stealthily across the front lawn.

The magnolia trees, every branch adorned with bountiful blooms and strong leaves, stood proud and elegant along both sides of the driveway. Pine Creek Farm was bursting at the seams with vibrant summer colors, the sweet scent of honeysuckle and relaxed guests.

And on June 11, Oliver turned three months old.

"Good job, sweet boy. Now, try again."

Mallory, sitting on a blanket in the front yard in preparation for a picnic, smiled as Gayle lifted a blue teething ring toward Oliver. Oliver, seated comfortably in a soft bouncer between Gayle and Mallory, reached out with both hands, his fingers opening and closing as he attempted to grasp the teething ring.

"Keep going, my love," Mallory said, grinning. "You've almost got it."

At the sound of her voice, Oliver swiveled his head to the side. When his big brown eyes met hers, he smiled.

Mallory laughed, leaned over and kissed the brown curls that waved onto his forehead. It wasn't his first smile—not by a long shot—but she couldn't help but be surprised and delighted at the sight of every smile that curved his mouth.

He'd grown so much over the past three months. He ate and slept on a regular schedule now, sleeping through the night for at least five to seven hours. And, best of all, he recognized her face. His expression lit up every time she walked into view and Mallory couldn't help but feel a burgeoning sense of pride. She hoped she was a good mother. She tried every day to care for Oliver even better than she had the day before.

"There he goes," Gayle said, laughing. "He got a hold of it. Such a strong boy."

As if pleased with the praise, Oliver shook the teething ring in his hand and chortled, smiling wider.

"And look at those little feet go," Gayle said. "He might be a runner one day."

"That he might." Grinning, Mallory reached out and tickled the bottom of Oliver's bare foot.

Oliver smiled wider and wiggled.

"You're a busy little guy, aren't you?" Mallory teased.

If he wasn't smiling and waving his arms, trying to grab anything that came near him, his little legs were going a mile a minute, his feet pumping in the air wherever he sat or lay, as though testing out their strength and mobility.

"I think you're just excited to be outside again," Mallory said, tickling his toes.

And she couldn't blame him.

It was another beautiful day at Pine Creek Farm. Being early afternoon, the scorching heat of the summer day had not yet arrived. Instead, the air was warm and pleasant—even if it was a bit humid—the sky was clear and the sun bright, and the grounds were bustling with activity as guests strolled about the fields, fished in the pond or rode horses across the front field in a trail ride.

Mallory closed her eyes and inhaled deeply, breathing in a lungful of fresh country air. "Room to breathe," she whispered.

That's what Liam had promised Pine Creek Farm would offer her when he'd offered her the caretaking job. And that's exactly what Pine Creek Farm had delivered.

Liam. Her mouth curved in a dreamy smile as she thought of him. She'd found it increasingly hard not to think of him lately. There'd been no more kisses beside the firepit, or anything else that wasn't well within the confines of friendship. But... she still had the memory of that one soft kiss she'd brushed against his cheek and the warm feel of his hand beneath hers. And every day, as they cooked breakfast in the kitchen, ate lunch together and sat by the firepit at night, Liam had begun feeling even more like family.

Being in his company was easy. Comfortable. There was a peace between them that she'd never experienced with Trevor—or any other man before. She could close her eyes when sitting beside him by the firepit in the evening and feel completely at ease. Her affection for him had intensified and continued to grow a little more every day.

If only she knew how he really felt about her.

He hadn't mentioned the kiss since it happened, and he didn't seem likely to. The morning afterward, he'd greeted her with a smile downstairs as usual, and they'd gone about the day as they had all the days before since her arrival.

But there was something in his eyes now when he looked at her. And, on more than one occasion, she'd caught his gaze lingering on her. When she'd notice him studying her, he'd meet her eyes and smile, gazing just a bit more before he broke eye contact and moved on. Each time, she'd gotten the impression that he had something he wanted to say and a few times, she thought he might actually voice his thoughts.

But that hadn't happened. Whatever secrets Liam had in his mind or heart, he continued to keep them to himself.

"Mind if I join you?"

Mallory shook herself slightly at the sound of his voice and glanced over her shoulder to find him striding across the front lawn in her direction. "You know you have a permanent invitation," she teased, smiling.

He laughed and took his hat off and tossed it onto the edge of the blanket where she and Gayle sat, then sat down beside Mallory. "That's good to know. I noticed earlier that you were carrying one of Pam's baskets out here," he said, nodding at the large straw basket on the edge of the blanket. "I asked one of the hands to lead the trail ride this afternoon so that I could join y'all on the off chance that you might have food in that thing."

Mallory laughed, too. "Then you made a good choice because that's exactly what's in there. It's a beautiful day, the flowers are blooming and we thought you might enjoy a picnic outside."

Or, at least, she hoped so. One constant since the day she'd kissed Liam had been that he had never missed eating lunch with Mallory, Gayle and Oliver. No matter how busy things became at Pine Creek Farm or how many trail ride requests he had to fill for guests, Liam always made time to return to the main house to eat lunch with them, hold Oliver for at least ten minutes and share a laugh or two before returning to work.

"I look forward to seeing this little man every day." Grinning, Liam reached out and held up one finger close enough for Oliver to reach out and grab. Oliver accepted the invitation, his tiny palm wrapping tightly around Liam's finger. "He's getting stronger, isn't he?"

"He's a runner, too," Gayle said. "Look at those feet go."

Glancing down at where Oliver's feet kicked at a steady

pace in the bouncer, Liam chuckled. "I think you're right about that, Mom. He never slows down, does he?"

Mallory shook her head. "Nope. He's a busy little guy." She reached behind her and lifted the lid off a cooler, dug around in the ice and withdrew a cold bottle of water. "Need a drink?"

"I'd love one." Liam took the bottle from her, unscrewed the cap then tipped it back, drawing deeply.

He'd gotten a tan over the past couple of months. More than likely, the tan had developed during the long hours of leading trail rides in the afternoon. It suited him. With his blond hair, hazel eyes and sun-kissed skin, he looked healthy, energetic and happy.

Realizing she was staring, Mallory pried her gaze away from Liam, ducked her head then dragged the picnic basket close. "Pam dropped off more barbecue sandwiches this morning when she and Barbara came to visit Oliver. She said she thought you might like them since you and the hands enjoyed them so much last time."

Liam set the water bottle down on the blanket and rubbed his hands together. "Oh, you have no idea how much I want those right now."

Mallory smiled. "Hard morning?"

"Lots of trail rides," he said, accepting a sandwich, wrapped in plastic, as she passed it to him. "All of the guesthouses are rented out and several children arrived with the last two families that checked in. They're old enough to ride but they've never done so before so I had to give them several lessons before we took the horses out today."

"Did they enjoy the ride?" she asked.

Liam nodded as he unwrapped his sandwich. "One of the boys was a natural." He took a bite of his sandwich, chewed then swallowed before saying, "He took off on his own a time or two. I had to chase him down and was scared to death I wouldn't catch him before anything unwelcome occurred. I reminded him several times that horses—even the best of them—can be unpredictable."

"Always the protector," Mallory said softly. It was something she loved most about him.

His eyes met hers and she stilled, heat suffusing her cheeks. A slow smile spread across his face as though he could read her thoughts and knew exactly what she was thinking.

But he didn't know how she truly felt about him, did he? Gracious, she hoped not. She'd been very careful—especially after kissing him—to keep a healthy distance between them. To keep the relationship as it had always been before she'd kissed him—strictly on the level of good friendship.

But behaving like Liam's friend didn't keep her heart from longing to be something more.

"There he goes again," Gayle said, pointing at Oliver. "He caught it the first time I held it out to him."

Oliver kicked his legs in his bouncer and waved a second teething ring in the air with a bright smile as though in triumphant success.

Liam laughed. "Good job, buddy." He glanced at Mallory. "Do you mind if I hold him for a little while?"

She shook her head. "Not at all."

He put his sandwich down, wiped his hands on a napkin then reached out and lifted Oliver from his bouncer. Liam's hands, though big and strong, could not have been more gentle or loving than if he were Oliver's biological father.

The thought sent a wave of longing through Mallory.

"Has he had his lunch yet?" Liam asked, glancing at Mallory again.

She nodded.

"Good." He looked down at Oliver and smiled, drifting his thumb over Oliver's soft curls. "That means we'll have more time to hang out. Whatcha feel like doing today, buddy? Wanna see if we can spot any of those bunnies running around the front yard?"

Oliver cooed again and kicked his legs.

"I'd like to hold him again." Gayle looked at Oliver longingly.

"Well now," Liam said, smiling down at Oliver. "Mamas always come first." He turned to Gayle and handed Oliver to her, making sure Oliver was settled safely within her arms before releasing him. "Take all the time you want, Mom. I need to finish my sandwich anyway."

Oliver, seemingly just as happy in Gayle's arms as in Liam's, continued to coo as Gayle spoke to him.

"You're such a happy boy," Gayle said. "So friendly and easygoing. Nothing seems to ruffle you."

Mallory met Liam's eyes and smiled. He smiled back but there was a lingering sadness shadowing his eyes.

They'd both noticed that Oliver seemed to be the brightest spot in Gayle's day. Over the past week especially, Gayle had begun sleeping later and later every morning and became disoriented much more often. Two days ago, she'd declined Mallory's offer to go outside for the afternoon, which was unlike her. Normally, Gayle loved the outdoors and enjoyed their slow walks down the driveway beneath the magnolia trees.

But lately, that had changed. Her energy was depleted, she seemed less motivated to do anything—especially activities she used to love—and she smiled much less often.

Liam had become worried. Mallory could see it in his face every time he looked at Gayle. He watched her closely more and more every day, asking how she was feeling, if she needed anything and checking with Mallory for any changes—however small—in her behavior.

Mallory could imagine how difficult it must be for him to be unable to slow or stop the decline of his mother's health. Liam always took care of others before himself. It was his nature.

"I had a little boy like you once," Gayle said, gently tapping Oliver's chin.

Liam picked up his bottle of water, drank deeply then resumed eating his sandwich.

"Only," Gayle said, "he had blond hair instead of brown. He had big hazel eyes and the sweetest laugh I've ever heard."

Liam took another bite of his sandwich.

"And when he grew up," Gayle said, "he was tall. So very tall and strong. He took care of me, you know? He took care of the farm, the house, my magnolias. Liam was a perfect son."

Mallory stilled, her eyes darting to Liam.

He paused in the act of drinking water, then lowered his bottle to the blanket and looked at Gayle. "Mom?"

Gayle didn't seem to notice him speak. Instead, she continued looking at Oliver, her smile growing. "I can tell you're going to be like Liam. So loving, so kind. Always giving more than you get. Always doing the right thing."

A sheen of moisture glinted in Liam's eyes beneath the sunlight. He looked at Mallory, his mouth parting, but no sound emerged.

"I hope your little one grows up to be like Liam," Gayle said, looking at Mallory. "He'd be a blessing to you."

Mallory looked at Liam, the joy in his expression stealing her breath. "Yes," she whispered. "I hope, very much, that Oliver grows up to be just like Liam."

They stayed outside for a while, sitting on the blanket, watching Gayle play with Oliver. She never seemed to recognize Liam, who sat beside her, smiling with tears in his eyes, but she continued praising the man named Liam who she remembered as her son.

After a while, Gayle's speech began to slow and her eyelids grew heavy.

"Mom." Liam reached for Oliver. "It's about time for your nap. Why don't we put Oliver back in his bouncer and get you inside and up to your bed? You look tired."

Gayle blinked as Liam lifted Oliver from her arms and settled him back in the bouncer. "Yes," she whispered, as though in a daze. "I am tired."

Mallory rose to her knees. "I'll help you get settled in your ro—"

"That's okay," Liam said, smiling. "Let me do it this time?"

Mallory sat back down. "Of course."

Liam looked at Gayle. "What do you say, Mom? Would you mind if I walk with you inside and help you get settled for your nap? I can read to you for a little while, if you'd like." He winked at Mallory. "My voice may not be as soothing as Mallory's but I'll read to you as long as you'd like."

Gayle nodded. "That'd be fine. Thank you, young man."

Liam stood then bent, cupping his hands under Gayle's arms and helping her stand. He thanked Mallory for lunch then left, leading Gayle up the front porch steps of the main house.

Mallory, tears in her eyes, watched them leave then looked at Oliver, who cooed. "Yeah," she whispered. "I hope you grow up to be just like Liam."

TODAY HAD BEEN a good day. No, today had been a great day.

Liam brushed Sugar's back and smiled. The stable was quiet, all the hands having left an hour earlier to knock off for the day, and dusk was settling over Pine Creek Farm. With the sun dipping low in the sky, the hot summer air had cooled to a comfortable temperature and the dying sunlight hit the landscape just right, casting a pink glow across the sky and through the open doors of the stable.

It was as though God had decided to tie a beautiful bow on the gift he'd given him today.

Liam laughed, his heart full. His mother had remembered him. She may not have recognized his face, but she had remembered his name. More than that. She'd described the things she admired most about him. There had been love in her words—the emotion had gentled every syllable—and the expression on her face as she'd looked down at Oliver in her arms had been the same expression she'd had when she'd looked at him as a child.

He could remember those summer days of childhood and early teenage years clearly. The times during summer when he and Holt would go down to the pond, fish for hours, then haul their catch back up to the main house.

Their mom had always been waiting for them in the rocking chair on the front porch, watching the sun set and waiting for their silhouetted figures to emerge over the hill. And when he and Holt had reached the front steps, a mouthwatering aroma had drifted from the kitchen and through the screen door, wafting over the front steps.

Holt had always dropped his cooler of fish outside, kissed their mom's cheek then run inside to start eating the dinner she always had waiting for them. Liam, on the other hand, had taken both of their fish hauls to the sink at the back of the house and had cleaned and packed them in ice before coming inside to eat his dinner.

When he arrived, his mother would stand from the dining room table, walk across the room and wrap her arms around him. He could remember her kissing his cheek, smiling softly and saying, "My sweet Liam. Always doing the right thing."

He'd been loved—Liam blinked back happy tears—and remembered.

That thought alone was enough to fill his heart with joy. The knowledge that his mother, despite her illness, still cherished some memory of him safely in her heart. Mallory had been sure of it. What was it she had whispered near his ear when she'd kissed him all those weeks ago?

In her heart, she remembers. You're not the kind of man a woman could forget.

He closed his eyes and smiled wider, saying a brief, silent prayer of thanks for all of the blessings God had given him. And there had been so very many blessings lately.

A plaintive meow sounded behind him.

Liam stopped brushing Sugar and glanced over his shoulder to find Miss Priss sitting nearby.

She stared up at him, her wide, intimidating eyes unblinking.

"So, what's up?" Liam asked. "Did you come to visit me or are you looking for Mallory?"

It had to be the latter. The cat had grown quite fond of Mallory. It followed her around whenever she took Gayle for a walk across the grounds and lingered nearby when she rocked Oliver on the front porch.

The cat stared at him for a moment longer then blinked slowly, stretched out on its side then rolled over onto its back, exposing its furry belly.

Liam raised his brows. "Oh, you don't think I'm gonna fall for that, do you?"

Miss Priss stared at him.

"If I pet you," he asked, "you're gonna bite me, right? Maybe rip my arm off?"

Miss Priss blinked slow again then wiggled. The feline looked far too adorable in light of the menacing personality she harbored.

"All right," Liam said softly, lowering to his haunches. "I'll give you a chance. Just...be kind."

Hesitantly, he lifted his hand and reached out, steering clear of Miss Priss's belly—he was nowhere near brave enough to chance petting her there—and touched her head, stroking her fur ever so slightly.

Miss Priss remained still, then her eyes slowly closed and she nudged his hand with her nose.

"Will you look at that?" Liam said, smiling. "I'm growing on you, am I?"

As if in response, Miss Priss pressed her head into Liam's palm then rolled over and stretched her legs out, giving him free access to her back.

Chuckling, he petted her with more confidence now, stroking her thick fur in slow sweeps. "So we're friends now, hmm? Maybe you decided to cut me some slack on account of how fond you are of Mallory and Oliver." He grinned. "If so, I'll take it."

And he could understand. He'd grown more than fond of Mallory and Oliver over the past months. He continued petting the cat, his smile growing even more.

After a few moments, his cell phone buzzed in his back pocket and reluctantly, he withdrew his hand and stood. "Sorry, Miss Priss. I need to take this."

He pulled the cell phone from his back pocket and answered, grinning as Miss Priss stood, stretched then sashayed away.

"Liam?"

The urgency in Mallory's voice made him freeze. "What is it? Is something wrong with Oliver?"

"No. It's...it's Gayle."

His legs were already moving, carrying him swiftly out of the stable and across the grounds. "What do you mean? What's happened?"

Mallory didn't answer right away—her silence more than telling—and he walked faster. The whole sky had turned pink, the rosy light reflecting off the white siding of the main house, casting a strong glow across the front lawn. A chorus of toads and crickets swelled in the distance, blending with the panicked buzz in his ears.

"Just come quick, okay?" Mallory said, her voice strained. "Please hurry."

He disconnected the call, shoved the cell phone in his back pocket and ran. He took the stairs two at a time, moving as quickly as he could to the second story of the main house. Mallory was standing outside Gayle's room. Her lips quivered and her face was streaked with tears.

He stumbled and drew to a stop, his chest burning. "What is it?"

"She won't wake up," Mallory whispered. "I've tried CPR but... I think she—"

Liam, his heart pounding, walked past her, entered the room and sat on the edge of the bed beside where his mother lay.

"Mom?"

Her eyes remained closed and her chest still.

He touched her hand. It was cold. There was no pulse.

"Mom?" It was barely a whisper that didn't require an answer. He knew she was gone.

"I called an ambulance," Mallory said from near his shoulder. "They should be here soon."

Liam looked up, his eyes meeting hers. "At least she's at peace now."

"Oh, Liam," she whispered.

He faced his mother again and moments later, Mallory's hands settled on his shoulders and her temple pressed gently against his. They stayed that way for several minutes until the first responders arrived.

Liam went through the motions, keeping out of the way as the paramedics worked, accepting the news of his mother's death stoically and without surprise, then stepped aside as the first responders carried Gayle away.

The sun had set by the time the ambulance left. Liam watched it disappear around a curve as he stood on the front porch, then his knees seemed to buckle, and he sagged onto the top step and lowered his face in his hands. Heavy sobs wracked his body, and he covered his face, hiding the tears.

"Liam?"

Mallory sat beside him on the step, wrapped her arms around him and hugged him close, swaying gently from side to side. Her soft hands smoothed his hair from his brow, wiped the tears from his cheeks and held him close as he continued to cry. He buried his face against her neck, absorbing her warmth and strength, finding some comfort there.

He stayed in her arms for over an hour, allowing his tears to flow freely as Mallory held him and continued rocking gently from side to side. He felt wrung out now, all the tears having left him, embarrassment taking their place.

"I'm sorry," he rasped, lifting his head from her chest and easing away.

Mallory cupped his face and urged him to meet her eyes. "You have nothing to be sorry for, Liam."

"You loved her, too," he whispered, watching a tear roll down her cheek.

"Yes," she whispered brokenly. A second tear followed the first. "I loved her very much."

The pain in her eyes reflected his own. He lowered his head and brushed his lips across her forehead, trying his best to thank her without being able to say the words. When her eyes fluttered shut, he kissed the corners of her eyes, too, then drifted his thumbs over her cheeks, gathering her tears against his skin as she'd done for him.

On the step nearby, the baby monitor crackled and Oliver's cry emerged.

"I need to go to him," she whispered, pressing her cheek against his palm.

Liam nodded and released her. "Do you mind if I come?"

She stood and reached out, taking his hand in hers, and tugged him to his feet. They walked silently up the stairs, hand in hand, into the nursery. Oliver was crying louder now, his demanding wails filling the room.

Mallory walked to the crib, lifted Oliver in her arms and whispered soothing words as she carried him to the changing table. Liam stood close by as she changed Oliver's diaper, dressed him in a fresh onesie and lifted him into her arms again.

"Would you like to hold him for a while?" she asked.

Liam nodded and sat in the rocking chair, holding out his arms as Mallory settled Oliver against his chest. Oliver looked up at him, his heavy eyelids beginning to close and a sleepy smile crossing his face.

Liam sat there for a while, cradling Oliver in his arms and rocking gently back and forth in the same way Mallory had with him. Soon, Oliver had drifted off again, his pink lips parting and his soft breaths coming rhythmically.

The sight of Oliver, happy and healthy, breathing deep and even, soothed the pain in his heart.

What a blessing this was. To be surrounded by two people he loved after losing someone so dear. The thought evoked a fresh surge of tears and he blinked rapidly, drifting the back of his knuckles gently over Oliver's cheek.

"I love you, Oliver," he whispered softly. He looked up, met Mallory's eyes across the room and said the words his heart shouted loud and clear. "I love you both."

Liam said he loved us, Oliver.

It happened just a few minutes ago when he was hold-ing you. Just as simple and surprising as that.

Mallory looked up from the notepad, shifted to a more com-fortable position on the edge of her bed then continued writing.

We lost Gayle today. She had a great time playing with you outside earlier this afternoon, then she lay down for a nap and—

She wiped a tear from her cheek.

But she remembered Liam. She spoke of him today while she was holding you. She said all the things that I've noticed about him that are great. She said she hoped you'd grow up to be like him.
That made Liam happy. You should've seen his face.

It's hurt him so much to think that Gayle had no memory left of him but even though she didn't recognize him, she spoke of him. What a blessing for God to give Liam before Gayle had to go away.

Mallory closed her eyes and swallowed hard, silencing a sob. She glanced over her shoulder and looked across the hall, catching a glimpse of Liam as he continued rocking in the chair as he held Oliver in the nursery.

You're still with him now as I write this. Liam started crying again and I thought it best to give him some space and privacy. I left him alone with you for a while. He's been through so much today and I know you make him happy.

You're such a comfort to him. I could tell the moment I put you in his arms that you eased his pain. He's always wanted a son, I think. He loves you so much, Oliver. So very, very much.

And I love him, too.

Mallory bit her lip and looked out the window. There were no stars out tonight. Instead, clouds had rolled in, covering the moon, and it was darker than ever outside.

He loves you, Oliver. I have no doubts about that. But I wonder, if you weren't mine…if it were just me that had come to Pine Creek Farm, would he still feel the same?

I know Liam loves you, Oliver.

But would he still love me if I didn't have you?

CHAPTER TEN

BY THE NEXT AFTERNOON, Liam's brother, Holt, and Jessie arrived at Pine Creek Farm with their three children. Liam and Holt hugged immediately when Holt and his family entered the main house, then the two men walked up the stairs to Gayle's room and shut the door, grieving together in private, sharing memories of their mother and discussing logistics of the funeral, visitation and reception for friends and family that would occur at Pine Creek Farm over the coming days.

Downstairs, Mallory and Jessie spent some time together with the children in the living room, consoling them in the loss of their grandmother and leaning on each other for support in dealing with their own grief. When the children's tears had stopped, Mallory and Jessie prepared a light lunch, chatting as they worked to catch up on each other's activities over the past few months while Jessie and Holt's twin boys, Cody and Devin, entertained their younger sister, Ava.

Before long, Liam and Holt returned downstairs and joined everyone for lunch in the dining room. The meal was a silent affair, everyone doing their best to carry on in the absence of Gayle, but an empty chair that remained at the dining table was a constant reminder of how much they'd lost.

After eating, Holt's twin boys became antsy and in need of

a distraction. Liam, his eyes heavy and shadowed, suggested that he and Holt take the boys down to the pond to fish for a couple of hours.

"Are you sure you're up for that?" Mallory asked as he led the two boys toward the front door.

He paused and glanced over his shoulder at her, trying to smile but it was halfhearted at best. "It'll do us all good, I think," he said. "The sunshine and fresh air will help."

That, at least, Mallory could agree with.

Last night, after Liam had finished rocking Oliver back to sleep in the nursery, Mallory had tucked Oliver in his crib, kissed him good night then walked with Liam out into the hallway. Liam was no longer crying but he looked exhausted, and he'd watched her expectantly, studying her face silently, waiting for her to speak.

When she had remained silent and began fidgeting awkwardly with the hem of her shorts as they stood on the landing, he had said good-night and went downstairs to his room.

Mallory had stood there long after he'd left, knowing what he was hoping to hear from her, and disappointed with herself for not having the courage to say it.

She loved him—she had no doubts about the intensity of her feelings for him. Her doubts lay elsewhere.

"They'll be fine," Jessie said as the front door closed behind Liam, Holt and the boys. "Besides, with them gone and now that Ava's down for her nap, I'll have a chance to get to know Oliver a little better."

With that, Jessie stood and walked around the dining room table to where Oliver lay in his bassinet. Smiling, she gathered Oliver in her arms then returned to her seat at the table and cradled him close.

"He's so beautiful, Mallory."

"Thank you," she whispered.

Mallory smiled as Jessie combed her fingers lovingly through Oliver's dark hair, then walked over to the window.

She looked out at the front lawn, watching as Holt and Liam, the twin boys between them, walked across the grounds toward a small shed near the stable.

More than likely, Liam kept rods and tackle there. They would probably gather up fishing poles and bait then stroll back to the pond for an afternoon of fishing. Standing there, eyeing the two men from a distance, she had difficulty discerning the difference between Liam's and Holt's tall, muscular frames. They were so similar in stature and both reached out occasionally to ruffle one of the boy's hair affectionately.

"Jessie?" Mallory asked.

"Hmm?"

"Can I ask you something personal?"

"After all the questions I asked you when we first met at Hummingbird Haven?" Jessie glanced over her shoulder and smiled. "Ask away."

Mallory glanced once more at the two men and boys walking across the grounds, then faced Jessie. "How did you know Holt was in love with you?"

Jessie's brows rose. "Well, now, that's definitely a question."

Mallory winced and held up her hand. "I'm sorry, I don't mean to pry, I just—"

Jessie shook her head, looked down at Oliver and grinned. "We don't mind, do we, Oliver?" She looked back up at Mallory and laughed. "Well, I guess I knew when he told me so, for one."

The teasing tone of her voice coaxed a smile from Mallory. "Fair enough. But how else did you know?"

Jessie thought for a moment, then said, "It was the little things mostly. The way he was more concerned with my comfort than his. How he would go out of his way to make me happy and how considerate he was of my thoughts and feelings—especially when it came to the boys." She looked down at Oliver, a wistful expression appearing. "I'm unable to carry children of my own," she said softly.

Mallory frowned and glanced over her shoulder at the twin boys, who walked between Liam and Holt. "But I thought—"

"Cody and Devin are Holt's children and mine," Jessie stated firmly, "but biologically, they only belong to Holt. Holt left Cody and Devin with me at Hummingbird Haven not long after they were born. He wasn't ready to be a father then and I was just grateful to have the chance to be a mom. I wanted to adopt Cody and Devin but Holt came back right around the time I decided to file and told me he wanted to raise them himself."

Jessie shrugged. "We were at an impasse, you see? But I think that was God's way of nudging us together. We worked together to help the boys get to know him and keep them happy and I decided to give them up so Holt would be happy but as it turned out, Holt wasn't happy unless I was in the picture, too. We married, I adopted the boys and we both adopted Ava."

"Oh," Mallory said quietly. "But...say, for instance, that Cody and Devin hadn't been part of the equation. How would you have known that Holt really loved you?"

Jessie stopped rocking Oliver in her arms and shifted in her chair to face Mallory fully. "What's happened, Mallory? What are you really asking me?"

Sighing, Mallory bit her lip and hesitated. She glanced down at Oliver, who slept peacefully now, then summoned the courage to face Jessie again. "Liam told me he loved me last night."

Silence descended as Jessie absorbed the news. Her mouth opened and closed several times as though she meant to speak but thought better of it.

"Actually, he said he loved us," Mallory said, motioning between herself and Oliver. "Not just me—but *us*."

Understanding dawned on Jessie's face. "And now...you're wondering if Oliver weren't part of the equation, would Liam still love you?"

"Yes," Mallory said, her neck burning.

Jessie sank back in her seat, blew out a heavy breath and

cradled Oliver closer. "And this happened last night? After losing Gayle?" At Mallory's nod, she groaned softly and muttered under her breath, "I was afraid of this."

Mallory's frown deepened. "Afraid of what?"

Jessie blushed. "Oh, no—please, I didn't mean it that way. What I meant is, Liam and I had a conversation very similar to what you're suggesting a few months ago."

Mallory shook her head. "What kind of conversation?"

Jessie looked down, her gaze focused on Oliver. "A few days after you first arrived at Pine Creek Farm, I called Liam just to check in on you. To see how things were going. I could tell from the way he spoke that he was happy to have you here at the farm, helping with Gayle." She smiled gently. "And I know from the way Liam spoke about you and Gayle during later conversations, that Gayle truly benefited from you being here. But I can also tell that Liam was getting attached to the idea of you living here with Oliver."

Mallory looked at Oliver. "On a permanent basis, you mean?"

Jessie nodded. "When we spoke that day, he mentioned several things he planned to do in the future, like taking Oliver fishing, for one." She held up a hand. "Not that he'd even met Oliver at that time." She laughed self-consciously. "I mean, Oliver hadn't even been born then, but Liam was already making plans for having a little boy in his life."

Mallory sagged back against the window, her hands curling around the windowsill. "He was excited at the idea of having a baby around?"

"Yes," Jessie said quietly. "That doesn't mean that he only wanted the baby though. It's just...well, Liam has lived here at Pine Creek Farm his entire life. Holt has had a chance to travel, to tour the rodeo circuit, experience the world and decide what he really wanted out of life. Holt chose a life at Hummingbird Haven with me, the boys and Ava." She hesitated. "Thing is, I don't think Liam has ever really had that chance.

I mean, the chance to really think about what he wants out of life and choose his own path."

"Because he stayed with Gayle after his father left?" Mallory asked.

"In part," Jessie said. "But he also has another reason that may be influencing how he feels about you and Oliver. He had known Gayle was getting worse for quite some time now. He and Holt didn't speak of the possibility of her passing often, but they did on occasion. Liam knew he would lose Gayle at some point, and I think he wondered at times what would come next for him."

Mallory closed her eyes, her stomach sinking as she shook her head slowly. "And there I came, knocking on your door the night he stayed at Hummingbird Haven."

"Mallory, please don't misunderstand me. I don't mean to say with any certainty that that's the case. It's just that..." She grimaced. "Well, I care about you and Oliver, too—very much. And I know from experience that it's easy to get attached when you're helping others, like Liam has helped you. The last thing I'd want in the world is for you to be hurt or disappointed again. You asked me what I thought and I'm trying to be honest and open with my answer."

Mallory opened her eyes and looked at Jessie. "And that's what I wanted. I wanted your honest opinion and I'm grateful you gave it to me."

Jessie bit her lip, her gaze moving from Mallory to Oliver and back. "I don't know that I have the answers you're looking for and I don't want you to just blindly accept my advice. I'd feel so much better if you spoke to Liam about this."

Mallory glanced over her shoulder and looked out the window. Liam, Holt and the boys were out of sight now. "I know what he'll say if I ask." She looked at Jessie again. "The problem is, I just won't know if he truly means it. And then I'll be right back where I started."

Jessie was quiet for a moment then asked, "Do you love him?"

"Yes," Mallory whispered. "I love him very much."

"Then maybe..."

As Jessie continued to hesitate, Mallory pushed away from the window, straightened and gestured that she continue. "Please. Tell me. I'd really like to hear what you think."

Jessie sighed. "If you love Liam, maybe give him—and yourself—some time and space so that you can both reflect on what it is you each really want now that Gayle is gone."

Mallory rubbed her temples. An ache had formed there. It began to spread down the back of her neck at the thought of doing what Jessie suggested. "I need to leave Pine Creek Farm anyway," she whispered. "With Gayle gone, it's best that Oliver and I have a place of our own rather than live with Liam as we are now. I could find a place for Oliver and me temporarily until I decide on something permanent. Maybe check with one of the women in the ladies' group at the church I attend with Liam. That way, Liam will have the house to himself and can decide how he truly feels without our influence."

Jessie nodded slowly. "That might be for the best."

"What I'm afraid of," Mallory said softly, "is that he'll realize that he only loves Oliver. Then he'll change his mind about wanting me in his life."

Jessie smiled confidently, but doubt lingered in her eyes. "If he truly loves you, he won't."

"You change your mind about swapping out that worm for a cricket?"

Liam glanced to his left where Holt stood by his side in front of the pond at Pine Creek Farm. Holt's sons, Cody and Devin, stood on the other side of Holt, holding their fishing rods and watching their corks bob in the rippling water. They'd been fishing for over an hour but none of them had caught any bream yet.

Liam looked at his own fishing line, untouched by fish, which continued to float idly deep in the center of the pond.

"I just might change my mind. Can't do any worse than I am right now."

"Why ain't the fish biting, Uncle Liam?" Cody asked, frowning up at him from where he stood on the bank.

His nephew's disappointed pout made Liam smile. "It's the wrong time of day, I suppose." He tilted his head back and squinted up at the sky. "It's pretty hot out in the afternoon. Those fish are probably snuggled deep in that water, cooling off and taking a nap."

"So, when's the best time to try to catch them?" Devin asked, reeling in his line.

"Bright and early—first thing in the morning, dude." Holt reached down and ruffled Devin's hair.

"So, can we come out tomorrow morning?" Cody asked. "First thing? Bright and early, like you said?"

Holt shook his head. "I'm afraid not. Your grandmother's funeral is tomorrow and we'll be tied up with that most of the day."

The boys' shoulders slumped and they both faced the pond again, their sad eyes roving over the water.

Liam knelt, bringing himself to eye level with the boys. "Hey. There's a secret spot out here. One where I'll bet you'll get a nibble or two no matter how good the fish are sleeping."

The boys' eyes brightened.

"Where?" Cody asked.

"Show us," Devin said.

Liam pointed at a weeping willow tree on the other side of the pond, its droopy branches dancing lightly over the surface of the water with each push of the summer breeze. "Right there, under that tree. There's a tangle of roots at the base of that tree. Stand right smack-dab in the middle of them, throw your line out and I guarantee you'll get at least one nibble."

Devin yanked his line, reeling it in quickly, looped his hook onto the rod, then took off around the pond, shouting over his shoulder as he ran, "I'm getting the first bite!"

Cody followed suit, reeling in his line and darting after his brother. After a few steps though, he stopped abruptly, turned and ran back to Liam. He threw his arms around Liam's neck and kissed his cheek. "Thank you for showing us the secret spot, Uncle Liam."

Liam ruffled his hair and smiled. "You're welcome."

Those boys were so adorable, he found himself unable to deny them anything most days.

Cody took off again, joining his brother, and the two boys ran around the pond and set up below the weeping willow tree, casting their lines in and laughing as the corks bobbed in the water.

"Takes you back, doesn't it?" Holt asked quietly by his side.

Liam stood, reeled in his line and cast it out again. "That it does."

Cody and Devin were the spitting image of Holt. They reminded Liam of himself and Holt when they had been the same age, fishing together under the weeping willow, laughing and chatting, looking for some new trouble to get into on the farm. He and his brother had been inseparable at that age.

"Those were some of the best days of my life," Liam said. "When we were kids, the whole world was a playground. We could run at full speed for hours, without stopping."

Holt chuckled. "I'd like to see you try that now."

Liam raised one eyebrow. "I'd watch that, if I were you. I may be a few minutes older than you, but we're basically the same age."

They exchanged wry glances and laughed once more, but their laughter faded when the reason for their recent reunion returned fresh in their minds.

"I wish I'd known you were going to the funeral home this morning," Holt said. "I would've made sure to leave Hummingbird Haven a lot earlier so that I could go with you and help you with planning the funeral for tomorrow."

Liam shrugged. "It was mostly already handled. Mom took

care of things ahead of time." He sighed. "She was so afraid of leaving things behind that were unsettled and didn't want to cause me any extra work."

Holt nodded. "She always took care of us." He glanced at Liam and smiled. "And you took great care of her at the end, Liam. Thank you for that."

Liam stood there silently, reeling his line in a few inches, allowing his mind to rove over the past few months. "It wasn't only my doing," he said quietly. "Mallory was closer to Mom than just about anyone by the end."

"Jessie's been telling me over the past few months how big of a help you said Mallory's been for Mom."

"Yeah," Liam said. "She's been a lot more than a help."

They fell silent again, reeling in their lines and tossing them out twice to new spots in the pond.

Liam listened to the water lap against the grassy bank, thoughts tangling in his mind and intense emotions swirling in his heart. "I'm going to ask Mallory to marry me."

"Don't."

Holt's response was as blunt as Liam's statement.

Liam jerked in surprise, his brother's one-word admonishment making him bristle. "What do you mean, *don't*?"

Holt looked at him then, his hazel eyes—the exact same shade as his own—peering deeply into his. "You're in the midst of grieving, Liam. And so is Mallory. From what you and Jessie have told me, Mallory loved Mom just as much as we did, so she's gotta be hurting pretty hard right now."

"I know that," Liam said. "But that's all the more reason to—"

"No, it's not," Holt said firmly. "This is the worst possible time for you to propose right now. With Mom gone, her routine has changed and your whole life has changed. This isn't the best time to make a major decision—or commitment—like that."

"It didn't come to me overnight, if that's what you're assuming," Liam said sharply, facing the water again. "I've been thinking about it for quite some time."

"How much time?"

Liam shrugged.

"A few months, maybe?" Holt asked quietly. "Or just days after she got here?" When Liam didn't respond, he added, "Jessie told me that you and she had a talk a few months ago, not long after Mallory came to the farm and started taking care of Mom."

Liam tensed, his eyes closing slowly as he reflected upon the content of that uncomfortable conversation.

"She said you were already talking about spending time with Oliver," Holt said. "Already making plans for showing him around the farm when he was older and fishing in this pond like we are now." Holt sighed. "I'm not suggesting that you not ever ask Mallory to marry you—she's a wonderful woman and I'd be over the moon for you. All I'm asking is that you just take some more time. Time to adjust to what your life will be like now without Mom around. You can finally take the time to rest and do whatever you feel like doing without obligation or expectations."

Liam dragged his hand over his face. "I don't understand why you and Jessie are so hung up on me doing something different or leaving the farm and—"

"That's not it," Holt said. "Not it at all. We're just very aware of the fact that you've sacrificed a lot of years to take care of Mom and her childhood home. I can't tell you how much I still regret—" His voice breaking, Holt turned his head and looked away, staring across the grounds. After a moment, he faced Liam again. "Some days I wish I would've stayed with you and Mom after Dad left. If I'd stayed, you would've had more freedom then. You would've been able to travel or go to college or choose whatever you wanted to do in life. As things stood, after Dad left then I left, too, you were stuck with everything on your shoulders."

"I wasn't stuck," Liam said firmly. "I chose to be here."

"I don't mean to imply that you would've chosen to leave if I hadn't. I just regret not helping you as much as I should have." Holt tugged his line in, aimed for a new spot in the pond then tossed it out again. "I won't say that I regret the way my life's turned out though. And if I had the choice, I can't say that I'd go back and do things differently because if I did, I may have never met Jessie or had the boys."

Liam looked at the twins again. Cody was pointing at Devin's cork. They both jumped with excitement and leaned forward, staring at Devin's cork as it bobbed in the water.

"Devin got a bite, Dad!" Cody shouted across the pond.

Holt smiled and waved then called out, "Nice job, dude! Now keep your eyes on it and snatch the line in when the fish bites again."

The boys returned their attention to the cork, remaining motionless as they stared into the water.

Liam chuckled. "You got two fantastic boys right there." He smiled at Holt. "And you're a fantastic dad."

"You will be, too, one day," Holt said softly as he faced him again. "Or is that why you're so anxious to ask Mallory to marry you? Are you looking to be Oliver's dad right now?"

"I love Oliver," Liam said. "Any man would be lucky to be his dad. But that's not the reason. I love Mallory, too."

"But do you think she's ready for another husband?" Holt peered at him. "She accepted your job offer and came out here to start over and make a new life for herself and her baby. Are you sure settling down permanently in the first place she moved to, and remarrying after what she went through with her ex-husband is what she really wants to do?"

Liam gazed across the pond again. A hollow formed in his gut. "I... I haven't thought about it in that way."

"You're a good man," Holt said, "and I'd be shocked if Mallory didn't love you back. But this is her chance, Liam. This is Mallory's chance to start fresh and make a new life for herself. One where she's safe and in control of her own life. You know her better than me," he said softly, "but I wonder, if you ask her to marry you so soon after you've met, considering the circumstances, if you might not scare her away?"

Liam's throat tightened as he watched the boys whoop and holler, pulling hard on the fishing rods, reeling in a bream.

"All I'm saying is," Holt whispered, "don't propose yet. Not right now. Give it time until you—and Mallory—are certain it's what you both want and not just a result of circumstances."

Liam didn't respond—he couldn't. His throat had tightened and his mind reeled. He'd told Mallory he loved her, but she hadn't said it back. And now Holt was bringing a new doubt into his mind. In the beginning, he'd wanted to help Mallory out of kindness, sure. But now things were different. *He* felt differently and he hoped she did, too.

But considering all she'd been through and if what Holt said was true, Mallory may not want to marry again. Not now, or possibly ever. And the thought of losing Mallory and Oliver—especially so soon after losing Gayle—was too painful to bear.

CHAPTER ELEVEN

THE NEXT DAY, Gayle's funeral went as planned. The pews of the church were full of friends and family who mourned her passing. The sermon was beautiful and Liam, sitting beside Mallory and holding Oliver in his arms throughout the service, was able to hold back the tears that brimmed on his lower lashes each time he looked down at Oliver's smile.

It was a difficult day that Mallory knew Liam was anxious to put behind him.

After they left the church and returned to Pine Creek Farm, Mallory carried Oliver inside the main house, settled him in his bassinet in the kitchen and began pulling casseroles, ham and desserts that friends and family had dropped off out of the freezer and refrigerator and began warming them up.

"Here," Jessie said, striding into the kitchen and dropping her purse on the dining table. "Let me help you with that."

They fell into an easy rhythm, working fast and efficiently, laying out the food on the dining table, filling glass after glass with sweet tea and directing those who dropped in to pay their respects to Liam and the rest of the family to the refreshments. In between, they gathered up dirty paper plates and cups and tossed them in trash bags and loaded the dishwasher with used silverware.

Dozens of neighbors and friends continued to pour in, studying the pictures of Gayle that Liam had set out the night before and offering their condolences to Liam. Mallory thought he held up well through it all, remaining patient and polite through the deluge of visitors. He'd even laughed once or twice at something someone had said.

Despite everything going as planned, the day had been long and by the time the last round of guests had arrived, it seemed even longer.

"Why don't you take Oliver up to the nursery?" Jessie asked, taking the dirty plates Mallory carried out of her hands and putting them in the sink. "I can handle the rest of this on my own."

"But—"

"You've done enough," Jessie said firmly. "You've been at it all day and you look like you could tip over at any minute." She hugged her then smiled. "Go ahead. Go sit down with Oliver and put your feet up for a while."

Too tired to argue, Mallory complied. She picked up Oliver from his bassinet and carried him through the kitchen and into the hallway.

"Mallory." Liam walked out of the living room and joined her at the foot of the stairs. "Are you putting him down for a nap?"

She nodded. "He's worn out."

"I know the feeling," he said quietly. He lifted his hand and drifted the back of one finger down her cheek. "I think you do, too. You look exhausted."

Despite the circumstances, Mallory found herself smiling. "What a charmer you are."

He had the good grace to blush. "You know what I mean. You're always beautiful, Mallory."

Her smile faded and she looked down, watching as Oliver frowned and began kicking against her arms.

"Hey there," Liam said, gently lifting one of Oliver's hands in his. "You giving your mama a hard time? She's been taking care of everyone today, so you should cut her some slack, okay?"

Mallory's smile returned. "You know the feeling, don't you? You're always taking care of everyone else no matter the occasion."

Liam met her gaze, admiration in his eyes. "I can't thank you enough for all you've done the past couple of days. And what you did for Mom." His throat moved on a hard swallow. "I hope you know how much I appreciate all you've done."

"It's the least I could do," she whispered, "considering all you've done for us. Oliver and I owe you more than we could ever repay."

Liam frowned as he studied her expression. "Mallory—"

"I should put him down," she said, lifting her chin toward Oliver. "Before he starts testing out his lungs again."

Liam nodded then stepped back so she could climb the stairs to the second floor to the nursery. Voices from downstairs, slightly muffled, could still be heard on the upper landing. She shut the door behind her and the nursery closed around them like a soft cocoon, peaceful and quiet. She carried Oliver over to the rocking chair and sat down.

The day had taken its toll on Oliver, too. His eyes were heavy but he was fussy and unable to relax.

"I know, sweet boy," Mallory whispered, lifting him up to her shoulder and rubbing slow, gentle circles over his back. "We both have a lot on our minds, don't we?"

She'd barely slept last night, the conversation she'd had with Jessie about Liam yesterday still weighing heavy on her mind.

Right now she had a reprieve from the difficult conversation she knew she'd have to have with Liam, considering the house was full of family and guests. But once Holt, Jessie, their kids and all the rest of the family and friends left, she'd be on her own again with Liam. There'd be no way around it then. She'd have to have a conversation with him. They would have to discuss the future and her place in it.

The problem was, she was afraid. She was afraid of losing Liam and having to leave Pine Creek Farm.

But there were no other options, really. She needed to do as Jessie had suggested. She'd have to come right out and ask Liam how he felt about her. If he loved her—even without Oliver. And even then, if he answered the way she wanted him to and hoped he would, she wouldn't be sure if he truly meant it.

Because it's the right thing to do.

That's what he had said once. And that was who Liam was—a good man who could be trusted and depended upon. He would do the right thing in any situation, even if it cost him.

And doing the right thing in this situation wouldn't be enough. Not for her and not for Oliver.

"Oh, Oliver," she whispered. "How can we ever leave this place? How can we ever leave Liam?"

Oliver had grown quiet, his soft breaths coming deep and even between parted lips.

Sighing, she stood, carried Oliver across the room and placed him in his crib. He rolled his head to the side, pressed his cheek against the soft mattress and pulled his knees under his belly.

Mallory smiled. He looked so peaceful now, so at ease. She wished she could feel the same.

TWO DAYS LATER, when Holt, Jessie and their children said their goodbyes, climbed into Holt's truck and drove down the long driveway of Pine Creek Farm, Liam stood in the front yard and held Oliver in his arms then, too. He knew his brother and Jessie had work to get back to at Hummingbird Haven but he hated to see them leave all the same. Over the past few days, he'd grown accustomed to having his family with him, all of the guest rooms in the main house full and the dining table surrounded by the faces of loved ones at every meal.

It would be a long stretch before he saw his brother again. More than likely, the Thanksgiving holidays would be their next gathering.

He waved goodbye again, knowing the boys would be looking back at him from the rear window of the cab until the truck turned onto the highway and disappeared.

Oliver, feeling neglected, wiggled in Liam's arms, his bare feet kicking his elbow.

"He's getting fussy," Mallory said from where she stood by his side on the front lawn. "I think it's time to put him down for the night."

Liam drifted his finger over Oliver's soft cheek, watching as Oliver's eyelids closed slowly. "Yeah," he said. "I think you're right. He's had a busy few days with a lot of attention from a lot of new people."

Mallory walked with him as he carried Oliver up the front porch steps, into the main house then climbed the stairs into the nursery.

"He's been worn out with all the commotion lately," Mallory said, smiling as Liam settled Oliver in his crib.

And so was she.

Liam studied her face as she bent over the crib and drifted a kiss across Oliver's forehead. Mallory had borne the brunt of the workload over the past few days as they'd attended the funeral, prepared the house to receive friends and family afterward and continued to receive drop-in guests who brought various casseroles and side dishes for the family.

Mallory had truly been a blessing. She'd gone out of her way to take care of everything, refusing to allow Liam to do anything but focus on healing and spending time with his brother, nephews and niece. But yesterday, he'd reminded her that he would be returning to the normal routine as soon as Holt and Jessie left. Staying busy was the best way to comfort a broken heart and there was plenty to do at Pine Creek Farm.

"You might want to lie down, too," Liam said softly. "You've had a longer day than any of us have."

She'd risen early this morning and cooked breakfast for everyone, having set the table with place settings and plates almost overflowing with scrambled eggs, bacon and waffles prior to Liam waking and joining her in the kitchen. She'd cleaned the entire house afterward, too, changing the bed-sheets and towels in every guest room, washing laundry, and sweeping and mopping the floors. Every time he'd offered to help, she'd shooed him away, encouraging him to spend time with his brother, Jessie, the kids and Oliver in peace.

"I think you're right. I could use a nap," she said now, tuck-ing a strand of her long, wavy hair behind her ear. Her hand trembled. "But there's something I'd like to talk with you about first."

Liam smiled, but his stomach churned. "That sounds pretty serious."

Her cheeks reddened. "It is." She walked toward the door. "Do you mind joining me on the front porch? The sun's start-ing to set and it's cooler now."

Liam nodded and followed her out of the nursery and down the stairs. He sat in a rocking chair beside her on the front porch and they rocked silently for a few minutes, gazing out at the grounds, watching the hot summer sun dip below the horizon.

"You know I can't stay," Mallory said softly.

He continued rocking by her side, staring straight ahead in the same direction that she did. "Even without—" He cleared his throat. "There's still plenty of work available around the farm even without the caretaking position. Maintaining the guest rooms and guesthouses alone is a full-time—"

"I don't mean that," she said. "With Gayle gone, it's not like it was. We're not a married couple and it wouldn't be appro-priate. Especially now with Oliver here."

"I could reserve a guest house for you. You and Oliver could stay there, apart from the main house."

"I appreciate the offer, but that wouldn't really resolve the issue."

He frowned. "Then what is the issue?"

She stared back at him silently, then faced the setting sun again. "When you were Cody's and Devin's age or maybe when you were a teenager, what were your dreams for the future?"

Frowning deeper, he looked at the grounds again, too. "I don't know what that has to do with—"

"It has everything to do with it," she said. "Please tell me. I want to know."

He continued rocking, roving his eyes over the landscape, watching as the sky changed colors, turning from blue to gold, pink then red before finally giving way to a starry night sky.

"You don't know, do you?" she asked quietly. There was a rustle of movement by his side and he turned his head to find her looking at him again. "You've never really had the opportunity to choose what you want out of life, have you?"

A wry smile curved his lips. "You've been talking to Jessie and Holt, haven't you?"

"Maybe. But that's not why I asked."

"I don't know what you want me to say, Mallory."

"I want you to tell me what you want." A plea entered her eyes. "I want you to tell me that there's something that you've dreamed of having. That you've thought about what it'd be like after your mom was gone. That instead of taking care of others and always sacrificing for someone else, that there's something you really want of your own."

Oh, he wanted. He wanted so much.

He wanted to marry Mallory. He wanted to be a father to Oliver. He wanted the three of them to be a family. He wanted to fill the main house with more children and one day, hopefully, grandchildren. He wanted—

Don't.

Liam shot to his feet at the memory of Holt's voice. He walked over to the porch rail, leaned onto his hands and ducked his head. "I know what I want," Liam rasped.

"Please tell me."

"I want to marry you." He spoke before thinking better of it, then spun around, his breath coming in short, shallow bursts. "I want to be a father to Oliver. I want you and Oliver to be under this roof with me every day, every night, every morning. I want you to let me love you and Oliver with everything I've got because I can't imagine the future without you and him. I want to be there for you and Oliver for as long as I can, in every way."

His answer seemed to disappoint her.

She looked down at her hands, wringing them together in her lap, her eyes sad. "Why?" she asked quietly. "Because it's the right thing to do?"

"Mallory—"

"You told me yourself that that was why you offered me a job and decided to help me." She smiled, but there were tears in her eyes. "You're a good man, Liam. The best I've ever known. But I don't want to be a cause of charity for you. I don't want you to marry me out of loneliness and then regret your commitment later. And I don't want you to realize, when it's too late, that had circumstances been different, had we not met as we did, that you'd be making a very different decision right now as far as what to do with your future."

Liam lifted his hand in appeal. "I love you and Oliver."

Her chin wobbled and she closed her eyes briefly before meeting his gaze head-on again. "I know you love Oliver. But do you love me? Do you truly love me? Or are you just in love with the idea of having a wife and child?"

Her words caught him off guard. They evoked an unexpected surge of emotions—hurt, frustration, anger and...doubt.

"You realize," she said softly, "that everything you've said you wanted—every time you've said you love me—you've said it in terms of me and Oliver."

He remained silent, his heart pounding in his chest as he wracked his mind, reviewing his words, searching himself to see if there was any truth to her assumption.

"If we hadn't met as we did," she said, "and if it wasn't Oliver and me—if it was just me—would you still feel the same?"

If it was...just her? He hesitated, searching for the right words, but not finding them. Oliver was rooted in his heart as deeply as she was. It'd be impossible to imagine he didn't exist, and he had no desire to.

"I don't know how to answer you," he said quietly. "I don't know what you want me to say and I don't know that there is anything that I could say that would make you understand how I truly feel. To make you believe me."

Mallory stood and moved closer, her hand lifting as if to touch his face before lowering back to her side without making contact. "I just wanted to be sure that you believed it," she said quietly. "And I think I have my answer."

She stepped away and he moved to speak but—

"I want to be sure that having me in your life is what you really want and not a result of circumstances," she said. "And I need some time to do the same for myself. I need time to stand on my own feet with Oliver, move forward independently and do everything I can to ensure that neither one of us is choosing this out of loneliness or fear. I owe that to Oliver, at the very least."

He closed his eyes, wincing as a surge of pain streaked through him. She would leave now and take Oliver with her. And he had to let her go. It was the only hope he had of getting her to understand. To help her see what he already saw and know in her own heart what he already knew in his.

"For how long?" he asked.

She bit her lip. "I don't know. Long enough for both of us to heal and know how we truly feel."

He rubbed his forehead and sighed. "Where will you go?"

"I spoke with Pam yesterday and she offered me a room at her place until I'm able to find an apartment. I'll pack tonight and ask her to pick me and Oliver up tomorrow."

Liam nodded, his thoughts tangled and his heart aching. "I'll help you pack."

What else could he do?

THE NEXT MORNING, Liam loaded Oliver's crib into the bed of his truck, tied it down securely and watched as Pam loaded the last of Mallory's bags into the trunk of her car that was parked in front of his truck.

"I think that's everything," Pam said, closing the trunk of her car. She rubbed her hands together briskly and faced Liam. "Mallory's getting Oliver into his car seat now and should be out shortly."

Liam nodded, shoved his hands into his pockets and leaned against the front bumper of his truck. "When you're ready to leave, I'll follow y'all into town, carry Oliver's crib into your house and help unload the rest of the bags."

"Thank you," Pam said, smiling. "That's very kind of you."

Kind. Such a benign word. But for some reason, in that moment and after a night of tossing and turning to memories of Mallory's questions, it felt like an insult.

Though he couldn't blame Mallory for wondering if his feelings for her were genuine. He had, after all, invited her to Pine Creek Farm as a kind, helpful gesture. At the time, he hadn't expected to fall in love with her. And apparently, she was still under the impression that he felt responsible for her somehow and that his love for her stemmed from the fact that she was Oliver's mother.

But there was no truth to that. Unable to sleep, he'd left his bed last night, dressed and walked outside to the firepit. He'd stared up at the stars and had caught himself turning to the empty chair beside him, expecting to see Mallory's face, only to be reminded of the painful fact that she may never join him there again.

He turned away and stared across the field, where one of the hands led several guests astride horses across the grounds in a trail ride.

Pam's hand touched his forearm, her voice gentle. "I know this is hard for you, Liam. And I'm so sorry about Gayle. Please believe me when I say that Mallory is doing this for you just as much—if not more so—than for herself and Oliver."

Liam faced her again and managed to smile. "I don't mean to be difficult or sound put out. It's just a lot of change all at one time."

Pam squeezed his forearm. "I believe that's why Mallory is giving you both some space," she said. "She wants to see you happy just like the rest of us do."

Liam nodded but remained silent. What would make him happy would be to hear Mallory say she loved him. But, it seemed, he'd have to settle on waiting—and hoping—to hear that in time.

And if, after all she'd endured in her previous marriage, she needed time to feel comfortable entering a relationship with him, he'd give her as much as she needed.

The front door opened and Mallory emerged from the house, carrying Oliver, who she'd strapped into the car seat, to Pam's car.

Liam pulled his hands from his pockets and walked over to her. "Would you like some help?"

There were dark circles under her eyes, as though she'd struggled to sleep, too, but she issued a small smile. "Yes, please. Thank you."

Liam took his time installing Oliver's car seat in the back seat of Pam's car. He lingered for a moment, letting Oliver capture one of his fingers in his tiny palm, his heart breaking just a little more when Oliver cooed and smiled up at him.

"I'm afraid we have to say goodbye for now," Liam whis-

pered. He leaned farther across the back seat, kissed the soft
curls on top of Oliver's head then eased away. "I'll see you
again soon, little man."

Or, at least, he hoped so.

Mallory and Pam got into Pam's car and Liam returned to
his truck, cranked the engine and followed them into town to
Pam's house. When they arrived, he unloaded Oliver's crib
and carried it inside, then brought in the majority of the bags
Mallory had brought, trying to set everything up in the guest
room similar to the way it had been in the nursery at Pine
Creek Farm.

"I think that's all of it," Mallory said, walking into the
room, cradling Oliver in her arms. "Thank you for helping
me move, Liam."

He studied her face, stealing a few extra moments to memo-
rize her features. "You're welcome." He hesitated, then shoved
his hands into his pockets again and headed for the door. "I'll
leave so you and Oliver can get settled in."

"Liam?" Mallory curled her hand over the crook of his
elbow and looked up at him, her brown eyes dark with concern. "You're welcome to see Oliver whenever you'd like. Any
time, I mean it. Just give me a call and we'll arrange it."

He didn't quite know what to say, and he couldn't say what
he wanted. He couldn't tell her he loved her again and beg her
to stay. She'd asked for space and he'd given it to her.

"Thank you," he said finally.

"Take care of yourself, Liam."

He bent his head and kissed Oliver's forehead once more
then cupped Mallory's cheek in his palm and pressed his lips
to her forehead, too, closing his eyes and breathing her in.
"And you as well, Mallory."

WE LEFT PINE Creek Farm today, Oliver.

You're asleep now in your crib, in a guest room in Pam's

house. You went out like a light. You didn't fuss or cry. You settled right in.

I'm pleased your routine wasn't disrupted and that you feel comfortable in Pam's house, but the fact that you took to the change so easily scares me.

Mallory, seated on the edge of the bed in one of Pam's guest rooms, stood, set her notepad aside then walked across the room to the window. She pulled back the curtain slightly and looked outside.

She couldn't see the stars here. Not in the city limits of Pine Creek. Though it was a small town, there were streetlights right outside Pam's house, lining the wide suburban road. It was silent here this time of night. There were no toads or crickets singing by the pond, no crackling fire and no whisper of wind over fields.

Mallory returned to the bed, picked up her notepad, sat down and began writing again.

Pam's house is beautiful and comfortable but it's not the same as Pine Creek Farm. It doesn't feel like home to me. And Liam's not here...

She glanced at the hallway, at the open door of the guest room where Oliver slept.

You're still sleeping soundly as though nothing's changed.

Is Liam doing the same? Is he continuing his day and night as though nothing's changed? I know he misses you, but does he miss me at all?

That's what scares me, Oliver.

What if, after some time, he doesn't miss me at all?

CHAPTER TWELVE

THREE WEEKS LATER, Mallory toured a two-bedroom apartment within the city limits of Pine Creek. It was a ground-level apartment, which meant she wouldn't have to carry Oliver's stroller up the stairs on account of there not being an elevator. The living room was small but was large enough for a couch and a TV, and the two bedrooms made up for the lack of space elsewhere by being connected by a large Jack and Jill bathroom.

"There's a refrigerator and microwave in the kitchen," the landlord said, leading the way from the hallway into the kitchen. "But it's not fully stocked with utensils or pans, so you'll want to bring those and your own dishes."

Mallory glanced briefly about the room. It was clean and large enough to accommodate one person when cooking, which was all Mallory needed and could actually financially afford.

After leaving Pine Creek Farm, she'd stayed home with Oliver for the first week, spending time with him, helping him become familiar with the new surroundings and feel comfortable with Pam. But soon, she'd struck out on her own with Oliver, visiting addresses she'd found on the internet for available apartments and keeping an eye out for any local businesses that might be hiring. But the first order of business had been purchasing a car.

With the money she'd saved from working at Pine Creek Farm and from selling her old car, she had tucked away just enough to afford a small used sedan. It wasn't fancy but it ran smoothly, was dependable and got great gas mileage so she couldn't complain. It was a treat, really, being able to strap Oliver in his car seat, hop in the driver's seat and drive them a few blocks away from Pam's house to sit in the park, enjoy the birds singing and watch other kids play.

Mallory could go anywhere now. Aside from her budgetary considerations, she could live anywhere she wanted, work anywhere she wanted and schedule her days however she wanted.

She was in charge of choosing the decorations for the new home that she and Oliver would occupy. She could hang her clothes in whatever way she pleased or not hang them up at all. She could move about freely in town, not looking over her shoulder all the time, unafraid to meet new people and explore new pursuits.

She finally felt free to live the life she wanted.

Only, no matter how many apartments she toured or how many jobs she investigated as possibilities, her mind—and heart—always kept coming back to Pine Creek Farm. She missed the place she had begun to call home and most of all, she missed Liam.

"—and walking distance from the park," the landlord was saying.

Mallory shook her head. "I'm sorry, I didn't quite catch that."

The landlord, a young blonde woman with pretty green eyes, smiled. "I just said that the park is within walking distance from the apartment." She squatted down, bringing her eyes level with Oliver, who was cradled in Mallory's arms. "I bet you'd like that, wouldn't you? Living right next to a park? When you get a little older, you'll be able to slide down the slides and swing on the swings. You'd enjoy that, wouldn't you?"

Oliver, a bit grumpy on account of it being past his nap time, made a face then buried his nose in Mallory's shirt and cried.

"Oh, goodness," the lady said, standing upright and pressing a hand to her chest. "I didn't mean to upset him."

"You didn't." Mallory smiled. "He hasn't had a nap today, is all. We've been looking at apartments most of the morning and haven't taken a breath yet."

"Well, I hope you'll keep us in mind," she said. "We'd love to have you as new tenants."

Mallory asked a few more questions about the apartment, thanked the landlord for giving her a tour and asked for her card so that she could call if she decided to rent the apartment. Soon after, she took one last look around then left.

Early July was scorching in South Georgia, and she winced as she exited the apartment complex. Humid, sticky air enveloped her as soon as she stepped onto the sidewalk.

Oliver, feeling the heat as well, began to cry again.

"I know," Mallory soothed. "Let's get you in the car and turn on the air conditioner."

By the time she'd driven back to Pam's house, carried Oliver inside and placed him in his crib, he'd already dozed off.

"Oh, but he was tuckered out, wasn't he?" Pam asked, walking in quietly and peering into the crib.

"I kept him out longer than I should have," Mallory whispered. "I just didn't expect it to take so long to tour apartments. Once I started, it made sense to keep going until I reached the end of my list and get it all done in one day."

"Did you find a complex you liked?" Pam asked.

"There was one that's nice enough and within my budget," Mallory said as she fiddled with a teddy bear that she'd tucked into Oliver's crib. "It's right across the street from the park so we could walk there any time we'd like."

"That's good." Pam studied her face. "But you don't really sound too excited."

She wasn't. No matter how hard she tried to stay optimistic about moving into a new apartment, she still couldn't bring herself to stop thinking about Pine Creek Farm...and Liam.

"Well," Mallory said softly, "it's a big step. I want to be sure that wherever we move, Oliver will be happy and safe."

"I completely understand," Pam said, squeezing her hand. "And please keep in mind that you're welcome to stay here as long as you'd like. I love having a baby around the house!" She grinned. "Now, you've had a long day and Oliver's sleeping good, so why don't you join me in the kitchen for a cup of coffee and some fresh-baked chocolate chip cookies?"

Mallory smiled. "It's a bit too hot for coffee for me, but I'll definitely take you up on the cookies."

Pam laughed. "I thought you would. We both have a sweet tooth."

An hour later, they were still sitting in the kitchen, lingering over coffee, lemonade and cookies while Mallory shared the details of the apartments she'd toured earlier that day.

"So, were there any messages left for me while I was gone?" Mallory asked.

Pam scooped a spoonful of sugar into her coffee and stirred. "Don't you really mean to ask if Liam called?"

Mallory sighed. "Am I that transparent?"

"No, not at all." She smiled gently. "You're good at keeping your feelings close to your chest. But you seemed a bit down lately and you're not as enthused about the prospect of a new apartment as I thought you might be."

"I'm not, am I?" Mallory leaned her elbows on the table and propped her chin in her hands. "I just love Pine Creek Farm so much. I miss it so. And Oliver loved it there."

"And you loved living there?" Pam asked.

"Yes."

"And you love Liam, too?"

"Yes."

Mallory stilled, answering Pam's question before she could think better of it.

Pam looked at her face and winced good-naturedly. "I didn't mean to stick my nose into your personal business, but it wasn't hard to tell during the times that I saw you two together that you may have feelings for each other."

Mallory sagged back in her chair and sighed. "I miss him," she whispered.

"I know."

"I just want Liam to be happy," Mallory said. "And I want to do the right thing by Oliver. I just don't know if it's the right time. I mean, Liam and I met under unusual circumstances. I just had Oliver and am trying to be the best mother I can, and we both lost Gayle. I just...it feels like the timing is wrong."

"Oh, Mallory," Pam said softly. "I don't think any of us have any control over that. God tends to do things in His own time and I think it's better to lean on His judgement rather than our own."

Mallory nodded in agreement but remained silent.

"And how do you know that Pine Creek Farm isn't where God wanted you all along?" Pam asked.

Mallory turned over the possibilities in her mind, wondering if meeting Liam, moving to Pine Creek Farm to care for Gayle and falling in love with Liam had been part of God's plan all along. And...if Liam falling in love with her had been part of His plan, too.

The only question was: Was she ready to trust Liam's heart and embrace a new beginning with him?

"I tell you what," Pam said. "You need some time to yourself. Independence Day is tomorrow and Liam always throws a fantastic fireworks display for the guests at Pine Creek Farm. There's free admission and it's open to all residents of Pine Creek without the need of a reservation. Why don't you go? It'll give you a chance to get out of the house, spend some time on your own and see how you feel about returning to the farm...and possibly Liam."

Mallory hesitated. It was tempting, but—

"What about Oliver?" Mallory asked.

"I'll watch him, of course," Pam said, smiling. "I'll take any chance I can get to babysit that sweet child. So do this for me, please. At dusk tomorrow, you hop in that new used car of yours and drive back to Pine Creek Farm. Watch the fireworks, talk to Liam and see how you feel."

Mallory considered this. It would be nice to see Pine Creek Farm again and it'd be wonderful to see Liam. Her heart practically leapt at the thought. "Yes," Mallory said. "That's what I'll do."

THE CROWD AT Pine Creek Farm on July Fourth was a sight to behold.

When Mallory turned onto the long driveway of Pine Creek Farm the next night, two teenaged boys, holding flashlights, stopped her a few feet down the driveway.

"The back lots are full, ma'am," one of the teens said, leaning on the open window of Mallory's car. "You need to park in this field over here—" he swung his flashlight to the left "—if you want to stay."

Mallory followed the pool of light as it settled on the field behind him. There were two lines of parked trucks and cars and only a few spaces remained.

"Wait a minute," Mallory said, sticking her head out the window and peering through the darkness toward the main house. "You mean to tell me there are so many cars parked near the house that they're backed up all the way out here?"

"Yes, ma'am," he said.

"There are that many people here?" she asked. "I didn't think Pine Creek was that big."

He laughed. "No, ma'am. We get people coming here from all over for the Fourth of July. This isn't even as bad as it gets, from what I'm told. This is my first year working this event, but my friends worked here last year and they told me it was almost twice as bad that year as it is this one."

"Well, that's good," Mallory said, smiling. "Depending on how you look at it. For business, I mean."

Liam, she imagined, was probably very pleased with the turnout. The more exposure Pine Creek Farm received, the more reservations he was likely to book for the guesthouses and trail rides.

"I suppose so." The teen shined his light behind her car then waved his arm. "I'm sorry, but I got someone coming behind you, ma'am. If you don't mind pulling on in and getting parked?"

"Of course," Mallory said, driving the car forward and turning left into the field.

She parked as close as she could to the driveway, cut the engine then got out and walked slowly along the driveway toward the main house. It was almost nine-thirty and the stars were shining brightly. She could see them twinkling between the branches of the magnolia trees that stretched out overhead. She smiled to herself as she thought of the many times she and Gayle had walked the same path, admiring the blooms, chatting, and sometimes strolling in silence, just enjoying the view.

Oh, how she missed Gayle. She knew Liam must miss her, too. She wondered what he'd been doing these weeks that she hadn't seen him. For a while, she'd hoped he would take her up on the offer to see Oliver and had waited impatiently for him to call.

It was ironic, really, that she was longing for him to visit Oliver just so she could see him. She supposed that, in a way, she should take it as a good sign that Liam hadn't pursued seeing Oliver. That, at least, could mean that all the time he'd spent with her and Oliver, he may not have been spending it just to be around Oliver. Perhaps—or at least she hoped—he'd wanted to be in her company just as much, too.

She continued walking, thinking of the many evenings she and Liam had spent sitting beside the firepit behind the main house. Some nights, they sat outside for over two hours, looking at the stars, sometimes sitting in silence, and other times chatting about various things.

She missed that. She missed Liam.

By the time she reached the end of the driveway, the crowd had thickened, and people milled about the grounds, most of them heading around the back of the main house.

Mallory craned her neck, scanning the area for any sign of Liam. He was here somewhere, but it would be almost impossible to find him, given the number of people who'd gathered on the grounds.

"Ten minutes until the show," another teenager, a girl this time, shouted from the edge of the crowd. "Please make your way to the back field, find a comfortable spot and settle in. The show will start soon."

Mallory stepped aside as the rest of the crowd began to move toward the back field. She chose a different path instead, taking a detour through the stable. Not long after she'd entered the stable, she felt a familiar brush of fur at her ankle.

She looked down at Miss Priss, who wound around her legs and meowed. "Well, fancy meeting you here." She bent and scratched the cat's ears, laughing when Miss Priss tilted her head for a better angle. "Oh, you've missed me, huh? Has Liam not been giving you enough attention?"

She petted Miss Priss for another moment or two then walked to the back of the stable and stopped at Sugar's stall. The brown mare sniffed the air then walked over and poked her nose out, snorting softly when Mallory stroked her forehead.

"I've missed you, too," Mallory said. "Have you been taking good care of Liam since I've been gone?"

As if in response, Sugar nudged Mallory's hand, seeking more affection.

Mallory obliged, lingering by Sugar's stall for a few minutes more before the distant pop of firecrackers rang out in the distance.

"Well, I better go," she said, giving Sugar one last pat. "I might miss the whole show if I don't head over there now and snag a good spot."

She left the stable and walked across the field to the back of the main house. Overhead, pops, bangs and whistles continued to ring out, lighting up the sky with dozens of various colors. Mallory stopped near the firepit where several others had gathered, tipped her head back and watched as the fireworks display continued.

Each burst of bright color lit up the fields with dazzling light as it streaked across the sky. Murmurs of appreciation moved through the crowd and Mallory smiled, enjoying the dazzling display.

It went on for a while and Mallory stood still, taking it in, until a hand, big, strong—and familiar—covered hers and squeezed. She turned her head and looked up, finding Liam smiling down at her.

His mouth moved but the pops and bangs overhead drowned out his words, and she pointed to her ear and mouthed, *I can't hear you.*

Laughing, he dipped his head, brought his mouth close to her ear and said, "I'm glad you're here."

His soft breath tickled her earlobe. She smiled and resisted the urge to lift her hand and touch his face. To feel his warm cheek beneath her fingertips.

Dipping his head down again, he said, "This is the best part coming up. Keep your eyes right there."

He pointed at the sky and her gaze followed. Moments later, a new round of fireworks rang out, lighting up the sky with multiple colors that shimmered among the stars.

Laughing with delight, she glanced at Liam. He was still looking up and bright shades of pink, blue, red, white, yellow and purple glowed over his skin. He looked down then and met her eyes, smiling.

She savored the moment, holding his gaze and squeezing his hand just a bit tighter. The moment—surprising and unexpected—was perfect. She'd never felt happier or more hopeful. Standing there, on Pine Creek Farm, with Liam by her side, felt like home just as much as it always had.

Her heart overflowed.

Soon, the fireworks stopped, the lights that had glowed over Liam's skin faded and the crowd sighed with disappointment.

Liam looked down at her with a regretful expression. "I have to go. People will be leaving soon and I need to help direct traffic."

Mallory almost sagged with disappointment. "I should've come sooner."

He stared down at her, his mouth opening and closing as he hesitated, before he finally said, "Come back tomorrow. Or the next day. I'm always here."

Someone called his name and he squeezed her hand once more before releasing it and walking away, calling back over his shoulder, "Come back tomorrow, okay?"

He disappeared into the crowd before she could answer.

She fell in line with the rest of the crowd and walked slowly beneath the magnolias back down the driveway to her car. She lingered for a moment, casting her gaze across the landscape once more, then got in her car and drove away.

I SAW LIAM today, Oliver.

There was a fireworks display at Pine Creek Farm and it was beautiful. It was the first time in my life that I stood beneath fireworks with someone I loved by my side who loved me in return, the way I deserve.

I miss him, Oliver. I miss working with him, laughing with him and sitting under the stars by his side. My heart knows what it wants. And I hope he knows for sure that he wants the same, too.

This is the last entry I'll write, Oliver. I'm taking a chance I should've taken weeks ago.

I'm hopeful and happy. I'm ready to put the past behind me and move on. I want us to start our new life together and I want Liam to be a part of it, too.

CHAPTER THIRTEEN

TWO DAYS LATER, Liam waved at several guests who he'd led on a trail ride as they said their goodbyes, thanked him again and walked away to return to their guest houses at Pine Creek Farm.

"You've had a full day, haven't you, girl?" he asked, patting Sugar on her neck.

Actually, they had both had two full days. For the past forty-eight hours, Liam had done everything he could to keep his mind and hands busy. He'd mucked the stalls both mornings, led extra trail rides to get through the afternoon then washed and groomed the horses before retiring for the night.

It didn't make much difference, though. No matter how hard he worked or how busy he stayed, he still couldn't get Mallory off his mind...or heart.

He could still see her face as she'd smiled up at him beneath the fireworks display two nights ago. It had been a surprise to see her there. He hadn't heard from her since she and Oliver had left Pine Creek Farm weeks prior, and he'd had to stop himself on many occasions from texting or calling her.

Each time he was tempted, he reminded himself that she'd asked for space and time, and that he'd agreed to give it to her. He had no idea what the time they'd spent apart had done for

Mallory's feelings for him, but it had certainly cemented his feelings for her.

The house felt empty and lonely without her and Oliver. But it went far beyond that. He missed seeing her smile first thing every morning, bumping into her as they cooked breakfast and sitting peacefully by her side under the stars every evening. None of those memories had anything to do with Oliver but had everything to do with Mallory.

From the moment he'd first met her, she'd tugged at his heart. Initially, out of empathy but later, out of love.

He loved Mallory, with or without Oliver. But he'd rather it be with.

He'd wondered often over the past several weeks how Oliver was doing. Whether he'd grown, had begun developing new skills or if he still smiled often. He missed him so much and had, many times, thought of calling Mallory and accepting her offer to spend time with him. But that wouldn't do. Not when Mallory was under the impression that he only loved her because of Oliver.

It was Mallory who he wanted to see and he hoped she would realize that.

He thought she had, actually, when he'd spotted her in the field under the fireworks display on the Fourth of July. For a moment, he thought she'd returned to tell him she'd changed her mind. He thought she would tell him that she'd decided to stay. And the disappointment in her eyes when he'd had to leave had given him hope that maybe he was right. That maybe, eventually, she would decide to return to Pine Creek Farm.

But she hadn't called. She hadn't reached out at all since that night.

It wasn't a good sign in terms of her having changed her mind.

Sighing, he rubbed his forehead then led Sugar into the stable. He took his time untacking, washing and brushing her.

And after settling her in her stall, he lingered there, stroking her neck and back, praising her softly, and even taking the time to pet Miss Priss when she wound around his ankles.

He'd grown to love that cat. If nothing else, she reminded him of Mallory.

After a while, the sun dipped low against the horizon and the hands had knocked off for the day. Liam reluctantly made his way back to the main house, knowing what lay ahead of him. Every night since Mallory and Oliver had left had been lonely and, most nights, sleepless.

His heart just couldn't settle.

As he walked inside, the aroma of vegetable soup filled his lungs and he followed it to the kitchen. Nancy, the housekeeper he'd hired two weeks ago, was pouring a glass of sweet tea and placing it on the table by one place setting.

"I made soup tonight," she said, smiling. "I remember you mentioned that you like vegetable beef so I used one of your mother's recipes and whipped up a batch. There's cornbread, too, and sweet tea and cobbler for dessert." She untied the apron she wore, lifted it over her head and hung it on a hook by the refrigerator. "I'll be off then. Is there anything else you need before I go?"

Liam shook his head. "No, thank you. You've taken care of everything here, as always."

Nancy nodded and headed for the front door. "I'll be going then. My grandbabies are coming home this weekend so I need to tidy up my place, too."

"I hope you have a good visit with them," Liam said.

"Oh, I will," she said as she left, closing the front door behind her.

Liam chuckled at the thought of Nancy chasing around her young grandchildren. Nancy was in her mid-sixties, made the best lemonade and hula-hooped for exercise—he'd stumbled upon her routine in the front lawn when returning from the stable last week. All things considered, she probably made her grandchildren very happy.

Liam picked up a bowl from the table, carried it to the stove and dipped several spoonfuls of soup into the bowl. He returned to the table and sat down but after two bites of soup, his appetite vanished, as usual, and he sat back in his chair and closed his eyes, the silence in the house almost deafening.

He prayed every night for guidance, for what he should do to convince Mallory that he loved her. To find a way to reconnect with her and encourage her to give him another chance.

But she wanted space and hadn't called. Short of not respecting her wishes—which he wouldn't do—he didn't know what else he could do…except try to accept that God's plan for his future might not include Mallory.

He stood abruptly, carried his bowl to the sink, and set it down. There was no need to linger. He wasn't in the mood for dinner. Instead, he walked outside and went to the back of the house to the firepit, sat down in his chair and closed his eyes. The air was soothing, filled with the chirps and croaks of crickets and toads and the sweet scent of honeysuckle. It would be a perfect summer night, that was, if Mallory were there.

"Mind if I join you?"

He stilled at the sound of her voice.

"I've been told I have a permanent invitation," she added softly.

Liam stood and turned slowly, his gaze moving over her, taking in every detail. She wore shorts, sandals and a short-sleeve shirt. Her hair was loose, falling in waves about her shoulders. There was hope in her eyes and gentleness in her voice. She never looked more beautiful.

"I knocked on the front door, but you didn't answer," she said, "so I took a chance, hoping you were out here."

"I am."

She smiled slowly. "I see that."

Cheeks heating, he laughed as he met her eyes, hope swelling within his chest. "Did you just come for a quick visit?" he asked hesitantly. "Or do you have time to stay a while? If you're hungry, my housekeeper left a big batch of soup and cornbread." He smiled. "You're welcome to come in and join me. It'd be like old times."

"Like the night we first met," she said, smiling softly. "That sounds nice, but—" she moved closer, walking gingerly down the path and edging between the two chairs to stand in front of him "—I didn't come for dinner. I came because I was hoping we could discuss the future."

He bit his lip, almost scared to speak in case he scared her off or spoiled the moment.

"I've been thinking," she said, pushing her hands into her pockets. "About how much I love it here and how much I love you."

His breath caught and he smiled. "You love me?"

"Yes," she whispered.

She moved even closer then and one of her hands left her pocket, lifting toward him, her fist unfurling. A ring, a plain wedding band, rested in the center of her palm.

"It's not much," she whispered. "But it's the best I could afford. I'm starting over, you see? There are three things in my life that are valuable to me. One is my faith, which led me to a new life. The second is Oliver."

"And the third?" he asked.

"The third is you," she said softly. "I love you, Liam. And if you still feel the same," she said hesitantly, "I'd love to start a new life together with you."

He smiled, his heart fit to burst. "Are you asking me to marry you?"

She nodded, her hand trembling. "Yes."

He cupped her hand in his, removed the ring with his other hand and kissed the center of her palm. He glanced up at her, the excited relief in her eyes making him smile even wider. "There's nothing I want more in this world."

EPILOGUE

THE NEXT YEAR, August arrived at Pine Creek Farm and with it came a new tradition.

"What does the winner get, Uncle Liam?" Cody called out from where he stood beneath the weeping willow by the pond.

Liam smiled. "A mess of fried fish," he shouted back.

Cody, seemingly pleased with this answer, turned back to his brother, picked up his fishing pole and cast his line out into the water.

It was a beautiful summer day. There wasn't a cloud in the sky, the sun shone bright and the birds were singing. Even the weeping willow tree's branches danced in the breeze as though it were celebrating. It was a perfect afternoon for the first annual Williams family reunion.

"Dada."

Liam glanced down to where Oliver, holding tightly to both of Liam's hands, stood, balancing carefully in the grass. He was over a year old now and getting around pretty well. Liam had had to childproof just about everything inside the main house. Oliver was a curious little boy and enjoyed investigating everything he could get his hands on.

"Dada!" Oliver released Liam's hands and stretched out his arms in the universal sign of wanting to be picked up.

Liam's heart melted and he bent over, lifted Oliver up and settled him on his hip. "That's my boy," he said, kissing Oliver's cheek.

Even though Oliver had been calling him *Dad* for a couple of months now, he still felt an overwhelming sense of gratitude each time he heard Oliver say it. It was like a dream being a father. One of the greatest gifts God had given him.

"Did you save me a seat?"

Liam grinned and turned around. But the sweetest—oh, the sweetest!—gift of all was Mallory.

She strolled across the field toward him and Oliver, looking more beautiful than ever. Her wavy hair was loose, shining beneath the summer sunlight, and freckles—the cutest he'd ever seen—were sprinkled across her nose and cheeks.

It was the sun that did it. Several months ago, not long after they were married, she'd asked Liam to give her riding lessons. She'd been a natural and it hadn't taken long for her to begin participating in the trail rides he led at least twice a week and the more she rode, the more freckles appeared.

He cherished those afternoons, riding horses beneath the sun with her by his side. But his favorite part of each day was still their evenings spent by the firepit, sitting peacefully under the stars, holding hands and thanking God for the many blessings that continued to multiply in their lives.

Like today. Today, he not only had his wife and child by his side, but his brother, Jessie and their children, too. The farm was full of life and laughter and Gayle would be proud of them all.

"I was hoping we could get a clear view of the first annual fishing tournament," she said now, grinning.

"I saved the best seat in the house for us," Liam said, holding out his hand.

She slipped her hand in his and he led the way across the grass to a blanket he'd spread on a low hill that sloped just above the pond.

"Any clear winner yet?" she asked, sitting on the blanket.

"Not yet," he said as he settled Oliver onto her lap. "But there's a clear leader. Holt and the boys are neck and neck— each of them brought in three bream so far." He sat down behind Mallory and stretched out his legs, scooting close and smiling as she leaned back against his chest. "But Jessie and Ava have all three of them beat at the moment though. They've snagged at least twice as many as that already."

Mallory tipped her head back and smiled up at him. "Well, there's plenty of time for the boys to pull it off. We haven't reached the end of the contest yet."

Liam kissed her softly then wrapped his arms around her and Oliver, pulling them close, holding them safe in his arms and heart. "Yeah," he whispered, thinking of the many years ahead that would be filled with love and laughter. "This is just the beginning."

* * * * *